PRAISE FOR
ANNE GRACIE AND HER NOVELS

"[A] confection that brims with kindness and heartfelt sincerity. . . . You can't do much better than Anne Gracie, who offers her share of daring escapes, stolen kisses and heartfelt romance in a tale that carries the effervescent charm of the best Disney fairy tales."
—*Entertainment Weekly*

"I never miss an Anne Gracie book."
—*New York Times* bestselling author Julia Quinn

"For fabulous Regency flavor, witty and addictive, you can't go past Anne Gracie."
—*New York Times* bestselling author Stephanie Laurens

"With her signature superbly nuanced characters, subtle sense of wit and richly emotional writing, Gracie puts her distinctive stamp on a classic Regency plot."
—*Chicago Tribune*

"Will keep readers entranced. . . . A totally delightful read!"
—RT Book Reviews

"The always terrific Anne Gracie outdoes herself with *Bride by Mistake*. . . . Gracie created two great characters, a high-tension relationship and a wonderfully satisfying ending. Not to be missed!"
—*New York Times* bestselling author Mary Jo Putney

"A fascinating twist on the girl-in-disguise plot. . . . With its wildly romantic last chapter, this novel is a great antidote to the end of the summer."
—*New York Times* bestselling author Eloisa James

"Anne Gracie's writing dances that thin line between always familiar and always fresh. . . . *The Accidental Wedding* is warm and sweet, tempered with bursts of piquancy and a dash or three of spice."
—New York Journal of Books

Marry
in
Secret

ANNE GRACIE

JOVE
New York

A JOVE BOOK
Published by Berkley
An imprint of Penguin Random House LLC
1745 Broadway, New York, NY 10019

ISBN: 9781984802040

First Edition: August 2019

Printed in the United States of America
1   3   5   7   9   10   8   6   4   2

Cover design by Sarah Oberrender
Cover illustration by Judy York
Book design by Kristin del Rosario

For Janga

You wrote to me about my very first book. Your words were warm, encouraging, wise. You've written about every one of my books since. And you always see more in them than I do. I can't tell you what that means to an author, especially one on the other side of the world. So this book is for you, with my very sincere gratitude and love. I hope it measures up.

Anne

xx

Chapter One

❧

Happiness in marriage is entirely a matter of chance.
—JANE AUSTEN, *PRIDE AND PREJUDICE*

LADY ROSE RUTHERFORD WAS NOT A YOUNG LADY WHO dithered and, having made up her mind, she generally stuck to it. It was, she had decided, high time she moved on.

She was not generally superstitious either. But after refusing twelve offers of marriage, the thirteenth . . . well, it was bound to make a girl think. Especially since it came from a duke.

Even if it was the most careless, most dispassionate offer of marriage that a girl could ever receive. "Oh, and by the way, if you want to put an end to all this nonsense . . ."

The truth was, she did.

NOW IT WAS THE EVE OF HER WEDDING AND SHE'D PLANNED a quiet night in, a nursery supper with just her sister and her niece—who was more like a sister, really—toasting bread and crumpets before the fire. But instead of a cozy, quietly intimate sisterly celebration, it was turning into an argument.

"It's a civilized arrangement," Rose said.

"No, it's a mistake," her sister, Lily, insisted.

"I can't imagine why anyone would want to marry him," Rose's niece Lady Georgiana Rutherford said. "He's rude, he's arrogant and he doesn't care two pins for anyone. Why would you imagine he could make you happy?" She peered at the slightly scorched crumpet on her toasting fork, then, deciding it would do, reached for the butter dish. Behind her a large hound watched mournfully, doing his best imitation of a Dog Who Hadn't Been Fed in Weeks.

Rose threaded bread onto her toasting fork. "Nobody can make another person happy, George. The recipe for happiness lies within each of us and is unique every time." And if she told herself that often enough, she might even believe it.

George snorted. "That's as may be, but people can make other people *un*happy—and he will, I'm sure of it." Ever the cynic when it came to marriage, George had been betrayed by every man she'd ever known until her uncle, Cal, Rose's brother, found her and brought her into the family fold— the family she'd never known she had.

Lily laid a hand on Rose's arm. "Are you *sure* about this, Rose? Because it's not too late to back out."

Rose's expression softened. Her sister was such a dear, but really, there was no backing out at this stage. "No, Lily darling, I'm not going to back out. The contracts are signed, the banns have been called, the church is booked, my dress is finished, the guests invited. Discussion over."

"But you barely know him."

"And you hardly knew Ned Galbraith when you married him, and look how happy you are—not that I'm planning to fall in love," she added hastily. "I leave that sort of thing to you, little sister."

"But—"

"The point is, I need to marry someone and the duke is more than eligible—the match of the year, they're calling it." She needed to marry and get the waiting, the endless, fruitless waiting, over and done with. To start her life instead of . . . dreaming.

"Why do you even need to marry? In five years' time you'll be in full control of your fortune and you can do what you like." It was George's plan, they all knew.

"She wants children," Lily reminded her. She spread her toast with strawberry jam, cut it into four careful triangles and topped each one with a lavish dollop of cream.

Rose nodded. "I do, but it's more than that. Five more years of waiting, George? I'd go mad. I can't *bear* this life, where nothing interesting ever happens and everything I do is reported and monitored and judged. As a young unmarried miss, I am, oh"—she flung up her hands—"'*cabin'd, crib'd, confin'd.*' But as a dashing young matron I'll be my own mistress."

George shook her head and made a thumbs-down screwing motion. *Under the thumb.*

"Yes, but why the duke, Rose?" Lily persisted. "You don't love him, and he doesn't love you. I know you've turned twenty, but you still have plenty of time to find the right man and fall in l—"

"But I don't *want* to fall in love, Lily dear," Rose said gently. "Neither he nor I have any interest in that kind of marriage." It was the very reason she'd accepted his offer.

"Enact me no emotional scenes" was how he'd put it, and wasn't that a relief, when the others who'd proposed had vowed their undying love and devotion—and expected the same of her? Or said they did.

How dreadful it would be to marry a man who loved her, knowing that with the best will in the world, she could never return that love. She'd never been good at lying. She'd probably end up hurting such a man, and she didn't want to hurt anyone.

The duke, on the other hand, had been very clear—quite adamant, in fact—that he didn't love her, and that he wasn't looking for love—quite the contrary. What he wanted, he told her, was a courteous, unemotional, rational arrangement. And children. An heir, in particular.

Rose had decided she could live with that, and so she'd accepted.

So what if the rest of the world thought her calculating, cold-blooded and ambitious. She knew who she was. A marriage was made between two people, and if she and the duke were content with—actually *preferred*—a lukewarm pragmatic arrangement, it was nobody's business but theirs.

"But you don't know what you're missing," Lily began. "Love is—"

"Not for me," Rose said firmly. She knew exactly what she was missing. And was grateful for it.

"But you've never *been* in love, so how can you—"

"Drop it, Lily," George interrupted. "If she doesn't want to fall in love, she doesn't. You don't go on about love to me all the time. Why badger Rose about it?"

"I'm not *badgering* her," Lily said indignantly. "Besides, you and Rose are different."

"I know—you wouldn't catch me putting my fortune and my future into the hands of a man I barely know and don't much like. Or any man, for that matter."

"On the contrary, I'll be virtually independent. Cal has arranged the marriage contract and the settlements are very generous. And Aunt Agatha is over the moon."

George snorted. "Call that a recommendation? Aunt Agatha would happily marry you to a . . . a *cannibal*, as long as he was rich and titled."

Rose couldn't help but laugh. It was pretty close to the mark. "Nonsense. A cannibal would *never* meet Aunt Agatha's lofty standards of behavior. His table manners would be lacking, for a start."

"As long as he had a title and a fat purse, she'd forgive his peculiar eating habits," George said darkly.

"It's not badgering," Lily persisted. "When we were schoolgirls, Rose and I both dreamed of falling in love— we used to talk about it all the time, remember, Rose?"

Trust her little sister. Lily might not be able to read books, but she could read people, especially her sister.

But Lily didn't know everything.

"Yes, well, that was a long time ago. A lot has changed since then. I'm not soft and sweet, like you. I don't want the hearts and flowers. I just want to be married and get on with my life."

"You know he won't be faithful," George said into the silence.

Rose dusted crumbs off her fingers.

"You don't mind?" Lily said incredulously.

"It's the price of freedom."

"Freedom?" George echoed. "To be under a man's thumb?"

"I won't be under his thumb," Rose said. "We have an agreement. I'm to give him an heir, and he will give me the freedom to do what I like, as long as I'm discreet." Not that she had any intention of breaking her marriage vows. She took her vows seriously.

"That's horrid," Lily said, dismayed. "I can't believe you're being so . . . so cynical, Rose."

"Cold-blooded," George said.

"Practical," Rose corrected her. "I used to want too much out of life. I'm more mature now."

"Oh, but you *should* want more," Lily exclaimed in distress. "I never believed I could have even half of what I dreamed of, and then I met Edward. You never know what—or who—is around the corner."

Rose loved that her sister was so happy, but she knew it was not for her. She leaned forward and took Lily and George by the hand. "Please, my dears, let us drop the subject. I know this marriage is not what you hoped for me, but you'll just have to accept that I'm a cold-blooded creature who will marry a man she doesn't love for the sake of freedom, a beautiful home, and a very generous allowance. And babies." She ached for a child of her own, and seeing her sister-in-law, Emm, so rounded and glowing, her child growing within her . . .

Lily shook her head. "You can't have changed that much; I don't believe it. I don't understand why you're doing this thing, and I wish you wouldn't, but if it's what you want—what you really truly want, I'll say no more."

Rose gave her sister a one-armed hug. "Don't worry

about me, little sister. I'm going to be just fine." Dear Lily, so newly married and so deeply, joyfully in love. Of course Lily wanted the same for her sister.

But falling in love was the very last thing Rose wanted. She couldn't explain why to Lily and George—or anyone else. Not without stirring up . . . things better left untouched.

Love was simply too painful.

ROSE PAUSED AT THE CHURCH DOOR. LILY AND GEORGE fluttered around her, straightening the circlet of flowers in her hair, arranging the lace train of her dress. Rose stood, lively as a statue, and about as warm. "Now, don't be nervous," Aunt Dottie had said a few moments before. "It will all work out perfectly, trust me, my love. I have one of my *feelings.*"

But Rose wasn't the slightest bit nervous. It all felt strangely distant, as if it were happening to some other girl. She moistened her lips and waited.

George poked her head around the door, glanced in and pulled a face. "He's there."

"Well, of course he's there," Lily said crossly. Poor Lily. She'd been in a brittle mood all morning, trying to put a good face on a wedding she still had grave doubts about. Lily wasn't very good at hiding her feelings.

What if the duke hadn't come? He was notoriously unreliable about keeping engagements. What if he'd jilted her at the altar? Rose considered it briefly and decided that it would be embarrassing . . . and possibly something of a relief.

Nonsense. She needed to do this, needed to draw a line in the sand between her old life and her new. Cut the bonds of the old, and move on.

The church was full—Rose's friends and relations come to see her married, the duke's too, of course, and quite a few other members of the ton come to witness what some were calling the wedding of the season. Strangers had gathered in the street outside to watch and wait, in hope of some largesse in the form of a shower of coins from the happy groom.

It didn't feel real.

"Ready?" her brother Cal asked. She nodded and took his arm.

Now. She took a deep breath and stepped inside the church and stood blinking as her eyes adjusted to the dim light of the interior. A hush fell, followed by a susurration of whispers and rustling silk as the congregation turned as one to look at the bride.

The church smelled of flowers, spring flowers, and beeswax, brass polish and perfumes, a hundred clashing perfumes.

At the end of the aisle, in the dappled light of a stained-glass window, stood her future husband, the Duke of Everingham, looking bored. He'd removed his gray kid gloves and was slapping them in his palm. Bored and impatient.

At least he'd turned up.

The organ played a chord that swelled to a crescendo, then died, and then the music started and she was walking, walking like an automaton, toward the altar, toward her fate.

She felt everyone's eyes on her. She'd hardly slept. Did it show? Did she care if it did?

The duke stepped forward. Cal waited, his arm steady beneath her hand, ready to hand her over—like a parcel, *like a possession*, George had muttered once at another wedding they'd attended.

Rose glanced up and met the duke's gaze. Dark eyes, gray-green, and cold as the winter sea. Perfectly good eyes, but the wrong color. The wrong eyes.

She regarded them bleakly. Time healed all wounds. Or so they said.

The bishop, resplendent in his robes of gold and purple, cleared his throat and they turned to face him. For the marriage of a duke and the daughter of an earl, their usual minister wouldn't do, it seemed. Aunt Agatha's doing, no doubt.

Rose hoped he wasn't the kind of bishop who would give some long dreary sermon. She wanted this wedding over. Over and done with. No going back.

"Dearly beloved, we are gathered together here . . ."

The familiar words washed over her. She was calm, quite calm. Coldly, perfectly calm. Not like last time.

The bishop continued, speaking in those melodic rises and falls peculiar to ministers. Did they teach them that singsong cadence at minister school? *". . . not by any to be enterprised, nor taken in hand, unadvisedly, lightly, or wantonly, to satisfy men's carnal lusts and appetites . . . but reverently, discreetly, advisedly, soberly . . ."*

She shivered. Lord, but this church was cold.

". . . for the procreation of children . . ."

Children. Yes, think of that. Imagine swelling like Emm, round and glowing with joy in the child she was carrying. Not long for Emm now. Would it be a boy or a girl?

"Therefore if any man can show any just cause why they may not lawfully be joined together, let him now speak or else hereafter forever hold his peace."

Her fingers were freezing. She should have worn kid gloves instead of these lace ones.

The bishop paused for a perfunctory breath, then continued, *"I require and charge you both, as ye will answer at the dreadful day of judgment when the secrets of all hearts shall be disclosed, that—"*

"Stop the wedding!"

There was an audible gasp from the congregation, followed by a hush, as everyone waited to hear what would happen next. Rose's heart jolted—feeling as though it stopped. Heart in her mouth, she turned to stare at the man who'd just entered.

After a long, frozen moment, she breathed again. For a moment she'd imagined—but no. She'd never seen this man before.

The church door banged shut behind him, the sound echoing through the silent church.

"What the devil?" Cal muttered.

Rose fought to gather her composure, shaken by the brief flash of—whatever it was.

The stranger stood in stark contrast to the smoothly groomed and elegant congregation. He was tall and gaunt-looking, but his shoulders were broad—a laborer's shoulders. His clothes were ill-fitting, coarse, the trousers ragged and patched in places. He wore no coat. His shirt was too flimsy for the season and his shoes were of laced canvas, dirty and with visible holes.

If he knew he was grossly out of place in this, the most fashionable church in London, interrupting the most fashionable wedding of the season, he showed no sign, no self-consciousness.

He was heavily bearded. Thick hair rioted past his shoulders, wild and sun-bleached. The face above the beard—what she could see of it—was lean and deeply tanned, the skin stretched tight over prominent cheekbones. His nose appeared to have been broken at least once. The tattered shirt-sleeves revealed tanned, powerful-looking muscles.

No, she'd imagined that fleeting resemblance. But who was he? And what was he trying to do?

"Is this a joke?" the duke demanded of his best man.

"Lord, no, Hart—of course not. Nothing to do with me."

"Rose?" Cal asked.

Her heart was still pounding. She stared at the big ruffian who stood in the center of the aisle, shabby and confident, as if commanding it. He met her gaze with an assurance that shook her.

For a moment she wondered . . . But no. He was too brutal-looking, too rough, too wild.

"Rose?" Cal repeated.

She shook her head. "No idea."

The bishop surged forward. "Ho there, fellow, by what right do you seek to disrupt God's work?"

"By the right of law," the stranger replied coolly. "Lady Rose is already married."

A low, excited murmur of speculation followed his announcement.

Rose's heart almost stopped. He couldn't possibly know.

"Throw the dirty beggar out!" Aunt Agatha shook her stick at him.

"Rose?" Cal glanced at her, and despite the racing of her heart and the knotting of her stomach, again she shook her head. She did *not* know this man. How many times had she imagined—but no. No! It was some cruel, tasteless joke.

Cal snorted and raised his voice. "Is she now? And who is my sister married to, pray tell?"

A hush fell as everyone waited for his response.

"To me." His voice was deep, a little rough. Faintly surprised by the question.

There was a universal gasp, then a babble of amused and outraged speculation. Several people laughed. There were a couple of catcalls.

"That's *a lie*!" Dry-mouthed, breathless and suddenly furious, Rose moved forward.

"Stay here, Rose." Cal caught her arm and thrust her toward the duke. "Look after her, Everingham. I'll get rid of this madman. Galbraith?" Rose's brother-in-law, Ned Galbraith, nodded, and the two men approached the rough-looking stranger.

"Back off, gentlemen," the stranger warned with chilling menace. "I'm neither madman nor beggar. Lady Rose is indeed my wife." His bearing was in stark contrast to his ragged appearance. And he spoke with the crisp diction of a gentleman.

Cal frowned and glanced at Galbraith.

"What rubbish! Who the devil do you think you are, coming here to disrupt my wedding?" Furious at the sight of her brother's hesitation, shaken by the tall beggar's confidence and the cruelty of his lies, Rose shook off the duke's grip and marched forward. The duke tried to draw her back, but she evaded him and half ran, half stumbled up the aisle, almost tripping over her train. She pushed in between her brother and brother-in-law, ready to confront the big, weather-beaten stranger who was trying to ruin her wedding.

"What nonsense is this?" she snapped. "I've never seen you before in—"

White teeth glinted through the beard. "Ahh, that temper of yours, Rosie."

She froze. This man with the spare, rangy frame, the powerful shoulders, the crooked nose, and the wild sun-bleached hair, he wasn't . . . He couldn't be . . . He was nothing like . . .

She opened her mouth to repudiate him again—and met his gaze. Eyes of the palest silvery blue. She faltered. And in her memory the echo of her much younger self saying, *Like a summer sky at twilight.*

"Thomas?" she whispered, and fainted dead away.

ROSE'S BROTHER LUNGED FORWARD, BUT IT WAS THOMAS who caught Rose before she fell, caught her and clasped her to his chest. She was his and he wasn't going to give her up. He glanced down at her pale face, her skin pearlescent in the candlelight, the crescent sweep of sable lashes, the full, rosy lips parted slightly. Unconscious, but breathing evenly. His woman. His wife. Rose.

She hadn't recognized him . . .

The hostile circle of faces edged closer. Thomas eyed them coldly, silently daring them to interfere.

Rose's brother held his arms out. "I'll take her."

Thomas's hold on her tightened. "She's my wife. You heard her."

"I heard her call you Thomas. That proves nothing," he growled. But he made no move to wrestle her out of Thomas's arms. He couldn't, not in a church. And with such an audience. He faced Thomas with contained anger.

He must know who Thomas was. Rose's recognition, belated as it was, had confirmed it. It must be obvious to everyone. So why deny him? Why pretend?

Yet another person who wanted him obliterated? When would it end? Thomas tamped down on the familiar cold anger. He was home at last, in England, and Rose was in his arms. It was all that mattered to him. He would deal with the rest later.

The warm weight of her was almost shocking to his senses, the fragrance of her perfume, the silken texture of her skin, the fine-spun gold of her hair. She was still insensible, pale as paper, breathing gently. His grip on her tightened. It was shock that had caused her to faint, nothing more.

Four years . . .

A small, round, sweet-faced young woman pushed through the ring of male protectors. "What did you do to her?" she demanded fiercely. "Rose never faints!" She unstoppered a tiny crystal flask and waved it under Rose's nose.

He remembered seeing a miniature of her once, much younger but still recognizable. "You'd be Lily, then, Rose's little sister."

She snorted. "Everyone knows that."

"She used to worry about you. You were very ill."

She stopped waving the smelling salts under Rose's nose for a moment and glanced up at him, frowning. "Who are you—really?" It was a strange question. Who the hell did she think he was?

"Her husband."

"Nonsense." She shook her head vehemently. "If Rose were married I would know."

He frowned. "You didn't know?"

At that moment Rose jerked abruptly into consciousness. She sneezed, recoiling and shaking her head. "Ugh! Take that vile stuff—" She broke off, glanced at the concerned faces surrounding her, then up at Thomas. Her eyes widened and her mouth dropped open.

"How are you, Rose?" The words came out low, ragged and hoarse.

There was a long, fraught silence. Not a soul in the church moved. Everyone craned to hear what she would say next.

Her hand fluttered up, hesitated, brushed his cheek, a

moth wing of a touch, faint and fleeting, then drew back. "It *is* you, isn't it?" she said finally. "But you're . . . I thought . . ." And then she said, almost accusingly, "But you're supposed to be dead." She sounded . . . Was she *angry*? With him? For not being dead?

It wasn't the reaction he'd expected. He wasn't sure exactly what he'd expected, but somewhere in his imagination there had been joy, laughter . . . kisses.

Fool. Had the last four years taught him nothing?

She was getting married. Today. To someone else.

He'd upset her fancy wedding. His unexpected appearance had given her a shock. That was inevitable.

Still . . .

You're supposed to be dead. Was she angry with him for surviving? If so, she wouldn't be the only one. He wasn't going to apologize for it. He'd fought to stay alive, fought to get back to England. To Rose.

For a moment she clutched his shirt in a tight fist, her mouth quivering. Then, abruptly, she released his shirt and pushed at his chest. "P-put me down, please."

Several females now pushed past their menfolk and clustered around Thomas, clamoring, "Put her down!" and "Release her, you beast!"

He set Rose on her feet. She swayed. He barely had time to steady her when her sister and the other females closed around her in a protective clump and swept her away to the other side of the church.

You're supposed to be dead. What the hell had she meant by that. Did she *want* him to be dead?

It was not the homecoming he'd expected. Of course, some people reacted uncharacteristically to shock . . .

"Now look here, whoever you are—" her brother began.

Thomas turned and said crisply, "Commander Thomas Beresford, late of His Majesty's Royal Navy." His announcement sparked off a renewed buzz of controversy among the congregation.

People rose from their pews and pressed closer, the better to hear. "He's no officer," someone called out.

"For shame," a woman said.

"Toss the wretch back into the gutter." A silver-haired old lady gestured angrily with an ebony cane.

"Shoot the scoundrel," an old man shouted. A murmur of agreement followed.

Thomas turned and swept a cold gaze over the congregation, staring the crowd—the overfed, overindulged, smug society pets—down. The mutters died away, stares slid sideways and eyes failed to meet his.

His detractors silenced, he turned back to Rose's brother, who eyed him narrowly and said, "You claim to be married to my sister? On what basis?"

Thomas glanced at Rose, then back at her brother. "You're saying you didn't know? She never told you?"

A tall dark fellow—one of the family?—stepped forward and said quietly to the brother, "Cal, I think this is a conversation best conducted in private."

Rose's brother nodded. So that was who he was, Calbourne Rutherford, the brother who'd been away at war.

"The vestry?" the bishop suggested.

Rutherford agreed, then jerked his chin at Thomas. "Beresford?"

Thomas glanced once more to where Rose sat surrounded by her female relatives, watching him with wide, distressed eyes. Distressed for what reason? Because she was shocked at his return? Because he'd messed up her wedding? Because he wasn't dead? He couldn't tell.

Of course, he'd given her a shock, appearing so suddenly when apparently she thought he was dead. And in the middle of her wedding—which at least proved that she did believe he was dead. And looking as he did, with no time to shave and dress appropriately. And given how he'd lived for the last few years, it was no wonder she didn't immediately recognize him.

But it wasn't like Rose to stay silent or in the background. Not the Rose he remembered. Or the Rose who five minutes earlier had marched up to him demanding to know what he was doing, disrupting her wedding.

"Beresford?" Rutherford said again. Thomas gave a brusque nod.

"Coming, Everingham?" Rutherford addressed the groom—Rose's groom—who up to now had said not a thing. Thomas inspected him. Good-looking in an ascetic sort of way and elegantly, if severely, dressed.

Thomas wasn't impressed. If their places had been swapped, Thomas would never have stood by silently while another man claimed Rose.

"Duke?" Rutherford repeated. "Are you coming?"

Duke? Rose had been about to marry *a duke*? Might explain why she seemed so upset. Might explain the anger he'd heard in her voice.

Belatedly he recalled Ollie shouting something at him as he'd raced off, something about "the wedding of the season," but he hadn't stopped to listen. Ollie had just told him that Rose was getting married at eleven and Thomas hadn't waited to hear another thing. He'd taken off running, running like a madman, cutting through alleys and across parks.

He'd only just made it in time.

The duke turned a basilisk gaze on Thomas, raked him slowly from head to toe. Thomas, unmoved, gave him look for look. Rose was his. And nobody, not family, not a duke, not an angry congregation waving sticks was going to stop him claiming her.

The duke turned to Rose's brother and lifted one indifferent shoulder. "It's your mess, Ashendon, you deal with it."

Ashendon? Rose's father must be dead if Cal Rutherford was now Lord Ashendon. And what had happened to the older brother? Dead too, he supposed.

Not that it made any difference to Thomas.

The duke stepped forward and addressed the congregation in a bored voice. "Ladies and gentlemen, thank you for your attendance but I'm afraid your time—and mine—has been wasted. There will be no wedding today." He picked up his hat and strolled from the church, apparently oblivious of the murmurs and whispers that followed his progress, quite as if he hadn't just been effectively jilted.

His best man hesitated, then snatched up his hat and hurried after him. The door banged shut behind them.

Rose's brother swore under his breath.

None of the congregation moved. They were all waiting to see what happened.

The bishop opened the door to the vestry. A thin, elegant, elderly lady—the one who'd ordered him tossed back into the gutter—rose to her feet. "I will be part of this discussion," she declared.

The bishop smirked indulgently. "Dear Lady Salter, this sordid business is not for ladies. We gentlemen will sort it—"

Lady Salter. Thomas recalled that Rose had a sweet aunt and a scary one. He'd met the sweet one, so this must be Aunt Agatha.

She skewered the bishop with a glare. "Pshaw! I arranged a brilliant match for my niece—a duke!—and if some ragged scarecrow thinks he can set it aside with some spurious false claim . . ." She directed a contemptuous look at the scarecrow.

Meet the in-laws. The scarecrow couldn't help himself— he winked at her.

The old lady swelled with indignation, but before she could damn his impudence, the bishop distracted her by saying, "Lady Salter, this is a complicated matter better suited to a masculine understanding."

She fixed him with a scathing glare. "Masculine understanding? Pshaw! Weddings are women's business!"

The bishop opened his mouth, ready to argue the case, when a voice from the doorway drew everyone's attention. "I vouch for Commander Beresford and the truth of his claim." As one the congregation swiveled toward the speaker. Thomas's friend Ollie had finally arrived.

Ollie strolled down the aisle quite as if he weren't the cynosure of all eyes. "I gather you made it in time," he said to Thomas.

"And who might you be?" Ashendon snapped.

Ollie made a graceful bow. "Oliver Yelland of the Navy Board, at your service. Sorry I'm late. Things to arrange, cab to catch, jarvey to be paid."

"Yelland? Yelland?" Lady Salter said irritably. "Never heard of you. What are you doing, poking that long nose into other people's affairs? You have no business here, sirrah, so—"

"On the contrary, madam, business here extremely pertinent." His glance took in the group gathered by the vestry entrance. "Known Thomas Beresford any time these last ten years. Vouch for him absolutely."

At Ashendon's skeptical snort, he added, "Doubt my veracity? Admiral Sir Thomas Byam Martin—Comptroller of the Navy—will vouch for me."

"That's as may be, but what—" Ashendon began.

"Am a witness."

"Witness?" snapped Lady Salter. "This is a private family matter. We don't need any more witnesses." She shook her cane at the listening wedding guests. "We have far too many of the dratted things as it is. Now, be off with you."

"Witness to the bride's wedding," Ollie said sweetly. "The *original* one. I was Thomas's best man."

Ollie was enjoying this, Thomas could see. He liked a bit of drama, enjoyed stirring things up. But Thomas wasn't worried about proving his claim. He knew he was married to Rose.

It was Rose he wasn't sure of, her reaction—or rather, her lack of reaction. He could feel her watching him when she thought he wasn't looking, but she made no move to leave her relatives and come forward and stand with him. The Rose he knew, the Rose he'd married, hadn't been backward in coming forward.

Then again, people changed. Who knew it better than he?

"Where and when did this wedding take place?" he heard the bishop ask.

Thomas said to Ashendon, "You really didn't know about it?"

"No. And if my sister were truly married, why would she hide it from her family?"

Why indeed? Ashendon seemed sincere. But why would Rose have kept it a secret? The whole point of the marriage had been to secure her position.

It had seemed so right at the time. In the four years since, he'd never had reason to doubt that their marriage, hasty as it was, had been for the best. He'd thought it the best thing he'd ever done.

So why had she said nothing to any of her family? And why didn't she come to him now, stand with him in front of them all and explain that yes, they were married?

He glanced at her and caught her watching him. Their eyes met, clung, and then she dropped her gaze and moved back in her seat, out of sight. Failing to acknowledge him.

A familiar cold bitterness stole over him. *Et tu, Rose?*

The last four years should have prepared him for this. And yet it hadn't.

He'd come running in, full of expectation, expecting to surprise her, yes, but in a good way. Not this blank-faced silence.

"Genuine marriage all right," Ollie said. "Took place four years ago, small village church outside of Bath, St. Thomas's church—hard to forget that name, don't you think? Ceremony was conducted by . . ." He frowned and clicked his fingers. "Purdy or Proudy, some name like that. Old fellow. White hair, what he had of it. Nature's tonsure," he added, twirling his finger around the crown of his head.

"Bath?" Rose's brother turned to the bishop, a question in his eyes.

The bishop pursed his lips and nodded. "Cecil Purdue was the vicar of St. Thomas's in that diocese, but he's dead. Passed away last year."

"Purdue, that's the fellow," Ollie agreed. "Dead, eh? Not surprised. Getting on for ancient when we met him. But the wedding's recorded in the church register, all right and tight, eh, Thomas? Thomas?" He elbowed his friend in the ribs.

Thomas dragged his thoughts back into the present. "Yes. Rose has—had—a copy of her marriage lines." He'd ensured that, in case she needed to prove she was married. Instead she'd apparently never even mentioned it. Had she burned the precious document as well?

"Arrant nonsense!" Lady Salter interjected. "Four years ago, Rose was a sixteen-year-old schoolgirl. She couldn't possibly have married without her father's permission— and that I'm certain he would *not* have given!" She directed a scathing glance at Thomas and his witness.

"Such a marriage might not be legal," the bishop offered. "If the girl was underage, if she had no parental permission . . ."

"Rose?" Ashendon turned to his sister. "You haven't said a word. Is there any truth in this story?"

Thomas folded his arms and waited. What would he do if she denied it? The possibility hadn't even occurred to him. But then, nothing about this day had gone remotely to plan.

Finally, Rose stood, ashen-faced and with a troubled expression. She opened her mouth to speak, then pressed her lips together and nodded. She looked at Thomas for a brief moment, then her gaze dropped. An older woman put an arm around Rose and drew her back out of sight.

A cold fist clenched in Thomas's chest. It was as he thought. She was ashamed of marrying him. Regretted it. Wanted to deny it, but had been trapped into admitting it. It explained why she couldn't look at him, why she didn't speak.

Thomas's hands curled into fists. All these years, dreaming of Rose, dreaming of getting back to Rose, and now . . . this.

She hadn't told anyone about him. Not even her family.

She'd been about to marry *a duke*.

Cold, familiar anger coalesced in his belly. During the last four years there had been one attempt after another to obliterate him. But he had survived. He was not so easily destroyed, not so easily set aside. He would show them all.

But oh, Rose. It hurt. It shouldn't, but it did.

"It's a damnable blasted mess." Ashendon glared at the twittering congregation, so avid to hear every juicy detail, watching as if it were a play put on for their entertainment. Thomas would happily turn a hose full of cold seawater on the lot of them.

"Damned gossipmongering vultures," Ashendon continued. "Aunt Agatha's right. This is private family business. We'll sort it out at Ashendon House."

He turned toward the audience and raised his voice. "My apologies, ladies and gentlemen. As the duke said, the wedding has been canceled. Thank you for your attendance. The wedding breakfast is canceled. Your gifts will, of course, be returned."

He gave a nod to the small knot of females surrounding Rose. They immediately rose and hustled Rose out of the church. At the church door Rose paused, turned, gave Thomas one long, unreadable look, then disappeared into the daylight.

Once the bride and her female relatives had left, under Ashendon's gimlet gaze the remaining guests reluctantly dissipated, talking nineteen to the dozen in hushed, excited voices of the scandal they'd witnessed. The wedding of the season, in absolute, delicious ruins. It would be all over the ton by teatime.

Chapter Two

❧

How hard it is in some cases to be believed!
And how impossible in others!
—JANE AUSTEN, *PRIDE AND PREJUDICE*

"YOU STUPID, STUPID, *STUPID* GEL!" AUNT AGATHA BEGAN her rant the moment the door closed behind the Rutherford ladies in the large drawing room at Ashendon House. "A complete *waste* of a duke! All my efforts to arrange a splendid match for you—*weeks* of negotiation—down the drain. All eyes upon us, and then, the wedding of the season turned into a scene from a lowbrow farce!"

Rose sat silent on the sofa. She couldn't think of a single thing to say. Aunt Agatha's fury pelted against her like hail against a window, registering, but not touching.

Her brain had room for only one thought: *Thomas was alive. And she hadn't recognized him.*

How could she not have known him when he'd turned up at the church? She'd been so certain it was some dreadfully cruel joke. But how could it be, when nobody knew about her marriage?

No matter how wild his hair or thick his beard, no matter what he was wearing, she *ought* to have recognized him. Oh, there'd been that moment of hesitation, that flicker of doubt, but he'd been in her thoughts just moments before, and she'd convinced herself that was the reason.

A wife should know her own husband. Instead she'd effectively rejected him. Guilt flayed her.

Aunt Agatha continued, "If there was any irregularity in your marital status, why did you not inform us before it came to such a disgraceful—and public—scene!"

"Oh, be quiet, Aggie," Aunt Dottie told her sister. "Can't you see the gel's had a terrible shock?"

"She's not the only one, Dorothea! She's brought scandal on us all with her thoughtlessness! We'll be a laughingstock! I won't be able to hold my head up in public for, for *days*!"

"Oh, poor you," George muttered. Aunt Agatha gave her a baleful glare.

George had brought her dog in with her, Finn, the gangly Irish wolfhound. He sat with his head on her knee. Rose watched absently as George scratched him gently behind the ears.

"How do you feel, Rose, dear?" Emm asked, leaning forward. "You're looking very pale."

Rose couldn't answer. She didn't know how she felt. *Thomas was alive.* All these years thinking he was dead, and now . . .

She should be rejoicing—and she was. Or she would be, soon. When he arrived. When she could see him, touch him, speak to him in private. Know him again. Surely then, it would all come flooding back, the way it had been, four years ago.

And yet . . .

He'd changed so much.

He was so thin. She'd felt his ribs clearly when he'd held her against him. Thomas—*her* Thomas, the one she remembered—had always been lean, but in a slender, boyish kind of way. This Thomas looked somehow . . . gaunt, as if all flesh and softness had been burned out of him. And yet he also seemed bigger, tougher, harder. She thought of those hard, ropy muscles visible through the ragged shirt, the broadness of his chest and shoulders.

He'd aged too, much more, it seemed, than four years. And there were lines around his eyes, and shadows beneath them, as if he wasn't sleeping. She'd always loved his eyes—such an unusual silvery blue, like snippets of a summer sky at twilight. Their color hadn't changed, of course, but today it had been like looking into burning ice. There was a hardness there she didn't recognize . . .

That look he'd given her as she'd left the church.

When she was a little girl, before she and Lily had been sent away to school, an old lady in the village had died, and her cat, a small, sleek black-and-white tomcat had run off, probably because nobody had remembered to feed the poor little thing.

Rose had come across it in the woods several years later. She knew it was the same cat—the unique black-and-white markings were unmistakable. It was thin, with its ribs sticking out, yet it was bigger—rangy and ragged-looking. She'd called to it, but it no longer trusted people. It had hissed at her and vanished.

Something about Thomas reminded her of that cat.

Which was ridiculous. People didn't go feral. He was upset, maybe; angry at seeing her about to marry another man.

She needed to explain. She swallowed. It wasn't going to be easy.

Aunt Agatha raged on. "As for Ashendon, what on earth did he think he was doing, allowing that scarecrow to disrupt our wedding? His father would be turning in his grave. He would have known what to do."

"What could Cal do?" George objected. "It's not his fault that man turned up."

"If he'd done as I told him and thrown the wretched beggar back into the gutter—"

"It isn't as simple as that," Emm said. "It's perfectly clear that there *was* a wedding some years ago, but that Rose thought she was free to marry again. She has a lot of explaining to do, but not right now. She's in no state to explain anything yet. Let us wait until Cal and Ned arrive with Mr. Beresford and perhaps things will become clearer then—"

Aunt Agatha ignored her. "You should have denied him from the start, Rose. Swooning away like the veriest weakling only drew attention to—"

"Oooh, but the way he caught her and swept her into his arms when she fainted. And that burning, possessive look he gave her. Soooo romantic." Aunt Dottie heaved a gusty sigh.

"Doro*thea*!" her older sister snapped. "Don't encourage her. The gel has behaved disgracefully! To make such an appalling *mésalliance* behind everyone's back! If her father had found out he would have had the fellow horsewhipped and the wretched affair annulled! Rose should be a duchess by now, and instead she's, she's—"

"Oh, stop fussing over what can't be helped, Aggie," Aunt Dottie said.

"Can't be helped? Can't be *helped*? What nonsense, of course it can be helped!"

The auntly squabbles washed over Rose. Her hands, still clad in those absurd lace gloves, were shaking, and not with cold. Her mind was swirling with questions, impossible-to-answer questions.

Oh, Thomas. What was she going to do? What would she say to him? She had no idea.

The door opened and she tensed, thinking Thomas had arrived, but it was only two footmen bearing laden trays. "Ah, the refreshments at last." Emm seized on the distraction thankfully. "Lily, would you pour the tea, please? There's nothing like a nice cup of tea to settle the nerves, and we can all do with that. And perhaps we can refrain from squa— from any further discussion of Rose's situation for the moment. George, would you pass your aunt those cream cakes—and please don't feed them to the—oh, really, must you encourage that animal?"

"I dropped it by accident," George claimed. Finn, having devoured a little cake in one swift gulp, gazed mournfully at the spread, doing his usual impersonation of a dog who'd Never Been Fed.

Rose's tension eased a little as the flow of questions—

questions for which she had no answer—was diverted into a diatribe from Aunt Agatha on why Animals—especially Large Dogs—had No Place in a Gentlewoman's drawing room.

George listened with a bland expression and surreptitiously fed a biscuit to Finn. She glanced at Rose and winked.

Tea was poured and cakes, biscuits and cucumber sandwiches were handed around. Rose felt ill.

Thomas was *alive*. Where had he been all these years? What had happened?

Aunt Agatha waved away the cakes. "The marriage must be annulled, of course."

"Now, Aggie, didn't you hear Emm? Let's give Rose a little time to collect her thoughts before we decide what is to be done," Aunt Dottie said. "Rose, dear, you just drink your tea and eat one of these delicious-looking cakes, or perhaps a nice little sandwich—yes, I know you don't want anything, but trust me, you'll feel better with something in your stomach."

"And when you've finished your tea, you can explain how this appalling situation came to be," Aunt Agatha said. "The main question is whether we can convince the duke to forgive the insult and take Rose back. The poor man must be devastated."

George picked up a sandwich. "Devastated? He barely seemed mildly put out."

"Quite right. A true gentleman doesn't show his feelings." Aunt Agatha sipped her tea.

Aunt Dottie put a worried hand on Rose's arm. "You weren't in love with the duke, were you, my dear?"

Rose blinked, pulled back from the turmoil of her thoughts. "What? Oh. No."

"As it should be," Aunt Agatha said crisply. "People of our order don't marry for love."

"Piffle." Aunt Dottie selected a small cake bulging with cream.

Her sister turned to her in exasperation. "You never did

have the least grasp of reality, Dorothea. It's no wonder you never married. The chances you wasted—a duke, that marquess, several earls—"

"I'm perfectly happy with the choice I made."

"But you chose *none* of them."

"No." Aunt Dottie bit into her cream cake with a blissful expression.

Aunt Agatha rolled her eyes. "And look at you now, a pathetic old spinster!"

"That's a horrid thing to say!" Lily put a comforting arm around Aunt Dottie's waist.

Aunt Dottie chuckled. "Oh, don't mind Aggie, my love. She always gets crabby when her plans go awry. I'm perfectly happy with my life. I have no regrets, and I don't feel the least bit pathetic. Delicious cakes, Emm, dear. My compliments to your cook." She reached for another.

"There's nothing pathetic about being a spinster," George said. "That's what I plan to be—a happy spinster, unencumbered by a bossy husband. Mistress of my own fate. And with complete control over my own money."

"Don't be ridiculous, Georgiana!" Aunt Agatha snapped. "It is your duty—"

Emm set her teacup down with a clatter. "Rose, my dear, I'm sure you'll wish to change out of that dress. Come, let us go upstairs." She rose, a little awkwardly because of her bulk, and held out her hand. "No, Lily," she added, as Lily moved to accompany them. "Stay here with George, please, and entertain your aunts."

Rose felt an unworthy surge of relief. It was cowardly, she knew, but she wasn't yet ready to face Lily. Not alone. So much to explain, and no idea how to begin.

And that was just Lily. What about Thomas? What was she going to say to him?

Emm led her to the stairs. "Dear Dottie. You realize she's drawing your Aunt Agatha's fire deliberately?"

Rose smiled. George was too. "I know. Aunt Dottie is a darling."

Emm kissed her cheek. "She loves you, as do we all—even Aunt Agatha, though she'd never admit to such vulgar emotion. Now run along upstairs, wash your face—have a bath if you like—and change out of that dress. Come down when you're ready."

Rose gave her sister-in-law a rueful look. "And what if I'm never ready? Oh, Emm, what am I going to do?"

Emm hugged her gently. "I can't tell you that, my dear. You must look into your own heart, and decide for yourself what is right. Whatever you want, your brother and I will support you."

"But what if I don't know?" And oh, wasn't that a disloyal thing to say?

"Just take it one day at a time. There's no reason to rush into any decision—Mr. Beresford has been gone for four years, after all. A few more days or even weeks won't make any difference, will it?"

"I suppose not." Rose hooked her train over her arm and walked slowly up the stairs.

Emm must have rung for her maid, Milly, for she appeared a few moments later. With discreet sympathy, Milly refrained from asking questions as she helped Rose out of her wedding outfit.

As the heavy silk brocade was lifted over Rose's head, she felt a wave of . . . was it relief? She stared at the exquisite dress laid carefully across the end of her bed and felt not the slightest of regrets. Had she not wanted to marry the duke after all? Had she deluded herself?

Of course, she didn't know about Thomas then.

"I think I'll have a bath," she told Milly. She'd had a bath this morning, but somehow it felt right to bathe again. She sighed at her own foolishness. Did she think she could wash away the events of the day and start over? But a bath still felt right.

Rose sat at her dressing table pulling flowers and pins from her hair while the maid bustled about organizing things. She felt strangely distant from that woman in the looking glass. Who was she now? No longer Lady Rose Rutherford. No longer the bride of the Duke of Everingham.

The bride, undone.

In a small wooden box in the corner of the dressing table lay a plain gold locket on a fine gold chain. Her wedding ring was inside it, along with a lock of Thomas's hair.

She picked it up, let the locket dangle and spin on its chain for a long moment, then held it in her palm.

For the last four years it had hung between her breasts, hidden below her neckline of her clothes. She only ever took it off to bathe.

This morning—was it really only a few hours ago? It felt an age away—she'd wondered whether she should remove it for the wedding. Was it wrong to wear one man's ring while marrying another—even when the first man was dead?

The duke had stressed that love wasn't part of their arrangement, but even so, she'd decided it wouldn't be right to wear it. She'd taken the locket off, kissed it—kissing Thomas good-bye for ever—and put it away.

Mrs. Beresford—well, actually she was still Lady Rose, only Beresford now instead of Rutherford. A married woman again. Not that she'd ever felt like a married woman. She'd gone from schoolgirl, to secretly married schoolgirl, then back to schoolgirl again.

The marriage must be annulled, of course.

Of course Aunt Agatha would want that, and possibly Cal—maybe everyone wanted it. But what did she want?

And what did Thomas want? Presumably he wanted her, wanted the marriage to go on. But after that "stop the wedding" he hadn't said much. Or done much, apart from catching her when she fainted.

She hadn't said much either. Or done anything at all.

Footmen filled the bath with steaming water and left. Milly tipped in some bath salts, swished them around and adjusted the temperature of the water. Rose removed the last of her clothes and sank into the hot, fragrant water.

If anyone had told her that a woman who thought herself a widow—a widow of a beloved husband, at that—might feel . . . conflicted? Confused? Bewildered? on his return, she wouldn't have believed it.

Oh, her brain told her she was delighted, full of joy, relieved, thrilled—all the good, happy things that were to be expected, but instead she felt . . . numb.

She soaped her sponge.

Not entirely numb. More like a limb slowly coming back to life, pins and needles, only a hundred times worse.

She'd buried Thomas, in her heart and in her mind—at least she'd tried to. So hard. A part of her had been frozen solid, ever since she'd read that small paragraph in the paper: "*all hands lost.*"

Now he was back, and it was as if her heart were breaking all over again . . . Unbreaking. As painful as before, if not more so.

She sponged herself. Guilt tore at her for giving up on him, for the way she'd behaved after the news of his death. Guilt for never telling anyone else about him.

And guilt for not recognizing him when he'd spoken up in the church, for denying him—her own husband—in front of witnesses. Like Judas.

All the while preparing to marry another man.

She loved Thomas, of course she did. At least she used to.

But what had happened to him? Where had he been all this time? And why had he never sent word to her to let her know he was alive?

This spare, somber, wild-looking stranger . . . That he was Thomas, she had no doubt of, but was he *her* Thomas? He was, and he wasn't.

And that was half the agony.

If she let herself love him as she had before—blindly and completely, with her whole unfettered, unruly heart—how could she bear it if she lost him again?

What if he'd changed so much he was no longer *her* Thomas?

I used to want too much out of life.

The impulsive young girl who'd married Thomas was no longer the same, either.

Rose rinsed herself off and stepped out of the bath. Her family was downstairs, waiting for an explanation she didn't know how to make.

She dressed quickly.

Thomas would arrive soon. The explanations she'd have to make to him would be even harder.

She wanted to run away. *I'm more mature now.*

She pulled a face at the girl in the mirror, picked up the locket and fastened it around her neck. Then she straightened her dress, took a deep breath and headed downstairs.

"CAN'T STAY, I'M AFRAID," OLLIE TOLD THOMAS AS THEY emerged from the church into the fresh cool air. They paused on the church steps. Most of the spectators, deprived of both drama and the expected shower of coins, had drifted away. "Have to get back. Left m'office without notice. Admiralty frowns on that sort of thing." He fished in his pocket, produced an elegant silver card case and handed a card to Ashendon. "M'card, Ashendon. At your service any time."

Ashendon glanced at it and slipped it into a pocket.

Thomas had been given no opportunity to speak with Rose. She'd been hustled away in a carriage by the Rutherford ladies. Lord Ashendon had declared that they—meaning he, Thomas and the third gentleman, who seemed to be some sort of family connection—would follow on foot.

In other words, he wanted to interrogate Thomas in private, without Rose or any of the other ladies present. Or perhaps to dispose of him down a dark alley, Thomas thought grimly. He could try.

Ollie scribbled on the back of another card and handed it to Thomas. "M'lodgings, Thomas. Welcome to stay until you get something sorted out."

Thomas thanked him. He hadn't given any thought as to where he might sleep the night. Everything had happened in such a rush.

Ollie hailed a passing hackney and climbed nimbly into it.

Thomas watched him leave. Ollie, at least, hadn't let him down.

Thomas hadn't expected to find Rose the day he arrived. His immediate concern had been to make his official report to the navy, make arrangements for the return of his men and then set out to find her. He'd expected to go to Bath, where he'd left her, presumably in the house of her aunt. The nice one.

Apparently women didn't stay where you put them.

"This way," Ashendon said, and they began to walk. It was spring, and a fine, cloudless day, but the pallid sun barely warmed Thomas's skin. Hard to believe it was the same sun, the harsh, pitiless orb under which he'd toiled for the past four years.

He'd thought of Rose every single day.

Had she thought of him? He had to wonder, now.

He'd expected his first day back in England to be one of surprise, but also of welcome, of celebration; instead the day had been one shock after another. Bad enough that the navy had kept insisting he must be dead because their records said so, but not only did Rose also think he was dead—she'd never told a soul she'd even been his wife.

And yet his uncle and his cousin *knew* he was alive, knew he'd survived the shipwreck and had made it to what passed for civilization in that part of the world. They'd made no effort to bring him home—worse, they'd denied all knowledge of his very existence, he had no idea why— and in doing so had condemned him to an unimaginably brutal existence.

But that was a betrayal he'd confront another day. Revenge, they said, was a dish best served cold. He'd had four years to prepare for that.

Today was all about Rose, the woman who'd put Thomas behind her to marry a duke.

He'd imagined a joyful reunion. He'd expected her to throw herself into his arms. Instead she'd pushed at his chest and asked to be put down. And had said barely a word since.

One more illusion shattered.

Ashendon's sidelong glance was knowing. "Having second thoughts, Beresford? Regrets, already? Because you can leave now if you wish."

Thomas gave him a hard look. "I'm not going anywhere."

They turned a corner and crossed a busy street lined with prosperous-looking shops. He was aware of Ashendon's continued sidelong scrutiny, the suspicion, the waves of silent hostility emanating from him.

Thomas didn't much like the man, but he couldn't entirely blame him for his hostility. He'd feel much the same if some scruffy fellow had appeared out of nowhere, claiming to be married to his beautiful sister—a marriage he'd never heard of until today.

If that was even true.

Marriage to a duke was nothing to be sneezed at; it would be a social and economic coup, even for the daughter of an earl.

"You really didn't know? She never told you?" He knew he was repeating himself but he still couldn't make sense of it.

"About this so-called marriage? No, not a word. And she still hasn't confirmed it to my satisfaction. That nod could have meant anything. So we've only got your word that it took place at all."

And Ollie's, but Thomas had no intention of arguing his case. He knew he was married. He knew why they'd married in secret. The question was, why was it still a secret?

They walked on.

"I'll give you a hundred pounds to disappear," Ashendon said.

Thomas stiffened but kept walking. He wasn't even going to dignify that with a response—no, on second thoughts he would. He gave a contemptuous snort. "Is that all?"

Now it was Ashendon's turn to stiffen.

They crossed another street.

"Five hundred pounds."

"Only a monkey? You'd drop more than that in a day at the races or an evening over cards." He walked on a few steps before adding casually, "You don't value your sister very highly, do you?"

Ashendon's teeth were almost audibly grinding.

"Which brother are you?" Thomas asked. "The brother who never visited, or the brother who never wrote?" He knew perfectly well which brother Cal was, but people revealed more than they intended when provoked into anger.

"Damn you, I was at war."

"And soldiers can't write home? Or were you simply too busy and important to spare a thought for a pair of young half sisters fretting themselves silly over their big brother's safety."

Ashendon scowled but said nothing.

Thomas continued, "Rose hasn't exactly been blessed with the men of her family, has she? First her father sends her away from her home, exiles her for a flaw not her fault—"

"Not Lily's fault either!" the second man flashed.

Thomas said in a hard voice, "Their father didn't care about either of them, though, did he? Rose told me he said—actually said out loud in her hearing—that he had no time for girls. And her brothers apparently felt the same, not bothering to—"

Ashendon grabbed him and shoved him hard against some railings. "Damn your impudence! I'm *nothing* like my father or my brother. Rose knows I care for her. And you can be damned sure I'll protect her from your grubby little scheme, whatever it is."

Thomas gave him a long cool look and simply waited. He'd dealt with some ugly customers in his time, and Ashendon didn't worry him. Thomas could take him, but he had no intention of brawling in the street with Rose's brother.

After a few heavy breathing moments, Ashendon controlled his temper, released Thomas and stepped back. "No spine, eh?"

Thomas smoothed his shabby shirtsleeves, quite as if he wore one of Weston's finest coats. "Bad enough that I'm meeting my wife after four years' absence dressed like this"—he gestured—"I won't mark my homecoming by giving her brother a thrashing. Not today, at any rate. I might have found you wanting in the past, but she considered you a favorite—or at least she used to."

"She still does," the other fellow said, sounding amused. "When it suits her."

Thomas turned to him. "And you are?"

"Galbraith, Ned Galbraith. Lady Rose's brother-in-law." He made no move to offer his hand.

"Lily's husband?"

Galbraith raised a brow at the familiar address. "You know my wife?"

Thomas shook his head. "I never met Lily until today. She was ill when I was courting Rose. But Rose spoke of her often."

"*Courting?*" Ashendon snapped. "There was no 'courting.' Courting happens with a family's permission—out in the open, under the eyes of a chaperone, not in a series of secret blasted assignations with a schoolgirl too young to know better. And don't refer to my sister as 'Rose,' dammit—she is Lady Rose to you."

"Actually," Thomas said coolly, "she is Mrs. Thomas Beresford, my wife."

"That's yet to be proven."

"Let us not stand here brangling in public," Galbraith suggested. Ashendon glanced at him, then gave a grudging nod. They all moved on.

"You claim you just arrived in London today," Galbraith said. He wasn't quite as hostile as Ashendon, but his skepticism was obvious.

"My ship docked this morning."

"After an absence of four years?"

"That's right."

"Where were you all that time?" Ashendon asked.

"Abroad."

"Care to explain?" Galbraith said.

"I was unavoidably detained." It was the truth, after all.

"What the devil does that mean?" Ashendon snapped. "Unavoidably detained by whom? Doing what?"

Thomas didn't answer. He walked on. His business was his own affair.

"And when you arrived, you went straight to the Admiralty?" Galbraith prompted.

"Yes, to report. As is my duty."

Beside him, Ashendon snorted. "And they just happened to say to you, 'Oh, by the way did you know, Lady Rose Rutherford is getting married today?'"

"No," Thomas said. "They kept insisting I must be dead."

"I can see their point," Ashendon muttered.

Galbraith ignored him. "Dead?"

"Because that's what my file said."

"The official mind," Galbraith murmured. "How did you convince them?"

"I wondered whether my friend Oliver Yelland might still be working there. If he was, he could confirm my identity. When I left England he was about to take up a minor position in the Navy Office. It was my good luck that he was still there, and was working today." Thomas had had the devil of a time convincing the clerks in the front office to send for such an important person as Ollie had apparently become. A faint smile teased his lips. The memory of their shocked faces when Ollie had given him the prodigal's welcome.

"And he told you about the wedding?" Galbraith prompted.

"Exactly."

"Bit of a coincidence," Ashendon muttered. "The so-called witness to your so-called wedding."

"Wasn't it?" Thomas agreed smoothly. "And lucky. Otherwise your sister would have committed bigamy." He let that sink in.

They reached another corner, and Thomas halted. He'd been aware for some time of the looks the three of them had received from people in the street; two elegantly dressed gentlemen and one scruffy sailor.

Dammit, whether she wanted to acknowledge him or not, he wasn't going to face Rose like this. A man had his dignity. Ollie would help him out. He turned around and started back the way he'd come.

Ashendon grabbed him by the arm. "Where the hell do you think you're going?"

Thomas wrenched his arm free. "I'm damned if I'll face my wife looking like this. I need a bath, a shave and a change of clothes."

Ashendon's chin jutted belligerently. "If you for one minute imagine I'm going to let you waltz in, disrupt my sister's wedding, cause a frightful scandal and then just disappear, you can disabuse yourself of that little notion right this minute. You're not going anywhere. We'll see this thing out to the end."

Thomas narrowed his eyes. "I'll go where I damned well please, when I damned well please. And right now I'm going to have a bath and a shave."

"And a haircut," Galbraith added. They both swung around and stared at him. "If I were returning to my wife after an absence of four years," he said mildly, "I wouldn't wish to look like that. Or smell like that."

"Smell?" Thomas frowned, resisting the impulse to sniff himself.

"Slight odor of fish," Galbraith explained.

"Whose side are you on?" Ashendon growled.

"I'm thinking of Rose. She's about to introduce Beresford to the family and explain her actions of four years ago. Spare her further embarrassment if he looks presentable, at least." He added quietly, "She's a girl of some pride."

Ashendon grunted.

Galbraith murmured, "Softhearted girl, your sister. Easier to reject a clean, respectable-looking man than a fellow who looks desperately down on his luck."

"Maybe." Ashendon gave Thomas a dirty look. "I'd

rather not introduce him at all. Send him on his way, pay the bastard off, and if there is a marriage, get it annulled."

"Rose might have something to say about that," Galbraith said. "She didn't exactly reject him."

She hadn't exactly embraced him, either, Thomas reflected. But he didn't say anything. He'd decide what to do once he'd talked to Rose.

"I can handle Rose," Ashendon said.

Galbraith looked amused. "There's a first time for everything, I suppose." He looked pointedly at Ashendon and waited.

"Very well, dammit," Ashendon said reluctantly. "We'll take Beresford to his hotel, and he can bathe and change."

"I don't have a hotel," Thomas said. "And until the Navy Board sees fit to release my back pay, I am entirely without funds. All I currently possess are the clothes I stand up in." The look of disgust on Ashendon's face was almost enjoyable. He thought Thomas was trying to push up the price of his bribe. "But I'm sure Ollie will lend me what I need."

"And we're supposed to await your pleasure while you find your friend and titivate, are we?" Ashendon snapped.

"You don't have a choice," Thomas pointed out. "I'm doing it whether you want me to or not."

"No need to find your friend," Galbraith said. "My house is just down there." He gestured.

"I know that, what of it?" Ashendon said impatiently.

"Beresford can clean up at my place. My valet will take care of him. And find him some clothes. We're much the same height."

They both stared at him, Thomas with wary surprise, Ashendon with outright disbelief.

"Decent of you, Galbraith," Thomas said. "My thanks." Was Galbraith playing some deep game or showing genuine goodwill? Time, he supposed, would tell.

They walked the short distance to Galbraith House and Galbraith sent for his valet, a short, nattily dressed man. "Mr. Beresford requires a bath, Enders."

The valet glanced at Thomas, hesitated, then an impassive expression—almost wooden—dropped over his face, like a theater curtain closing. "Very good, sir."

"And a shave and haircut," Thomas added.

A flicker of expression crossed the valet's face before returning to wood, almost stone. "Of course, sir." He bowed, a very correct bow that somehow conveyed that if his employer wished to ask his Very Superior Valet to clean up A Scruffy Beggar, then, against his better judgment, the superior valet would comply. But it had better not become A Habit.

"He'll need a change of clothes, too. See if you can find something of mine to fit him," Galbraith added.

The valet bowed again. "Very good, sir." Meaning quite the opposite. "If you would come this way, sir?"

WHILE BERESFORD WAS UPSTAIRS CLEANING UP, NED'S butler, Fenchurch, provided them with a cognac and left them to ponder the situation.

Ned sipped his cognac. "Not exactly how we expected the day to turn out."

Cal grunted and stared into the fire.

"Think there's anything to his story?"

"I do, dammit," Cal said. "You didn't really know Rose back then. She was completely uncontrollable. Sneaking out and getting herself married to some impossible blackguard was exactly the sort of thing she'd do."

"So you'll accept it?"

"No. It's a devil of a tangle, but I swear I'll get her out of it." Cal stared into his glass, brooding. "Somehow."

There was a long pause, then Ned said, "I find his approach interesting."

"Interesting?" Cal snorted. "I can think of a better word. Infuriating. Inconvenient. Impossible. I'd like to strangle the swine."

"As I recall, you almost tried."

"Can't blame me. Fellow's got a damned cheek."

"Didn't seem to bother him, though, did it? Not afraid of you, was he?"

Cal shrugged. "Didn't fight back."

"Chose not to," Ned said with meaning.

Cal cast him a swift glance and scowled. "Damned provocative."

"Mmm. That's what I find interesting."

"Eh?"

"I think he's doing it deliberately."

"Doing what?"

"Stirring you up, trying to provoke you."

Cal snorted. "Trying? He's damned well succeeding."

"You're too close to the situation. Think about it. He's testing you."

"Testing me?" Cal sat up indignantly. "Why the devil should *he* be testing *me*?"

"That's what I find interesting. If he was trying to get himself accepted by Rose's family, one would expect him to be more conciliatory, even ingratiating. But he's not."

"Quite the opposite."

"Exactly," Ned agreed.

"Hmph. He's too damned sure of himself."

The two men sipped their cognac thoughtfully. "The way he handled your attempt to bribe him was interesting, too," Ned said after a while.

Cal snorted. "He knows she's worth more than that. That's why he's being so blasted annoying—he wants more money."

"Not so sure about that, myself. Think he's winding you up." Ned crossed his long legs and settled back in his chair. "It must have occurred to him, if it hasn't yet occurred to you, that as Rose's legal husband, he's already entitled to the whole of her fortune."

"Not if I get it annulled."

Ned shrugged. "Think there's a good chance he'll end up as our brother-in-law."

"Over my dead body."

Ned looked amused. "Hope it won't come to that."

There was a short silence, then Cal said, "Where do you think he's been all this time?"

Ned pursed his lips, considering. "He's dashed reticent about it. Got to be something shady."

Cal nodded. "And his reappearance—timed perfectly for the *speak now or forever hold your peace* part—too blasted melodramatic for words. Got to be calculated for maximum impact."

"And in front of half the ton—no chance of hushing it up now."

Cal grunted agreement and lapsed into another long brooding silence. Then he said, "You're sure Lily didn't know about this wedding? Those girls would happily lie through their teeth for each other."

"No. I saw Lily's face when it all came out. She was as shocked as you and I."

"But if it was a real marriage—and it does sound like it was—why would Rose keep it a secret all these years?"

Chapter Three

❧

Doubts are more cruel than the worst of truths.
—MOLIÈRE

"IT WAS WHEN YOU HAD THE MUMPS—REMEMBER, LILY?
More than half the school was ill—your entire dormitory—
and those of us who'd had them already were sent home." The
bath had helped. She'd given her situation a lot of thought
while she was bathing—it was amazing how water helped
clear the mind as well as the body—and realized there was
only one thing that mattered: that Thomas was alive.

Lily nodded. "And you went to stay with Aunt Dottie, but—"

"And you know how Aunt Dottie likes to visit the pump
room every day," Rose continued hurriedly. She knew what
Lily was going to say. Why hadn't she told her afterward?
Rose had no answer to that. She wasn't entirely sure herself.
All she knew was that at first she hadn't wanted to speak of
it to anyone, had wanted to hug it to herself as a most delicious, exciting, intensely private secret.

And later . . . Well, later she hadn't been able to speak of
it at all.

It was so painful, dredging up these memories, memories she'd never thought would see the light of day again.

She'd buried them in the deepest, darkest corner of her mind and sealed them over with ice, frozen deep and cold and safe, never to be recalled, never to torment her again. No one would ever know, ever suspect. But now, the fragile shell had been cracked open and she was having to bare her secrets, her precious, private moments, to the harsh, if loving, exposure of family judgment.

Because Thomas was alive. *Remember that.* He was *alive.*

Aunt Dottie nodded. "I do enjoy the company at the pump room, it's true. And that was such a difficult time for us all." She turned to the others in the room and explained. "Poor little Lily took the mumps very hard—some people just sail through them, but not Lily. She was so sick they wouldn't even let us visit. Poor Rose was beside herself with worry, weren't you, dear? So I took her out as much as I could."

"Yes. And that's where I met Thomas."

"At the pump room?" Lily exclaimed in surprise.

Rose nodded. "His friend, Mr. Yelland—the man who came to the church today, remember?—had been ill, and was recuperating under the supervision of a Bath physician. Taking the waters twice daily, bathing in the hot springs, that kind of thing. Thomas had been given leave while his ship was in dock for repairs, and he came to Bath to see how he was getting on."

"And?" George prompted.

"We met, and fell in love."

George pulled a skeptical face. "Just like that?"

"Just like that." Even now, after all those years had passed, Rose could remember the absolute certainty she'd felt, almost from the moment they met, that she and Thomas were meant to be together for all their lives.

And Thomas had seemed to feel the same. Napoleon had just been defeated—or so they'd thought at the time— and Thomas was making plans to leave the navy and make a home with her, perhaps to manage one of his uncle's estates.

But later, she'd wondered whether perhaps Thomas hadn't felt quite the way she did . . .

Aunt Dottie nodded understandingly. "Young love, I know."

Aunt Agatha snorted. "Young nonsense, more like! To make such an appalling *mésalliance* behind everyone's back! If her father had found out, he would have horse-whipped the fellow and sent him on his way! Rose should be a duchess by now, and instead she's, she's—"

"Oh, be quiet and listen for once, Aggie. And don't ridicule what you don't understand. The heart wants what the heart wants." Aunt Dottie continued, "Of course, it was very naughty of you to sneak out and make a secret marriage, Rose dear, but Aggie is quite right; your father, God rest his soul, would never have allowed it—"

"I should think not!" Aunt Agatha snapped. "A penniless nobody!"

Rose flashed her a hard look. "Thomas is *not* a nobody to me."

"Well said, my love." Aunt Dottie patted Rose's knee. "So I quite understand why you did it in secret. It is very hard when you're young and in love, and you think nobody understands or will listen."

"Pshaw! Don't imagine it has slipped my notice that *you* are the one at fault here, Dorothea! You were in charge of Rose at the time. It is your disgracefully lax guardianship that is at the root of this calamity."

"Pooh! We don't know that it's a calamity at all. We haven't even heard the poor boy's story yet."

"Of *course* it's a calamity, you ninny! We lost *a duke!*" Aunt Agatha snapped.

"Pfft! Who cares about dukes?" Aunt Dottie dismissed an entire class of noblemen with an airy wave of her hand. "Love is far more important. I must say, I don't much like that beard, but he has lovely eyes, your Thomas. And those shoulders . . ."

Aunt Agatha swelled with outrage, but before she could scald them all with vitriol, Emm intervened, saying in her best schoolteacher voice, "Stop teasing your sister, Dottie. Go on, Rose, I can understand you falling in love—I did it myself at your age, quite disastrously as it happened—but what prompted you to make a clandestine marriage? Why did Mr. Beresford not apply to your father—or Aunt Dottie at the very least—for permission to court you? Why hide it from everyone—even after the event?"

"And not even tell *me*," Lily said in a low voice. "I wouldn't have told."

"I know." Rose squeezed her sister's hand in mute apology. Looking back, she hadn't really meant to keep it such a secret, not for so long. At first it was simply because falling in love with Thomas had seemed so magical, so precious and private—too private to share. She wanted to hug it to herself, to revel in the secret joy of being in love. Of being married to the most wonderful man in the world.

Besides what would be the point of telling anyone at that stage? Thomas was away on his ship, so it wasn't as if they could commence their married life together. And if her family had learned she was married, apart from the dreadful fuss they would make, Rose knew she'd be pulled out of school, separated from Lily, and she couldn't allow that to happen. Lily struggled in school, and Rose had to be there to protect her.

Then the news had come that Thomas's ship had gone down. All hands lost . . . Dead.

For the next few weeks she'd been too busy hiding her grief. Because if anyone discovered she'd been secretly married, the fuss she'd dreaded would happen anyway—and to what end? If Thomas were alive it would have been a different matter, but he was dead, dead and gone, and the prospect of going over it all again, explaining to Miss Mallard, to her father and Aunt Agatha—the thought of them all picking through the ashes of her dreams with their horrid, suspicious minds—was unbearable.

She might have shared her secret with Lily at that point, but Lily was staying with Aunt Dottie at the time, slowly recuperating from her very severe reaction to the mumps—

she'd almost died—while the rest of the school returned to their lessons.

And then . . . No, she couldn't bear to speak of that. Not now. Maybe not ever.

Afterward, she couldn't bear to have it sullied by a lot of questions. The kind of suspicious, ugly questions she was facing now. So she'd done her best to bury her dreams along with her husband, buried them deep and covered them with ice as best she could. Never to speak of them again.

And now Thomas had returned from the dead . . .

"I cannot think well of him for going behind everyone's back," Emm said. "You were, after all, just sixteen. He was much older, and an officer."

"He was twenty-three," Rose said. And even at sixteen she knew what she wanted.

Emm raised her brows. "Really? He looks much older."

Rose nodded. "He's changed a lot. That's why I didn't at first recognize him." The knowledge of that failure twisted inside her once more.

"It's obvious why he married her in secret," Aunt Agatha declared. "He was after her money, of course."

"He wasn't," Rose flashed. "He knew nothing about my inheritance."

"Don't be naïve, child, of course he did."

"He didn't, I'm sure he didn't. Or if he did, it made no difference." Thomas was unlike any other man she'd ever met. He hadn't seen her as the Earl of Ashendon's daughter, or the Rutherford heiress, or even as the latest beauty—he'd looked at her and seen Rose, the person, the girl with hopes and dreams and fears and insecurities.

"Then why make such a hasty, havey-cavey marriage?"

"It wasn't havey-cavey. There wasn't time. Thomas had to leave. He'd been called back to his ship." And she knew if she'd told anyone in her family—even Aunt Dottie— there would be a grand fuss and they'd step in and prevent the marriage, and she *wanted* to be married to Thomas, she really did.

"So? That's no reason to rush you into marriage. He at least should have known better."

"He wanted it as much as I did, but it wasn't for the sake of my inheritance, it was because—" She broke off, biting her tongue.

"Because?" Aunt Agatha raised a sardonic brow.

Rose felt her cheeks heating. She looked away. It was all sounding so tawdry now, and it wasn't, it hadn't been. Her time with Thomas had been beautiful.

"Hah! He made sure of you, didn't he?" Aunt Agatha said knowingly. "The villain, seducing an innocent young gel. I devoutly hope Cal is giving the fellow a thorough horsewhipping at this very minute."

Rose turned in distress to Emm. "He won't, will he, Emm? I don't want him to hurt Thomas."

"Hush now, it will be all right," Emm said soothingly. "Cal isn't such a brute." But she didn't sound completely confident.

"Thomas didn't seduce me," Rose admitted, her face flaming. "I wanted it too. We were *in love*! He married me to protect me, to protect my honor, in case—" She stopped.

"In case you were caught with a bast—" Aunt Agatha began.

"It wouldn't have been a bastard!" Rose felt her face crumpling. She fought it. "Because he *married* me!"

"Pah! He married you, gel, because—"

Emm cut her off. "That's enough! All this happened in the past and there's nothing any of us can do to change it. Recriminations are both pointless and unnecessarily hurtful. It is Rose's welfare now that must concern us, and how we—and she—are to go on in the future. And until Cal and Ned return with Mr. Beresford—and until Rose gets a chance to talk with Mr. Beresford alone, and decides what she wants, nothing can be decided." She glanced at the ormolu clock on the mantelpiece. "I cannot think what can be keeping them so long."

"A good horsewhipping, I hope," Aunt Agatha muttered.

* * *

GALBRAITH'S VALET TOOK THOMAS UPSTAIRS TO A SMALL
dressing room. Indicating a plain polished dressing table
with a chair facing a looking glass, he said, "If you'd care
to wait here, sir, I'll arrange your bath." Without waiting for
an answer, he hurried off.

It was a gentleman's dressing room, elegantly appointed
but plain and practical, containing, as well as the dressing
table, two large wardrobes, a high chest of drawers, and a
comfortable-looking armchair and small table next to the
window. A large enameled bath sat before the fireplace,
currently empty.

Thomas wouldn't have minded a fire. His clothes were
thin and he hadn't yet acclimatized.

He wandered to the window and gazed out at the vista
of roofs and chimneys, the faint haze of smoke, even in
spring, a glimpse of waving treetops indicating a nearby
park. In the street below, carriages rattled past, and a nurse-
maid strolled along with her two young charges, heading
for the park, no doubt. Two servants bustled past, baskets
in hand, heading for the market perhaps.

All perfectly ordinary sights, but not to Thomas, not today. *London. England. Home.* He couldn't quite believe it.

"I thought we could trim your beard and cut off the
worst—er, the better part of your hair before the bath, sir,"
Enders announced from behind him. "Let the hot water
soften the bristles." He waved Thomas to the dressing table
and opened a leather case containing shaving implements
and scissors. Two footmen arrived carrying large cans of
steaming water and began to fill the bath.

Thomas sat and for the first time in years saw his reflection.

Good God! Was this what he looked like now? He stared.
Lord, if he'd seen a drawing of himself—one of those clever
charcoal drawings that artists did in the marketplace for a
few coppers—he wouldn't have known himself.

No wonder Rose hadn't recognized him. He looked like a wild man. A savage. He recalled the expressions of those people in the church when he'd turned and faced them down. He grinned. They must have thought him a barbarian come among them.

His grin faded. This was who he was now, who he'd been for most of the last four years. This grim-faced, barbaric-looking savage. And the change wasn't only skin deep.

No wonder her family had banded around her. Protecting her from him.

She'd been about to marry a duke.

Did she love the fellow? Impossible to tell.

Irrelevant now anyway, now that Thomas had returned.

Her family wanted him gone, that was clear. Of course they'd want a duke instead of the man they saw now.

No matter. He'd fought tooth and nail to get back to England, and he'd fight tooth and nail to keep Rose—as long as she wanted him, that is.

And that was the question. Did she want him? Or would she side with her brother to have their wedding annulled so she could marry her duke?

If she didn't want him, if she wanted her duke and all he could offer, did Thomas have the right to keep her? Legally, perhaps, but morally? Did anyone have the right to hold another person against their will?

But as well as rights, Thomas had obligations. And in his current situation he needed Rose—and her fortune—more than ever.

He stared again at the man in the mirror. He wasn't exactly a bargain. The contrast between him and her duke couldn't be stronger; the duke was rich, established and titled. Thomas was impoverished, homeless, forgotten and disowned—repudiated by his closest relatives.

And damaged, let's not forget that, he reminded himself.

Was he even fit to live with her, after the life he'd lived?

Did he have a choice?

A different man, a better man would offer to release her from her vows, those vows forced by circumstance and youth and impulsive, reckless lovemaking. Let her go to her precious duke, who couldn't even be bothered to fight for her.

Thomas was no longer that man.

He was going to fight for her. Her and her fortune.

Footmen came and went, emptying cans of hot water into the bath. Clean, steaming hot water. Thomas couldn't wait to immerse himself in it. He was once fastidious, but that was in another life. In the last years he'd learned to be grateful for a dousing in cold seawater.

And if he smelled of fish afterward, it was still an improvement.

The valet picked up a small pair of silver scissors, ran his gaze over Thomas and pursed his lips distastefully.

"Sorry-looking specimen, aren't I?"

The valet jumped, as if the table had spoken, and all expression dropped from his face. "Not at all, sir," he lied smoothly.

"Been at sea a long time. Washing in cold seawater just doesn't do the trick."

"Indeed, sir." Standing well back, the valet gingerly picked up a strand of Thomas's hair between thumb and finger and snipped at it with a tiny pair of silver scissors. From his expression, he half expected Thomas's thick bush of hair to attack him. Or perhaps it wasn't the hair that concerned him.

"You need not worry," Thomas said dryly. "I take good care to ensure I carry no . . . livestock on my person."

In the looking glass, the valet's gaze met his. "Sir?"

"I'm very particular in that respect." He couldn't blame the man. Anyone would expect a man of Thomas's current appearance to be slovenly in his personal habits. But despite his current appearance, Thomas was as clean and vermin-free as he could possibly make himself.

Enders seemed to accept the assurance. He moved closer and snipped at Thomas's hair and beard. Clumps of sunbleached hair dropped to the floor. It was dark underneath.

The valet stepped back. "There, that will do for now. I'll

trim your hair properly and give you a nice close shave once you've had your bath, sir." He frowned, as if to say something, then closed his mouth.

"What is it?" Thomas said, and when the man didn't answer, he said, "Spit it out, man, I'm beyond being delicate about my situation."

"Well, sir, I just wondered, wouldn't you be more comfortable if we sent for your own clothes? I mean, Mr. Galbraith is about your height, but you're a good deal thinner than he is, except across the shoulders. And what about shoes?" He looked doubtfully at Thomas's tattered canvas shoes.

"Everything I own is at the bottom of the sea." Thomas stood and stretched. "I've been wearing borrowed clothes ever since."

The valet's eyes widened. "Oh, so you were *ship-wrecked*, sir." His tone was relieved, as if Thomas had achieved a sudden respectability he had hitherto lacked. "In that case, I'm sure Mr. Galbraith's wardrobe will do very nicely." He bustled about, pulling out underclothes, stockings, an immaculately pressed white shirt, breeches, a waistcoat, a starched muslin cravat and more, draping them carefully on the chair beside the window in the order in which Thomas should don them.

He eyed Thomas's feet with a worried expression. "I'm not sure what we'll do about shoes for you, sir . . . There's a pair of boots that I think might fit you. We bought them last year but the leather stretched and they're now a little loose on Mr. Galbraith. We'll try them on after your bath, sir." Now that he knew the reason for Thomas's ragged appearance, he seemed to regard him as a worthy challenge, rather than an unpleasant duty.

He fetched towels, sprinkled some bath salts in the bath, swished the water around and indicated a little stool on which sat a dish with soap, a sponge, a little nailbrush and a back scrubber. He reached for Thomas's coat to help him out of it.

Thomas stepped back. "That will be all, thank you, Enders." He had no intention of letting Enders or anyone see him naked.

Enders looked puzzled. "But do you not wish for my assistance, sir? Your back scrubbed, or—"

"No. I shall ring for you when I'm ready." He waited for the valet to leave. Let the man assume he was overly modest or religious or something.

"Very good, sir. You might want to make use of this on your hands." Enders handed him a pumice stone, bowed and departed, closing the door behind him.

Thomas looked down at his hands. Not the hands of a gentleman. Scarred and callused; the nails were clean but broken. These hands had held Rose. The rough paws of a bear, handling a . . . a butterfly.

He stripped quickly and stepped into the hot water, sinking into it as deeply as he could. The tub was large but not quite large enough to sink his whole body in. Still he wasn't about to complain. He lay there soaking up the delicious sensation of clean, hot water for several minutes, then picked up the soap, lathered himself all over and scrubbed himself from head to toe. Then he applied the pumice stone.

By the time he'd finished he'd scrubbed his skin almost raw. He gave a distasteful glance at the murky bathwater, then saw that an extra can of hot water had been left beside the bathtub. He stood and rinsed himself down with the clean water, and finally, for the first time in God knew how long, he felt clean again. Better than he had in weeks. Months. Years.

Feeling like a new man, he dried himself and dressed in the drawers, undershirt, shirt and stockings that Enders had laid out for him. He found a tin of tooth powder and rubbed it on with his fingers, then rinsed. Picking up a small looking glass, he examined his teeth. Still all there and in good order—a legacy from his father.

Seamen were notorious for bad teeth—mostly a result of scurvy—but Thomas's father had taught him young to care for his teeth as well as his diet, and showed him how to make an emergency toothbrush out of a chewed twig. It had served him well these last years.

There was a small jar of cloves, and he chewed one to sweeten his breath while he finished dressing. The buckskin breeches were loose around the waist, and he adjusted the buckle at the back to tighten them. The coat, however, was too small across the shoulders. He set it aside. In stockinged feet and shirtsleeves, he rang the bell.

Enders arrived almost instantly, bearing a tray with a steaming jug of water, a shaving brush, razor and leather strop. He nodded at Thomas with brisk approval. "Ready for your shave now, sir?" He shook out a large sheet and draped it around Thomas to protect his clothes.

As he lathered up the soap, Enders said with barely repressed excitement, "They are saying belowstairs that you are Lady Rose's long-lost husband, sir."

"That's right."

"Lost at sea, were you, sir?"

"Correct."

"They're saying you burst into the church just as—" A hard look from Thomas stopped Enders in midstream. He had no intention of providing further fuel for servants' gossip.

Enders bit his lip and set about shaving him. "Terribly romantic for you and Lady Rose, sir," he murmured after a while. "We're all very fond of her here. Such a beautiful young lady, and she and Lady Lily are so close. Don't worry, I'll do my best for you, sir. You won't believe the difference."

As the valet shaved him, Thomas watched his face slowly emerge. He still looked strange to his eyes—older, thinner. Harder. For the first time he saw the resemblance to his father that people used to comment on—apart from the broken nose and the thin silvery scar that curled down the side of his face and around the jaw.

He stared at his reflection and knew that the relatively civilized man he saw there was just as much a lie as the savage. The truth was somewhere in between. Years of being treated as less than human. Could a man ever really come back from that?

Did he have any choice?

"A regular application of lemon juice will help fade that unsightly tan," the valet assured him. He wiped Thomas's face clean with a hot, damp towel, then patted on a fresh-smelling cologne that left his skin tingling. "Now for your hair, sir. The Windswept do you think, or the Brutus? Or perhaps a Bedford Crop—you certainly have the bone structure for it."

Thomas wasn't listening. He was thinking of the way Rose's family had looked at him, the way Rose had looked at him. That whole congregation clad in silk and satin and lace, smelling like a garden. And him in rags, looking like a savage and smelling of fish.

"The Brutus, perhaps, sir, with just a hint of the Bedford?" the valet continued. He considered Thomas's reflection. "No, your hair is lovely and thick, with just that hint of curl that other men envy. I think we'll create a style of your own, sir."

Thomas didn't care. He let the fellow get on with it. The valet snipped busily. Thomas, deep in thought, stared unseeing at his reflection.

What was he going to do? For the last four years he'd had a single goal in mind—getting back here. And now that he'd achieved it, he felt strangely hollow. It didn't feel like a victory at all.

"There you are, sir." Enders fetched a hand mirror and held it for Thomas to see his head from all angles. "Perfect."

Thomas eyed his new haircut sourly. "What the devil is that supposed to be?" His hair was all curled and puffed up. He might as well be wearing a bird's nest.

Higgins chuckled indulgently. "Oh, you navy men. I assure you, sir, this style is all the crack. You look quite dashing, if I say so myself—or you will once you are fully clothed. Lady Rose will be all admiration."

Thomas doubted it. He scowled at his reflection. Fashionable or not, he'd rather look like a savage than wear a bird's nest. He raked his fingers through his hair, ignoring the valet's whimpers as his fashionable arrangement was ruined. He grabbed a handful of artistically arranged curls. "Cut all this off."

"Oh, but—" Catching his eye, the valet broke off. "Very good, sir." Dolefully the man chopped away under Thomas's supervision, until all the feathery bits were gone, and Thomas had a plain, short, rather brutal-looking haircut.

"That's better." He was what he was, and the sooner people realized it the better.

The valet sighed, folded away the protective sheet and fetched a pair of braces to hold up the too-loose breeches. Next he produced a shining pair of boots that he assured Thomas were too big for his master and therefore surplus to requirement—besides being insufficiently stylish. These boots, the valet confessed apologetically, had not been made by Mr. Hoby. They were, he confided, A Mistake.

Thomas pulled them on, then stood and took a few paces around the room. It felt odd to be wearing boots after all this time, but they fitted perfectly.

Enders then tied Thomas's neckcloth in a complicated knot, buttoned him into a waistcoat, squeezed him into Galbraith's coat—apparently it was all the crack to wear your coat skintight, as long as you didn't split the seams— handed him a handkerchief and a hat and sent him on his way.

Clean, close-shaved and well-dressed, Thomas felt up to anything. He walked downstairs to join his brothers-in-law, one at least of whom seemed to want to kill him, and both of whom wanted to be rid of him. He didn't care.

They could do no worse to him than had already been done. And he'd survived.

IF THOMAS HAD EXPECTED LORD ASHENDON AND GAL-braith to compliment him on his transformation from shabby seaman to well-groomed gentleman in breeches and gleaming boots, he was doomed to disappointment. Both gentlemen looked up as he entered. Galbraith scanned him briefly and gave a brisk nod.

Ashendon's expression was ice cold. "A thousand pounds."

Thomas curled his lip. "Paltry." Assurances or explanations would never convince Ashendon that Thomas hadn't married his sister for the money, so why not make her high-and-mighty brother stew? Besides, now he did need her money.

Ashendon swore under his breath, then continued his interrogation. He didn't even offer Thomas a seat but prowled back and forth in front of the fireplace, hurling questions at Thomas.

Thomas was soon fed up with it.

"Yes, I knew who she was—the beautiful Lady Rose Rutherford, daughter to the Earl of Ashendon and heiress to a considerable fortune—of course I did. Her aunt Dottie made—"

"Lady Dorothea to you," Ashendon snapped. Thomas's transformation had apparently exacerbated an already bad mood. Or maybe he was always a bad-tempered bastard.

Thomas eyed him coolly and continued, "She made no secret of it. She was bursting with pride in her lovely niece—and why not? But that wasn't why I married Rose."

"It was out of the pure, disinterested goodness of your heart?" Ashendon said sarcastically.

"Of course it wasn't. I wanted her."

"And had no interest in her fortune."

Thomas shrugged carelessly, knowing it would annoy Ashendon. But then he was annoyed, too. The reason he'd married Rose in a hurry and in secret four years ago was not one he was proud of—but what did it matter now? The world—and Thomas, and no doubt Rose too—had changed, but the fact was they were married.

"Of course her fortune will come in useful. I'm not a wealthy man. My father was a younger son and died at sea when I was a boy. I was raised on the goodwill of my uncle, but he sent me to sea when I turned sixteen. I've known all my life that I must make my own way in the world." He let that sink in, then added, "But her fortune was not why I married Rose."

"I don't believe it."

"Believe what you like, it makes no difference. But it's no compliment to your sister to assume a man would only marry her for her money."

"I don't. But a naval officer who would coax a schoolgirl into a clandestine marriage without her family's knowledge?"

"I was twenty-three, a mere boy."

"You were an officer. You should have known better."

He should have, of course. An officer, yes, but at the time he'd thought himself a man, fully grown and mature. Now with the hindsight of experience he could see he'd been a boy, but a boy full of good intentions, just the same.

He'd been young, and relatively inexperienced in the way of women, and Rose had been so ardent and eager and lovely. He'd been dazzled, entranced, and unable to resist her, even though he knew she was too young and innocent to know the possible consequences of what they were doing.

And once the deed was done . . . well, Thomas knew his duty. "I married her for her own protection—giving her the protection of my name. In case."

Thomas saw the moment when Ashendon realized what he was admitting to. "You filthy, lustful swine!" Ashendon's fist slammed into him.

Thomas saw the punch coming but made no attempt to dodge it. Delivered with fury, strength and no small degree of skill, it sent him reeling. He staggered back, steadied himself against the wall and straightened, but made no move to retaliate.

Ashendon waited, and when it was clear Thomas had no intention of fighting back, his lip curled with scorn. "Still a coward, I see."

Thomas felt his jaw gingerly. "I probably deserved that." Or at least his twenty-three-year-old self had. No brother could be blamed for reacting so to the news that his innocent young sister had been seduced. In Ashendon's place, Thomas would feel much the same.

"Probably? You deserve a horsewhipping."

Thomas narrowed his eyes. "I don't advise you to attempt it." He'd allowed that one punch, but that was his limit.

Galbraith intervened. "Now, now, gentlemen, we're not here to brawl."

"I know I shouldn't have lain with your sister," Thomas said, "but once I had, I did my best to protect her from any consequences of our imprudence. It was the only honorable thing to do, to give her the protection of my name."

"Honorable?" Ashendon practically spat the word. "You smooth-tongued villain, prating of honor and love! You seduced a young girl and married her for her fortune!"

Thomas didn't respond. It might not have been true back then, but he'd be lying if he claimed that Rose's fortune wasn't very much on his mind now.

"Gentlemen, gentlemen," Galbraith interrupted again. "Going over old ground is pointless. We need to sort out what is to be done about the situation."

"Nothing to sort out," Thomas said. "I married her, and I'll fight tooth and nail to keep her."

"Fight?" Ashendon made a scornful sound. "I'll believe that when I see it."

Thomas gave Ashendon a level look. "I haven't yet begun to fight."

"Well, I'll fight to ensure that she's free to choose her own husband."

"She's already chosen. She chose me."

"It's my job as head of Rose's family to protect her and—"

"I'm Rose's husband. I will decide what's best for her."

"I've only been a member of this family for a short time," Galbraith interrupted, "but one thing I've learned is that Rutherford ladies don't take kindly to being told what they can and can't do. Shall we go to Ashendon House and let Rose speak for herself?"

Chapter Four

❧

Know your own happiness. Want for nothing but
patience—or give it a more fascinating name: Call it hope.
—JANE AUSTEN, *SENSE AND SENSIBILITY*

THE DOG HEARD THEM ARRIVE FIRST, PRICKING HIS EARS
and then scrambling to his feet, facing the door with an
expectant expression and a gently wagging tail. Then came
the rumble of deep voices and the sound of crisp masculine
footsteps.

The men had arrived. Finally.

All conversation died. Every face turned toward the
door.

Rose had, quite unconsciously, been pleating the fabric
of her dress between nerveless fingers. She looked down at
the crushed fabric and tried to smooth it with her hands. It
was one thing to change out of the dress she'd put on to
marry another man; it was quite another to greet this one
wearing a badly crumpled gown.

Oh, what did it matter? He was here. Thomas was here.
Any moment now he would step through that door.

She still didn't know what she was going to say to him.
Or even how she felt. She was as skittish as a kitten. And
possibly even . . . shy?

Which was ridiculous. She was the boldest of the Rutherford girls—everybody said so. She was never shy, never nervous.

She never fainted either, except that today she'd fainted—in church, of all places.

And she never let Aunt Agatha intimidate her, and yet earlier she'd allowed her to rant on for what seemed like hours.

The door opened. "Ah, here you all are," Cal said.

Rose swallowed. Her heart was thudding so hard it was a wonder the others couldn't hear it.

"What took you so long?" Emm asked. "I thought you'd be here ages ago."

Cal jerked his head at Thomas. "Beresford wanted a bath." He sat on the arm of Emm's chair, snagged a sandwich and munched it down in two bites.

Ned entered and seated himself next to Lily.

But nobody took any notice of them. All eyes were on Thomas, who'd just stepped into the room.

And what a sight he was. Tall and freshly shaven, with his dark hair cut short in a brutally masculine crop, he looked . . . *Beautiful,* Rose thought. A crisp white shirt emphasized his deep tan and, unfashionable as that was, it highlighted the blazing intensity of his silvery blue eyes.

They burned into her, those eyes. For a moment it felt as though there was no one else in the room, just Rose and Thomas. Thomas and Rose.

"Oh, my," Aunt Dottie murmured. "Doesn't he clean up a treat?"

Rose breathed again. He did, oh, indeed he did. He was wearing a neatly knotted neckcloth, a plain dark waistcoat and fawn breeches tucked into gleaming black boots. A tightly fitting coat in dark blue emphasized a pair of powerful shoulders, muscular arms and a deep chest.

He stood, surveying the inhabitants of the room with unconscious arrogance. As if commanding the deck of a ship. Or facing a firing squad.

Her cheeks heated. This wasn't the boy she'd fallen in love with.

This was a man.

Thomas's gaze devoured her. Her skin prickled with awareness. She couldn't look away. Without the beard and the wild sun-streaked hair, she could see his face properly now: the long angular jaw, his cheeks hollowed and thin, so thin, the skin stretched tight across his cheekbones.

A pale, narrow scar ran down from his ear and curved around his jaw. Who had done that to him? And his nose, his once beautiful straight nose was now a little crooked, as if someone had broken it. Though she had to admit it didn't detract from his looks at all. Quite the contrary.

And his mouth . . . Oh, dear God, his mouth . . .

A delicate shudder rippled through her as she recalled that mouth and what he could do with it. Fighting a blush, she glanced down, hoping nobody had noticed. Having just admitted to her female relatives that she'd lain with him— before marriage!—they were sure to be watching her closely.

"Well, Ashendon, don't sit there gobbling sandwiches," Aunt Agatha snapped. "Introduce us."

Cal, recalled to his duties, introduced Thomas to everyone. Thomas responded politely enough, though in a curt, no-nonsense manner. Was he just going through the motions? Was all his awareness directed at her, as hers was to him?

Part of her wanted to rise from her seat and drag him off, to be alone with him, to talk, and touch, and know him again. Another part hesitated, dreading the explanations she was going to have to make. This Thomas wasn't the same as her Thomas. He seemed so much bigger and tougher and somehow . . . remote.

Oh, Thomas. She'd let him down in so many ways. Her mouth wobbled. She clamped down on it.

George's dog, Finn, rose and approached him, his claws clicking on the parquetry floor. He sniffed at Thomas's boots. Thomas glanced down but otherwise didn't respond.

"Please be seated, Mr. Beresford." Emm indicated the chair next to her, on the opposite side of the room from

Rose. She signaled to the butler who hovered in the doorway. "A fresh pot and more sandwiches please, Burton."

Thomas took the seat offered. Finn followed him. Thomas offered his fingers to sniff, then absently fondled the dog's rough head.

"His name's Finn," George said gruffly. "He doesn't usually take to strangers."

Aunt Agatha cleared her throat. "Well, Ashendon, I must assume since you have brought this fellow into your home that you consider there is some truth to his sorry tale."

"I *told* you there was," Rose said. "And don't call him 'this fellow.' His name is Mr. Beresford. And it's *not* a sorry tale!" She wasn't sorry—well, she was about some things. But sorry she'd married him? Not at all.

"I do not recall addressing you, Rose." Her aunt raised her lorgnette. "In my day, young misses spoke only when spoken to."

"But I'm not a young miss, am I? I'm a married woman." There, she'd claimed him.

Aunt Agatha thinned her lips. "That remains to be seen." She turned back to her nephew. "Ashendon?"

Cal nodded. "I'll investigate the claim, naturally—"

"Naturally. We cannot let Rose be brought to ruin by an *adventurer.*"

Thomas made no attempt to defend himself. His expression was flat and hard, his eyes unreadable. Rose looked at him, wishing he would deny the accusation—he wasn't an adventurer, not the way Aunt Agatha meant it—but instead he sat there, looking grim and unapproachable, saying nothing.

Cal continued. "But it seems very likely that a wedding was performed, and I expect there will be evidence to support it. Do you have your marriage lines, Rose?"

Rose nodded. Did he want her to fetch them? Why hadn't she thought to bring them down before? Her mind was so scattered.

"Documentation aside, I cannot believe such a ceremony can be legal, however," Aunt Agatha said. "Rose was a minor at the time, and it took place without permission from her father or any other guardian. An annulment is the only option—"

A nerve flickered in Thomas's jaw, but he still didn't speak.

"Despite the fact that consummation took place—and worse, *before* the wedding," Aunt Agatha finished acidly. "Did he tell you that, did he, this seducer of innocent gels?"

"I told you, it wasn't like that!" Rose flashed. "If anything, I seduced *him*." She was shaking.

Thomas finally spoke. "I take full responsibility for what happened." He didn't even look at Rose. He seemed quite indifferent.

Aunt Agatha snorted. "I'm sure you do, knowing it will strengthen your grubby case. But no matter what you say, we will press for an annulment."

"I tend to agree with you, Aunt Agatha," Cal said. Emm and Rose began to speak at the same time, but Cal gently squeezed his wife's shoulder and continued, "But four years have passed since the wedding ceremony, and with half of London being informed of it this morning, there is no hope of quashing any scandal. I think it must be up to Rose and—actually, as far as I'm concerned, it's entirely Rose's decision."

"I agree," Emm said. "If she wants an annulment, we will press for it. If she wants the marriage, it stays."

Rose sat back. Her decision? What about Thomas? Didn't he get to decide too? She glanced at him. He looked so stern and forbidding, she had no idea what he was thinking.

"Nonsense! We know what's best for her. Rose is still a gel and she will do as she's told."

Cal said dryly, "Oh, yes, she's famed for her obedience."

"Oh, do be quiet, Aggie," Aunt Dottie said. "This isn't your decision. Cal is the head of this family and if he says it's up to Rose, it's up to Rose." She turned to Rose. "So, Rose dear, what do you want?"

There was a long silence.

Rose swallowed, and opened her mouth, then closed it.

Before she could make any decision, she needed to explain some things to Thomas—admit one particular thing—and afterward, well, it all depended on how he reacted. Now, with her entire family looking on, she had no idea what to say.

Thomas said nothing, but those blazing blue eyes bored into hers. She dropped her gaze and saw his big, battered hands clench into fists.

Battered hands? Old scars, white against the tan. How had that happened? And when? They were waiting for an answer, but her mind was full of questions.

"It's not fair," Lily said suddenly. "It's been four years since she and Thomas have seen each other and you haven't given them so much as a moment alone. Rose is still coming to terms with the fact that the man she thought was dead is alive. With so little warning, and with all of us staring at her, how can she possibly think clearly about what she wants?"

Rose gave her sister a grateful look. She should have said that herself, but she was not herself at all today.

"Lily's right," Emm said. 'The last thing we want to do is rush you into any decision, Rose dear. Take as long as you need. A day, a week—as long as it takes."

"The longer the better," muttered Aunt Agatha. "Better yet, let Cal arrange an annulment and you will have all the time in the world to come to your senses."

Rose closed her eyes. All this sniping and arguing and pushing for an annulment would go on forever, unless she stopped it. She couldn't bear any more uncertainty, any more waiting. She'd waited for four long years and now it was over. Thomas had returned to her, and if he didn't want to stay married to her, he shouldn't have stopped the wedding.

And if he wasn't the Thomas she remembered, so be it. People changed.

She was married to this tough-looking, enigmatic man with the eyes that burned, and if she could see nothing in him of the charming boy she'd married four long years ago, if he was gaunt and taciturn and somehow . . . hardened, what did it matter anyway? She wasn't the same girl he'd married.

Whatever had happened, whoever they were now, she and Thomas would cope. She couldn't go backward—the past was the past—she could only move forward and hope for the best.

She'd heard a military man say once that it didn't matter what decision you made, the important thing was to make the decision, and then throw everything you had into making it work.

She opened her mouth to speak.

"If you try to annul this marriage against our wishes"—Thomas addressed Cal in a deep, harsh voice—"I will fight you all the way. And I warn you now, when I fight, I fight to win." His eyes were hard, bleak, silver shot with blue, and Rose was reminded again of that feral cat.

"So do I," snarled Cal, bristling.

"It will be a very public fight," Thomas said silkily. He glanced at Aunt Agatha. "Will that please you, Lady Salter?"

She swelled with outrage. "Impudent jackanapes!"

"Stop it!" Rose jerked to her feet. Her voice shook—she was far more nervous now than when she'd been about to marry the duke—but she managed to say, "There will be no fighting. Four years ago I made vows before God, and it doesn't matter what has happened since, I'll honor them."

There was a short, shocked silence, then a babble of talk.

"You don't know what you're saying, gel," Aunt Agatha began.

"You're still in shock, give it a week," Cal said.

"Are you certain this is what you want, Rose?" Emm asked.

Rose wasn't certain, but then life wasn't certain, was it? She'd lost Thomas once, and if there was the smallest chance of getting him back—and surely, somewhere inside this grim, taciturn stranger was the man she'd fallen in love with—she wasn't going to risk turning him away.

And anything was better than watching her family tearing themselves apart.

Rose shook her head and said in as firm a voice as she could muster, "There will be no annulment. Thomas Beresford is and shall remain my husband."

"That's the way," Aunt Dottie said. "Good girl."

There was another short silence, then all eyes turned to Thomas.

THOMAS IGNORED THE SILENCE THAT HUNG IN THE ROOM. He stared across at Rose, staggered by what she'd just done. She'd honor her vows to him? Just like that? When only a few hours ago she'd been about to marry a duke?

Why would she do such a stupid thing?

He'd been certain she'd take the offer of annulment.

She was as pale and washed-out now as she had been when she lay unconscious in his arms. Her voice had trembled as she spoke the words, but she'd said them clearly and without equivocation. She would honor her vows.

He had a flash of memory of Rose on her wedding day— the first one—when a radiant young girl had pledged her heart to an idealistic young man. She'd been blazing with joy that day, like a thousand candles lit her from within.

Today she looked like a girl going to her execution.

He'd come prepared to wrest her—and her fortune— from the protection of her family. He'd told himself he was justified in doing it, that she'd moved on, forgotten him, wiped him from the record. That it was just another betrayal in the long line of betrayals.

And now this, an offer that took his breath away with its preposterous generosity.

In his determination not to let Ashendon get the better of him, to hold on to the rights that were legally his, Thomas had all but forgotten: Rose wasn't just a rich society heiress who could solve all his problems; somewhere, underneath that composed ladylike exterior, she was still the rash, warmhearted, ridiculously generous girl he'd married, too tenderhearted and impetuous for her own good.

If he'd been fool enough to anticipate a joyful homecoming—which he wasn't, thank God—his reception by her and her family would have taught him better. If she'd thrown herself into his arms, kissed him, if she'd even recognized him at the beginning instead of staring across the aisle at him like a frozen doll . . .

But she hadn't. In the old days he'd been able to read her easily; every mood, every thought was reflected in her eyes. Now what she thought, what she truly thought, was anyone's guess.

It should have made it easier to think of her as a means to an end. And for a while, it had.

But now she'd risen to her feet, pale but determined, and in the face of clear family opposition—and all common sense—she'd offered to honor her long-ago vows. Giving him herself and everything she owned on a plate, no questions asked.

It was insane, dammit! She'd done it again, thrown herself impulsively away on a man she barely knew without giving any thought to what was prudent or practical. Or wise.

If she thought Thomas was the same man she'd married, she was in for a rude shock.

The waiting silence pressed against him, expectant, hostile.

She'd said nothing of love. She only spoke of honoring vows. Of duty.

The Rose he'd married was a deeply romantic young woman who lived and breathed love—love for her sister, love for her family, and once, an eon ago, love for him. For Rose, duty had never come into it.

He hardened his heart. He needed her and her fortune and would do what he must to secure his rights and fulfill his obligations. Four years of brutality and hardship burned the softness out of a man. A good thing too. To survive, a man needed to be ruthless.

"Thomas?"

He opened his mouth to accept her offer—and made the mistake of looking at her again. And saw the trembling mouth, the fingers tightly knotted in a fold of her dress, the eyes full of . . . he didn't know what. Some emotion he didn't want to know about.

His own duty was clear. But dammit, he couldn't do it, not while she was looking at him with those wide blue eyes, full of . . . he didn't want to know.

He swore long and hard under his breath, then heard himself say, "You do me great honor by your decision, Rose, but your family is right."

"What do you mean? I said—"

Now he was the insane one, blowing a fortune down the wind when he so desperately needed it. But he couldn't seem to stop himself. "Things have changed. *I* have changed, and so have my circumstances. When you married me I was a young man with what I thought would be a bright future ahead of me. I had a career, the support of my family, a home. I have none of that now." What was he doing, confessing all this—and in front of her family? Ammunition against him.

She bit her lip. "I don't understand."

He hardened his voice. "I can give you none of what that duke could. You'd be better off with him."

"She would be—infinitely better off!" Lady Salter interjected. "As long as the duke can be brought to reconsider her after such a scandal."

"If he were in any way worthy of Rose, he'd be here now, begging her to take him back," Thomas snapped. "He'd never have let her go in the first place."

The old lady looked taken aback. Ashendon raised his brows.

Rose shook her head. "But Thomas, I've already decided. I said—"

"You said everything that was honorable, but it's a mistake. I'm not the man I was. Not the man you married." Bile stung his throat. What was he doing? Throwing it all away in a stupid fit of . . . gallantry? Insanity?

But the words kept coming. "These past four years have

been . . . difficult. I've changed. Not just outwardly." He swallowed. "When a man is pushed to the brink . . ."

"Thomas, what are you saying?"

"You were just a girl. You made an impulsive promise based on a false premise, and now you believe you have no choice but to keep it. But it's not true. You can do a lot better than me now."

There, he'd done it, overturned all his plans in a stupid fit of . . . stupidity.

"Oh, splendid young man," Lady Dorothea murmured.

Behind him, Ashendon growled, "Changed your tune, haven't you, Beresford? Whatever happened to 'fight tooth and nail to keep her'?"

Without turning his head, Thomas responded. "I was prepared to fight you, Ashendon, prepared to fight any other members of Rose's family, but . . ." He lifted his hand in a futile gesture. There were no words to explain what he'd just done.

"Well!" Lady Salter raised her lorgnette and subjected him to a thorough scrutiny. "Well!"

"Thank you, Mr. Beresford," Lady Ashendon said at last. "It's a very gallant—and unexpected—offer."

"Don't you *want* to stay married to me?" Rose asked abruptly. Her face was white and tense.

"Of course," he assured her, managing to make it sound like a meaningless gallantry. "But I rushed you into marriage once. Your brother claims he can have it annulled. I don't know if that's possible, but if it is, if you have a chance to start again fresh and leave an impulsive youthful mistake behind you . . ." He spread his hands in a *why not?* gesture.

Her brow furrowed. "You think our marriage was a mistake?"

He looked away and didn't answer. He'd burned his boats. No use trying to mend them now. It was the very opposite of what he'd intended.

It was one thing to claim that which was his by right. It was quite another to have a trembling young woman offer him all she was and all she owned, simply because of a promise she'd made when she was sixteen. He'd sunk low in the last four years, but not that low.

The door opened and two footmen entered carrying tea trays and more food. Tea was poured, and cakes, sandwiches and little pastries handed around. The tense atmosphere eased slightly with the clatter of crockery and the tinkling of teaspoons.

"Have one of these excellent cream cakes, Mr. Beresford. I've eaten far too many already today, but they're so delicious." Lady Dorothea offered him a plate. And a warm, dimpled smile. It was a clear welcome.

"Thank you, no." He was too tense to eat a thing. Besides, his stomach wasn't yet ready for rich food like cream. But Lady Dorothea kept fretting that he was too thin and wasn't eating, so to please her he took a cucumber sandwich.

"Well then, Mr. Beresford." Lady Salter addressed him peremptorily. "Who are your people?"

His people? Good question. Four years ago his understanding of who he was and who his people were had turned to bitter ashes. "I'm an orphan. I have no family."

Ashendon's look was sharp. "You mentioned an uncle before. You said he'd raised you."

Thomas nodded. "He washed his hands of me some years ago."

Ashendon's gaze sharpened. "Why was that?"

Thomas lifted an indifferent shoulder. "I cannot say." And wasn't that the truth? It had shocked him to the backbone at the time. Four years later, the hurt and shock had burned away. Bitterness and cold rage sustained him these days.

Rose suddenly asked, "But where were you all this time, Thomas? What kept you from coming home?"

"I was unavoidably detained." It was the truth, after all. He had no intention of saying any more.

"Were you a prisoner of the French?" she asked.

"The war is long over," Ashendon said curtly. "Most prisoners of war were released years ago."

Everyone waited for Thomas to explain. He picked up a cucumber sandwich, ate it, then sipped his tea.

"Couldn't you have written, at least?" Rose said eventually.

Ashendon watched him with narrowed eyes.

"Not all places have a postal service," Thomas said.

She frowned, obviously unsatisfied with his responses, but said no more.

"Beresford, Beresford," Lady Salter pondered aloud. "Would that be the Gloucestershire Beresfords or the Norfolk Beresfords?" Why the hell did she want to know? Hadn't she realized he'd given up her precious niece?

"Neither." In the direst of circumstances, both his uncle and cousin had betrayed him, so Thomas sure as hell wasn't going to claim them now.

She sniffed. "Pity. Some connection to the Gloucestershire Beresfords, and in particular to the Earl of Brierdon, might have helped with this mess—if Rose decides to go ahead with the marriage, of course."

Lady Georgiana made a contemptuous sound. "I don't see how. Unless the earl wanted to advise Mr. Beresford on the tying of his neckcloth, and the use of champagne in boot blacking."

Thomas put down his cup with a clatter and stood abruptly. He'd had enough of this, this sitting around drinking tea and parrying pointless questions. "I'll take my leave now. Thank you for your hospitality, Lady Ashendon." The irony of the polite meaningless phrase. He'd ruined everyone's day, and they all knew it.

And with no help from anyone else, he'd even ruined his own plans.

Rose jumped up. "I'll see you out."

Ashendon made as if to stop her, but his wife laid a hand on his knee and murmured something, and he subsided. She nodded at Rose, who led Thomas from the room.

WITHOUT A WORD, ROSE WALKED TOWARD THE FRONT door. Was she insulted by his rejection of her offer? Relieved?

Thomas couldn't tell. The warm, vibrant, outspoken girl he'd married had changed, become this frozen young ice queen. She was just as beautiful as ever—more beautiful—but he'd never fallen in love with her face. It was Rose herself, full of life, fearless and bold, who'd entranced him back then.

Three paces from the front door, he caught her hand and turned her around to face him. "I meant what I said in there, Rose. I'm no longer a man to build a future with. You always craved freedom, so take it while you have the chance." Because any minute now he was going to regret what he'd done.

She turned his hand palm upward and stared at it, her face troubled. "Your hands, your poor hands, Thomas."

His hands, his damned, ruined hands. His calluses must have been rough against her soft skin. He tried to pull free, but she hung on and grabbed his other hand as well. "What happened to them?"

"Nothing."

"But they're so rough. And the scars—"

"I'll get some gloves." Damn, that valet was right. He should have worked that pumice stone harder.

"Don't be silly, that's not what I'm talking about. I want to know how they got that way."

"It doesn't matter," he said in a hard, no-argument voice.

A spasm of emotion flickered behind her eyes and was gone. She dropped his hand and turned abruptly away, but instead of opening the front door to send him out into the street, she opened a door to the right and gestured for him to follow her inside.

It was a small anteroom, furnished with a pair of stiff-looking tapestry-covered armchairs, a matching sofa and a couple of small tables. A small window opened onto a narrow side street. She walked to it and stood with her back to him, gazing out, though at what, he couldn't imagine: All he could see was the side wall of the next house. He closed the door behind him.

She turned and faced him, her arms folded defensively beneath her bosom. "Are you angry with me, Thomas?"

He blinked. "No. Why would you think—"

"Because I was about to marry again?"

"No, I—" He broke off. Perhaps he was a bit angry. But mostly with himself, not her. And the damnable situation, for which neither of them was responsible.

His uncle and his cousin were, ultimately.

She waited. He didn't say anything. She turned back to gaze out of the window where there wasn't a view. "They said you were *dead*, Thomas. Not merely missing. Not even lost. They said your ship was sunk, at the bottom of the ocean, and all hands drowned."

"So I gather. But six of us managed to survive. Just me and five ordinary seamen. Three of us could swim, and we kept the others afloat, clinging to wreckage until we were washed ashore."

"Where? Where did you land?" She still had her back to him.

"Does it matter?"

Her silence told him it did.

If he gave her a name it wouldn't help. It would only lead to more questions and more, until she'd end up with a disgust of him. Better to have her angry.

"No place you'd ever heard of. A desolate land at the ends of the earth." A blasted, benighted, hateful place.

It seemed to him her spine had further stiffened against him. "No letter? Not even a message? If I'd known . . ."

"No." The fact was, he'd sent two letters, neither of them to her. Much good they'd done him.

"Was it difficult for you?" Maybe it wasn't. If she'd told no one . . .

One shoulder hunched in a brittle, dismissive movement. "I managed."

A flicker of anger caused him to say, "By not telling anyone about me? About our marriage? What was I, a dirty little secret you did your best to forget?"

"No," she said after a long silence. "But I did decide it was better not to tell." She paused and just as he decided she'd said all she wanted to, she continued. "You don't know what it was like back then. If they didn't know they couldn't *fuss*, couldn't ask me endless, impossible questions. If they'd known, they would have dragged me out of school, sent me who-knew-where, separated from Lily, left her alone in that dreadful school—and to what purpose? You were *dead*, Thomas," she repeated in a hard little voice. "So what was the point?"

What was the point? The brutal truth.

He should leave now before he said something he would regret. Make a clean break of it. She'd dealt well enough with his death; his departure from her life now would make little difference.

He regarded her stiff back and couldn't keep the bitterness from his tongue.

"Did you even weep for me, Rose?" he asked, apparently needing to twist the knife in his heart one more time.

For a moment he didn't think she'd heard. That, or she was going to ignore his question, his stupid, pointless, painful, irrelevant question. He'd made his decision. Why string it out?

"Weep for you? *Weep for you?*" She turned and, appalled, he saw that her face was drenched in tears.

"Rose?" All this time, giving him her rigid spine, tossing questions at him in that stiff little voice—no outward sign of distress—and yet her face and the neck of her dress were wet with tears.

A hollow opened up inside him, edged with panic. He hated it when women cried. And this was Rose.

"Weep for you, you big idiot?" She rushed at him and thumped him on the chest. Tears poured down her cheeks. "Why would I weep? What a stupid question. Weep? I was furious with you! Furious!" She pummeled his chest with angry, ineffectual fists. "You showed me a glimpse of heaven and then you left me. Left me!"

She went to hit him again and he caught her fist in his

hand. "All alone with nothing—not even the slender hope of 'missing.' They said you were *dead*, Thomas! Drowned. All hands lost! In black and white they said it, printed in the newspapers! Just two weeks after our wedding!"

Helpless, guilty, paralyzed by her distress, he muttered, "I'm sorry." He wasn't even sure what he was apologizing for. Dying? Not dying? Making her cry?

"'Dirty little secret'—how could you even *think* such a thing? I just hadn't had *time* to tell anyone. I had to wait until Lily was better—you *know* how sick she was, and she's my beloved sister so of course I had to tell her first. And then—you were dead. And she was still away, recuperating, and I was stuck back in school, in a dormitory with five other girls."

Her face twisted with emotion. "So who could I mourn with, who could I share my grief with—a pack of giggling schoolgirls, girls who would happily pick my life to bits for their entertainment, like, like chickens?"

Did she mean him to answer? How could he? He couldn't imagine.

"There was no one, Thomas! No one! One day you were there, filling my life with joy, and then—you weren't. It was as if you'd never existed. Except . . ." Her voice broke, and she touched the place over her heart. "Here. And in my dreams."

She subsided against his chest, clutching his coat for support, clinging to him like a drowning person as great wrenching sobs shattered in waves though her.

Thomas couldn't speak; there was a lump in his throat as big as a fist.

He eased her onto the sofa and sat awkwardly holding her—he had no idea what to do. The man he used to be would have hauled her into his arms and kissed the tears away. The man he was now sat on the sofa, racked with tension, forcing himself to be distant and impersonal.

He'd let her go. Against all his best interests he'd pushed her away—for her own sake.

He'd thought he'd never forget the taste of her, or the

scent, but in the life he'd led, it had been such a struggle to hold on to even the smallest of sense memories. The best he'd been able to do was to preserve in his heart and mind the *idea* of Rose. The memory of her laugh, her smile, the way she gave herself wholly, joyfully and without reservation.

Shame flooded him. He'd forgotten this, the actuality of her, the warmth, the scent, the passion of her.

Helpless and aching, he sat patting her back, making vague, deep, *there-there*-ish sounds. It was what you did when women wept, wasn't it? When you couldn't hold them as you wanted to.

At last the jerky sobs slowed, then stopped. For a long time the silence was broken only by the sound of ragged breathing—Thomas's was almost as ragged as hers—and the distant rattle of carriages in the street outside.

Spent, she leaned against him, making no move to pull away. After a few minutes, she turned her tear-drenched face up to him. "I'm sorry, I don't mean to be such a watering pot. I never cr—"

"Dry your eyes." He made his voice hard. He thrust his handkerchief into her hand. "It's all over now." He released her and slid to the end of the sofa. "It's over," he repeated. "It was a bad time, but you have the opportunity now to put all that behind you and make a new life for yourself."

She sat up, wiping her eyes. "What are you saying?"

"Accept the annulment your brother says he can get you. Marry someone else." Someone better.

She smoothed the damp and crumpled handkerchief over her lap. "Are you truly going to abandon me, Thomas?"

He didn't meet her eyes. "I'm giving you a choice, the choice I didn't give you four years ago."

"I made the same choice you did." She waited a moment, then added, "I'm still prepared to honor those vows."

He didn't answer, couldn't look at her—if he did, all his resolve would go up in smoke.

There was a short, hurt silence. "Then why did you come to the church today? Why stop the wedding? Why turn my life upside down if you were just going to walk away?" Beneath the pain and the bewilderment was a faint thread of anger. Good. Anger would make her stronger. "You know why."

"Apparently I don't. You need to explain it."

"To prevent you from committing bigamy." He hadn't even thought of it until Ollie had mentioned it. And bigamy had had nothing to do with Thomas's desperate race from the Admiralty offices to St. George's church in Hanover Square.

"I don't believe that's the reas—" She broke off. "Is that a bruise?" Her eyes narrowed and she reached out and touched his chin lightly. "It is, and a fresh one at that. How did that happen?"

He pulled away. "It's nothing."

Her expression darkened. "It was my brother, wasn't it? He hit you."

"No. It happened earlier, in the street. I—I tripped. On a cobblestone."

"I don't believe you. Is that it? Why you're pushing me away. Because my brother is bullying you? Because if that's it, you must ignore him. He's just trying—"

He rose from the sofa and addressed her as he would men on a ship. "It's nothing to do with your brother. The fact is, my situation's changed. I have no fortune, Rose, no job—I'm out of the navy—and no home. I cannot support a wife."

"Pfft!" She made a dismissive gesture. "I have money enough for both of us. I'm an heiress, remember?"

He didn't say anything. He'd taunted her brother by pretending to be the kind of man who'd live off a woman, forgetting that he could no longer afford such scruples. And for a while there he'd even thought he could become that kind of man. Until he'd looked into her eyes and realized he couldn't.

"Thomas?"

Why did she keep arguing? Much more of this and he'd weaken, take her and all she had to offer, then shatter her dreams and ruin her life. Again. "You're in no state to decide anything. You need time to settle, to think it through, discuss your situation with your family."

She stiffened at his tone. "And if we decide my future is to be a duchess?"

He shrugged, as if it would mean nothing to him. "Then so be it."

Her fingers curled into fists. "You'd be happy with that, would you?"

He opened his mouth to assure her he would, but he couldn't make himself say it. "You're free to choose."

"Free?" She was angry again. "We are *married*, Thomas."

"We were, but—"

"But what?" She narrowed her eyes. "Is it *you* who wants to be free?"

He didn't answer.

"Is there someone else? Another woman?"

"No! Of course not!"

"Then I don't see the problem. Unless you no longer want me."

He closed his eyes. How could she possibly think that? Not want her? For so long he'd ached for her, dreamed of returning to her, making a home with her in some green and pleasant English valley, raising a family.

And then the fantasy had withered, leaving a bitter husk of a man driven by rage and dreams of vengeance . . . And today the last remnant of his dreams had turned to ash.

"I'm . . . damaged, Rose. Not the man I was. Not the man you married."

"Damaged?" Her eyes widened with concern. "How? What—"

"Not a physical problem. But"—he shook his head wearily—"I'm not fit for marriage to someone like you anymore."

"Someone like me? What do you mean?"

But he wasn't going to try to explain. "Just take the annulment, Rose."

"Are you really going to do it, Thomas? Just let them annul us and walk away?" Her voice shook with disbelief.

"It's for the best." And then, because he couldn't make himself walk away from her without one last touch, he touched her cheek lightly with the back of one finger. "Be happy, Rose."

"Rose?" Her sister, Lily, stood in the doorway. "Sorry to interrupt, but Cal, um, wants to see your marriage certificate. They, he sent me—they're wondering what was keeping you." By the end of her speech she was flushing.

Rose sighed. "Because of course I need a chaperone to be alone with my husband. I'll be so glad when everyone stops fussing. All right, Lily love, I'll be there in a minute."

Lily nodded and withdrew, but she left the door ajar. Deliberate, Thomas assumed. She'd be waiting in the hall.

"You'd better go, then," Rose told him. "They'll all be out here soon. I'll see you tomorrow."

Had she not listened to a thing he'd said? "I'm not coming back tomorrow. Talk the situation over with your family—they want what's best for you."

"And what if I need to talk to you again?"

He hesitated. He didn't want to talk to her again.

She persisted. "What if I need you to sign papers or something?"

"Send someone with a note. I'm staying with my friend Ollie. Your brother has the address."

She sniffed. "You don't imagine Cal would give it to me, do you? Don't you have a card?"

He fished in his pocket and pulled out the card Ollie had given him, memorized the address and handed the card to her. "I meant what I said. You owe me nothing. Think carefully about what you want."

She followed with a mutinous expression. "And if I already know what I want?"

His face was grim. "Think again. Listen to your family, Rose. Make the wise decision. Take the annulment."

Chapter Five

❧

THE FRONT DOOR SHUT BEHIND THOMAS. "I'M SORRY,
Rose. Cal would have come except we—well, Emm—
decided it would be better if I—" Lily broke off. "Rose,
you've been crying."

"I know." She was exhausted and yet . . .

"But . . . you never cry."

"I know." She hesitated, then added, "I haven't been able
to. Not properly. Not for the last four years."

Lily's eyes widened as she took in the implications of
that. "You mean . . . ?"

Rose nodded. "I think I must have bottled it all up. But
just now, when Thomas and I were talking, the tears just . . .
came. I couldn't help it. I wept all over him, Lily, noisily
and messily—years' worth of tears just pouring out of me."
The violence and intensity of it had shocked her. But now
she felt strangely calm. Wrung out, but calm.

She pressed her palms to her cheeks, still trying to take in
all that had happened. "I'd forgotten crying could do that."

"Do what?"

"Be such a . . . such a relief. Afterward." Not during. During had been terrifying.

Lily laid a worried hand on her arm. "Are you all right now?"

Rose nodded. "It was quite frightening at first—I couldn't seem to stop, Lils. It was like something had taken me over. I wasn't in control at all." She hated losing control, but there was no denying that something had loosened inside her. She felt somehow cleansed. Except . . .

If only Thomas hadn't stopped her from telling him everything . . .

Lily hugged her. "I know. But you'll be all the better for it, trust me."

Rose wasn't so sure.

"How did he take it? They say most men hate women crying—well, you know how Cal is—but Edward doesn't seem to mind a bit."

"You don't fake tears with Edward, do you?" Rose asked curiously. Lily had the ability to weep at will. It had proven useful in their early disputes with their brother. Cal simply fell apart at the first sign of feminine tears.

"No, of *course* not. I'd never do that to him. Though it's tempting, because the few times I have cried in front of him . . . Oh, he's just lovely, Rose. So tender. And afterward . . ." Her lips curved in a tender, secret smile.

Rose understood. She couldn't put words to the way it felt, having Thomas just holding her so quietly, patting her back so awkwardly and sweetly with his big battered hands. He was, she suspected, as appalled as Cal but trying to hide it. She'd felt the tension in him.

If they'd been truly married again, if they'd had a bedroom to retreat to . . .

Instead he'd become all bossy and officious, moving physically away from her, telling her to put the past behind her, to forget what happened, and forget him. Why? What had changed?

"I think Cal hit Thomas," she told Lily. "On the way here. Thomas's poor jaw has a nasty bruise. He wouldn't admit it, of course, but I could see perfectly well that it was fresh. It was changing color right before my eyes."

"I'll ask Edward about it. But why would Cal hit him, and then bring him here? It doesn't make sense."

"I don't know, but sometime between the church and here"—Rose narrowed her eyes thoughtfully—"or sometime since he arrived, Thomas was made to change his mind."

"*Made* to?" Lily looked dubious. "He didn't seem like the kind of man who would be *made* to do anything."

Rose grimaced. "He's not. Or at least he never was in the past."

"He didn't seem at all bothered by Cal or Aunt Agatha, and they were openly hostile to him. I thought him rather intimidating, to be honest. That grim expression and those cold, cold eyes—" Lily broke off, flushing. "Sorry, I'm sure he's perfectly nice once you get to know him."

Rose smiled. "He is, and you will." She was determined on it.

Lily regarded her doubtfully. "But he told you to take the annulment. I'm sorry, Rose, I couldn't help but overhear, I wasn't eavesdropping—"

"It's all right. And I know what he told me. What I don't know is why. He spouted some nonsense about having no fortune and no job and no home—but I'm an heiress, and he knows it. We'll have plenty of money. So it can't be that."

Lily said hesitantly, "Edward says a real man doesn't take money from a woman. He's arranged for my inheritance to be put in trust for me and our children."

Rose stared. Could that possibly be it? Some stupid male pride thing? She couldn't credit it. Would Thomas put his pride before their happiness? Surely not.

But it was certainly worth considering. "You've become very wise, little sister."

Lily flushed with pleasure. Rose nodded toward the closed door of the drawing room. "Now, tell me, what are they saying in there?"

Lily wrinkled her nose. "It's not good. Emm is still saying you must decide—"

"Good, then—"

"But Cal and Edward and Aunt Agatha are still talking about an annulment—Aunt Agatha is utterly determined on it. She keeps saying to Cal"—her voice took on the cadence of Aunt Agatha's—"'What is the point of being an earl if you can't pull strings to free your sister from the machinations of a blackguard!'"

"Well, they shan't. I won't let them. And Thomas is *not* a blackguard. And he certainly doesn't machinate, or whatever the word is."

"They don't trust him, Rose. Most of them think he's a fortune hunter who deceived a vulnerable schoolgirl."

"But they heard him refuse me."

Lily grimaced. "They're saying it's a clever ploy on his part—though Aunt Dottie doesn't agree. They also think there's something fishy about where he's been these last four years, and that he refuses to explain. And they don't like the timing, how he managed to turn up at the perfect moment—and attired in such a way—to create the maximum scandal."

Rose frowned. Put like that, it did look rather damning.

"Oh, and Cal says until he sees your marriage lines, he won't be convinced there was a wedding. And if there was one, it might not be real."

"In that case, I'll fetch them right this minute. Come with me?" Linking arms, they hurried upstairs. Rose rummaged in the small wooden box where she kept her jewelry and other precious things. The document was at the very bottom.

She tipped everything onto her bed. The certificate came out last.

"Here it is." She unfolded it and looked at her signature and Thomas's. "There, that should convince our dear, suspicious brother." She refolded the document and started repacking the little wooden box. Lily sat on the bed, watching. "You said most of the men and Aunt Agatha are against Thomas, and Emm is on the fence. What about the others?"

"Aunt Dottie thinks he's very handsome, and that it's all wonderfully romantic. She says she has one of her 'feelings' about him."

Rose chuckled. "The darling, of course she does. And George?"

Lily dimpled. "She says that Finn likes him and that Finn is a very good judge of character."

Rose laughed again. "Good old Finn." She sobered then. "And you, Lily, what do you think?"

Lily hesitated. Her gaze dropped and in a low voice she said, "I don't know what to think. I still don't understand why you never told me, Rose. Didn't you trust me?"

"Oh, Lily. It wasn't that at all." At the hurt in her sister's voice, Rose found herself blinking back tears again. Such a day she'd had. She was feeling completely storm-tossed, *in alt* one minute, despair the next. All the pain she'd repressed over the years, spilling out. Scalding her again—and spilling over everyone.

She climbed onto the bed beside Lily and took her hand. "I'm sorry I never told you, Lils. I just . . . couldn't. By the time you were well enough to be told, so much had happened it was all too painful to speak of."

"I wouldn't have told. I'd never betray you."

"I know, darling, but you were still so very frail. I didn't want to burden you with my troubles. I don't think you realize how close to death you came—you nearly died, you know."

Rose had already lost Thomas, and then . . . He wasn't all she'd lost.

So the thought of losing Lily, as well . . .

"It was better—or so I thought at the time—to just pretend it had never happened. I'm the one who's supposed to look after you, remember?" She grimaced ruefully. "Who would be sixteen again? I thought I knew everything then."

"It's all right." Lily gave her a comforting hug, then tilted her head and regarded Rose thoughtfully. "You know, I think I knew there was something wrong back then. When

I came back to school after recovering my health, you were . . . different."

"I was? How?" She'd tried so hard to not let anything show. It had been hard, so hard having to keep it all inside her. But the consequences of letting it out were—had seemed at the time to be—unthinkable.

"Oh, on the surface you seemed the same, but for a while there it was as if you were . . . I don't know, acting a part—the part of lively Rose Rutherford. There was something a little frenzied about it. You were doing all the usual things, and yet there was something missing. It was as if a light had gone out inside you."

Rose bit her lip. Such wisdom from her little sister. It was exactly how it had felt. But there was more to it than Lily knew.

"You never said anything."

Lily shrugged. "I thought it was because I'd been so sick—I know I was horridly weak for ages afterward, and I hated how I'd made everyone so anxious. So I didn't want to bring it up again. And later I wondered whether something horrid had happened at school while I was away. You always did try to shelter me from anything nasty that happened, didn't you?"

"And I always will."

"I don't need to be sheltered anymore. I can look after myself. And besides, I have my darling Edward now. He would slay dragons for me."

Rose loved her sister's glowing confidence. Lily was so happy in her marriage.

Would Thomas slay dragons for Rose? The old Thomas would have. But this Thomas? She thought of his bruised jaw. She wasn't sure of anything anymore.

She picked up her marriage certificate and linked arms with her sister. "Now, let us screw our courage to the sticking point and beard our own dragon in her den. Aunt Agatha might spit fire but she won't change my mind. Please tell me you'll be on my side, even if still have doubts."

"Of course I'm on your side," Lily assured her. "Always."

* * *

"You *what*?" Ollie's eyebrows almost disappeared into his hairline. "Are you *mad*? You're married to one of the most beautiful, lively, well-born gels in the ton—an heiress to boot—and you encourage her to *get an annulment*?"

"It's the right thing to do." Rose was lucky in that she had a family in a position to pull strings to free her. Most people didn't have that option. Annulments were almost impossible to get.

"Because she has a fortune and you're broke?" Ollie eased the cork from the bottle of claret he'd selected for the first part of the evening. He held the bottle up to the light and scowled at it. "I ought to let this wine breathe, but you've given me such a nasty shock I'm in need of immediate sustenance."

He poured out the wine and took a deep draft. "Pride, that's what your problem is."

"No, it's—"

"Pride. You think you've got nothing to offer her."

"I haven't." Thomas took a sip of wine and put his glass down. After four years without alcohol, he seemed to have lost the taste for it.

Ollie made a rude noise. "Fiddlesticks! Girl's an heiress, isn't she? You're her husband, so everything she owns is yours by legal right. It's blasphemy, that's what it is. Pride and blasphemy!"

"*Blasphemy?* What on earth are—"

"The whole reason God created heiresses," Ollie continued severely, "is to bring comfort and joy and ease of living to poor sods like you and me. Most men—any poor fellow with a grain of sense, in fact—would jump at the chance to marry an heiress, even if she was cross-eyed, hook-nosed or hunchbacked—probably—but your heiress is a well-connected, gloriously sweet beauty!"

He made a disgusted gesture. "You don't mind goin' around wearing some other feller's breeches and boots, but you're willin' to slough off—yes, slough off!—a perfectly lovely girl—a girl who loves you, too—at least she did four years ago—because you're too stiff-necked to live off her fortune! Four years ago it didn't bother you, and as far as I can see, nothing's changed."

Thomas was the one who had changed. Four years ago he'd married Rose. Looking back he wondered whether he'd been in love or simply infatuated, but one thing was clear in his mind: The catalyst to their hasty secret marriage, at least in his mind, was the fear that she might be with child. Their unequal positions had paled before the prospect of pregnancy and the disgrace that would follow if she remained unmarried.

But pregnancy hadn't happened, and now he was even less of a desirable prospect than he was back then. Back then he had family, a career, expectations. Now he was nothing but a piece of human flotsam. Jetsam.

The irony was that now the idea of Rose's fortune was almost as enticing as the prospect of having her again. But somehow he couldn't bring himself to use her like that.

Ollie regarded Thomas with a jaundiced expression. "See, this is what happens to fellows when they've been at sea for too long. They might *appear* to be perfectly sane—especially when they get themselves cleaned up and stop looking like a dashed savage—but scratch the surface and they turn out to have rats in the attic!" He poured another glass. "Rats. In. The. Attic!"

He added accusingly, "Do you *know* how many men have begged Rose Rutherford to marry them? Offhand I can think of at least ten. And they're just the lucky ones who made it past that watchdog of a brother of hers, the Earl of IntimidAshendon."

Thomas shrugged. He didn't want to think about it.

"She'll go back to Everingham, I expect. If he'll have her." Ollie swirled his wine. "Complete and utter waste. He's so full of juice already that he wouldn't notice whether she brought a fortune or not, the insufferable prig. Now someone like me, for instance—"

"Is he?"

"Who?"

"The Duke of Everingham? Is he an insufferable prig?" He needed to know. Because if Rose was going to marry him . . .

Ollie pulled a face. "Not really. Bit of a cold bastard by all accounts—not that I move in his circles. But when a man as rich as that snaps up the prettiest heiress in the ton, got to despise him, eh?" He drained another glass. "Damned wasteful."

Silence fell, broken eventually by the sound of a cat yowling on a roof nearby.

"Blasted cats," Ollie muttered. "So, plans. My half day tomorrow, how about I show you round a bit, put you down for my club, get my tailor to measure you up, that sort of thing."

Thomas eyed his friend's extremely natty coat. "Until I ascertain the state of my accounts, I doubt I can afford your tailor. Or your club."

Ollie sat up, shocked. "Can't keep goin' around in another fellow's castoffs. Best order everything you need, the sooner the better. Weston for coats, Hoby for boots—"

"These boots will do for the moment."

The look Ollie gave him reminded Thomas of a Latin teacher he'd once had. "They won't, you know. You need more than one pair, and a variety of other shoes as well. You're not striding around on the deck of a ship now, you know."

For most of the last four years Thomas had worn no shoes at all. Ollie would be horrified.

"Society judges by appearances—remember the reception you got yesterday when you arrived looking like a wild man? Unless you want to be fobbed off on the lowliest clerk, you need to dress—and act—like a gentleman."

"I have more important things to do than go shopping. I have business to discuss at the Admiralty." And not just for back pay. His men needed rescuing. "And then I'll visit my bank—I had a small amount saved before my ship went down."

Ollie shook his head pessimistically. "Good luck with that."

"What do you mean?"

"Clams, the lot of them—navy, banks, lawyers—they all hate coughing up money. It'll probably take forever—especially since they've got you down as a dead man. Lord knows where your savings have gone—into some deep dark vault, I'll be bound, and you'll have to produce yourself in triplicate, stamped with the king's seal and escorted by two bishops and your old nanny before they'll even let you in the door."

Thomas laughed.

"Don't mean to pry," Ollie said after a moment, "but wasn't there an uncle or some such relative on the horizon? I'm sure you mentioned him once or twice. Might he be able to bail you out? Or at least make you a loan?"

Thomas shook his head. He'd never been the sort to puff off his grand relations in front of his friends, and now that he'd been rejected by his family, that was a relief. "Not possible, I'm afraid." He wouldn't ask his uncle for help now if he were dying. Not that he'd get any if he did.

"Well, if you want my advice, you'll order whatever duds you need and hope the bank and the Admiralty have come through by the time the bills come in."

"What if they don't?"

"Delay, man—what do you think half the gentlemen of London do? Order a new coat, and delay. Something will turn up, count on it."

BY THE TIME ROSE WENT TO BED, SHE WAS EXHAUSTED. Such a day full of turmoil and emotion. She should have collapsed, senseless, but instead she tossed and turned restlessly, unable to stop the thoughts and arguments that raged in her mind.

It couldn't possibly be simple masculine pride stopping Thomas. After all, it wasn't as if he'd be having to run to her every time he wanted any money—legally it was all his.

In fact, legally it was his already. Unless the annulment came through.

She was the one who'd be dependent on him. That was why George refused to consider marriage—she vowed never to be dependent on a man.

Rose hugged her pillow, turning over the events of the day.

Thomas had run to the church—he was panting when he got there.

He claimed it was to stop her from committing bigamy, but his eyes had blazed with light when she first saw him. Before she'd fainted.

Later, they'd been grim and hard.

Something had happened between him and Cal on the way back from the church. They were like two dogs circling each other, stiff-legged and braced for a fight.

He'd handled her family well—even Aunt Agatha—until . . . until Rose had said she would honor her vows. And then he'd turned her offer down. Why?

To be noble? She pondered that.

Thomas had always been protective. One of the reasons for their hasty marriage was because of the possibility of a baby—he was determined to protect her good name. But what was he trying to protect her from now? Himself?

This mysterious "damage" he'd mentioned? Not physical, he'd said, so presumably he could still father children. She could see he'd lived hard in the last four years, but that was no reason to call off a marriage. It was certainly no reason for her to abandon him. Quite the contrary.

Assuming there wasn't another woman, Rose could only think of two reasons why Thomas would urge her to take an annulment—male pride, because he'd come down in the world since they'd married, or the one she feared was the real reason: Thomas no longer loved her.

People could change a good deal in four years. He'd changed physically, but that didn't count. It was how people were inside that mattered. One of the things she'd always loved about Thomas was that he'd seen *her*, the Rose that she was inside. Other people saw the Earl of Ashendon's daughter, or the heiress, or admired her face or her eyes or some such silly thing that had nothing to do with who she really was.

But Thomas had, from the first, looked past all those superficial things and seen her—flawed, impatient, hot-tempered, restless, vulnerable, impulsive Rose—and loved her anyway. Loved her for the very things others criticized her for. His first words to her in the church had been about her temper, delivered with a smile.

She didn't think she'd changed very much. Not in the essentials, surely?

But maybe Thomas had changed inside, and didn't want her anymore. He'd spoken no word of love to her, had barely even touched— Oh! She sat up in bed, her eyes wide open in the dark.

She'd spoken no word of love to him, either. She hadn't hugged him, hadn't kissed him, hadn't told him how happy she was that he was alive, that he'd come back to her.

In the church she'd denied him initially, and then she'd fainted. Then she'd sat like a stuffed dummy while everyone else argued the point. Later she'd defended him to her family, but he hadn't witnessed that.

And when she and Thomas did finally get to speak in private, had she embraced him then? Had she kissed him and hugged him as she longed to do? No, she'd wept all over him like the veriest ninny, thumping him as if blaming him, blaming him for dying. And for coming back.

Rose punched her pillow. What a fool she'd been! A selfish, thoughtless, witless, self-centered, triple-toffee-coated idiot!

The clock in the hall chimed three. Rose pulled the covers back up around her and lay in bed, making plans.

The rest of the household was still asleep when Rose slipped out of bed three hours later. She washed quickly and dressed, then tiptoed downstairs. Rain was pelting down, and she muttered a curse and took an umbrella from the stand in the hall. It would be difficult to find a hackney at this hour of the morning and in this weather.

Tilting the umbrella in the direction of the rain, she set off, telling herself it wasn't all that far to walk and her jean half-boots were her most comfortable shoes.

THOMAS WOKE SLOWLY, CONSCIOUSNESS PEELING LANguidly back in layers, like floating to the surface of a deep lake. Rose curled naked in his arms, soft and sweet-smelling in the aftermath of making love, his own body tight and aching, hungry and unsatisfied . . .

It took him a while to realize it was a dream.

At least this had been a good dream. He dreamed all the time, but the good ones were few and far between. Barely a night passed when he wasn't jerked from sleep, sweating and shaking. And the fear, even though it was imaginary, took a long time to fade.

He lay on Ollie's *chaise longue*, listening to the rain pelting steadily against the window. That was what had caused this dream, of course, memories of that cramped little bed in his room in Bath where they'd first made love, while outside the rain had pelted down, battering the windows while they, blissful and enchanted, entered a world of their own making.

Life had seemed so simple then.

But that was the past, and it did no good to yearn for what would never be again. He'd learned that the hard way.

He drew the blanket around him and listened to the sounds of the city stirring. How long since he'd heard those sounds? Water gurgled noisily down the pipes from the roof, wheels splashed through puddles. He'd never realized how joyous rain could sound. Living in a parched land made you see things differently.

As always, his thoughts turned to the men he'd left behind.

Nearly four years since he'd seen any of them. Dodds,

Jones, O'Brien, Dyson and young Pendell. How were they faring? Were they even still alive?

He'd promised to get them home, assured them repeatedly that he'd take care of them, to trust him. And here he was, safe and warm in bed, listening to rain, English rain.

And where were they? Had their wives married again? Did their children call some other man Papa?

He had to bring them home. Somehow.

He'd visit the Admiralty offices again this morning. Yesterday his mission had been cut short by the news of Rose's imminent wedding and his race across town to prevent it.

Now more than ever, it was urgent he convince the navy to rescue his men. Now that he'd blown the chance of getting the funds he needed from his rich wife.

Ah, Rose. It was for the best, he told himself.

What time was it? The rain had turned the morning sky bleak and gray, and without the sun it was hard to tell time. Downstairs he heard the knocker sound, then the porter's voice and a low conversation—an early tradesman perhaps. The conversation became an argument, then he heard footsteps running up the stairs and a shout, "Oy, miss, stop. You can't go in there—"

The door to Ollie's apartments flew open.

"There you are." It was Rose, damp and triumphant. She dropped a battered umbrella in the corner, declaring, "Umbrellas these days have no stamina! The wretched thing blew inside out and look at me, I'm completely drenched." Locks of wet hair clustered around her face like the fronds of a sea anemone. She looked enchanting.

"What the devil—" Thomas sat up, clutching his blanket around him.

The porter followed her in. "I'm sorry, sir, I did tell the young person—"

"Young person?" Rose said indignantly. "I'm a young lady!"

"Young lady, my fat aunt!" The porter's wife, a small, stocky troll with an impressive bosom, wheezed into view. Dressed in a violently pink wrapper with her improbably red hair tied in dozens of rags, she confronted Rose, arms akimbo. "You're no better than you ought, you are, pushin' your way into a gentleman's abode at this hour! Now take yourself off, you brazen young hussy! This is a respectable establishment, and I won't have no—"

"I am this gentleman's wife!" Rose declared.

"Pfft! A likely tale. Now don't you back her up, sir—Mr. Yelland knows full well we don't allow females—"

"Thomas, am I or am I not your legally wedded wife?" Rose asked, spearing her fingers through her hair and feathering it out.

Thomas was very tempted to deny her, the minx, but the porter's wife was regarding him gimlet-eyed and he found himself saying, "She is, Mrs. Baines, I'm sorry—"

"What's all the blasted commotion?" Ollie stuck his head out. "Can't a man sleep in his own apartm—" Seeing Rose, he turned bright red and snatched the nightcap off his head. "Morning, Lady Rose, Mrs. Baines," he muttered, and retreated into his bedchamber like an appalled tortoise.

"*Lady* Rose?" the porter's wife said suspiciously, but her eyes were popping.

"Yes, I was Lady Rose Rutherford, but it's Mrs. Beresford now," Rose explained, apparently deciding the correct form of address would only confuse the woman. "My husband and I have only just been reunited after four years apart."

She made an apologetic moue. "Was it *very* wrong of me to come at such an early hour? Only I've missed him so, and I didn't sleep a wink last night, and this morning when I woke, well, I just couldn't stay away a moment longer."

She gave a sigh worthy of an orphan in a melodrama and directed a brave-but-woebegone look at the porter's wife. "But if you say I must go, Mrs. Baines, I will. I wouldn't want to sully your fine establishment's excellent reputation with my thoughtless and impulsive behavior."

But Mrs. Baines wasn't born yesterday. "Married, you say?" Her gaze dropped to Rose's hand. "Where's your weddin' ring, then?"

"It's here." To Thomas's surprise Rose pulled a locket from her neckline, opened it and pulled out a gold wedding ring—the one he'd given her; he recognized the design. "We married in secret, you see. I have a *very* strict and cruel guardian and if he discovered Thomas and I were married, well, he would have locked me up in a horrid dark chamber in the basement. With spiders and rats."

Mrs. Baines pursed her lips, unimpressed. "I don't reckon I'd blame him. Lady or not, I reckon you're a right handful, but since Mr. Beresford swears you're his legally wedded wife"—she darted a severe glance at Thomas—"I'll say no more. Come along, Baines." She swept to the door, then turned back and wagged a minatory finger at them. "But no joinin' giblets, you understand, or I'll be giving notice to Mr. Yelland, and that would be a shame, 'cause he's never given me a moment's trouble. A proper gent *he* is!"

The door banged shut behind her.

Rose turned to Thomas. "*Joining giblets?* Does that mean what I think it does?" He nodded and she collapsed on the *chaise longue*, gurgling with laughter. Having fought to keep a straight face throughout the entire exchange, Thomas couldn't help but join in.

Ollie poked his head out again and peered around with a hunted expression. "Has she gone?" Assured Mrs. Baines had left, he emerged, fully dressed and almost perfectly groomed.

"Terrifying woman, but does an excellent job." He picked his hat off the hat stand and said to Thomas, "Tell Baines when you want your breakfast. Mrs. Baines is a fine cook—and Baines will bring it up."

Thomas sat up. "Aren't you staying?" He had no desire to be left alone with Rose, especially not in the mood she was. And with him in his underwear and thoughts of "joining giblets" flying around.

"Good lord, no. No desire to play gooseberry." Ollie ran a hand over his chin. "Going out for a shave. Planning to go in to work early, catch up on a few things. Will eat my breakfast out. See you this evening." He gave Thomas a meaningful glance.

Ollie never allowed himself to be shaved by strangers. And he never ate his breakfast out or went in early to work. "There's no question of playing gooseberry," Thomas said firmly. "Lady Rose is leaving—"

"But Mrs. Beresford is staying," Rose put in with a bright smile.

"Quite right," Ollie said. "You just stay here with *your wife*, Thomas. And remember what I said about the purpose of God's creations. Use your head. And no *rats in the attic* this time." On this obscure message, he left.

Rose glanced at the ceiling. "Are there rats in the attic?"

"Yes," Thomas said curtly. "Close relations of the ones in your cruel guardian's dungeon basement."

She giggled. His body tightened at the sound. How often in the past had he imagined hearing her laugh again? A mountain brook burbling through river stones, sunlight dancing on the water. But the reality of it was so much warmer and more enticing.

He stood up—she was too damned close for comfort— and gathered the folds of his blanket more closely, aware that underneath it he was wearing only a pair of drawers and an undershirt. And that he was already half aroused. "What are you doing here, Rose, alone and at such an hour?"

"Here, you need to tuck it in better." She stepped close and with nimble fingers arranged the blanket around him, knotting a corner over one shoulder, and tucking fabric around his waist. "Like this. It's a cross between a Scottish kilt and Roman toga. Lily and I used to love playing dress-ups."

"Leave it." The touch of her hands, the brush of her fingers against his skin, the scent of her, damp hair and warm, fragrant woman—he couldn't bear it. He stepped back and said in a stern voice, "You shouldn't be here, Rose."

She scanned his face. "You look tired, Thomas. Are you not sleeping well? Is the *chaise longue* uncomfortable? It's too short for you—"

"It's fine." The truth was he could sleep anywhere. Just not for long. "Why are you here?"

"I had questions," she said airily. "Is this what a bachelor's apartment looks like? I must say I expected something a bit more . . . decadent. This is very neat and nice, isn't it? But then, Mr. Yelland is quite a particular gentleman, isn't he? I imagine other bachelors might be more—"

"Rose." It was a warning.

"Yes, Thomas?" she said in an innocent tone, her wide blue eyes dancing with mischief.

"You shouldn't have come."

She batted her eyelashes. "Really, Thomas?"

"I thought we'd agreed, you'd talk to your family and think seriously about accepting an annulment."

She made a careless gesture. "I talked, I thought and I don't want an annulment."

Why could he not make her understand? He wasn't the man she'd married. If she ever learned what he'd been, what he was now . . . He was doing this for her own good. He tried again. "Four years ago you married me without a thought for the future, and you ended up in . . . in limbo. Now you're being as reckless as ever." Throwing herself, body and fortune, into the ring, without a thought for the consequences.

"Thomas, I know what I want."

He shook his head, unconvinced, and she narrowed her eyes at him. "You think I haven't thought about this? I'm not a child, you know. I know that people change. I don't think it matters, that's all, not unless we want it to. Is that what you're saying, Thomas?"

"I think you're reacting to the situation without consideration of what is practical."

"Practical!" She snorted. "I was on the verge of marrying for practical reasons when you came back. I want something more than practical now, and I want it with you."

"I'm not who you think I am."

She threw up her hands in frustration. "Oh, will you please stop saying that? Nobody is who other people think they are. Everyone has secrets. And everyone lies." She walked over to the window and stood staring out over the bleak prospect.

She was right. Everyone had secrets, but some were worse than others. And it was time he shared some of his.

"I have . . . other obligations," he said.

She narrowed her eyes. "Children?"

"No, nothing like that."

"And you said there wasn't another woman."

"No, of course not."

She sat down and smoothed her skirts over her knees. "Then what are they, these obligations?"

"Do you recall me telling you about the five other men who were shipwrecked with me?"

She nodded.

He told her then about his men, about Dyson, the oldest, a big bluff northerner, the backbone of the crew; about O'Brien, a wiry little weasel plucked from the stews of London by a press-gang in the last weeks of the war. Bitter and hot-tempered, he'd nevertheless made a surprisingly good seaman and had proved unexpectedly resilient in the ordeals that followed their wrecking.

Then there was Dodds, big, bald, bandy-legged and easygoing. A joke for every occasion, that was Dodds. He left a wife and two children behind.

Jones had no family; he was a good-looking charmer with a woman in every port.

Lastly there was Jemmy Pendell, the youngest, a boy of nineteen on his first voyage, leaving a new wife behind with a baby on the way.

Pendell was the one who broke his heart the most. The others were hardened men who knew the risks. Pendell had been an eager young boy, naïve and enthusiastic, off on his big adventure before settling down to raise his family.

"I want to bring them home," he finished.

Her face softened. "Of course you do."

"It's going to cost money."

"Naturally. But where are they?"

"The Barbary Coast."

"And they need money to pay their fare home?" She wrinkled her brow. "Couldn't they . . . I mean, if they're sailors, couldn't they work their passage home?"

"They could if they were free to leave. They're not."

Her eyes widened. "They're prisoners?"

"Worse." He didn't want to tell her, but he forced it out. She had to know. "They're slaves."

"*Slaves?* But how—?"

"It's how things work along the Barbary Coast. Piracy is rife. Slavery is a way of life and has been for centuries. After we were shipwrecked and the six of us made it to shore, we were captured by local tribesmen." He paused, remembering how they'd been stripped of all their clothes and made to walk for hours, days across the burning sands, starving, thirsty, burned raw by the sun, their feet raw and blistered.

"They took us to the nearest big town." A journey that had taken several weeks across the desert. Their captors weren't deliberately cruel—they were poor, almost as ill-fed as Thomas and his men—but the journey had almost killed the Englishmen with their fair skin and their soft-soled feet.

Thomas had kept them alive by sheer willpower, coaxing, bullying, carrying them at times, and keeping hopes alive with his promise, his absolute, unshakable promise that if they could only make it to civilization, he would get them home.

He'd convinced their captors that his uncle would pay a good ransom, that he was an English lord and would pay.

His captors had believed him. His men had believed him. Thomas had believed it himself, poor fool that he was, because he thought it was the truth. He'd imagined himself loved, valued, wanted.

"They have a system there, where those who believe they can command a ransom are housed by the sultan—he's the fellow in charge. He takes charge of all incoming slaves and collects a percentage of the profits. It's a filthy system, the trade in human cattle, but all very businesslike."

"So, this sultan?" she prompted.

"We didn't meet him. We stayed in his palace, though, where his deputy, the caliph, lived. He allowed me to send a letter home, explaining what had happened and asking for a ransom to be sent."

"So what happened?"

"After a month, a letter came from my uncle."

"And?"

"It said the man calling himself Thomas Beresford was no kin of his; he was a scoundrel, not to be trusted; and there would be no ransom forthcoming."

She gasped.

"It never occurred to me that my uncle would refuse." It had shocked him so badly he was certain it must be a mistake. "But I saw the letter myself. My uncle had signed it himself—I recognized his hand."

"The caliph wasn't happy—all that time feeding me for no result—but after some persuasion he allowed me to send another letter. This time I wrote to my cousin. I was certain he'd pay, but . . ." He clenched his fists, bafflement and fury surging up as it always did. "The same kind of letter came back. Disowning me and refusing to pay."

"Are your relatives poor, then?"

He tried to keep the bitterness out of his voice, but it spilled over anyway. "Far from it. They could have paid the ransom a dozen times over and not even noticed."

"Then why would they refuse?"

He looked away, unwilling to show her the hurt he still felt. The hurt that he was determined to stifle with rage. "That's the question that's been eating at me ever since."

"Had you fallen out with them? Quarreled?"

"On the contrary. I would even have said—before this— that we were quite a close family. Fond of one another." He'd spent his boyhood looking after Gerald, especially at school, and his uncle, well, his uncle had been as much a father to Thomas as his own father.

He gestured, a mix of bewilderment, frustration and anger. "I'll get to the bottom of it eventually." He'd beard the old man in his den and demand an explanation.

"I wish you'd written to me. I would have paid."

"By that time the caliph had no patience for any more letters. And so we were sold." It was the last he'd seen of young Pendell, thin as a rake, shaking like a leaf, trying hard to look brave, stepping up to the auction block in chains. His grand adventure over.

"As slaves," she breathed, horrified. "Oh, Thomas, I'm so sorry."

There was a short silence. She rose and walked back over to the window. "Thomas, the 'damage' you spoke of, did you mean because of your experiences as a slave?"

He hesitated before attempting to explain. He hated having to talk about this, would rather they both went on pretending it had never happened. But he supposed she needed to know. And then, with any luck, she'd leave the question alone and he'd never have to speak of it again.

"Yes. Being a *thing* that someone owns, that they can do what they like with, it . . . changes you. You can never be the same person again." How could he explain to this lovely, glowing, sheltered girl the depths of degradation to which he'd sunk? It just wasn't possible. And he didn't want to try, didn't want to drag her down to that awareness. Because if she knew, if she understood what he'd been, what he'd done, she'd never look at him the same way again.

Chapter Six

❧

And listen why; for I will tell you now,
What never yet was heard in tale or song.
—JOHN MILTON

ROSE WANTED TO HUG HIM, KISS AWAY THE PAIN, PRETEND it was all over, that it didn't matter. But they weren't children to kiss it better and make it all magically go away. Terrible things happened. So did wonderful things. And for both there were consequences we had to live with.

"The thing is," she began slowly, "everything that happens to us in life changes us, for better or worse. It isn't only the bad things. I've changed, too, in ways you might not like."

He shook his head as if that weren't possible. But he'd made his confession and now she would make hers. And then, perhaps, they could both move forward.

"You said yesterday that when we married I'd made an impulsive promise based on a false premise. What did you mean by that—a false premise?"

It took a moment before he responded, and when he did, it sounded as though he didn't understand the purpose of her question. "That you might become pregnant. We thought marriage would protect you in that eventuality, but since it didn't happen . . ."

Raindrops trickled down the windowpane, gathering in tiny rivulets. She traced them with a finger. "But it did."

There was a short, shocked silence. "Rose?" He took three steps across the room, grabbed her by the shoulders and pulled her around to face him. "You had *a baby*?"

"No. I lost it. I miscarried a few weeks after you . . . after I heard your ship had gone down."

He stared at her, dumbfounded, and she shifted under the pressure of his hands on her shoulders. Would he blame her, the way she'd blamed herself? Losing the one small piece of him left to love . . .

"My God. I had no idea. . . . Why didn't you tell me?"

She just looked at him. He hadn't been there when it happened, and since he got back, where had been the opportunity? She wasn't even sure it was the right thing to do, to tell him now, on top of his own horrific revelations, when everything was still so uncertain and he was still, apparently, pushing her away. But if she didn't tell him now, when could she?

Rain pelted cold and relentless against the window.

He drew her to the *chaise longue* and seated himself beside her, holding her hand tightly in his big rough paw. It was so comforting, and yet it made her want to cry. But she was determined not to cry all over him again.

"Tell me what happened."

"I was back at school. Lily was out of danger then, but still convalescing at Aunt Dottie's. At first I didn't even realize I was with child. If it hadn't been for one of the maids . . ."

She turned to him and said almost savagely, "Why is it that girls are never taught anything useful? We're not even permitted to know how our own bodies work!"

She'd been throwing up into her chamber pot every morning for a week, thinking she was coming down with something—since the mumps outbreak, everyone in the school was very sensitive to any sign of ill health. But the queasiness passed once she'd vomited and so she thought nothing of it—until the next morning, when it returned. And the next . . . And still she didn't realize the significance.

Why would she, motherless, and being educated in an establishment staffed by spinsters, where such things were never discussed, never even acknowledged? They probably knew no more than their pupils.

It was Ella, the quiet little maid who lit the fires and scrubbed the floors and emptied the chamber pots who'd first shyly approached her and asked if perhaps miss might be in the family way. Rose had stared at her blankly, and Ella clarified, "Have you lain with a man, miss? Might you have caught a baby?"

Caught a baby?

Ella was the second oldest of ten, and she'd quietly explained that her mum had thrown up just this way, every time a baby started growing inside her.

"I was so happy when I realized it. Your baby, Thomas, our baby. I'd lost you, but you'd left me a little piece of you to love and protect. But then . . ." Her voice broke.

His arm slipped around her and tightened. "Tell me." His voice was ragged and deep.

"I lost it." There was no point going into the gory details. Waking in the night, just before dawn. Cramps, like knives cutting into her. And blood, terrifying blood.

He muttered something she didn't catch. "Go on."

"Ella, the maid, helped me through it."

She'd come into the dormitory at dawn to light the fire and saw what was happening. Her mother had lost several babes too early, and she'd explained to Rose that she was losing the babe.

The pain was bad, but the worst pain of all was knowing she was losing the last remnant of Thomas.

He held her tucked against his chest, just breathing, and they were silent for a long time. She leaned against him. He was so big and warm. She'd forgotten what a comfort it was just to be held.

"I can't imagine what it must have been like," he murmured into her hair. "And nobody else knew?"

"Not a soul. You couldn't keep a secret in that place. They would have thrown me out, married or not, pregnant or not. Miss Mallard's Seminary for the Daughters of Gentlemen prides itself on keeping young ladies pure, ignorant of anything to do with life and skilled in the more useless feminine arts."

"You couldn't tell your family?"

She snorted. "They'd have been just as bad. They would have whisked me off somewhere horrid. You never met Papa, but he was the sort of father who liked hunting and fishing, thought girls were a blasted nuisance and preferred them packed away and out of sight so he didn't have to bother with them. Cal was away at the war, and my older brother—George's father—was built in the same mold as Papa, only Henry was lazier and even more selfish."

She thought about Henry. It occurred to her that she was actually the second one in her family to have made a secret marriage. Though Henry had behaved disgracefully, whereas she . . . well, the jury was still out on that.

"Do you know, he never met or even acknowledged George, though he did at least marry her mother. I believe her grandfather forced him at gunpoint. But Henry kept the marriage secret and never went near George, left her to make her own way in the world. Cal only found George by accident after Henry died and Cal came back from the war and discovered he'd become the earl."

Rose would never have abandoned her baby, never, no matter what her father and the rest of them said or did.

"What about Aunt Dottie? Surely you could have gone to her. She seems as soft as butter."

Rose smiled. "She is. Aunt Dottie is a darling, but I doubt she could keep a secret, and once it was out, Papa and Aunt Agatha would have been the ones to decide what would happen to me." She shuddered. "I wasn't going to risk that."

"I'm so sorry. You had no one to turn to, and I—"

She reached up and put a finger against his lips. "Hush, it's all in the past now, and besides, I did have someone. I had Ella."

"Your friend, the little maid?"

"She was wonderful. She kept my secret, explained to me

what was happening and how to deal with it, and helped me through it without any kind of fuss or bother. She was the same age as me, and could barely read and write, but she knew so much more about life." She looked at him. "When I have daughters I'm going to make sure they know everything they need to know—and more."

He didn't respond.

"She left at the end of that year to get married. I gave her a set of warm woolen blankets and a teapot with pretty cups and saucers—she loved pretty things. Miss Mallard was shocked and told me it was far too extravagant for a maid-servant, but I didn't care. Ella was my friend."

Rose glanced up at him with a speculative expression. "I also gave her twenty pounds just for her, to spend on what she wanted, and not to tell her husband about. Women should have their own money and not have to ask their husband or father for every penny."

She waited for him to comment, but he didn't. They hadn't ever discussed the money issue. A woman's entire fortune belonged to her husband, and he could administer it as he saw fit. She hadn't given it much thought in the past, but George's insistence that she was keeping her fortune and not letting any man get his hands on it had given her food for thought.

Thomas would be a generous husband, she was sure, but what if he wasn't?

"So you stayed in school," Thomas said. "I thought you hated it there."

"Oh, I did, but Lily needed me." She turned her head to look at him. Could she trust him with Lily's secret? She decided against it. Lily's inability to read was her secret to reveal if she wanted to.

"Besides, I was better off being in school, having to keep up a front, keeping busy." Pretending everything was all right. She'd been so desperately sad after she'd lost the baby, drained and miserable and utterly despairing. Most days she hadn't even wanted to get out of bed. But she'd forced herself to go on.

Only Lily had noticed that she wasn't herself, but she'd said nothing. Rose wished now she'd told her sister back then, but she'd felt as though she were drowning in misery, and feared she would drag Lily down with her.

She was never going to let herself get into such a state again.

"At school there's always something one has to be doing, and they don't give you any choice. Besides," she added, trying to brighten what was turning out to be a very depressing conversation, "Miss Mallard's remedy for what she called 'girlish megrims' was a tablespoon of cod liver oil, and let me tell you, Thomas, that stuff tastes dis*gusting*." She pulled a face.

There was just one last thing she had to say to him, and then . . . she'd have done what she had to. Not quite expiation, but as close as she could come.

"I'm sorry I lost our baby, Thomas."

He lifted his hands helplessly. "It wasn't your fault. These things happen."

Outside the rain hurled itself against the windowpanes, rattling the windows in their frames.

"I didn't even cry for the baby. I wanted to. Ella kept telling me to have a good howl, that it would do me a power of good, and I tried, I really did. But somehow, I just . . . The tears wouldn't come." She shook her head, bewildered. "I think I'm just naturally hard-hearted."

"You're nothing of the sort." He hugged her tighter, stroking her hair with impossibly gentle, rough-skinned hands.

"I'm sorry about yesterday. I think you got four years' worth of tears in one burst."

"Four years?" He twisted in his seat and stared at her, shocked. "You mean you hadn't cried—"

"For four years? No." She was hard-hearted, she must be. "Not since . . . ?"

She nodded. "Something inside me got, I don't know, blocked. And yesterday, for some reason, it unblocked itself. So I'm sorry if I embarrassed—"

"Oh, for God's sake, you have nothing to apologize for—nothing!" He pulled her into his arms and kissed her.

SHE TASTED OF RAIN AND REGRET, AND FAINTLY, ENDEAR-ingly, of tooth powder. She slipped her hands over his chest, along his bristle-roughened jawline and burrowed her fingers into his hair, drawing him closer.

The taste of her, familiar, beloved and at the same time tantalizingly exotic burned through him. He'd married a girl; she was all woman now. He cupped her face in his hands, and she shivered, and abruptly he recalled his damned rough-skinned hands. "Sorry," he murmured, and pulled them off her satiny-soft skin.

"No." She grabbed his hands and put them back, pressing her palms over his. "I like the feel of them, of you touching me."

"But they're rough." And her skin was so soft.

"I don't mind. I like it." She rose on her tiptoes to cover his mouth with hers. He groaned and angled his mouth to go deeper, exploring her, remembering, learning her again.

An aching need, one that he'd lived with for four long years, rose up and engulfed him. Heat spiraled through him, heat and hunger and need, desperate need.

She clung to him, pressing herself against him, showering him with kisses and caresses, with that heedless, bountiful, exuberant passion he remembered so well. Offering her all.

The ache in him grew, a kind of madness, burning away his resolve to protect her, dissolving all awareness except that he had her in his arms at last, Rose, his wife. He was all naked hunger and heedless, selfish greed. He pressed her into a lying position, positioning himself over her, lavishing kisses on her mouth, her neck, the delicate line of her jaw, working his way lower.

A loud banging at the door jolted him into sudden awareness. Without any further warning the door flew open. "Your brrrreakfast," Mrs. Baines announced dramatically. She eyed them with beady, knowing suspicion.

Scraping together some semblance of control, Thomas rose, his breath ragged. He clutched his blanket around him, hoping the thick folds would hide the evidence of his arousal. He felt like a naughty schoolboy caught out.

Rose remained draped languidly across the *chaise longue*. She stretched, smoothed back her hair and sat up, smiling, looking like the cat that ate the cream.

"We didn't order breakfast," Thomas pointed out. Truth be told, he was almost grateful for the interruption. Another few minutes and he'd have taken Rose on the *chaise longue*—and she would have done nothing to stop him. Quite the contrary, she was all eager encouragement. In that she hadn't changed.

She was very bad for his self-discipline.

"I always bring Mr. Yelland his breakfast," the porter's wife said. "I don't hold with my gentlemen going out without their breakfast. Put it on the table there, Baines." Her husband sidled meekly in, carrying a large tray containing several covered dishes and a large coffeepot.

"Mr. Yelland left earlier," Thomas told her.

She snorted. "Think I don't know that?" She slanted him a glance that told him she knew exactly what he'd been up to and she weren't having none of it. "I don't expect your young lady, I mean your *wife*"—there was a world of sarcasm in her voice—"will want any, so I'll show you downstairs now, miss." She gestured to the door.

"On the contrary, I'm utterly famished," Rose said immediately, bathing the hostile little troll with the warmest of smiles. "You're a perfect angel, Mrs. Baines. Everything smells divine."

The perfect angel scowled. "Butter wouldn't melt . . ." she muttered.

"Oh, is there butter, too?" Rose said with all the innocence of a kitten. "How delicious. I do like hot buttery toast, don't you? And what's under these?" She lifted the covers. "Ooh, sausages and bacon and eggs, Thomas—your favorites. And loads of lovely fresh toast, and is that a pot of marmalade? Lovely." She sighed and added guilelessly, "But no giblets today, it seems. Oh, well, another time."

Mrs. Baines swelled with indignation. "Barefaced cheek . . ." She looked at Thomas, who was trying to maintain a straight face, and said severely, "I hope for your sake she's not your wife, sir, 'cause if she is, she's going to lead you a right merry dance. A right merry dance." She stomped to the door, saying, "Baines will be back to collect the dishes." The implication was left hanging: *Which won't give you time to get up to anything else.*

Rose skipped to the door and, thanking her charmingly for the lovely, lovely breakfast, closed it after her.

"You, miss, are a minx," he told her.

She laughed. "I can't resist it when people like that get all stuffy and bossy and interfering. But she's right, I probably will lead you a merry dance. Now come on, let's eat this food before it gets cold."

He didn't respond. A merry dance with Rose; it sounded like heaven. But she still thought him the man he'd been. The man he was now was a recipe for heartbreak. He'd hurt her enough already.

She was so brave. Dealing with a miscarriage with only a young maidservant to help her . . . And that cod liver oil—he could read between the lines there.

And she thought she must be hard-hearted . . .

"I'm sorry for leaving you in such an appalling situation. For leaving you to deal with it all on your own."

"Let's not worry about the past." She looked up at him with a smile that almost broke his heart. "It was nobody's fault. And anyway, you're here now. I won't be on my own again, will I?"

It was a stab to the heart.

"How many sausages?" she asked, preparing to serve him his breakfast.

"None, nor any bacon. I'll just have an egg and some toast, thanks."

She frowned. "Is that all? Cal would eat at least three

sausages and some bacon and a couple of eggs. And then toast."

"It's all I want." His stomach couldn't take rich, fatty food at the moment. It was still getting acclimatized.

"You're very thin, Thomas. Is something wrong? You're not ill, are you?"

"No, no, I'm fine." It was just years of poor food and harsh conditions. Nothing he needed to tell her about.

She was chatty over breakfast, he learned. She talked of her plans for the day, and asked about his. He mentioned Ollie's determination to get him to order new clothes, nothing else. He wasn't up to telling her his real purpose. He hoped he wouldn't have to.

She told him how she rode in the park with her family most mornings, weather permitting. "It's lovely. You should join us."

He pushed his plate away and said wearily, "There's no point, Rose. This"—he gestured between them—"isn't going to work."

"To quote Aunt Dottie, 'piffle!'"

He stood up, shoving his chair back angrily. "Four years ago you married me without a thought for the future, and you ended up in . . . in limbo. I made you pregnant and left you to cope with the consequences on your own."

"I managed."

"Then when I returned, I destroyed the advantageous marriage you'd arranged—"

"To a man I didn't love."

"—and left you at the center of a scandal. Now, because I ki—because of what happened just now—"

"You mean when you kissed me, and I kissed you back? When we kissed each other, Thomas, is that what you mean?"

He closed his eyes. "You're impulsive, reckless. Making a bad decision on the basis of a few moments of . . . emotion."

"Pooh! I'm not such a ninny. A few kisses won't turn my head, even if they are"—her gaze dropped to his mouth—"yours." Her lips curled into a knowing little smile that caused a ripple of desire to curl right through him. He stamped down on it.

"I know what I want, Thomas. I always have. And I think you want me too, but you've got some maggot in your brain telling you it's wrong. But it's not. I knew four years ago we were meant to be together, and I feel it just as strongly now. Yes, we've both been through some difficult times—and don't think I haven't noticed you haven't told me very much at all about what happened to you, yet, but I can be patient."

He passed his hands over his eyes. What to do with such a woman?

"You do want me, don't you, Thomas?" she asked softly. He opened his eyes and she was there in front of him, a breath, a touch away. The unique fragrance of her teased his senses. Before he could react she rose on her tiptoes and brushed her lips lightly over his. "Don't you, Thomas?" She kissed him again.

He groaned. A man could only stand so much. He hauled her into his arms and kissed her again. Just once. A last desperate kiss. A kiss to last a lifetime.

He released her and stepped back, breathing heavily, putting what he hoped was a safe distance between them.

She smiled confidently up at him. "That's better. So, it's all settled, then."

"No. This changes nothing."

She laughed. "Thomas, you can't kiss me like that and then try to convince me you don't want—"

"That was a good-bye kiss. I mean it, Rose," he said firmly. "You can't base your life on, on a whim, a couple of kisses. I won't let you."

"No, Thomas." Her voice was demure, but there was nothing demure about her expression.

"At the very least, you need a period of sober reflection."

"Yes, Thomas." Her eyes danced, anything but sober. She was every inch the bewitching minx he'd fallen in love with.

But he was a weary husk of a man with a dead stump for a heart. And obligations elsewhere.

He hardened his voice, needing her to understand. "I would be six kinds of villain if I allowed you to base your decision on . . . emotion."

"Yes, Thomas." She rose on her toes and planted a swift kiss on his mouth.

"Stop it, Rose—I'm serious here."

She tried to look serious, but he wasn't fooled for a minute.

"Promise me you'll give it a few d—a week before you decide. And listen to your family. Give their opinions serious consideration."

"Serious consideration." She repeated it like an obedient schoolgirl, her expression showing she was anything but.

He had to get her out of here. If she looked at him like that for an instant longer he wouldn't be answerable for the consequences. "I'll see you in a few days. Or a week."

"Come riding with us tomorrow. Seven o'clock, Hyde Park—weather permitting."

He stamped down on the temptation. "Good-bye, Rose."

Her laugh was soft, pure, delectable mischief. "See you tomorrow, Thomas."

He closed the door behind her and leaned against it. He'd failed her once; he wouldn't fail her this time. For all her experience, she was still something of an innocent, and he had to protect her, even if from himself.

Especially from himself.

A knock came on the door. He wrenched it open. "I told you—"

Baines recoiled, holding up his hands in a gesture of peace. "Just came for the dishes, sir. I saw the young lady leave, but if it's not convenient . . ."

Thomas sighed and waved the man inside.

THE RAIN HAVING EASED TO AN OCCASIONAL SPATTER OF drops, Rose walked home, pondering the situation. What was Thomas so worried about? Was it simply an excess of nobility? Imagining she cared a lot more about social status than she did? The duke had given him ideas, perhaps, but she'd only agreed to marry the duke because he'd assured her he didn't love her and preferred she didn't love him. Which she didn't.

Give her a poor and loving Thomas any day over a rich, phlegmatic duke.

Fresh from Thomas's embrace, she couldn't conceive of agreeing to such a cold-blooded bargain. And yet she had. Thomas's return had shattered the shell she'd built around herself, the shell she hadn't even realized existed. She felt more alive now than she had in forever.

She gave a little skip. Thomas kissed like a dream. She couldn't wait to get him back in the marriage bed.

She entered the house quietly, wanting to avoid any questions about where she had been. She washed and changed, and came downstairs again as if she'd slept in and had only just woken up.

Following the sound of voices, she found Emm, Cal, George, Lily and the two aunts seated in the back drawing room. Emm had her writing desk out and was poring over sheets of paper, making notes. Cal too had a list in front of him. George was sorting papers, Aunt Dottie and Lily were winding wool and Aunt Agatha was peering through her lorgnette, overseeing whatever it was that Emm was doing.

Emm looked up with a warm smile as she came in. "Ah, there you are, Rose dear. Did you sleep well?"

"Very well, thank you, Emm." It was a lie, but she felt as refreshed as if she had slept beautifully. Kissing Thomas had that effect on her. Her blood was fizzing like champagne. She sat down beside Emm. "What are you doing?"

"Going through the lists."

"What lists?"

Emm gave her a dry look. "Canceling a wedding turns out to be just as much work as planning one, if not more. The food was easy. Thank goodness we decided on a small family wedding breakfast. The servants took what they wanted and distributed what was left to the poorhouse."

"Oh." Rose hadn't thought of the trouble she was putting everyone to. "What can I do to help?"

"I can deal with most of this." Emm gestured to several closely written sheets. "This list is for the return of the wedding presents. George is helping with that, and Lily will be wrapping them back up."

"Here's your job." Emm passed Rose a thick list of names and addresses. "It's the list for the cancellation of the ball—all the people we invited and all those who accepted. You'll need to write to all of them; you know how people change their minds. We can help with the addressing, but the notes of apology will need to be in your hand."

"You're canceling the ball?" Rose took the list and glanced at it without really seeing it.

"Unless, of course," Aunt Agatha said in a withering voice, "you think we should hold a ball to celebrate a wedding that didn't happen."

"Everyone needs to be notified to let them know it's off," Emm said. "Oh, and Cal, while I remember it, we'll need to cancel the musicians too."

Cal grunted and scribbled something on a piece of paper.

Rose stared at her elderly aunt. A slow smile grew on her face as it all came together in her mind. "What a wonderful idea, Aunt Agatha. Thank you. It's the perfect solution."

Aunt Agatha lifted her lorgnette and stared at Rose through it. "What are you talking about, gel? What solution?"

"Not to cancel the ball."

Emm looked up, surprised. "But we must."

Aunt Agatha sat forward in her chair, suddenly intent. "Unless you've decided to be intelligent, that is. Is that it, gel? If the annulment can be hurried through—Ashendon, you can get onto that immediately—and the duke agrees to go ahead with the marriage—we'll need to speak with him—"

"No, Aunt Agatha." Rose interrupted her gently. "That's not what I meant. I'm sorry to disappoint you, but I won't agree to an annulment. I made sacred vows to Thomas Beresford and I mean to keep them."

The old lady's thinly plucked brows snapped together. "But the fellow refused you, said he was willing to let you go. I heard him myself."

"I know, but he only said that because he thinks he has nothing to offer me. He's very noble, my Thomas."

Aunt Agatha sniffed. "Or very clever."

"You don't know him yet," Rose said. "But when you do, you'll like him, I'm sure."

Aunt Agatha dismissed that possibility with a sharp gesture. "That remains to be seen. Your insistence on being stubborn and foolhardy is one thing; the matter of the ball is quite another. Naturally we must cancel it, and the sooner the better. Why on earth would we continue with a ball that was to celebrate your marriage to the Duke of Everingham?"

"To celebrate the return of my husband, Thomas Beresford, from the dead?" Heart in mouth she glanced at Emm and Cal, beseeching them with her eyes.

Aunt Agatha snorted. "A ball, for a *nobody*?"

Rose kept her voice even. "As I've said before, Aunt Agatha, he's *not* a nobody to me." Her aunt eyed her balefully.

George spoke up. "Besides, if nobody's ever heard of him, all the more reason to introduce him, don't you think?"

Rose smiled at her. "Exactly." Dear George could always be relied upon to enter the lists against Aunt Agatha.

Aunt Dottie clapped her hands. "I think it's a splendid idea. I do so enjoy a ball. Remember the one Edward's grandfather held for Lily and Edward? Simply delightful. And now another one, in London, and at the height of the season. It will make a wonderful splash."

"That was the intention, Dorothea," Aunt Agatha said acidly. "When we were celebrating *a duke*."

"How much better," Aunt Dottie declared, "to be celebrating love, and a man's return from the dead. Sooo romantic." She pulled out a wisp of lawn and lace and wiped her eyes with it.

"I think it's a lovely idea," Lily said. "Clever, too. It will make it clear to the ton that we are welcoming Mr. Beresford into the family."

"Are we?" Cal grumbled. "I don't want to welcome the swine anywhere."

"Are you sure about this, Rose?" Emm asked quietly. "Not about the ball, but about the marriage."

"Very sure, Emm. I know I was young when I married Thomas, but truly, he is the man for me."

Aunt Agatha made an exasperated sound. "But you know so little about him, child—he has no family, no background—"

"You can tell he was well brought up," Rose said. "His manners are impeccable. And he was an officer in the navy."

"And where has he been the last four years?" Cal snapped. "Not with the navy, that's certain. Did he explain that while you were talking to him yesterday?"

"No."

"And did he explain how he intends to support you?"

Rose lifted her chin. "I have a fortune. We can live on that."

He rolled his eyes. "Like a lamb to the slaughter. I ought to wash my hands of you." But it was clear he wouldn't. Her brother was very protective, and while his hostility toward Thomas was distressing, she was sure eventually the two men would come to like and respect each other. But in the meantime . . .

"That reminds me," Rose said. "Did you hit Thomas yesterday? He had a fresh bruise on his jaw."

Her brother's eyes grew flinty and hard. "Why, what did he say?"

His attitude confirmed in Rose's mind that he had. "He said he tripped on a cobblestone, but I don't believe a word of it. You hit him, Cal, didn't you? Well, I won't have it, do you understand? Thomas is my husband and the sooner you accept that, the better."

Her brother said nothing. He folded his arms and sat with a mulish expression.

Emm picked up her pen. "Well, do we go ahead with the ball or not?" She looked at Cal, who threw his hands up and muttered, "Oh, why not? If she's so determined to have him, we might as well try to put a good face on it."

"Nobody will come," Aunt Agatha warned.

"Nonsense! Of course they'll come, Aggie," Aunt Dottie said. "Everyone will be bursting with curiosity, desperate to meet the man who not only returned from the dead, but who in doing so displaced a duke so dramatically. It's going to be a delicious squeeze." She rubbed her hands together. "Such fun!"

Emm looked down at the papers spread before her and nodded. "Very well. The wedding gifts will have to be sent back regardless, but we will go ahead with the ball. We'll need to inform all our invited guests of the change of plan. We can get new cards of invitation printed, of course, though it will be a frightful rush. And Rose, you will have to write all the notes explaining. I warn you, there are hundreds. George, you can address them, and Lily, I rely on you to seal the notes with that pretty gold wax—I hope we still have enough of it left." She made a note to check. "Oh, and Rose, when you see Mr. Beresford next, ask him if there is anyone he would particularly like invited." She separated several sheets from the pile. "All these arrangements can remain as they were, thank goodness."

"And before any of those notes are sent out, Rose will have to apologize to the duke," Aunt Agatha declared. "In person."

Rose grimaced. There was no getting out of that one.

THOMAS SPENT THE NEXT TWO DAYS GOING FROM ONE ADmiralty office to another. He came away in the late afternoon of the second day seething with fury and frustration. His back pay wasn't the issue—that would take time, but eventually the navy would cough up.

It was the men he'd left behind that were the sticking point. Five British seamen, held in appalling conditions in a foreign country. Surely the navy had an obligation to rescue them?

Apparently not.

What exactly are these conditions?

He couldn't say, exactly, but—

You haven't seen them for almost four years? My dear fellow, you must see how impossible it is for us to act after all this time. Apart from the cost, anything could have happened to them. No, no, no. Quite impossible.

Again and again the message was the same. It was unfortunate, but nothing could be done.

But Thomas was committed to getting those men back to England. He *needed* to get them home. Safe, as he was. They were his responsibility. They were *the navy's* responsibility.

But was anyone in the whole blasted Admiralty concerned for the fate of five ordinary seamen that they'd written off as drowned four years ago? Not one sympathetic ear could he find.

Oh, he'd been given a vastly better reception now that he was clean-shaven and dressed as a gentleman, but still, his concerns were dismissed. He'd demanded to speak to men of higher and higher rank—and each time he was—eventually—granted an interview. But each man pointed out to him the impossibility of his mission, that in this postwar environment the navy was shedding men, that it was a pity, but when a man joined the service he knew the risks. *Fortunes of war, you know.*

And when he'd pointed out that it was peacetime now, and that several of these men had been press-ganged, forced into the navy against their will, that only made several of the smug bastards more adamant. *Nothing can be done, dear fellow. Think of the costs. And even if we could afford the ransom, even if we could spare a ship to send on this wild-goose chase, what guarantee is there of finding them after all this time? No, it's a demmed pity, but there it is.* As if his men deserved their fate, and press-ganged men, well, what did it matter? Not proper seamen, were they?

Finally he'd seen the most senior admiral in the place, semiretired but bristling with self-importance and gold braid.

No no no. I'm sorry, dear fellow, but we sent Exmouth to clear out several nests of those villains several years ago—bombed the living daylights out of Algiers—you didn't hear about that? Tremendous victory, thousands freed, hundreds of our fellows brought home. Cost us a fortune—which we don't have now the war's over. But we made our point. Couldn't possibly justify any further expense, especially not for a mission to rescue a handful of ordinary seamen who might not even be alive, what?

And then as the admiral's aide was showing him out, the old fellow had added, *Different if they were officers, of course. Might have been able to do something then.*

Thomas had to leave. It was that or commit murder.

HE CALLED IN ON HIS BANK ON THE WAY BACK TO OLLIE'S, hoping for some good news there. He gave his name to the clerk and asked to speak to the bank manager. The bank manager emerged from his office and approached Thomas with a smile.

"Mr. Beresford, how very good it is to see you."

Thomas shook the hand the man offered. "Yes, as you can see, I'm not dead, after all."

The manager gave him an odd look. "No, quite. I can see that. Were you after an advance? Because you're earlier than expected—quarter day is not for several weeks yet."

"Quarter day? I'm not sure I follow you, Mr. . . . ?" He hadn't made any kind of appointment, so how could he be early?

"Filbert, Matthew Filbert, sir. You won't remember me. I was just a clerk when you were in here last. But I'm very glad you've come. There's a small matter I need to discuss with you. Will you step this way, please?" He ushered Thomas into his office and shut the door.

Thomas proceeded to explain his situation. Filbert's eyes almost popped.

"You mean, you were reported dead? For the last four years? Bless my soul, what a shocking situation. I had no idea. But how—?" He broke off, frowning, then rang a bell. A clerk arrived a moment later. "Be so good as to fetch the Beresford account files," Filbert told him.

A few moments later the man returned bearing a heavy, clothbound ledger. He laid it on the manager's desk and withdrew. Filbert leafed through it and muttered something under his breath.

"You say you were reported dead four years ago?"

"That's correct."

"And that until three days ago the navy had you listed as dead—definitely dead, not merely missing?"

"Definitely dead. There were witnesses to the destruction and sinking of our ship, and they reported it as sunk with all hands lost."

"But you survived?"

"Yes. I and five others managed to make it to shore."

"Ah, so you've been back in England all this time."

"No, we were trapped in a hostile country for the last four years—the other five men are still there. I escaped, and arrived back in England three days ago."

Filbert frowned over the account book, and Thomas added, "What is all this about? I assume you were notified of my so-called death. I understand there might be some difficulties in releasing funds immediately, but I assure you, I am Thomas Beresford."

"Yes, yes, I know that. I recognize you from before, sir." Filbert tapped the ledger book. "But if you've been 'dead,' how is it that you have been withdrawing funds from your account every quarter day for the last four years?"

"What? I haven't!"

"Well, someone bearing your signed authority has. Every quarter day, the money held in trust for your allowance is deposited in your account—"

"You mean the money from my late mother's trust fund? I thought that could not be touched until I turn thirty."

"Yes, yes, that one can't. I'm speaking of the allowance your uncle set up when you first went to sea."

Thomas stared at Filbert, his brain reeling. "You mean he didn't stop it? He continued supporting me financially?" Four years ago, Uncle Walter had rejected Thomas's appeal for ransom in no uncertain fashion, denying any knowledge of him, refuting any claim Thomas made of him and ending with a statement that Thomas was not even a member of his family.

And yet, according to this man, he'd continued to pay Thomas's allowance into his account? It made no sense.

"Yes, it's paid into your account every quarter day, and three days afterward, your agent arrives bearing your authority and withdraws it all."

"What? That's ridiculous. I don't have an agent and I've never signed any authority."

For answer Filbert passed over a small sheaf of documents. "Is that not your signature?"

Thomas examined them. Each one was an authority to pay the bearer the entire quarterly allowance, and was signed by . . . Thomas. If he didn't know better, the signatures would have fooled even him. He swore and pushed them back across the desk. "I agree it looks like my signature, but I swear to you I never signed any of these. I've never authorized a payment to any other person. I didn't even know that my uncle was continuing to pay my allowance."

Filbert looked skeptical.

"Dammit, I haven't even been in the country! How the hell could I sign those blasted things when I was imprisoned on the other side of the world?"

Filbert pursed his lips. "Can you prove you were out of the country?"

"I have a witness to my return, and I can prove the navy has me listed as dead—will that do?" Filbert hesitated, and Thomas added, "Dammit, why would I be claiming such a thing if all this time I'd been signing those notes and collecting my allowance? What would be the point of my coming here—to tell you I'm not dead? When you never imagined I was dead in the first place?"

Filbert pursed his lips. "There is that. It is most perplexing."

"It's more than perplexing," Thomas said grimly. "Someone has been systematically stealing my money— and with the bank's connivance."

"*Connivance?*" Filbert was shocked. "Never that, sir. Oh, no, no, no! Never call it connivance. We were *deceived*—you must admit that is a very convincing facsimile of your signature. I shall instigate an immediate investigation. Never fear, we will get to the bottom of this, sir, be assured."

Chapter Seven

❦

He was not an ill-disposed young man, unless to be rather cold hearted, and rather selfish, is to be ill-disposed…
—JANE AUSTEN, *SENSE AND SENSIBILITY*

"WILL YOU COME WITH ME TO VISIT THE DUKE?" ROSE asked George. "I need a break from writing all these wretched notes." She stretched her aching fingers. She'd been writing notes for the last day and a half and was only three-quarters through the list of people who needed to be notified of the change of purpose of the ball.

"Why do you want to visit him?" Caution laced George's voice.

"I need to apologize to him, about, about the . . . the cancellation of the wedding." So awkward. She couldn't even think of a polite phrase to describe what had happened.

"Can't you just write him a nice apologetic letter?"

She could, of course, but she felt she owed it to him to apologize in person. "I think what happened caused him a lot of embarrassment. A letter seems insufficient." And rather cowardly.

"It wasn't your fault. You were as surprised as anyone when Mr. Beresford turned up. And the duke didn't seem embarrassed to me. More irritated."

"Whatever he felt, I still need to apologize. In person."

George wrinkled her nose. "So why do you need me? I was going to take Finn for a walk."

"I cannot call on an unmarried man, not in his home, not by myself."

"Why not? You're married, after all. And you said you'd be free once you were married." George was refreshingly indifferent to the niceties of social conventions.

Rose laughed. "Not quite that free. Please come, George. Emm is taking a nap—this baby makes her so tired—and Lily is off somewhere with Edward, which only leaves you or Aunt Agatha to accompany me, and if she comes she'll make me feel like a naughty schoolgirl."

Aunt Agatha had indicated she would come again in the late morning, before visitors started arriving—a lot of curious Claras had called the previous day, wanting to sniff out the details of the scandal, and they were expecting even more today. Rose wanted to have the apology over and done with before she arrived. Otherwise Aunt Agatha was sure to insist on going.

And if Aunt Agatha accompanied her she would be sure to treat Rose like a naughty schoolgirl instead of a grown-up married woman. Besides, it was Rose's problem, and she would deal with it herself.

George might hate polite social calls, but there would be no better companion for such a visit. She wasn't the slightest bit intimidated by the duke and didn't understand why everyone else found him so formidable. That attitude would help Rose through an interview she dreaded.

George sighed. "All right, but can we take Finn? With all the rain we've had, he hasn't had a proper run for two days."

"Of course. We can cut across Berkeley Square, and he can have a bit of a walk there, then after I've spoken to the duke, we can go for a lovely long walk in the park and he can really stretch his legs."

Ten minutes later, dressed in hat, gloves and warm pelisse and carrying an umbrella each, they set out for the duke's residence, Finn leading the way.

* * *

"LADY ROSE BERESFORD AND LADY GEORGIANA RUTHER-ford to see the duke." Rose handed the butler her card. This was another thing she needed to do: have new calling cards made. The "Duchess of Everingham" ones she'd ordered would be no use to anyone now.

"I shall inquire whether His Grace is at home." The man clearly knew who she was, even though she'd never actually visited the duke at his home. And though he was perfectly polite, he managed to convey, in that subtle way that only the best butlers could, that he did not approve of her visiting his master, respectable companion or not. Nor, his glacial expression conveyed, was Rose forgiven for effectively jilting his master the previous day.

He stood back to allow Rose and George to enter. George gave him a friendly nod and handed him Finn's lead.

The butler looked at it as if she'd handed him a live snake.

"It's all right, he doesn't bite," George assured him. "Not unless I tell him to."

Holding the lead between thumb and finger, the butler pulled a bell cord, and a liveried footman appeared. "Take care of this . . . creature," the butler told him, and handed him the lead.

Finn happily went with the footman, his tail wagging slightly, his claws clicking on the marble floor, his muzzle high as he snuffed the air for potential treats.

The butler turned back to Rose and George. It was clear that Finn's presence had sunk their credit with him even lower, if that was possible. "Would you care to wait in here, ladies?" He ushered them into the drawing room, a large, elegant salon papered in cream silk with a discreet gold pattern. Despite the lateness of the season, a fire burned merrily in the grate, and a big bay window overlooked the street.

Rose sat on an elegant straw-colored settee and looked

curiously around. Everything was of the first elegance. Strange to think this might have been her home, her butler. But she had no regrets.

George stood in front of the fire and hitched the back of her skirt up, the better to warm her legs. Emm had mostly managed to break her of the habit of wearing breeches under her dresses—unless she was riding—but George, who'd spent most of her early years dressed as a boy, still complained that dresses were drafty, cold and illogical, and only good for summer wear. If that.

George glanced around and grimaced. "All this white and gold. A bit bland, don't you think? And no books anywhere to be seen."

"I keep my books in my library," a cold voice said from the doorway. They turned and Rose could see from the direction of his gaze that even though she'd been quick to drop her skirt, the duke had noticed George's unladylike pose.

"Shall I have a footman stoke the fire for you?" he asked sardonically.

George's grin was entirely unrepentant. "No thanks, I'm nicely warmed up now."

If Rose hadn't been so nervous she might have laughed. Instead she clutched her reticule to her chest with cold fingers and waited.

The duke eyed George with a steely expression, then turned to Rose, who had risen at his entrance. "To what do I owe the honor of this visit, Lady Rose—or do you prefer Mrs. Beresford now?" The words were silkily polite, but there was an acid undercurrent to their delivery. He knew perfectly well she was still Lady Rose; only her surname had changed.

Like his butler, he had not forgiven her.

Rose stiffened her spine. She'd come here to apologize, but she was not expecting forgiveness.

She glanced at George. They'd discussed how to handle it on the way over. George obediently wandered to the far corner of the room, picked up an ugly, though probably priceless statuette and proceeded to demonstrate fascination and obliviousness. Not particularly successfully, but it would do.

"I came to apologize for what happened," Rose told him baldly. "I'm sorry you were embarrassed."

He gestured for her to be seated. "I was not embarrassed."

He was going to be difficult; she told herself he was entitled to be. "Disconcerted, then."

"Not at all."

"Upset?" she said edgily.

"Hardly." And before she could go on, he said, "We made an agreement to marry. It was at that point you should have told me you'd already been married. You knew perfectly well that given my position, I expect to marry a virgin. Given that you weren't, I must consider I had a lucky escape."

Rose gasped. "But I have only ever lain with my husband, and that was for just two weeks. And since then I've been celibate for four years!"

"Nevertheless, not a virgin." He rubbed his long fingers together as if ridding himself of dust.

"Why should *she* be a virgin? You're not!" George burst from her corner.

He barely turned his head, but his heavy-lidded glance was icy. "You cultivate an interest in my sexual exploits, do you, Lady Georgiana?"

George glared at him. She clutched the statuette in her fist, almost as if she might throw it at the duke. Rose prayed she wouldn't.

The duke shrugged with an ineffable air of cynical ennui and continued. "Virginity is a requirement for any bride of mine. There must be no question of the paternity of my heir."

Rose swallowed her temper. He was right. "I should have told you," she admitted.

"I appreciate that a *lady*"—an ironic two-edged cut aimed at both Rose and George equally—"might feel too delicate to speak of such matters as virginity, but your guardian had no such excuse. There was no mention of such a thing when we were drawing up the settlements."

"Cal didn't know," she said quickly.

A dark brow winged upward.

"I never told him, never told any of my family." She swallowed. "I married in secret, and just a few weeks later my husband was reported dead. Cal was away at the war at the time, and . . ." She made a vague gesture. "By the time he came back there didn't seem to be any point in telling him."

"And Lady Salter? Am I to understand that all the while she was promoting the match, she was also ignorant of your true state?"

"Yes. Nobody knew, nobody at all. I am the one to blame—the sole person responsible. I deceived everyone, including you. I'm so sorry."

There was a long silence. He crossed one long, booted leg over the other and contemplated his foot. "Secret from everyone? To what purpose?" he said eventually, sounding less sardonic and more curious.

She shook her head, not knowing how to explain, especially to such a cold man. But she was here to make amends, so she forced herself to try. "It was too painful to speak of. I tried to put it out of my mind."

"Successfully, I gather."

Remembering her thoughts during the first part of the wedding ceremony, she said nothing.

There was another long silence. Coals hissed and settled in the fireplace.

The duke rose to his feet. "So you came to apologize. I accept your apology. Was there anything else?" He was reaching for the bell pull as he spoke, clearly intending to end the interview.

"Well, actually . . ." Rose fished in her reticule. "I wanted to give you this, in person." She handed him a folded note. "It's about the ball. The one we planned for the week after next."

His brow rose. "Canceled, I presume."

"No, it's going ahead. We're going to use it to introduce Thomas, my husband, to the ton."

He didn't even glance at her note. "And what has that to do with me?" The cutting tone was back.

She took a deep breath. "I'd like you to come."

Her words hung in the air.

"Let me get this straight. The ball that was intended to celebrate my wedding—the wedding that ended in a debacle before it even started, the wedding that was touted as 'the wedding of the season' and is now being spoken of as 'the scandal of the season'—that ball? And you want me, the jilted groom—is that the right word? *Jilted?* Or perhaps *spurned* is better. Or what about *supplanted*? Yes, *supplanted* will do nicely—so you want me, the supplanted groom, to come and give the newly reunited happy couple my blessing? In front of all the ton?"

Rose swallowed. Put like that, it did seem rather outrageous. "Yes?" she said in a small voice. "Please?" It would help smooth things over wonderfully.

He gave a harsh bark of laughter and rang the bell pull.

"If you came, you could demonstrate to the ton your supreme indifference," George said helpfully. "You'd like that, wouldn't you?" He gave her a cutting glance, but otherwise ignored her.

Seconds later the butler appeared in the doorway. "Show these ladies out, Fleming," the duke said. "Good day, Mrs. Beresford, Lady Georgiana."

"So you think someone's been masq'rading as you?" Ollie, sprawled almost horizontally in an armchair, regarded his wineglass somewhat muzzily. They'd eaten their dinner at Ollie's club and had now retired to Ollie's apartment to drink port. Quite a lot of port, after a very excellent claret at dinner.

"Forging my signature and stealing my money, certainly." Thomas was as much bemused by the fact that his uncle had continued paying his allowance as by the knowledge that someone else had been systematically robbing him for the last four years. Who could it possibly be?

And why would his uncle keep paying an allowance into his account when he knew for a fact that Thomas couldn't touch it? Because as far as Uncle Walter was concerned, Thomas was still rotting on the other side of the world. He'd gone out of his way to ensure it.

It made no sense.

He was going to have to go to Gloucestershire and confront him. He wasn't looking forward to it.

"The bank manager agreed to advance me some money, so I'm in funds again, at least."

"Good work. How d'you get on at th'Admiralty?"

"It's hopeless. I practically battered down every door there; none of the bastards is the slightest bit interested." He was going to have to find the money elsewhere.

A sly little voice in his head kept reminding him that while his marriage remained unannulled, he was, legally, entitled to full control of Rose's entire fortune. But he'd wrecked her life enough; he wasn't going to rob her as well. There had to be another way.

"Good thing you decided to be sens'ble then," Ollie said drowsily.

Thomas thought for a minute but couldn't make sense of his friend's words. "In what way sensible?"

"Staying married to your heiress."

"But I'm not. Her family want better for her than I can provide and I agree. I've advised her to agree to an annulment."

Ollie heaved himself up sufficiently to turn his head. "Then why are they holding a ball for you?"

"A ball? What the devil are you talking about?"

"The Ruth'fords are holding a ball th'week after next to introduce you to the ton. Cel'brate your return from the dead or some such thing."

Thomas had never heard anything so ridiculous. "You're foxed."

"Got invited to it myself. 'S up there." Ollie gestured vaguely to the mantelpiece. He peered blearily at Thomas. "What? Di'n't you get an invitation? Poor Thomas, left out of his own ball." He sank back into his chair, chuckling.

Thomas found the invitation on the mantelpiece. He opened it and read it swiftly. Sure enough it invited Ollie to attend a ball at Ashendon House in a fortnight's time, to celebrate the return of Lady Rose Rutherford's long-lost husband, Commander Beresford, late of His Majesty's Royal Navy.

He stared at it, turned it over, read it again. It had to be a hoax.

"Did you write this? Is it your idea of a joke?"

Ollie snorted. "Zif I'd joke about such a thing. No, looks to me like the girl's d'termined to have you after all, and has talked the family around. So, old friend, all your troubles are over. Lovely girl, rich wife, aaaall settled. Except—oh, no!" He sat up, suddenly serious.

Thomas blinked at his friend's sudden urgency. "What?"

"You don't have a thing to wear! I'll introduce you to m'tailor first thing in the morning."

"Not first thing."

Ollie regarded him with owlish surprise. "Why? What could be more important than ordering your clothes for the ball?"

"A ride in the park." Thomas tapped the invitation thoughtfully. He'd given her fair warning—more than fair; he'd told her repeatedly—but she'd gone ahead regardless and declared her marriage to the whole world.

Be it on her own head. She was stuck with him now.

THOMAS RENTED A HACK, A BAY GELDING WHO WOVE through the morning London traffic without turning a hair at dogs or barrow-boys, wagons or anything else.

He arrived at Ashendon House just before seven o'clock, just as several grooms trotted up, leading a string of thoroughbreds. Whatever else he was, Ashendon was a good judge of horseflesh.

The front door opened and the Rutherford ladies, dressed in stylish habits, hurried down the steps. "Thomas! You're joining us! I'm so glad," Rose exclaimed.

He greeted her family members and was rewarded by a warm response from her sister and niece and the big gangly hound, a brusque nod from Ashendon and a slightly less stiff one from Galbraith.

The gentlemen tossed the ladies into their sidesaddles. Thomas was surprised to see Lady George mounted on a spirited black stallion that looked far too strong for her. He danced and shied and caracoled, but she only laughed at his antics, seeming quite unworried. All the Rutherford ladies, it seemed, were at home in the saddle.

The small cavalcade set out, two by two, Lady Lily with Lady George, the hound at her heel, followed by Rose and Thomas, then Ashendon and Galbraith. A dour-looking Scottish groom came up in the rear.

Thomas could feel the eyes of his brothers-in-law boring into his back.

Rose gave him a sunny smile. "Isn't it a glorious morning?" She was dressed in a blue habit that matched her eyes, trimmed with silver in a vaguely military style, with a saucy shako perched on her head.

"Wonderful," he responded dryly. She looked glorious, but the day was gray and chilly, with a brisk breeze sending the clouds scudding across the sky. The middle of spring; to Thomas's bones, it felt like winter.

Rose leaned across and said softly, "It's a bit like a school crocodile, going in pairs, I know, but once we get to the park we can spread out and be more private."

He was glad to hear it. He had no intention of saying what he had to in front of her brother.

"You said you wouldn't visit. What changed your mind?" she asked as the gates of the park came into view.

He gave her a sideways glance. "Ollie received your invitation."

"Oh, good. You got yours, too, of course."

"There wasn't one for me."

She turned in surprise. "You mean we didn't send you one?"

"Apparently not."

She gurgled with laughter. "George," she called. "We forgot to send Thomas an invitation."

George turned her head. "He doesn't need one, he's the guest of honor."

Rose laughed again. "There's your answer. You're the guest of honor."

"When were you going to tell me?"

Her face was full of mischief. "When I saw you next, of course."

"And if I didn't visit? What if I decided to go to the country and didn't hear about the ball? What if I didn't turn up?"

She gave another merry peal of laughter. "That would have been embarrassing, wouldn't it? I'd get an even worse reputation than I already have for being careless with bridegrooms, and Aunt Agatha would crow with triumph." He was humbled by her utter confidence in him, but it was foolish.

They passed through the gates of Hyde Park and their pace picked up. At this hour the park was virtually deserted, the earth fragrant and damp after the recent rain and the grass so green it almost hurt Thomas's eyes. He'd forgotten grass could be so green.

Lady George twisted around in her sidesaddle, winked at Rose and called, "Cal, race you to the big tree on the other side of the park." And before her uncle could answer, she was off and racing, riding like fury, *ventre à terre*, her dog streaking along beside her.

Ashendon, cursing reckless young women who obviously wanted to break their necks, set off after her. Galbraith, chuckling, joined his wife. They rode off together, leaving Rose and Thomas alone with the grim Scottish groom.

"That's Cal sorted," Rose said with satisfaction. "And Kirk won't bother us. He looks fierce but that's just an expression he uses to intimidate people. He's really very sweet. Now come along, a quick gallop to blow away the cobwebs and by the time Cal gets back we'll be nicely out of sight and able to talk."

She urged her mount to a gallop and headed in the opposite direction from her brother. She was almost as good a horsewoman as Lady George. Thomas's horse had to struggle to keep up. The Scottish groom followed, hanging back discreetly.

It was exhilarating, the race across the fragrant earth, the pounding hooves, the wind cold in his face, the heat of the horse beneath him, the laughing girl just ahead of him. It more than blew the cobwebs away, it blew away the years. He just wished he had a decent horse.

They reached a pretty copse of trees, and Rose slowed and then drew her horse to a halt. She took one look at his mount and laughed. "Your poor horse, Thomas. Next time we'll arrange for you to ride Emm's horse—it needs to be exercised more, now that Emm's in no condition to ride." She unhooked her leg from the sidesaddle and slid gracefully to the ground. She turned to the groom with a smile. "Kirk?"

"Aye, Lady Rose." He came forward and took her reins, waited for Thomas to dismount and took his as well, then withdrew to a circumspect distance where he could watch but not hear.

"Good morning, Thomas," she said demurely, then reached up and planted a kiss on his mouth that was anything but demure.

Too aware of the watching groom, and with the proposition he was about to put to her weighing heavy on his conscience, Thomas resisted the temptation she offered. He took two steps back. "You're determined to go ahead with this marriage?"

She nodded and said softly, "I told you before, Thomas, I'm not giving up on you."

Wind stirred the branches, sending a spatter of raindrops from the wet leaves. "Then don't say I didn't warn you."

Her mouth tightened. She waited. "Is that all you have to say?"

He didn't say anything. He'd said all he had to say.

She tapped her foot, a sure sign of rising temper. "How about 'Thank you, Rose, for having faith in me, thank you for deciding to keep the vows you made me in that little church outside Bath'?"

"I am honored by the faith you have in me. But as I've told you repeatedly, I think it's misplaced."

"Well, we'll just have to agree to disagree, won't we?" She glared at him, and then suddenly a smile broke through, like sunlight through the clouds. "Oh! We're having our first fight, aren't we? Like a proper married couple. But I'm too happy today for a proper fight."

She linked her arm through his and started to walk. "Now, is that the only reason you came today, to be all surly and disagreeable and"—she slanted a sultry glance his way—"delicious?"

Delicious? "What a revolting notion! I am not—men are *not* delicious."

"Oh, pooh, what would you know? You're a man." She led him down a narrow path. The garden path, Thomas thought to himself. This merry dance he'd been warned about and seemed utterly unable to resist.

They reached a small rustic bench beneath a spreading beech tree. She wiped it with a handkerchief, picked up a fallen leaf and sat down, patting the seat beside her. "So we're only going to flirt now, is that it? No kissing or anything? I don't mind—I adore flirting with you—but I can't help feeling there's something more serious on your mind."

There was.

"Do you know who administers your fortune?"

She didn't blink, just thought for a minute, twirling the leaf gently between finger and thumb, and said, "I think it's Phipps, Phipps and Yarwood. At least that's who the family has always dealt with." She nodded. "Yes, I'm sure it's them."

"Would you go with me to see them? And bring your marriage lines?"

She gave him a long thoughtful look, then nodded briskly. "I will."

"Just like that? No further questions?"

"I trust you, Thomas." She twirled the leaf between her fingers again. It flew out of her hand and floated to the ground. "I know there's more you're not telling me, but I won't pester you about it. You'll tell me when you're ready." Her confidence in him was breathtaking.

He wasn't sure he would tell her. And she sure as hell shouldn't trust him—trust anyone so blindly with all her worldly possessions. Though legally all she owned was already his. It was the way of the world.

But the ways of the world were neither fair nor just. He knew it better than most.

He rose. "Can we visit Phipps, Phipps and Yarwood? Today, I mean." The sooner he got it done the better.

"Yes, of course. I'm quite looking forward to it. I've never been to a lawyer's establishment before. Places like that don't encourage females to visit."

Arm in arm they walked back to where Kirk was waiting with the horses. "We'll go straight after breakfast. You'll take your breakfast with us, of course."

"Er." He'd as soon take his breakfast with a tiger as eat with Cal Rutherford glowering at him.

"You're family now, remember," she said firmly. "You eat with us. It's time Cal faced facts and accepted that you're his brother-in-law."

Thomas resigned himself to a bout of indigestion.

"DO YOU KNOW WHAT THAT SWINE HAS DONE?" CAL glared at his brother-in-law, Galbraith. He was on his way to his club and had bumped into Galbraith in the street.

"No, but I feel sure you're going to tell me."

"I've just been to see the family lawyers—nothing too important, just some leases that need renewing—and *he* had just been there. With my sister!"

"Unusual."

"Yes, poor old Phipps was still reeling at having a lady visit his dusty offices. But that's not the point. The old fellow was so discombobulated, he let it slip that that blackguard was dipping his dirty great fingers into Rose's fortune."

Galbraith shrugged. "The marriage is legal—you checked, remember? He's entitled to do whatever he wants with it."

"He's given orders to have a third of it converted into gold, to be collected by him the day after the ball."

Galbraith narrowed his eyes. "He's going to bolt with it."

"My thoughts exactly."

"But why only a third? Why not take the lot?"

"How do I know how a scoundrel's mind works? And there's more, I'm sure, but Phipps suddenly realized he shouldn't be telling me—as if I haven't been managing the girls' fortunes all this time! He clammed right up, the blasted old pettifog. Wouldn't say another word. Apologized for his indiscretion. Begged me not to mention it to a soul." He glanced at Galbraith's raised brow and snorted. "You don't count—you're family."

"So is Beresford—Rose made it clear at breakfast, remember?" He grimaced. "Quite bossy when she gets her teeth between the bit, that sister of yours."

"Yes, well she's going to be left high and dry by that villain if we don't do anything about it."

"We? Who said anything about *we*? In any case, what can anyone do? The law is on his side."

"The law is an ass." Cal glowered, brooding at the passersby. "What are you doing hanging around in the street, anyway?"

"On my way to Jackson's. Felt like some exercise. Thought I'd have a bout or two with the master."

"Perfect! I'll come with you. No need to bother with Jackson, I'll give you a couple of rounds myself. Exactly what I'm in the mood for. If I don't punch someone soon, I'll explode."

"What an irresistible prospect," Galbraith said dryly. "I can't wait."

*   *   *

"TOLD YOU YOU SHOULD HAVE ORDERED NEW DUDS straightaway. You'll be lucky if Weston gets that coat finished in time."

Thomas shrugged. "If not, I'm sure I'll find one somewhere."

He wasn't all that interested in clothes, to tell the truth. He'd dropped in on the bank on the way to meet Ollie and had been stunned by some unexpected news.

"Not like Weston's," Ollie insisted. "Still, we've got most of it under control now—wonderful how an incentive of the folding sort can hurry things along."

"Yes, wonderful," Thomas murmured, not really paying attention. The bank manager had told him the investigation was proceeding, and he'd let Thomas know the moment there was news. In the meantime he needed to talk to Thomas about his mother's legacy.

Thomas knew almost nothing about it. He knew there was one, of course, but since his uncle had invariably referred to it as "your mama's little legacy" and described it as "paltry" he'd always assumed it would be negligible—a handful of shares, perhaps, and a few pieces of jewelry. Uncle Walter had promised that whenever Thomas married or decided to leave the navy, he would be provided for in a much more substantial fashion.

But according to the bank manager the legacy was quite a handsome one, enough to support a wife and family in comfort, if not in style. And that was not all.

"So," Ollie said. "What shall we do this afternoon? Feel like dropping into the club again?"

Thomas shook his head. Ollie's club was also Ashendon's club, and he'd rather not bump into Rose's brother again today. Breakfast had been grim enough. The looks that man could give while cutting up a sausage . . .

For himself, Thomas didn't mind, but Rose had fretted. She wanted her brother to treat him like, like a brother. Fat chance. Ashendon had hated Thomas from the beginning and Thomas hated him right back.

If it weren't for Rose . . .

"What about popping into Jackson's, then? Introduce you to the great man, watch a few bouts, maybe spar a bit, drink a few mugs of blue ruin? It's just around the corner."

Thomas had heard about the famous boxing club but had never been. "Sounds good."

JACKSON'S BOXING SALOON SMELLED OF MEN AND SWEAT, a combination that sent a prickle of tension rippling down Thomas's spine. He thrust the memories aside.

Ollie was clearly a regular, for he was immediately hailed by several gentlemen and enjoyed himself hugely, introducing Thomas to this fine fellow and that. "And look, Thomas, there's the great man himself, Gentleman John Jackson, over there talking to—Oh."

Thomas looked, but the group surrounding Jackson concealed him from view.

"Time to go," Ollie said.

"What? But we just got here."

"Come back another time. Too busy today. Don't want to be late for dinner." He tried to push Thomas toward the door.

"But it's nowhere near time for din— Ahh." Ollie's sudden desire to leave became clear. Talking to Gentleman Jackson were Galbraith and the Earl of Ashendon.

Ashendon spotted Thomas at the same moment. He said something to Galbraith and stalked toward Thomas with a grim expression.

Ollie tugged at Thomas's sleeve. "Come away, Thomas. I don't like that look in his eye."

Thomas shook him off. As far as he was concerned Ashendon always had that look in his eye. "Ashendon." He greeted his brother-in-law coolly.

Ashendon's eyes were chips of ice. "Come for a bit of a

spar, eh, Beresford? I've just been trying to persuade Galbraith into going a few rounds with me, but he's strangely reluctant. Perhaps—"

"We were just leaving," Ollie said hastily.

Ashendon curled his lip. "Now why does that not surprise me? Not interested in a round or two, Beresford?"

"Not today," Thomas said easily. He wasn't going to fight, not with Rose's brother. Too personal.

"Frightened of losing to me again? Third time's the charm." Ashendon was being a jackass, but if Thomas fought him, it would only worsen matters.

Thomas eyed him coldly. "You don't want to fight me."

"Oh, but I do." Ashendon smiled, all white teeth and pseudo-cordiality. Scenting a challenge, several onlookers edged closer.

"If I fight you"—he raised his voice slightly—"I want it known that it's not my preference. I don't fight for pleasure." And that was fair warning.

Ashendon's smile was triumphant. "Here and now?"

He shrugged. "Here and now." He didn't know what was up Ashendon's arse today, but the continuous, barely veiled hostility from the man was, he told himself, an attempt to protect Rose, and Thomas couldn't fault the intention even if the methods were insulting.

Galbraith strolled up with Gentleman Jackson. "My sister-in-law's husband, Jackson, Thomas Beresford, new to London." The two men shook hands.

"Beresford has agreed to go a couple of rounds with me, Jackson," Ashendon said. "What do you say? Will you referee?"

"A friendly bout, eh?"

"*Very* friendly," Ashendon purred.

Jackson eyed Thomas shrewdly, his gaze dwelling on Thomas's chest and shoulders. He nodded to Thomas. "Lord Ashendon has the advantage in weight, sir, but you're much of a height, and I'd say you'd strip to advantage." He turned to Ashendon. "I'd be happy to referee, my lord. Step this way, gentlemen."

He directed a space to be cleared in the center of the room. He glanced at Thomas and pointed to a bench. "You can leave your things over there, sir."

Ashendon, already half stripped, tugged off his shirt and undershirt, revealing a powerful chest and arms. He removed his boots and stockings, then strolled to the center of the room naked but for a pair of breeches.

As Thomas stripped off his coat, waistcoat and shirt, Ollie poured advice into his ear. "He's a damned good fighter, light on his feet, but solid with it. Good science—he has a punishing right. A nasty left hook, too, so watch out for it."

Thomas pulled off his boots and stood up in breeches and a sleeveless undershirt.

"Shirt and stockings," Ollie prompted, holding out his hand and snapping his fingers.

"I'll fight like this."

Ollie frowned. "Can't fight in stockings. You'll slip."

Thomas shrugged. He tucked the top of his stockings under the hem of his breeches and firmly retied the ties. It would have to do.

"But Ashendon's in bare feet. He'll have the advantage."

Thomas stood up. "I'm ready." He strolled to the waiting circle, made up of watching gentlemen. Bets were already being made. From the murmurs that accompanied Thomas's arrival, it was clear Ashendon was the favorite.

Jackson glanced at his feet. "You don't want to remove those stockings?"

Thomas shook his head. There were more murmurs, and more bets were laid.

"Gloves or bare knuckles?" Jackson asked. An assistant stood by with boxing gloves. Ashendon waved them away. "Bare knuckles." He looked at Thomas with a challenge in his eye. Thomas shrugged and the gloves were taken away.

Jackson explained the rules, gave a brisk nod, and a bell sounded.

Fists raised, they circled each other warily. Thomas wasn't new to fighting. He'd first learned to fight at school, defending his cousin, Gerald, from bullies. Gerald was the elder, but he was delicate and artistic, and a magnet for the nastier types.

Then in the navy, Thomas had been inducted into the rougher kinds of fighting, the kind that waterfront thugs indulged in. Years battling the French—and fighting off occasional pirate attacks—had hardened him further. And then there were the last four years, that had been about one thing only: survival. By any means he could.

Ashendon moved, his fists held high. He swung the first punch: a left-handed feint, followed by a swift uppercut to the jaw.

Thomas blocked it.

Watch an enemy's eyes, not his body.

Ashendon swung again. Thomas was ready for it. It glanced off him.

Back and forth they danced, feinting, punching, blocking.

The earl fought like a gentleman. Thomas was almost bored. But he went through the motions, his temper under firm control.

"Fight, damn you!" Ashendon snarled.

He gave the earl a hard punch to the nose, and connected. Blood spurted.

"First blood to Beresford." Money changed hands.

Ashendon checked his nose—not broken—and dashed the blood away. He came at Thomas in a rush. They grappled, punching, hitting, bones against flesh. Thomas heard something rip.

"You bastard, I know what you're up to," Ashendon growled in his ear as they grappled. "I'll stop you, if I have to kill you to do it." He punched Thomas hard over the eye, opening up an old wound, then disengaged abruptly, shoving Thomas back, sending him into the ring of cheering, laughing spectators.

Thomas wiped the blood from his eye and pushed the spectators roughly away. He stepped forward, the taste of hot, coppery blood in his mouth.

"Had enough?" Ashendon's chest was heaving but his lips curled in scorn.

Thomas's fist shot out. Ashendon's head snapped back. He reeled, spitting out blood but no teeth, then came back, fists swinging.

Punches flew thick and fast.

Thomas's next blow sent the earl staggering, down on one knee. He rose slowly, wiping away blood and sweat, a ploy to catch his breath.

"Had enough?" Thomas taunted. He'd had enough of this gentlemanly playing at fisticuffs.

The earl's face darkened. He came at Thomas, fists flying.

Thomas met him head-on. *Kill me, will you?* He pounded into the earl, bone against flesh, relentless, focused, vicious, punch after punch, smashing hard into him, driving him back.

A bell sounded, loud and insistent.

"Thomas, Thomas, that's enough." Ollie's voice. He tugged at Thomas's arm.

"It's over, sir." A different hand on his shoulder, heavy, authoritative. Thomas twisted around, ready to fight this new enemy. "Easy, easy there, sir. It's over." It was Jackson.

Thomas straightened, catching his breath. The red haze slowly cleared from his brain.

Chapter Eight

❦

**Nothing has proved him unworthy; nor has anything
declared him indifferent to me.**
—JANE AUSTEN, *SENSE AND SENSIBILITY*

JACKSON'S BOXING SALOON HAD GONE SILENT. THE
cheering, jeering spectators stood motionless, staring at
Thomas as if they'd never seen a man fight before.

He looked at his opponent. Ashendon was still standing,
but barely. He was swaying on his feet, spattered with blood
and dark bruises.

Jackson's eyes were dark with understanding. "Best to
stop it before it got out of hand, sir."

Thomas nodded wearily. He hadn't wanted to fight at all.
But the taste of blood in his mouth, the threat to kill him . . .
rage, long suppressed, had broken free . . .

Jackson raised his voice. "Since both gentlemen are still
on their feet, I declare this friendly bout a draw." There was
a groan and a mutter of complaint from the spectators.
Jackson, unperturbed, simply held up his hand. "My club,
my decision." He turned to Thomas and Galbraith. "Nicely
fought, gentlemen."

Thomas turned toward his bench. The crowd parted silently before him, all eyes. A low murmur of comments
followed his passing. Thomas ignored them. Ashendon

walked slowly to his bench, leaning heavily on Galbraith. He looked a mess.

Rose's brother.

Thomas hesitated, then approached. "Are you all right?"

"What do you care?" Ashendon snarled.

"You're my wife's brother," Thomas said, and when the earl didn't respond, he added, "You forced this fight on me, remember. I told you I don't fight for pleasure." He glanced at Galbraith.

But Galbraith was looking elsewhere. He nudged Ashendon, who followed Galbraith's gaze. His eyes narrowed. "You swine. Now it all makes sense."

Thomas glanced down. One of his stockings had slipped down in the fight and lay scrunched, half off, almost below his ankle. He yanked it up and tucked it back under the hem of his breeches. But it was too late. They'd seen.

Damnation.

Ollie returned with water, cloths and vinegar for Thomas to clean himself up with. "Never knew you could fight like that, Thomas. Took my breath away. Dashed glad I'm your friend and not your enemy."

He hovered, passing Thomas vinegar-soaked cloths and chatting excitedly, reliving the highlights as he'd viewed them. Thomas dressed in silence, cursing Galbraith's sharp eyes.

Galbraith approached. "I'll fetch a cab. Your choice whether we go back to my place or Ashendon House."

"Why should we go—" Ollie began.

"Ashendon House," Thomas said wearily. Might as well get it over and done with.

THEY ARRIVED AT ASHENDON HOUSE AFTER DROPPING Galbraith off at his own house on the way. "I'll bring Lily," he said. "This looks like a family affair, and she won't want to miss out." He glanced at Thomas for confirmation, and Thomas shrugged.

But if any of them thought that the revelation of secrets

would be top of the agenda, they reckoned without the women of the family. Lady Ashendon took one look at her husband, exclaimed faintly and whisked him upstairs to have his injuries tended to, overruling his objections in a no-nonsense voice. "I'm not fussing, Cal, merely being practical. Now don't be a baby . . ."

Rose did likewise, escorting Thomas to her bedchamber, where she bathed each cut in vinegar and applied a pungent unguent to every cut and bruise she could find, scolding him all the time for being so foolish as to fight her brother and at the same time exclaiming in distress over every little mark as she tenderly rubbed on goo.

"Take off your shirt," she instructed when she had finished with his face and his bruised and scraped knuckles.

He hesitated but decided that she was going to find out anyway. He shrugged off his shirt, and she continued applying her potions.

A sudden still silence told him she had seen his back.

"Thomas?" she whispered. "Oh, Thomas."

He didn't say anything. What was there to say? What was done was done.

"When you told me . . . I didn't think . . . never imagined." Her voice broke, and he slipped an arm around her waist.

"Don't upset yourself, love, it's all long in the past." Several months at least.

"It's wicked what they did to you, wicked!" She gingerly touched his back. "Does this hurt?"

He almost laughed. He could barely feel it. The scarring had made his skin as tough as an elephant's hide. "No, it's just ugly, that's all."

"It's not ugly, it's—" She broke off. "It's evil." She bent and he felt a warm, damp flutter on his back, then another. She was kissing his back, his ruined back. And there were tears. He felt them.

"Don't weep for me, Rose," he said huskily.

"I'm not," she lied, wiping her eyes. "I'm angry. Nobody has the right to do this to another person."

She continued tending to his cuts and bruises in silence. When she was finished she helped him back on with his clothes. "Thomas," she said decisively, straightening his neckcloth. "We must bring your sailors back immediately. As soon as possible."

He noted the *we* and started to smile, then winced as his cut lip sent a message of disapproval. No smiling for a few days at least.

They joined Ollie, Galbraith, Lily and George downstairs in the drawing room. A short time later the earl and countess joined them. Ashendon was still a mess, only now he looked even worse because the unguent his wife had applied was green. His handsome face was bruised, swollen, lopsided and greenish.

Thomas told himself it would be ignoble to enjoy it. He failed; nobility had never been his forte.

"My, my, you two did have a time of it," Lady George commented. She eyed their injuries with interest and added cheerfully, "That lot will have scabbed up beautifully by the day of the ball."

"The ball!" Lady Ashendon and Rose exclaimed in unison, and looked at each other in dismay.

"Oh, why must men be so foolish!" Lady Ashendon said crossly. "As if fighting ever solved anything."

The butler and a footman entered with tea and refreshments—sandwiches, little savory pastries, dainty fruit tarts, curd cakes and more. Lady Ashendon was a superb hostess. Ashendon gave the butler some invisible signal and he immediately poured brandy for all the men, leaving the women to their tea.

"So, why have you brought us all here, Cal?" Lady Ashendon asked.

CAL LOOKED AT THOMAS. "GO ON, YOU MIGHT AS WELL admit it, now that we've seen what those boots are hiding."

"Admit what?" Thomas took a bite of a savory pastry.

"That you're a convict."

Rose shot from her seat. "Cal, he is *not*! How dare you make such a vile accusation! Thomas is a man of honor."

Cal barely glanced at her. "He's got scars around his ankles, Rose. Manacle scars, the kind convicts get from wearing a ball and chain."

Rose turned to Thomas. "More scars, Thomas? Oh, that's wicked." She ached for what he had endured.

Cal sat forward. "What do you mean, 'more scars'?"

Rose glanced at Thomas, silently asking permission to tell them. He gave it with an indifferent lift of one shoulder. "He has whip marks on his back," she told Cal. "Dreadful scars."

"I'm not going to ask how you came to see his naked back," Cal said thinly. "But I will point out that convicts get whipped for bad behavior."

"So do slaves," Thomas said. "Especially ones who repeatedly try to escape."

"Slaves?" Cal stiffened. "Are you saying you've been *a slave* for the last four years?"

"*'Unavoidably detained,'* he told us," Ned murmured. "It fits."

They stared at Thomas in silence, taking it in.

"How?" George asked. "How did you become a slave?"

Thomas then told Rose's family the story he had told Rose earlier, about the shipwreck on the Barbary Coast, how he and five men made it to shore, their capture by nomadic tribesmen, the journey across the desert and their eventual sale as slaves. He'd only given her the bare bones, and he gave her family even less detail.

He also left out the bit about his uncle refusing his ransom. Rose wondered why, but she didn't question him. It could wait.

When he'd finished everyone sat back, their expressions varying from horror to pity. All except Cal, who continued to eye Thomas with suspicion. "Then explain, if you can, why you've arranged for a large proportion of my sister's fortune to be converted into gold—"

Honestly, her brother was like a dog with a bone sometimes. He never let go.

"—and made ready for collection the day after the ball."

The day after the ball? Rose blinked. There had been no mention of that when she and Thomas had talked his plans over. Nevertheless she wasn't going to raise it with him while Cal was in this hostile mood.

"Because he needs it to bring back the other five sailors, of course," she said. "What did you think?"

Cal said sharply, "You knew about this?"

"Of course. Thomas told me all about it." Almost all.

Cal snorted. "And you, of course, believe every word he says."

"I do, as it happens," Rose retorted, "and don't you dare tell me I'm being naïve. I know him, you don't."

"So you're willing to be impoverished on his say-so?"

"As a matter of fact Thomas signed it back over to me this morning—my entire fortune—all except the funds he needs for the rescue of those sailors." She smiled at her sister. "Much as Ned did with Lily's fortune."

"You did what?" Cal stared at Ned, who smiled and shrugged as if he'd done nothing special. Cal turned back to Thomas. "Why would you do such a thing?"

"I have a legacy coming to me when I'm thirty from my late mother's estate," Thomas told him. "It should cover what we need. And I just found out today, there's a house." He glanced at Rose. "It's only small, and I have no idea what condition it's in, but it's not far from here. We can go and look at it if you like."

"A house!" Rose was thrilled. She was fed up with living in her brother's house, especially since he kept on being so horrid to Thomas. "Where is it? Can we go and see it to-day? Do you have a key?"

And suddenly, just like that, the whole discussion of Thomas's apparent perfidy was over. Everyone was much more interested in this house of Thomas's. Or had decided to be in order to put a stop to the unpleasantness. Because it was the ladies who now took over the conversation.

"You only just found out about it, Mr. Beresford?" Emm asked.

He nodded. "My mother died when I was young. I barely remember her, and my father was away at sea for much of my childhood. I knew my mother had left me a legacy; I just never knew the details."

He turned to Rose. "She left this house for the use of her beloved governess for her lifetime. Once the old lady died, it was to come to me, free and clear. The governess died some time ago and the house has been sitting empty for a month." He stood. "It's on Bird Street and I have a key. Would you like to see it?"

He didn't need to ask twice. Rose jumped up. "I'll fetch my hat and pelisse."

"Can I come too?" Lily asked. "I love looking at houses and seeing how they can be made nicer."

"Of course, the more the merrier," Rose said. "I'd love your opinion, Lily darling—you did such a lovely job with your own house."

"Then I'll come too," Emm decided. "As long as it's not too far."

IN THE END, THEY ALL WALKED AROUND TO BIRD STREET: Rose, her sister Lily, Lady Ashendon and Lady George, who said she wasn't much interested in houses but could do with a walk. She brought, of course, her faithful hound. Galbraith came too, for escort purposes, he explained; he and Lily would walk home later. Even Ollie, having nothing better to do, trailed along.

It wasn't quite what Thomas had envisaged, this family excursion to inspect the house, but that was the Rutherford family, he was learning. They did everything together. It wasn't at all what he was used to.

Ashendon, of course, didn't go. Claiming they had no need of him, he took himself off—for a nap, or a hot bath, Thomas suspected, watching the stiff way he walked. He himself was a little stiff, but he hadn't taken the hiding Ashendon had.

Bird Street was only a ten-minute walk from Ashendon

House. "It's prettier than I expected," Rose said as they approached it.

It was small and white, a narrow, three-story building, with five steps leading up to the front entrance. Wrought-iron railings protected the front, with steps at the side that led below street level to a tiny courtyard and an entrance into the domestic area, the kitchens and scullery.

On either side of the front door sat two heavy terra-cotta pots in which sat two wilted bushes. More sad-looking pots were arranged in the little courtyard below—Thomas recognized a bay tree and a rosemary bush among them, all looking distinctly neglected. George immediately decided to weed and water the poor things and commandeered a rather surprised Ollie to fetch and fill a bucket with water.

Inside, Thomas was relieved to see, the house was neat as a pin, a little dusty but otherwise immaculate, though the air was stale with disuse. The ladies explored, directing Thomas, Galbraith and Ollie to open windows to let fresh air in.

It was very much an old lady's house, crammed with fussy little bits and pieces and a variety of spindly, mismatched, old-fashioned furniture that Thomas wouldn't be game to sit on. Some of the stranger-looking pieces sported animal heads and feet.

"It's charming," Rose declared after the first whirlwind tour. "It has such potential." She and the other women then went through the house more slowly, room by room, exclaiming, discussing and planning. Rose, having brought a small notebook and pencil with her, listed what was to be kept (very little), what discarded (most), and what was to be done to each room (everything).

Thomas watched, fascinated. It bore some resemblance to a military campaign.

Ollie, having been directed to move furniture, roll up rugs, open windows and carry buckets of water for thirsty plants, suddenly remembered he had an urgent appointment (unspecified) and left.

Galbraith, hands in pockets, leaned against the mantelpiece and observed indulgently. "Give the ladies their head," he recommended. "Lily redecorated my house from top to bottom. Made it a place a man could come home to—wanted to come home to. Turned a house into a home."

A home. Thomas thought about that. A place nobody could deny him. It had an appeal, even if he hadn't ever thought of a small fussy house as the kind of home he'd feel comfortable in. He'd always thought of Brierdon Court as home. Until it wasn't.

"Cal's a good fellow," Galbraith continued. "Tenacious, and can be irritatingly dogged when he gets a bee in his bonnet—as he has about you—but I couldn't ask for a better friend. He's just very protective of his family, especially his sisters."

"I know." Thomas might find Ashendon irritating in the extreme, but he couldn't fault his protectiveness toward Rose.

"He won't hold his thrashing against you, either."

Thomas raised his brows. He'd believe that when he saw it.

"He can be a stubborn bastard, but underneath it all, he's fair-minded. He knows he forced that fight on you. You warned him. Can't blame you for what happened."

Thomas said nothing. He wasn't even sure what had happened. He couldn't explain it if he tried.

"Saw a bit of that sort of thing during the war," Galbraith continued quite as if they were having a nice cozy chat instead of a gratuitous one-sided conversation. "Put a man through hell, and then push him too far and he snaps. So, the galleys, was it?"

Thomas's head snapped up. "How the hell did you know?"

Galbraith shrugged. "Educated guess. Can't imagine house slaves being kept permanently in chains, for a start, and those scars on your ankles are from long-term wear. Then there's the breadth of your shoulders, the state of your hands, general physique. So, I'm right, eh? How long?"

"Three years."

Galbraith whistled. "You must be damned tough, to survive that long. How did you escape?"

Thomas's smile was humorless. "A slight irony. We were attacked by pirates. I was, at the time, rowing in a pirate galley." When he'd been sold, in a vicious act of revenge by his owners ashore, the galley captain had wanted to use him as a navigator—British naval men were valued for their skills. But Thomas had refused to work in the service of pirates so he'd been tossed in the galleys as a lesson. The captain had expected him to relent after a short time at the oars, but . . .

Ashendon wasn't the only stubborn bastard around.

At the time of the attack, Thomas had thought his time had come. It was utter chaos, blinding smoke, the clashing of scimitars, the roar of guns, men yelling, screaming . . . praying. The galley slaves had stopped rowing and sat in their fetters, chained together, unable to move or fight, just waiting to live or die—for many of them it made no difference which.

And then, a giant African, bare-chested and with a gold earring, had leapt down among them and raised a huge, gleaming axe. "Nobody move," he'd yelled in Arabic. Thomas braced himself. It wasn't as if he could move—he'd been chained to his oar and his fellow slaves for months. Death by axe would be swift, at least—it was better than rotting in the galleys until he died. Or went insane as so many did.

The axe flashed in the sunlight and came crashing down between Thomas and his neighbor, missing them by bare inches. It severed the chain that linked each row of slaves together—one chain, looped through each man's manacles, binding them together until someone in the row sickened and died, or went mad and was tossed overboard for the sharks. Sharks always followed the galleys. They were well fed, especially in the summer.

It had taken a few seconds to realize what had happened: the big man hadn't missed—he'd freed them. Thomas worked feverishly, dragging the heavy chain through each loop—his fellow rowers were panicking, impeding his movements through sheer disbelief and fear. Finally he pulled the chain free and stood up.

The African had moved systematically through row after row, his big axe cutting through the chains that bound each row of slaves. And then, chaos of a different kind as the slaves freed themselves and joined the fighting, barehanded and savage against their former masters.

Thomas learned later that the big man had been a galley slave himself. "Join us and live free," he'd said to Thomas, but Thomas still couldn't bring himself to prey on other ships.

"I could have joined the men who freed me," he told Galbraith, "but I wanted to come home. So I hopped from ship to ship, mainly fishing vessels, working my passage until I found a ship that was heading for England." Back to Rose.

"Not much of a storyteller, are you?" Galbraith commented dryly. "Left out all the interesting bits."

Thomas shrugged. Pity was not an emotion he courted. And if people learned the details . . . Disgust was also something he'd rather not see in their eyes. Bad enough that Galbraith had worked out that he'd been a galley slave. The lowest of the low. Utter degradation.

"And these five men, the ones you left behind, they weren't working the galleys like you?"

"No, they were lucky. They stayed ashore."

"Because you were recalcitrant, and kept trying to escape?"

"Something like that."

Galbraith gave him a shrewd look. "In other words, not at all. There's a whole other story there, I suspect, but I can see you're determined to play oyster. I gather you haven't told Rose much about your experiences."

"No, and I don't intend to." He refused to . . . to contaminate her with the depths to which he'd sunk.

Galbraith chuckled. "I can see you haven't been married long. Women have a way of finding things out, and Rutherford women have a knack for getting to the heart of things. The very things you're determined never to speak of . . ."

His eyes darkened and for a moment Thomas could see that Galbraith was far away in some other place and time. He straightened and added briskly, "At any rate, I know what it's like to lose men for whom you feel responsible. If there's anything I can do to help, count me in." The man was utterly sincere, Thomas realized with a shock.

"Thank you." He didn't know what Galbraith could do, but he appreciated the offer. And the implicit suggestion of friendship.

"You don't need to do everything by yourself, you know," Galbraith pointed out. "You're part of this family now." He glanced toward the stairs, and his rather austere face softened. "Speaking of which, here come the ladies. Brace yourself, Beresford, for talk of papers, *chinoiserie*, faux patterns, fabrics, motifs, flocking, bas reliefs, *trompe l'oeil*, and other matters incomprehensible to the masculine brain. So, my love." He greeted his wife as she entered the room. "Enjoying yourself?"

She hurried across to him and slipped her arm through his. The affection between them was obvious. "Oh, Edward, it's going to be such fun. Rose and I have been making such delightful plans."

"You won't recognize this house when I'm finished with it, Thomas," Rose declared, waving her little notebook.

"You won't," agreed Galbraith mock gloomily. "My advice is to stay far away while the transformation is being achieved. In fact, flee the country, my good fellow, while you can."

"Oh, hush, Edward, it's going to be quite charming," Lady Ashendon said, laughing. "But now my dears, we must leave. We have just enough time to change for dinner."

Rose linked her arm through Thomas's. "I'll stay here with Thomas a while," she said. "We have things to discuss. He can walk me home later."

"Will you be home for dinner?" Lady Ashendon asked.

Rose glanced at Thomas and squeezed his arm. "Probably not." She was blushing.

Thomas did his best to look indifferent.

"Very well, then," Lady Ashendon said tranquilly. "I'll see you later. Good evening, Mr. Beresford."

Thomas watched as the Rutherford ladies collected their things, arranged their hats, pulled on their gloves and left, with Galbraith and the dog as escorts.

He could hardly believe Lady Ashendon had allowed him and Rose to remain in an empty house unchaperoned. It was final, tacit acceptance of their marriage.

Finally, blessedly, Thomas and Rose were alone.

ROSE WALKED HIM THROUGH THE HOUSE, EXPLAINING THE changes she wanted to make.

"Sounds good," he told her. "Perfect," and "Just right."

"And here"—she opened a door leading to a room that would make a small dressing room or a large closet—"we're going to put the stables."

"Very nice," he said.

"Hah!"

He eyed her warily. "Hah?"

"I knew you weren't listening. Don't you care what our home looks like?"

He grimaced. "Not really. No, no, I'm sorry, I don't mean that, it's just that—"

"You don't care."

He shrugged. "I'm sure whatever you decide will be perfect. Colors, curtains, carpets—I never notice stuff like that. As far as I'm concerned, the important thing about furniture—a bed, for instance—is not the carvings on the bedposts, or the hangings or the covers, only"—his expression was darkly intent—"who's in it."

She felt herself blushing. "Who's in it?"

"Exactly." He jerked his chin toward the line of doors down the hallway. "Which room was it that had that big bed in it with the blue hangings?"

She pointed. "That one—Thomas!" she shrieked as he scooped her up and marched purposefully toward the room she'd indicated.

"Hush, woman, I'm showing you what I mean about beds."

Laughing, she wound her arms around his neck and kissed his chin. "I wondered how long it would take you." She and Lily had earlier made up the bed with clean sheets, in expectation of just such an occasion.

"Four blasted years," he muttered.

"Thomas!" She grabbed his chin and turned his face toward her. "It's been four years for you?"

"Yes."

She hugged him tightly. "Oh, Thomas, I'm so glad."

"And you?" His voice was hesitant.

"Of course," she said indignantly. "You were the only man I ever misbehaved with, and you're still the only man I've ever wanted." She tugged at his neckcloth and tossed it aside, then started on the buttons of his waistcoat.

"I wouldn't have blamed you if you had, you know."

"And I wouldn't have blamed you." She hoped it was the truth, but when it came to Thomas she did have a jealous streak. She hugged him again. "But I'm so glad you didn't."

He kissed her, a hard swift kiss that sent shivers down her spine. "Ouch."

"Ouch?" she queried.

He touched his mouth gingerly. "Forgot the split lip." He kissed her again, more carefully.

"Oh, dear, yes, I forgot about the fight. Do you hurt anywhere else?" she asked anxiously.

A smile grew, starting in his eyes and curving his poor battered mouth. "Oh, dear yes, I have the most terrible ache," he murmured. "Low down." And she knew with a shiver of delight that it had nothing to do with the fight he'd had.

"Here?" she said, sliding her hand down to his stomach.

"Lower." His voice was deep and husky.

They reached the bedroom; he kicked open the door and dropped her on the bed. She bounced slightly. "Comfortable?"

She looked up at him looming deliciously over her. "Not

very." The mattress was rather lumpy now that she came to think of it.

He lay down beside her. "And now?"

"Hmm." She pretended to consider. "A bit better."

"And what about now?" He gathered her hard against him. Through their clothes she could feel the firm evidence of his desire.

She smiled and reached down to stroke her hand over him. "Much better."

His mouth lowered to hers and she hummed in pleasure and opened to him. He tasted dark and masculine, familiar and yet wildly, excitingly different.

They kissed and caressed, exploring each other, tasting, relearning each other, remembering and discovering, but all too soon the urgency to make love built.

Rose tried to unbutton him, but it wasn't easy, and he tried with her, but what with petticoats and pantaloons and chemises and corsets and ties and hooks and laces, she was not so easy to unwrap either. They slid off the bed and worked feverishly to strip each other of their clothing, until they stood facing each other, eyes locked, naked.

He devoured her with his eyes. She devoured him, first with eyes, then with mouth and hands. His body was proud, erect—he was magnificent, her Thomas.

And then they were kissing, and touching and stroking and squeezing. And somehow they were on the bed, rolling, writhing, shuddering, and it was all heat, and hardness, and wetness and aching, yearning desperation.

"I can't—it's not going to be pretty, Rose. Four years, remember?"

She wrapped her legs around his waist. "I remember. Hurry."

He surged into her, and she arched beneath him, feeling her body stretch to accommodate him. Ah, Thomas, it had been so long. Too long.

He started moving within her then, and the ache and stretch and pull, and oh, oh, the power. It built and crested, too soon, too fast and he collapsed, shuddering on top of her. She didn't care, for Thomas was hers again and it was glorious.

She lay, legs locked around him, his head buried in the curve between her neck and her jaw. She stroked his hair, his poor ruined back, his magnificent shoulders.

He stirred. "I'm sorry, I came too soon—"

"Hush. It doesn't matter."

"It might take a while—"

"Don't worry. I'm fine." And she was, more than fine. She was just happy to have him here, naked and sweaty and sated in her arms. Skin to skin. Her Thomas.

She lay, dreamily content, running her hands over his body, feeling his breathing gradually slow, and the loosening of the big, hard body as he drifted into sleep.

The scars around his ankles were ugly, purplish. Obscene. She ached for him. He was so thin, every rib distinct, yet the muscles on his arms were hard and powerful. And brown. His whole upper body was brown. What kind of work had he been doing?

She tried to imagine it. And couldn't.

And then she too drifted off to sleep.

THOMAS WOKE SOME TIME LATER. HE WASN'T SURE HOW much time had passed, only that he'd slept, after failing to bring her to climax. She was sleeping now, lying bonelessly half beneath him, one slender leg hooked over his. His wife. Lord, but she was a dream come true, all silken skin and warm, soft curves.

He gently caressed the silken curve of her hip and bottom, and felt her waken and shiver beneath his touch.

His hands. Dammit. He pulled them back. When would he remember?

"Don't," she said sleepily. "I like the feel of your hands on me."

He didn't believe her. She was just being kind. He didn't want kind, not from her.

Her eyes opened a slit. "Remember before, back in Bath,

how much I used to like the rough texture of your unshaven chin?"

He remembered.

A knowing smile curved her mouth. "A little friction can be a fine thing, Thomas." She took his hand and placed it on her breast. He stroked his palm slowly across her nipple and she moaned and moved sensually against him. Her shivers, he saw now, had nothing to do with distaste for the roughness of his hands and everything to do with desire.

He stroked down her belly, along her thighs, back and forth, teasing, arousing. She moved restlessly, her legs trembling. She clutched his hair with desperate fingers, pulling his head down to her mouth, muttering, "Now, Thomas!"

He kissed her, then let his mouth follow his hands, lower and lower. He parted her trembling legs and slipped between them.

"Thomas!" she gasped. "What are you—?"

The sweet-salt taste of her stung his lip and it was a gift, a healing. She was roses and new-baked bread . . . and woman. His woman, his Rose.

She squeaked as his tongue found her most sensitive spot, and then clenched her eyes shut, emitting little gasps and moans as her body vibrated with pleasure.

He teased her to desperation, her legs thrashing around him, and then he sucked hard. With a faint scream she bucked beneath him and almost came off the bed. He entered her then, in one smooth powerful motion, and drove them both to a shattering climax.

When he woke for the second time, it was dark. Faint light from a three-quarter moon was all that lit the room. He slipped out of bed and groped around until he found some candles and a tinderbox on the mantelpiece. He wrestled with the tinderbox, striking and striking the flint, but the spark never caught. He muttered a curse. He hated these things, had never been good with them, and hadn't touched one in years.

A soft chuckle came from the bed. "Don't bother trying

to light a candle. We can dress in the moonlight." She slipped from beneath the covers and came to him, naked and lovely and unashamed, a goddess of moonbeams and shadows, and slipped her arms around him. "I'm so very glad you came home to me, Thomas." She kissed him softly.

His arms locked around her. It still felt like a miracle. Even more so with her in his arms.

After a moment she spoke. "That thing you did, with your mouth." He could feel her blushing in the darkness as she said it. "I didn't know people did such things."

"Men talk." And then he realized she was asking him an indirect question. "I've never done it before, but when I heard it described, I wanted to try it with you. Did you mind?"

She laughed and rubbed her cheek against him, a sensuous little cat. "What do you think?" And something tight inside him unraveled a little.

They talked as they dressed, the soft dark and the empty house seeming to invite confidences. Until Rose came to the subject of his scars.

"I was looking at those frightful marks around your ankles while you were sleeping, Thomas. Were they painful?"

"No." Until they rubbed his skin raw and the seawater got in. He pulled on his breeches and fastened them.

"Didn't it make it hard for you to walk around?"

"Yes, that was their purpose. So we couldn't move." He found one of his stockings, put it on, then pulled on a boot.

"But how could you do your work?"

"It was sitting-down work." He groped around on the floor, searching for his other stocking. Where the hell was it?

"What kind of work were you doing?"

"Rowing. Now that's enough—"

"Rowing?" She gasped. "You were *a galley slave*?"

"I don't wish to talk about it."

"But—"

"Ever." He found the blasted stocking and dragged it on.

"But, Thomas—"

"Look, first Galbraith was in my ear about it, and now you. That's enough. I'm not discussing it."

"You told Edward? Before me?" Her voice sounded hurt. He cursed himself.

"He told me. He guessed." And he'd had no plans to tell her at all.

"But how?"

"I don't know how and I don't care," he lied. "Now, I said that's enough, Rose. Are you finished here? Got all you need? Are you ready to go home?"

There was a short pause, and when she finally spoke he heard a thread of anger in her voice. "I'm not nearly finished with you, Thomas Beresford, but you're right, I'd better go home. I have no idea what the time is, and I don't want Emm to worry. Will you stay to supper?"

"No. Thank you." He was aware he sounded like a brute: curt, brusque and ungrateful for the generosity she'd shown him. It was natural for her to be curious, but he couldn't bear to talk about it with anyone, let alone Rose.

"You should eat some supper. You're too thin."

"My body is still adjusting to English food. I'll have toast or something at Ollie's."

"Ollie's, yes. When do you think we'll be able to move into this house?"

He shrugged, even though it was too dark in the room for her to see. "Whenever you decide it's ready, I suppose. Seeing as you've taken it on as a project." He sounded callous, as if he didn't care. He did, but he was rattled. She'd caught him unaware. That was the trouble with making love—it relaxed a man, made him talkative, unwary.

He'd planned never to let her know he'd been a galley slave, the lowest of the low, barely existing, laboring in stinking, unbearable servitude. And instead he'd blabbed it without thinking, while looking for a damned stocking.

"In that case, I'll let you know." She was cross with him, but she'd get over it. She didn't hold a grudge, his Rose. She was as direct in her anger as in everything else. Thank God for it. He knew where he stood with Rose.

But he wasn't giving in. Some things were simply too . . . private.

ROSE SAT CURLED UP IN HER BED, HUGGING HER KNEES, brooding. One of the things she'd always loved about Thomas, back when they first met, was that they could talk about anything. They'd talked about everything under the sun. She told him about her family, how worried she was about Lily who was so sick, about the rest of her family, the people at school.

She'd talked to him about things she'd never spoken about to anyone else—dreams, random thoughts, worries—and he shared his thoughts and ideas with her.

She knew about his childhood, his mother dying, his father's naval career and Thomas's thoughts about following in his footsteps. He'd told her about the uncle who'd taken him under his wing, the cousins he'd grown up with, Gerald with whom he'd gone away to school, and Ambrose, his uncle's illegitimate son.

It had sounded like a relatively carefree and happy childhood and a close-knit family—so why had his uncle and cousin turned their backs on him? Such a ruthless and hard-hearted act of abandonment. It made no sense to her, but perhaps there was something he wasn't telling her. He'd been quite closemouthed about them to her family, too, telling them he had no family.

Who was this uncle? Thomas had only ever spoken of Uncle Walter—no surname or title—and Gerald and Ambrose. And though he'd referred to his home with obvious fondness, he'd never mentioned the name of the house, or even a town or village nearby. Just *home*. Which had become no home at all.

She'd always assumed that it was accidental that he hadn't originally mentioned them by name; now it seemed deliberate.

And now, he'd practically bitten her head off for asking

about something that had happened to him, something serious and hurtful that she needed to know about.

She'd shared the trauma of her miscarriage with him. That was his business as much as hers. And how he got his dreadful scars was something she needed, as his wife, to understand.

He'd talked about it with Ned, but he couldn't talk about it with her. That hurt. But maybe it was a male thing. She would ask Ned about it in the morning.

SHE BROACHED THE MATTER WITH HER BROTHER-IN-LAW and sister when they were out for their usual morning exercise in the park. They'd been for a good fast ride—it was the only time it was possible, when the park was almost deserted—and had blown away the cobwebs and given the horses and Finn a good run. Now while George and Cal were flinging a stick for the dog, Rose and Lily and Ned were letting their horses amble slowly along as they talked.

"I know he talked to you about it, Ned, for he told me he had, but when I asked him about it he just clammed up. And when I persisted he got quite short with me."

"He didn't exactly tell me about it, Rose. I made a good guess and surprised him into admitting it. We never actually discussed it."

That made her feel a bit better. But not much. "But why would he not want to tell me about it? I don't understand."

Ned hesitated. "It's not a very nice topic for a lady."

She gave him an indignant look. "I'm his wife. If he had to endure it, I can certainly bear to listen to it."

Ned grimaced. "I didn't mean that, exactly."

Lily leaned forward. "Perhaps he feels ashamed of what happened to him, Rose. Or guilty."

"Why would he feel guilty? Or ashamed? It wasn't his fault."

"People feel shame for all sorts of reasons," Lily said

quietly. "For things they did, for things they couldn't help, and sometimes, for things that were done to them."

"Lily's right," her husband said. "Beresford has lived through unimaginable hardship. And squalor."

Rose looked at him. "Squalor?"

"Think about it. Those unfortunate fellows are chained to their oars for months at a time, day and night. Think what that means."

Rose thought about it. Her insides curled with horror as she pictured it.

"It's brutal and relentless and utterly inhumane," Ned continued. "So he escapes from that—and it can't have been easy—and he looks at you and he sees a lovely young woman who he imagines is untainted by life. Is it so surprising that he doesn't feel worthy?" Lily reached across and took her husband's hand and squeezed it.

Ned kissed his wife's hand. "But the love of a good woman is a miraculous thing."

Lily said softly, "Don't give up on him, Rose."

The horses walked on. Rose, deep in thought, pondered shame and guilt. All her life her sister Lily had felt guilty and ashamed because no matter how hard she tried, she still couldn't read. It wasn't her fault, but emotions didn't work on logic.

And after she'd lost the baby, Rose had been racked by guilt and shame—she still was in unguarded moments— and yet she knew she'd done nothing wrong.

And Ned? He was a war hero—she didn't know what he could feel shame or guilt about, but it was obvious he understood it from personal experience.

She could see now why Thomas might not want to talk about what had been done to him. And why he'd been like a bear with a sore head when she'd persisted.

"I knew there was a reason why Lily loves you, Ned." She leaned across and kissed him on the cheek. "I love you too."

She smiled at her sister. "And I won't give up on Thomas,

of course I won't. I won't push him to talk, either. Not until he's ready."

He needed to talk, she was sure of that. It would help release some of those dreadful bottled-up feelings. Like lancing a boil to let out all the muck and poison. She knew. She'd kept four years of grief bottled up inside her. And what good had the bottling-up done her?

Ned rode off to join Cal and George, and Lily and Rose continued on their leisurely amble. Even though Rose saw her sister most days, she still missed her, missed having her to talk to any time, day or night. Marriage separated the most devoted of sisters.

"After I lost Thomas, I told myself I never wanted to fall in love again, that loving someone and losing them was just too painful." She glanced at Lily. "I know, but I believed it, truly believed I could—and should—go through the rest of my life avoiding the glorious highs for fear of the terrifying, devastating lows. A life that was calm, safe, dull—it's what I thought I wanted."

Lily smiled. "And now?"

"Thomas walked back into my life and it just . . . went up in smoke, all my firm, safe resolutions. I'm back in, Lils, up to my neck, in over my head, out of my depth. It's terrifying, and yet . . ." She made a helpless gesture. "I'm ridiculously happy."

"I know."

"He's not the Thomas I married, but that doesn't seem to matter—he's still the man for me. There's so much I don't know—where he's been, what he's done, what he even believes anymore. But it just doesn't matter. It's just . . ." She gestured helplessly, groping for the way to explain her mixed-up feelings.

"There's more of him to know, more of him to love?"

Rose looked at her sister. "That's it exactly. How did you know?"

Lily smiled. "Because that's what it's like with my Edward."

Chapter Nine

❦

Ah! There is nothing like staying at home for real comfort.
—JANE AUSTEN, *EMMA*

ROSE WAS DETERMINED TO MOVE INTO THEIR NEW LITTLE home before the ball, and her enthusiasm fired up the other women in her family. Lily, of course, having already redecorated her husband's family home, was more than willing to lend her a hand and share her expertise. George decided to help, not because she cared about the interior of a house but because she wanted to avoid the fuss about what she insisted on calling "The Ball Not to Celebrate a Duke."

Even Emm, almost wholly concerned with the ball, couldn't resist popping around to Bird Street once or twice a day to see the progress made and to contribute to the discussions. She was usually accompanied by a couple of footmen bearing baskets of refreshments.

"Are you sure you're not overdoing it?" Cal said when she returned home one afternoon. "As far as I'm concerned the ball and Rose's house can both go hang. The only important thing is you."

Emm laid her hand on her swollen belly. "And the baby."

"That too, but you most of all."

She smiled. "It's fun, and you know I like keeping busy.

Besides, it's better than sitting around waiting for this little one to arrive."

He snorted. "Preparing for the ball of the season is hardly 'waiting around.'"

She laughed. "Burton is in his element—he has everything and everyone running like clockwork. First thing in the morning the girls deal with all the mail that has come in, and really there is very little for me to do. Besides, it's so interesting watching the girls working together. Lily is the artistic one, and Rose the decisive one—and the one who gets everyone moving."

"And George?"

"Would you believe George has discovered a passion for gardening? She's turning the little courtyard at the back into such a pretty space."

Cal's brows rose. "That's a surprise."

"She's a hard worker, Cal. Did she have a difficult early life? She never talks about the years before she came to us."

"She did. From all I could make out, my damned brother left her alone, to sink or swim."

"Well, she's done very well. They all have. You wouldn't believe the progress they've made in only a few days."

"I would. We're paying a fortune in labor. I don't know how many men we've got working around the clock to get Beresford's blasted house ready."

"It's Rose's home too, and you don't fool me one bit, Calbourne Rutherford. You arranged all those workmen, I know. And paid for them yourself."

"Just eager to get her off my hands," he said gruffly.

"Nonsense. You want your sister to be happy as much as I do."

He frowned. "Yes, but *is* she happy, Emm? Is that fellow going to be good to her?"

"It's not going to be all smooth sailing," Emm mused. "But I think she loves him, which has to count for a lot."

"But does the villain love her?"

"I don't know. I hope so. Rose might seem confident and self-sufficient, but she badly needs to be loved."

* * *

CAL WAS WRONG WHEN HE CLAIMED THAT ROSE SPENT her days at Bird Street, "harrying workmen." There was no harrying; she merely knew what she wanted and was determined to get it.

She was loving every minute of it—even when things went wrong, such as when the paperhangers hung the sitting room paper upside down. Yes, it was a subtle design—cream flocking over a lovely pale green background—but surely anyone could see that was a stylized pineapple! And that the frill of leaves or spikes or whatever you called them went at the top.

As for the excuse that the wretched men had never eaten a pineapple or even seen one—well, that was no reason for them not to know their business! Luckily she'd discovered the error in time, and made them pull it off and start again, this time with the pattern right side up.

It was Thomas's house, but she was the one who cared about how the house looked—Thomas would probably have just cleared out all the fussy little ornaments and replaced the furniture with something more solid, and that would be that.

"Close your eyes," she told him.

Thomas obediently closed them. He'd taken to dropping into Bird Street every evening. They'd fallen into a routine—first Ned would come to collect Lily and he'd walk her home, and George and her dog back to Ashendon House. By then all the workers had left, and Rose was alone in the house. It was then that Thomas came to her, ostensibly to see the progress of the house renovations before walking her home, but really, Rose knew it was to see her. It was heartwarming how hard he pretended to be interested. The ground floor was still in chaos, with ladders and builders' tools and curing plaster and drying paint the only evidence of progress. But it was going to be lovely, she was sure. Only one room was completely finished; Rose had made it her priority.

"Keep them closed." She led him up the stairs to the room in which they'd first made love. "And now . . . open."

It was the same room, but what a transformation. Rose was delighted with it. She'd had the heavy old-fashioned paper stripped and replaced it with a light cream one, making the room much lighter.

The big four-poster bed remained, but she'd had the base restrung and fitted with a new mattress with a warm woolen base and a feather topping, thick as a cloud. It was made up now with fresh cotton sheets, plump new pillows and beautiful soft blue bedclothes.

She'd had the old felt matting ripped out and now a beautiful cream-and-blue Aubusson rug lay in its place. The heavy old blue bed-curtains were gone and the bed was hung with gauzy white drapes. She would order warm ones for the winter, but for the time being these were perfect, letting the breezes circulate on hot summer nights.

She was looking forward to hot summer nights with Thomas.

"What do you think?"

He nodded his approval, then looked at the bed and considered it thoughtfully. "It looks different."

"Yes, it has a new feather mattress and new covers. And new curtains, of course."

"That might explain it." But his frown didn't lift.

"Is there something wrong?"

"I'm not sure." He seemed very serious. "You know my attitude toward beds."

For a moment she couldn't think. Then she laughed. "Oh, you mean, it depends on who's in them?"

"Indeed. Shall we?" He held out his hand as if inviting her to a waltz and led her to the bed. It was exactly the reaction she'd hoped for.

There was none of the frenzied desperation of last time. He undressed her himself, taking his time, lavishing her with his attention, slow, intense and deeply thrilling.

One by one her garments came off. He tossed them carelessly aside, his intent gaze never lifting from her. She felt it like a caress.

And when finally she stood there naked before him, his eyes burning into her with such heated concentration, she had never felt so beautiful.

Outside the sun was setting, the last golden rays piercing the clouds, staining them crimson and silver and purple. It bathed the interior of the room with a pearly light. Thomas was a dark silhouette against it, solid, mysterious, enticing.

He reached for her, and she smiled and held him back with one finger. "My turn now." His skin was firm. Heat poured from him. She reached for his buttons.

His coat, waistcoat, neckcloth and shirt went first, the same slow, teasing process that she had endured. He hurled his own clothes aside with a little more impatience than he'd shown with hers. She had him remove his boots next. He yanked them and his stockings off, tossed them aside and reached for her.

"Not yet." She gazed at the smooth planes of his chest, marked in places with fading bruises and a few silvery old scars, the cause of which she didn't want to think about. Scarred or not, he was beautiful. She shivered in anticipation.

"Are you cold? I could—"

She laughed softly. "I'm not the least bit cold."

"Really?" She felt his dark gaze shift to her nipples thrusting hard and aching toward him.

She stroked them lightly and her mouth curled in a slow smile as his whole body stiffened. "They're not cold."

His fingers opened and closed, but he clamped them to his side and stood like a soldier, waiting to be called for action.

She unfastened the fall of his breeches and pushed them down his legs. He breathed a gusty sigh of relief, kicked them away and drew her against him.

"And now, my beautiful, teasing witch . . ."

He was fully aroused and she was ready, more than ready for him. She twined her arms around his neck and pulled him down onto the bed.

He bent and kissed her nipple. "You're right, it's not cold at all," he murmured in mock surprise. He traced his tongue around it in lazy, leisured circles, teasing and arousing until she was trembling with need.

She'd forgotten, all the time he'd been lost to her, what it was like to lie with Thomas, the intensity and focus he brought to it—or perhaps he hadn't, back then. He might have been more spontaneous. And she'd been so innocent. Anything he did back then—everything he did—was new and exciting.

Now, it was different, he was different—and ohhh!

"Thomas!" His mouth closed over her breast, and she clutched at his shoulders, his hair, his back as she arched and trembled.

His mouth was hot and demanding. His hands were everywhere, those big gentle, hard-skinned hands, caressing her breasts, slipping between her thighs, curving around her hip, her belly, her buttocks. Urgency followed their path, welling up from deep within her. She writhed with pleasure, hunger, need.

Her breath caught on a series of jagged, rising peaks. Heat poured through her and her thoughts fragmented under his ravenous sensual assault. Wave after wave of sensation, she let herself float, responding helplessly to the wordless, insistent demand of her body, the relentless passionate drive of his.

She was beyond thought, beyond speech. Finally, gratefully, he was positioned over her, his heavy maleness pressed against her entrance.

She pressed her heels into the mattress, pushing up against him in silent urgency. He paused, and it was as if they trembled together on the edge of a cliff. Then he surged into her, hard and sure, and she found his rhythm. Higher, harder, faster until together they . . . shattered.

* * *

AFTERWARD SHE LAY RELAXED IN HIS ARMS, A LITTLE sleepy, a little dreamy. "So what have you been up to while we've been transforming this house?"

"Fittings," he said in a dark tone that made her giggle. "Endless, dreary fittings. I have been stuck with pins, plagued with patterns, and as for the debate between knee breeches or full-length trousers—"

"Ollie has been cracking the whip, has he?" Belatedly she recalled that it was not the most felicitous of jokes to make. "I mean—"

"The man is obsessed. He is determined I shall not disgrace him at this ball of yours."

"Don't you mean disgrace me?"

He looked down his nose at her. "You, my dear deluded young lady, are not my sartorial advisor; you are merely my wife."

She giggled again. "And what else have you done today?"

"Oh, this and that. Various arrangements." He trailed his fingers down the line of her spine.

"What sort of arrangements?" She waited for him to explain, but the chatty Thomas of old seemed to have disappeared. It was a little like coaxing an oyster to talk.

"What did you arrange?"

"A fellow in Ollie's office has been helping me trace my men's relatives to check that they're all right."

"Oh, that's a wonderful idea. How far have you got?"

"It's slow progress. Only one so far, Dyson's wife. We've learned that his mother has died, but she was very old and she passed away peacefully in her sleep. His wife has been pretty stretched, I gather, without the earning power of her husband, but she's managing."

She raised herself on one elbow. "You didn't let her know her husband is alive? And that you're planning to bring him home?"

"No. I don't want to raise false hopes. She'll be all right now."

All right now. She was learning to read between Thomas's lines. "You sent her some money, didn't you?"

He shrugged. "It doesn't take much to keep a family going."

She lay back down with her arms around him and snuggled her cheek on his chest. "I love you, Thomas Beresford. You're a good man."

Thomas stroked her hair and didn't respond.

SHE LIKED TO TALK AFTER THEY MADE LOVE. THOMAS preferred to lie there in silence, stroking her warm, silken skin. Lord, was there anything softer than a woman's skin? To say he'd missed her, missed this, was the most ludicrous of understatements.

"Tell me about Mogador." She stroked his chest, rather like petting a cat.

He stiffened. For a few moments he didn't say a thing, but he could feel her waiting. "I told you I don't wish to talk about it."

"You said you didn't want to talk about being a galley slave. I was just wondering what Mogador was like. I've never been to another country." Her voice was soft, soothing in the darkness. "The sultan's palace, for instance. Was it glamorous, like something out of *The Arabian Nights*? Or was it a disappointment? But if you don't want to talk about it . . ."

He didn't want to talk about any of that time, wanted to wipe it from his mind—if only he could. The nightmares continued to haunt him. They'd fade eventually, he was sure. They had to.

Still, it was natural for her to be curious, and his period at the sultan's palace was one of the better times. And after the bedsport he'd just had, he was feeling relaxed and loose and as close to happy as he'd been in years. If he couldn't talk about it now, when could he?

"It was the sultan's palace, but the caliph was the fellow I dealt with. He lived there, part of his job, I suppose, and the sultan lived inland, in another city. It was a magnificent place, especially after we'd spent so long sleeping under the stars or, if we were lucky, under canvas." Or in a filthy crowded pen, like animals.

He shoved that memory aside.

"I only saw a small part of the palace. My men and I were kept in one section—the simplest and plainest. I was held separately from them, and treated better, not just because I was an officer but because I'd stressed that my uncle was a great English lord who'd be happy to pay our ransom. They're very class-conscious, it turned out, even though it's not their system. Or maybe it was just the promise of the money."

"Whichever it was, it was good strategy on your part to claim kinship to a great English lord," she murmured.

"Strategy, yes." He glanced down at her. "Isn't it time for you to go home?"

"No, everyone else is out at a concert. We have plenty of time. Go on."

"The palace is set high, a magnificent white building overlooking the island and the sea. I detected some European influences. There were big European-style windows, for instance, and some European furniture, though it was just for show, a sign of affluence—chairs that nobody sat in, for instance. They do everything on the floor: sitting, eating, sleeping."

"It sounds quite primitive."

"It's not, not at all, it's just a different way of living. The interior is like Aladdin's cave in its riches and beauty. Marvelously colored tile work and extraordinary mosaics, floors and columns of polished marble and other beautiful stone. Both floors and walls were scattered with gorgeous thick carpets and hangings, all in the richest colors, some made of silk." He'd forgotten about the beauty of the place. His last years had been so ugly, they'd blotted out the marvels he'd seen. And the kindness he'd experienced. The caliph had been good to Thomas, insofar as his job allowed.

His voice warmed as he remembered. "There were intricately carved screens over the windows, even the interior ones and some doorways—the most remarkably detailed craftsmanship in both wood and stone. And whole rooms for bathing, with deep tiled pools and carved ceilings." Even he and his men were given access to a small stone room just for bathing. "I wouldn't mind something like that here."

"It all sounds very beautiful and exotic."

"It was—but don't forget, it was the sultan's palace. The ordinary people don't live like that."

She circled one of his nipples with her fingernail. "And the ladies of the palace. Were they very beautiful and exotic, too?"

The faint *meow* in her voice surprised a chuckle out of him. He rather liked that she could be jealous of unknown foreign ladies. "I didn't see any."

"What, none at all?" She didn't believe him.

"They keep their women hidden from the sight of infidels and strangers. The women lived in one of the other sections of the palace and I didn't ever see one—not even the caliph's wife, or wives. I suppose some might have been watching us from behind those screens, women there presumably being as curious as women here," he added teasingly. She nipped him lightly on the chest in punishment.

"So you saw no women at all in the whole country?"

Just one woman and he preferred not to think about her. "Women in the streets are heavily veiled. All you can see is a pair of dark eyes, and sometimes not even that."

She wrinkled her nose. "I don't think I'd like to be hidden away like that."

"No, you're too independent. But"—he shrugged—"different lands, different customs." He'd been to places where the women went bare-breasted and were thought quite modest by local standards.

The room was dark now, the quiet stillness broken only

by their voices. It was peculiarly conducive to intimacies, but they were starting to venture into uncomfortable territory. "Isn't it time to go home now? Aren't you hungry?"

"No, Emm brought over some delicious food for luncheon and I ate like a pig. What about the food there? You said you were finding it hard to adjust to English food. Was it so very dreadful?"

"Not at all. I ate with the caliph several times and the food was wonderful—very sophisticated and exotic. Most of the time though, my men and I ate very simply—rice, lentils or beans with vegetables, though prepared differently from the way we would have them."

"Better or worse?"

He thought for a minute. "Better. They use spices, even for the simplest meals."

"Then why are you having trouble with English food?"

"I'm not. I just find some things a bit rich and fatty, that's all. Now I really think it's time we left."

And he slipped out of bed and groped around for his clothes, cursing under his breath. Either he was going to have to get better at using a blasted tinderbox to light a candle, or he'd need to be tidier with his clothes.

The real solution, he knew, was not to lie in bed so long, talking. Especially about things that . . . stirred up memories. It was just that Rose was so damned irresistible.

THEY WALKED BACK TO ASHENDON HOUSE, ENJOYING THE warm evening. "I hope the weather is like this for the ball," Rose said. "I'm looking forward to it, aren't you?"

Thomas didn't answer. She turned to him with a sudden unwelcome thought. "You can dance, can't you?"

"Hmm? Yes, I can dance."

But there was enough vagueness in his response to prompt her to ask, "Well enough for a ball?"

"I think so. As long as it's the hornpipe." He turned a worried face to her. "They do play that at London balls, don't they? It's my best dance."

She had a moment of sheer horror before realizing he was teasing her. "You brute! It's no joking matter," she told him severely. Then a giggle escaped her. "You must ask Aunt Agatha that question, but only when I'm there. I can't wait to see her face. Or hear her response." Aunt Agatha was still far from reconciled to Rose's choice of husband.

"Get behind me, Rose," he said quietly. He was looking at something up ahead.

"What?"

He thrust her against a wall, stepped in front of her and raised his voice. "Don't come any closer."

"What? Who are you talk—?" She broke off as two men stepped out of a shadowy lane, one wielding a cudgel.

"No danger, gov'nor, just hand over the readies and we'll be off."

"I'm a poor man," Thomas said. "I have nothing for you."

Rose was shocked. Thomas sounded almost frightened.

The second man laughed, a nasty sound. "Poor, eh? Well, your pretty little bird don't look too poor to me. Hand over your jewels, me sweet, or we'll take—"

"No." Thomas moved hesitantly toward them, fumbling in his pockets. "Here, I have a little money. Just don't hurt—" He kicked the man with the cudgel. His knee popped and he went down with a shout. He'd barely hit the ground when Thomas was onto the second man, slamming fists into him once, twice, three times, sending him sprawling into the gutter. The first man stirred. Thomas snatched up the cudgel.

"Want me to bash your brains in? Or do you have enough sense to clear out while you're still in one piece?" He stepped forward threateningly and the two villains took off, limping and hopping as fast as they could go.

He watched them go, then tossed the cudgel into the gutter. He straightened his neckcloth and smoothed his coat back into place. "Now, where were we? Oh, yes, you were urging me to ask Lady Salter about dancing the hornpipe at your ball." He offered Rose his arm, quite as if he'd never heard of such a thing as a fight.

"Thomas, that was amazing." The whole thing had

taken a bare few minutes. If she'd blinked she might have missed it.

"I'm sorry you had to witness that. I'd heard that the gas lighting had more or less kept the criminals off the better streets, but I see now that was an exaggeration."

"Thomas, you drove off two men with your bare hands."

He looked up at the moon. "A few more days and it will be full."

"I thought at first you really were frightened, but that was just a ploy, wasn't it? Lulling them into a false sense of superiority."

"Am I allowed to know what color your dress is?"

"My dress?" She glanced down at her dress. It was quite obviously the same it had been all day. It was blue when he'd taken it off her, and it was still blue when she'd put it back on and he'd helped to fasten it. "I don't understand." He'd just beaten off two vicious thugs. Why was he talking about her dress?

"Your dress for the ball."

"For the ball?" She stared at him. "Thomas Beresford, there is no way I can believe you have any interest in the color of my ball dress."

"Of course I do."

"Why?"

He looked perplexed for a moment—grappling for a reason, she was certain—and then he said, "Ollie will want to know."

"Ollie will want to know?" she repeated.

"I'm sure of it."

She burst out laughing. "That's ridiculous."

"No, I assure you—"

"Thomas, it's all right. You obviously don't want to talk about the fight, and I'll try to respect your wishes. But just let me say this: You were magnificent. And you can babble all you like about ball dresses and the moon, but I know you're a hero." She slipped her arm through his. "My hero."

But thrilled as she was with his swift and valiant defense of her, she could see now how he'd been able to defeat Cal.

And there had been a brisk savagery about the way he'd dealt with those thugs that was a little bit unsettling.

It was a reminder that she didn't know very much about this man, her husband. He was darker and more complex than the Thomas she'd married. One minute lighthearted and teasing, the next dealing out swift and savage retribution, and afterward, seemingly unaffected by the violence and talking nonsense about dresses.

PINEAPPLES ASIDE, THE HOUSE REFURBISHMENTS WERE all going well. Her marriage was another matter. Oh, Thomas was doing all the right things, doing everything he was asked to do. And the lovemaking was wonderful.

But Rose couldn't rid herself of the feeling that there was something missing.

When they were first married it had been so joyous and spontaneous. They'd talked and laughed and made love, and talked again, and everything was spiced with the excitement of the forbidden, of secrecy.

Of course it was different, she told herself. They were no longer as young and carefree as they'd been back then, and after what Thomas had experienced, after what they'd both experienced, of course they'd changed.

But some part of Thomas still seemed somehow locked away from her. Distant. He was playing the dutiful husband role, but was his heart really in it?

It wasn't just that he didn't much like to talk about his experiences. There were times when she wondered if she'd forced him back into this marriage, whether he'd wanted her to get that annulment. Whether he'd only married her in the first place because it was the honorable thing to do, in case she was with child.

At the time she'd believed that he loved her as much as she loved him.

Now she found herself wondering. Had he really only stopped the wedding to save her from committing bigamy?

What if all the time it had been protectiveness on his

part, not love? Gallantry rather than passion. Duty, leavened with desire, but not love. Was he now putting the best face on it that he could?

In odd unexpected moments, these doubts arose to torment her. She shoved them aside. Marriage took time, everybody said so.

Cal had married Emm for purely practical reasons, she reminded herself, and Rose had watched as they grew from strangers into lovers. Nobody seeing Cal and Emm together now would doubt that they truly loved each other.

And Ned. He hadn't even noticed Lily the first few times he met her. Their marriage was forced by scandal, but a blind man could see that Ned doted on her now.

Rose ached for Thomas to look at her the way Cal looked at Emm, the way Ned looked at Lily.

She had been so confident that a marriage of convenience was what she wanted, that she didn't want love. Because love was too painful.

But that was the duke. And this was Thomas.

And love was still painful.

What happened in the bedroom was bliss, to be sure. In the bedroom, Rose felt sure that Thomas loved her the way she loved him—even if he never said the words.

He was a good husband. He was loyal and honorable and she loved him with all her heart. If he didn't feel quite the same, if his heart was a mystery to her, it shouldn't matter. They were married.

In any case, actions spoke louder than words. It was foolish to crave the words. If Thomas did not speak them, he had his reasons. She had love enough for both of them. She would not give up on Thomas.

THOMAS LAY SATED AND RELAXED, ROSE CURLED AGAINST him. The lovemaking was getting better and better as they learned each other's bodies, what they liked and how best to please.

Soon they would officially move into the house together,

then the grand ball shortly after that. And then . . . well, then he'd be setting off to bring back his men.

And though he had mixed feelings about returning to Mogador, he was feeling pleased with the progress he'd made. He'd tracked down two more wives and arranged for them to be taken care of. Only young Jemmy Pendell's wife and baby to be found now.

The last man, Jones, wasn't married and though he probably had unknown bastards scattered around the world, there was no way of tracing them, and Jones probably wouldn't thank him if he did. A bachelor gay and determined to stay one, was Jones.

Rose's question came soft and inevitable, out of the dark. "When you were in Mogador, how many times did you try to escape?"

He sighed. He'd expected more questions. Rose was determined to find out all about the life he'd led in the last four years. He couldn't blame her. She had a right to know about the missing years. And though he found it uncomfortable, he forced himself to do it.

"Only twice. It's hard enough to escape from your master—only the most trusted slaves are permitted outside the home compound. Then if you do escape, it's almost impossible to find a ship that will take you—you need a permit to leave, you see. And the waterfronts are well patrolled by the sultan's guards. Both times I was caught and returned to my owner." And was given a thorough beating—sometimes two, one from the guards and one from his owner—but Rose didn't need to know that.

"And after each attempt I was sold on. Nobody wants a troublesome slave."

"Were any of your owners kind?"

"*Kind* wasn't quite the right word, but decent, yes; for the most part I was reasonably well treated. My last owner, Sidi Achmed, was a good and decent man who treated all the people of his household well and fairly."

"What happened?"

"He sickened and died, quite suddenly, and we—all the household slaves—were left in the hands of his widow."

"What was she like?"

"Not kind, for a start; in fact, *kind* is the very last word I'd use to describe her, or her spoiled bully-boy of a son. She and her son shared a taste and a talent for cruelty." Conditions for the household slaves worsened considerably under their rule.

"The boy was sixteen, and Sayida—that's how we had to address her; it means *madam*—indulged him in everything. Nothing was too good for Adil." Whatever he wanted, he took, and he took great pleasure in cruelty.

"None of the female slaves was safe from him, not even the twelve-year-old kitchen girl, though I did my best to protect the child." All it did was make Adil more determined to torment Thomas in whatever way he could, usually by torturing things that were smaller and weaker and couldn't fight back—he didn't dare take on Thomas himself; he knew Thomas wouldn't hold back, regardless of the threat of punishment.

"It was the women who suffered most under Adil, until the little sod realized I was fond of animals."

"He sounds appalling."

"His mother was just as bad. Two months after her husband died, Sayida decided it was time for me to warm her bed."

She rose up on one elbow. "What did you do?"

"What do you think?"

Her eyes widened. "Thomas, you didn't."

"Rose, I didn't." He leaned down and kissed her nose. "Of course I refused." Without apology or grace. No flowery excuses, just a blunt refusal. And when she persisted, plunging her hand into his loincloth and handling him like an animal, he shoved her off him, saying, "Touch me again like that and you die." But Rose didn't need to know about that humiliation.

"You weren't tempted? She wasn't pretty?"

He made a scornful sound. "She was pretty enough on the outside, but inside she was poison through and through." From then on his life became one long round of hard work, semistarvation and beatings. "The more I got to know her, the more I understood why Sidi Achmed had turned up his toes and died so easily. It must have been hell being married to her."

"She and her son sound like a dreadful pair."

"They were. He had me beaten one day for refusing to call him *sidi*—which means 'lord.' I put on my thickheaded Englishman guise and pretended I didn't understand the order." Thomas smiled grimly at the memory. "He'd summoned the whole household to witness my punishment. But when he'd finished with the beating, I told him in perfect, fluent Arabic, in front of everyone, 'Sidi Achmed was a good man; he would be shamed a thousand times over if he knew the vile creature his son has become.'"

His expression hardened. "It was war from then on."

She nuzzled her cheek against him.

"The last straw came when I came across Adil beating up a frail old man." His stomach clenched at the memory. "Nasr was a gentle old scholar, Rose, a Greek, I think. He'd been with the family sixty years—imagine being a slave for that long. He'd taught Sidi Achmed his letters and later Adil. He must have had a fine brain, for he'd overseen the family business all that time, and it had thrived. He kept the account books, conducted all their correspondence—he spoke and wrote at least four languages. But by the time I arrived the poor old fellow was nearly ninety, and his mind was going."

Rose hugged him silently.

"You'd think he would have earned an honorable retirement, but gratitude wasn't in that woman's vocabulary, nor her son's," Thomas said. "That day, I heard the old man crying out in the courtyard and went to see to him. That little worm was beating him, kicking him, punching, hitting him with a stick—a stick! And laughing, as the poor confused old fellow wept hopelessly and tried to dodge the blows."

Her eyes darkened with sympathy.

"Years of faithful service and this was to be his old age. Bad enough to be confused and forgetful, but being endlessly tormented by a vicious young thug? For reasons that made no sense? It was unbearable."

"Poor old man. What did you do?"

"I dragged him off the old man, seized his stick and was about to give the evil little rat the thrashing of his life when the other slaves stopped me. They dragged me away and kept me in the lockup until I calmed." By doing so, they'd saved Thomas's life, for the punishment for hitting the owner's son would surely have been death.

"Oh, Thomas. What did they do to you then?"

"Sold me to the galleys, to the master with the most vicious reputation—a pirate. And you know what? I was better off there."

"You don't mean that, surely?"

"I do, because hideous as that existence was, it was from the galleys I eventually escaped, and thus made my way back to England, and you, my sweet Rose." He kissed her.

Chapter Ten

❧

It is well to have as many holds upon happiness as possible.
—JANE AUSTEN, *NORTHANGER ABBEY*

"DID YOU SEND THIS?" ROSE ASKED THOMAS WHEN HE called in around noon a few days later. He'd arranged a delivery of wine and spirits—he was stocking the cellar—and had come to supervise the unpacking and storage of the wine.

"What is it?"

She showed him an elegant wooden box, shallow and divided into segments, each one containing a piece of beautifully made and arranged marzipan fruit. There were grapes, apples, pineapples, peaches and more, colorful and lifelike.

"Very fancy," he said.

"Isn't it? It came with this card." She passed it to him.

Welcome to your new home. He turned the card over and frowned. "There's no name."

"I know, I thought it strange but perhaps whoever sent it forgot to sign it. Or maybe the shop mixed things up. It was on the doorstep when I arrived this morning."

"Odd. Oh, well, I expect someone will mention it and then we'll know. In the meantime, they look very fine and expensive, so enjoy them."

She wrinkled her nose. "I don't much like marzipan. I thought you might enjoy them."

"I used to love it when I was a boy, but these days . . ." He grimaced. "A bit sweet for me. Anyone in your family?"

She shook her head, then became aware of the young apprentice paperhanger watching, clearly listening in. "Was there something you wanted, Peter?"

He reddened. "Sorry, m'lady, just, I never seen anything so pretty. Are they some kind of sweet?"

"Yes, marzipan. Almond paste and sugar, shaped to look like fruit and painted with vegetable dyes. See?" She held it out so he could see into the box.

Peter edged forward, barely able to take his eyes off the glistening sweets. "That there's a pineapple, ain't it? And there's a peach. And cherries, like they was just picked off a tree."

Rose glanced a silent question at Thomas, who nodded. She handed him the box. "Here, Peter, they're yours."

The young man's eyes almost popped. "Mine, m'lady? You mean it?"

She smiled. "Take them home to your mother or your sweetheart, and enjoy them with our compliments."

"Thank you, m'lady, sir." He closed the box carefully and hurried away.

"Nice thing to do," Thomas said. "Thought you were dark on paperhangers these days."

She laughed. "He wasn't the one who got the pineapples upside down."

The wine merchants arrived and Thomas went off to supervise the unpacking and stowing of the wine in the cellar. He'd had wine racks built earlier.

Rose was preparing rooms for the servants: fresh paper for the women, paint for the men, a rug on each floor and warm blankets for the beds. Emm had stressed to her that you got the service you deserved—Emm recalled her own time as a lowly teacher, living in a cold attic room with no heating and inadequate bedclothes. It had made quite an impression on Rose and she resolved to ensure that her own servants were as comfortable as she could make them.

Not that she had any servants yet—the domestic agency that had supplied servants to both Emm and Lily was sending applicants to be interviewed tomorrow. Emm was going to sit in on the interviews with her.

THE WINE MERCHANT'S CARRIER AND HIS MEN FINISHED unloading the wine. Thomas paid them and they departed. He surveyed the filled racks with satisfaction. Would they ever drink that much wine? Still, wine was an investment for the future.

"Excuse me, sir." It was the wine carrier.

Thomas turned, surprised. "Did you forget something?"

"No, but there's a lad lyin' on the ground out back, lookin' right poorly. Thought you ought to know."

Thomas hurried upstairs and went through the kitchen into the backyard. Young Peter lay sprawled, half curled on the cobbles, retching in a pool of vomit. A few of his fellows were standing back, doing nothing.

"Good God!" Thomas examined him. "You"—he stabbed a finger at a nearby workman—"is there a doctor around here?"

"It's all right, sir, the lad don't need a doctor," the foreman said. "He's just reapin' his reward for being a greedy guts." He pointed at the overturned box of marzipan lying a few feet away. "He ate all them fancy sweets, all by hisself." He bent to pick one up.

"Don't touch that!" Thomas snapped. It wasn't simple overindulgence; there was foam coming from Peter's mouth, greenish-yellow foam. "This boy is seriously ill. Now where's the nearest doctor?"

"There's a Scotsman lives not far from here," one of the men offered. "He's good but he don't have much to do with nobs."

"Fetch him," Thomas ordered. "Tell him there's a boy here been poisoned."

"Poisoned?" The foreman blanched and took a step back.

"A guinea for you if he's here within the half hour." The man raced off.

Thomas fetched a damp cloth and wiped Peter's mouth. The boy was barely conscious. He moved him away from the soiled area but left him on the ground. It wasn't cold, and he had no idea what to do, whether it was safe to move him. From the look of the lad's vomit, there wasn't much remaining in his stomach.

But you never could tell with poison.

He picked up the box of marzipan and carefully replaced the spilled sweets. Only three left. It might turn out to be overindulgence, but he didn't think so. He closed the box and slipped it into his coat pocket.

"AND YOU SAY THE BOY'S STILL ALIVE?" OLLIE ASKED. Thomas had told him all about the incident over a glass of wine, late that night.

"The doctor has high hopes of his recovery, but as he doesn't know what the poison might be, it's hard to say. He took one of the sweets and a sample of the vomit to test."

He showed Ollie the box and the card, which he'd also collected. "I don't suppose you know of anyone who could find out more about this?"

"Not my area," Ollie said regretfully. "Figures, numbers, I'm your man. Poisons? Assassinations? You need Ashendon."

"Ashendon?"

Ollie nodded. "Not that he's involved anymore, but he *knows* people." He tapped the side of his nose significantly. He pushed the marzipan box distastefully away. "Take that thing to Ashendon. He's your man."

Thomas didn't like the idea of asking Ashendon for anything, but someone had sent these filthy, poisoned, harmless-looking marzipan sweets to Rose. It could have been her lying there on the cobbles, vomiting her heart out. It didn't bear thinking of.

If anyone was motivated as strongly as Thomas to track down the villain, it would be Ashendon.

Peter was still alive the next morning, though still a very sick boy. Thomas spoke to the boy's widowed mother and discovered that Rose had been by earlier with a basket of food. It turned out that Peter was the breadwinner for his mother, younger brother and two sisters. Apparently Rose knew this. How, he had no idea.

Thomas assured the boy's mother that he would cover the costs of Peter's medical treatment and that the family would be looked after. He slipped her five pounds to make up for the loss of the boy's wages and left quickly to avoid her embarrassing gratitude.

He then called on Ashendon. He explained what had happened—Rose had already told him some of it—and showed him the box, the sweets and the card. He finished by saying that Ollie had suggested he consult Ashendon because he "knew people."

Ashendon neither confirmed nor denied it. He questioned Thomas about the incident. "You don't have any idea who sent it?"

"No."

"Who hates you, who have you offended?"

"*Me?* I've offended nobody—apart from you. Why would I be the target? I know practically no one in London. I've been at sea since I was sixteen, and missing for the last four. Hardly anybody even knows I'm alive, remember?"

Ashendon raised a sardonic eyebrow. "Apart from everyone my sister sent an invitation to. Several hundred people at least, knowing Rose."

"Oh. I hadn't thought of that. But I don't know anyone in the ton." His old friends, apart from Ollie, were all either at sea or dead.

"I can't think of anyone who'd wish to harm me." *Uncle Walter?* he thought suddenly. But he couldn't imagine it. Failing to act to save someone on the other side of the world was a far cry from actively attempting to kill them. In any case, what would be the point?

Then he wondered about the attack by the two thugs.

Ashendon eyed him shrewdly. "Thought of something?"

"Not really." He explained about the attack, but the more he talked the more certain he was that it was a simple robbery.

"Saw them off by yourself, did you? Unarmed?"

Thomas shrugged. He didn't need to point out to Ashendon that he knew how to fight. The man's face was still covered in scabs and fading bruises, courtesy of Thomas.

"No one has any reason to harm me," he repeated.

"So you think it was aimed at my sister? Rubbish. Who would wish to harm Rose?"

He was right; nobody in their right mind would want to harm Rose. Then again . . . "What about the duke, the one she was going to marry? Would he be the sort of man to want revenge? Because if you wanted to harm us both, that would be a way to do it."

"Everingham? I can't see it, myself. He doesn't seem the type, but it's worth keeping in mind. Leave it with me," Ashendon said. He refused to say more. Rose's brother was a very irritating man.

THE DAY FINALLY ARRIVED FOR THOMAS AND ROSE TO MOVE into the new house. Everything was ready. In a rather prosaic arrangement, they'd agreed to meet at the house at two. Rose said she didn't want any fuss, but Thomas had brought a bunch of flowers and a special bottle of champagne to celebrate—the vintage was the year they were married.

He arrived early, as was his usual habit, bringing his belongings in the portmanteau Ollie had lent him. Ollie had come too, curious to see the refurbished house—and to take his portmanteau back.

Thomas unpacked—it took ten minutes—and then the two men went downstairs. It didn't seem right to open the champagne without Rose. He'd stocked the cellar a few days earlier—a masculine contribution to the setting up of the house—and recalled he'd bought a case of very good brandy. He found a bottle and poured out two glasses. Very fine glasses, too, he noted.

Nothing had escaped Rose's attention in furnishing this house. It was complete in every detail. He felt slightly guilty that he had done so little to help but told himself that women enjoyed these things. Nesting.

His plans for the rest of the day involved a quiet drink with Ollie and then a slightly less quiet afternoon in bed with his wife. Rose and her sister-in-law, the countess, had interviewed potential servants, and a cook, two housemaids and a general manservant were due to arrive tomorrow, so Thomas was looking forward to his last day alone with Rose in the house.

His time as a domestic slave had made him realize how much servants got to know about their masters. Most people never thought about it but very little was truly private.

Rose had left the hiring of a valet to him, but he'd leave that task until afterward. Not long now . . .

"To the new house and a more comfortable bed than my old *chaise longue*." Ollie raised his glass and sipped. He raised his brows, sipped again, then eyed his glass with approval. "Very fine brandy this."

"Yes, now that the war's well behind us we're getting good French brandy again—legally." Thomas didn't drink very much these days, had lost the taste for it, but a good, well-stocked cellar was a necessary part of any gentleman's house.

"I heard you found the last seaman's wife. Good timing that," Ollie said. Jemmy Pendell's wife and little daughter had been found at last.

"Yes, the confusion was because the address was Newport, and we didn't know which Newport it was, there being several towns called Newport in the kingdom."

"That would explain it. Wouldn't say no to a top-up." Ollie held out his glass.

"It was the Newport in Gloucestershire we wanted."

"Ah. Well, now that's done, and you're all settled in here, you can relax and enjoy the ball."

"Mm." Thomas grimaced. He wasn't looking forward to the ball. Large noisy gatherings never used to bother him, but these days he found them rather . . . unsettling.

A little clock on the mantel chimed the hour and Thomas gave a start. "Blast! Rose will be here any minute and I forgot to explain about the color of her dress. If she mentions it to you, just tell her I forgot to tell you."

Ollie frowned. "Forgot to tell me what?"

"The color of her ball dress."

"Why the devil should you have told me that?"

"Because I told her you wanted to know."

Ollie's eyes almost popped. "You told your wife that I wanted to know what color her ball dress was going to be? Have you got rats in your attic? Why the devil would I want to know that?"

"I don't know. I just told her you did."

"Why?"

"It was all I could think of at the time."

"You know what?" Ollie said after a solemn consideration of the facts. "Either you really have got rats in the attic, or you've been hitting too much of this very fine brandy."

Before Thomas could explain this aberration, the front door opened and a carnival arrived—at least that was what it sounded like. The entire Rutherford family, including aunts, husbands and dog—as well as a handful of footmen and maids from Ashendon House—swept in like a flood, bearing flowers, food, more champagne and gifts.

And just like that, it turned into a party. Thomas could see his afternoon in bed with his wife slipping away. Then he realized he would have the whole night with her, their first ever, and cheered up.

Once the initial excitement had calmed and while the women were off examining every nook and cranny, Ashendon drew Thomas aside. "That marzipan was poisoned, all right."

The doctor had said the same when Thomas spoke to him. "What kind of poison?"

Ashendon's lips tightened. "It's not clear. But that lad is

lucky to be alive. If he'd only eaten a few pieces, he wouldn't have thrown up and the poison would have entered his system. As it is, he must have vomited most of it out."

"So his greed saved him," Thomas said. "And not just him—if he'd taken the box home to share, his whole family could be dead." It was a sobering thought. "Any luck tracing the box and the card?"

Ashendon shook his head. "The marzipan is from a known confectioner—there is a small symbol imprinted on the underside of the box that we were able to identify and trace—but the shopkeeper has no recollection of who bought it, and the card is not one of theirs."

"So we still have no idea, then."

"No."

"OUR FIRST PARTY. WASN'T IT CHARMING?"

"Very." Their last guest had just left. It was Ollie; Thomas practically had to push him out the door.

"All these flowers, and the baskets of fruit. Don't you love fresh fruit?"

"I do indeed." The day was over, the house smelled of fresh flowers and Thomas was finally alone with his wife. He reached for her. Smiling, she danced out of reach.

Rose in a happy mood was irresistible. He was feeling rather mellow himself after a brandy, a couple of glasses of wine and some delicious food. His digestion was returning to normal—huzzah!

"Would you wait down here for a while, please, Thomas?" Her smile was bewitching. She clearly had something planned. "Come up in fifteen minutes."

Why not? They had the whole night ahead of them. He poured himself another brandy and settled down to watch the clock. Fifteen minutes later he climbed the stairs and knocked.

"Come in."

Their bedroom was a bower of flowers and light—there were vases of flowers and glowing candles everywhere.

"Makes a change from groping around in the dark, doesn't it?" Rose said. He turned to tell her he'd enjoyed groping her in the dark. And his throat dried.

She was wearing the flimsiest, frothiest, almost transparent scrap of white lace and dark red netting. He stared, unable to summon a thought or a word. The blood had rushed from his brain to his groin.

She seemed rather pleased with his reaction. "Like it?" She twirled around. "Delightfully improper, don't you think?"

His throat produced some sort of noise.

She giggled. "My dressmaker, Miss Chance, made it."

He finally found his voice. "She forgot to add the dress."

She giggled again. "Do you object to my choice of attire, sir?"

"I most emphatically do not." He flung off his coat and prowled toward her.

Laughing, she skipped to the other side of the bed. "Good, because I have two more of these outfits. You'll see them eventually. But not tonight."

Which was a good thing because Thomas had no patience for a fashion showing, not right now, no matter how charmingly revealing they might be. He was ready for action.

He unbuttoned his waistcoat and tossed it aside. "It's 'an outfit,' is it? I would have thought it was more like a handkerchief."

She picked up a pillow and smoothed it into place. He had no idea why. The pillows would all be messed up the minute they hit the bed. She held one of them in front of her and plumped it slowly, eyeing him provocatively over the top of it. Ah, that was why.

He lunged toward her.

She threw the pillow at him and, giggling, scrambled across the bed, giving him a sight of naked pink buttocks framed in gauzy burgundy froth. It forced a groan from him. He dragged his shirt over his head, yanked off his breeches and boots and dived toward her.

He caught her and they went rolling across the bed. "So,

wench, you would defy me." Apparently he'd become a medieval warrior.

"I would, sirrah. You are a brute and a cad and a varlet!"

He frowned. "Do you know what a varlet is, wench?"

She paused, sitting atop him, clad in a whisper of nothing, and chewed her lip in a way that had him groaning again. "No, actually, come to think of it, I don't. What is a varlet?"

"A very small var," he said, and rolled over, capturing her beneath him. "Now I have you." Medieval Thomas was back.

Smiling, she pulled his head down to lavish luscious, unhurried kisses on him. The taste, the scent and feel of her filled his senses. Medieval Thomas melted away.

They made love then, with much murmuring and laughter and tenderness. Leaving that flimsy excuse for a nightgown on her, he caressed her through the gauze and lace; a different kind of textural arousal that left her purring and eager.

She reached for him, sure and confident, smiling with catlike satisfaction when she felt his heat, his hardness, his readiness. She explored his length, squeezing, stroking, driving him to the brink.

"Now, Thomas." He entered her slowly, smoothly and felt her thighs lock around him. They had all the time in the world and he wanted to make it last, but she was eager and demanding and his body took over.

Power and intensity roared through him, and she arched and shuddered around him as he took them over the edge together. And collapsed.

In silence he gathered her to him, and in silence they lay, entwined. His heart was full to bursting. He had no words.

All those years, dreaming of Rose, imagining coming home to her . . . He hadn't known the half of it.

BURNING . . . HE WAS BURNING UP. THE SUN, THE PITILESS sun. Sweat poured from him, dried as soon as it appeared.

No wind. And the stench, the endless, choking stench. Men rotting in their own filth.

They said you got used to it, stopped noticing it after a while. But he never would. Never could.

His throat was raw. Dry as bark. So hard to swallow. The water bucket . . . When would it come around?

Two rows in front the Swede was mumbling, raving in his insanity. The whip kept him rowing. For now. Much more of the madness and they'd throw him to the sharks. Insanity was a disease on the galleys; infectious, unsettling. Fatal.

The man beside him rowed like a grim automaton, a skeleton thinly wrapped in tanned leather, every bone showing, his back a network of silvery scars. He hadn't spoken a word in months. A Frenchman; they'd been enemies once. Here countries didn't exist. Were they still at war? Thomas didn't know.

Above him the captain called down to him. "Hey, Englishman, changed your mind yet?" Thomas looked up. The rhythm of his rowing never faltered. He knew better than to stop or even slow.

The captain drank a long draft of water, letting it spill down his neck and chest. Thomas's dry throat convulsed. The captain grinned knowingly. "Say the word, Englishman, and you could be up here now, drinking as much water as you wanted."

Come and be his navigator, he meant. Hunt down blameless ships, maybe even English ships. Join him in murder, and plunder, and rape . . .

"Thank you, no, Captain. I am content here." He returned his gaze to the bony spine of the man in front of him and rowed grimly on. He didn't know the man's name but he knew every bump on the man's spine. And every scar on his back.

"You're a fool." The captain poured the rest of the water out on the deck. The men nearest him licked at the escaping droplets in desperation. And received a kick in the face for their trouble.

Don't even think about it. If he took up the captain's offer, he'd lose his soul, lose his humanity. As a slave it was only his body they could torment . . .

"A sail!" the shout came.

An English ship? French? Spanish? American? He couldn't see. Not that nationality mattered to the pirates. Or the slaves.

"Faster!" The beat increased. His muscles screamed. "Faster!" The lash of the whip snaked across his back. "Faster!" Closing in on the target ship now. Hounds baying for blood. "Faster! Faster!"

"Thomas!"

He jerked upright. *Faster! Faster!*

"Thomas, wake up." Soft, fragrant arms closed around him. "You're having a dream."

He blinked stupidly, his heart racing. Disgust and dread and rage still clogged his throat.

Cool, gentle hands smoothed his damp hair back from his forehead. "It's all right, Thomas, it was just a dream. You're home now, safe."

Safe. The room smelled of flowers. And faintly of lovemaking. *Home.* The last few candles were guttering, a whisper of acrid smoke signaling their final passing.

His pulse slowed. He pulled her against him, breathing in her clean, sweet-smelling goodness.

"Sorry," he began.

"Don't apologize," she said softly. "Everyone dreams."

Not like Thomas, they didn't.

"Do you want to tell me what it was about? It can help, sometimes, I know."

"No!" He almost shouted it. God no. To bring that evil place into this . . . haven? He moderated his tone. "No."

"Then lie down now and go back to sleep. And try not to think about anything except being here, safe, with me." She pulled him down on the pillows beside her and drew his head to her breast. He lay in silence as Rose held him and caressed him. Slowly the dream faded, and with it the sense of filth and unworthiness and desperation.

Thomas slept.

*   *   *

THE EFFECTS OF THE DREAM MIGHT HAVE PASSED IN THE
night but the memory of it hung over Thomas in the morning. As soon as he woke, he slipped out of bed and went
downstairs, naked—they had no servants as yet—and
scrubbed himself from head to toe in the secluded backyard, rinsing off in cold water from the pump.

It was irrational, he knew, but he needed to clean away
the stench of memory along with the sense of filth, and
unworthiness.

Tipping a last bucket of cold water over himself, he
shook his head clear, like a dog shaking off water, and
found Rose leaning against the doorpost, watching him.
She was wearing slightly more than last night, but not
much—another confection of lace and gauze designed to
go over the original tiny scrap. Or maybe the word was *with*
rather than *over*, for it hardly hid anything. He was already
aroused—despite the cold water.

"I hope you won't be wearing that in front of the servants," he said.

She tilted her head and eyed him cheekily. "I won't go
wearing this in front of the manservants if you promise not
to walk around like that in front of the maids."

He glanced down, and she laughed and tossed him a towel.

"I wish now I hadn't asked Kirk to collect us here this
morning," she said. "He'll be here at eight, and we don't
have time to do anything but dress, I'm afraid."

They went upstairs to dress. "I'm sorry about waking
you last night," he said as he sorted out the clothes he'd
tossed down so carelessly the previous evening.

"Thomas, darling, dreams happen. You can't help them."
She slipped her chemise on over her head and fastened the
drawstring. "Do you have dreams like that often? Bad ones,
I mean."

He forced a smile and lied. "No, mostly I dream of you."

She wasn't fooled. "I'm serious, Thomas, how often do
you have nightmares?"

He pulled on his breeches. "Don't worry, I'll sleep in the other room."

She frowned. "You'll do nothing of the sort."

"I don't want to disturb you."

"It'll disturb me far more if you sleep in the other room." She stepped into the skirt of her riding habit and fastened it. "How often do you have bad dreams?"

He lifted a weary shoulder. "Often enough." He stamped his feet into his boots.

"Are they coming more often or less often since you arrived home?"

He thought about it. He hadn't had one for a few days. On the fishing boats, and when he first arrived in England, sleeping on Ollie's *chaise longue*, he'd been jerked out of sleep a couple of times a night, enmeshed in some frightful dream.

She could call them nightmares, but the things that came to him in the night had happened, they'd actually happened. Not so much dreams but haunting memories.

But come to think of it, in the last week or so they'd occurred less frequently.

"They come and go," he said evasively. "No pattern that I can see." Another lie. He knew full well what had brought on last night's little horror. He'd booked his passage. He was going back there.

"Perhaps if we look for a pattern we might find a way to make them come less often. It might be something you ate, for instance. You ate more than usual last night."

"It wasn't anything I ate."

"It's worth trying, though, isn't it?" She did up the buttons of her tightly fitted jacket, then pulled a brush through her hair. Effortless beauty at this time of the morning.

"What if they don't go away? What if they keep coming?"

She shrugged. "Then we learn to live with it." She gave him a stern look. "But you don't apologize for them, and you don't sleep in another room, is that understood?" She slipped her arms around him. "We're in this together, Thomas."

Thomas squeezed her tightly. The optimism of the ignorant. No point in arguing.

"Now hurry up. Kirk will be here any minute. I did say, didn't I, that he's bringing a mount for you?"

"No, you didn't." He dragged his shirt over his head, tucked it in, buttoned his waistcoat, and shrugged himself into his coat. It seemed to have a few wrinkles. Lying on the floor all night would do that, he supposed. Normally he was very neat and tidy with his things; most seamen were.

Then again, most seamen didn't have to contend with the sight of Rose dressed in nothing but a flimsy wisp of outrageousness and lace.

He brushed at the wrinkles with his hands. It didn't make much difference.

She looked at him and burst out laughing. "We're going to have to get you a valet, first thing. Today if possible."

"It can wait. There's no hurry."

She shook her head. "Thomas, you need a valet now. You'll need him to help you prepare for the ball."

"No, I can manage. I'll hire someone when I get back. No use having him kicking his heels and doing nothing while I'm away."

"Away?"

"Yes, I'm not sure how long I'll be. It depends."

ICE COALESCED IN THE PIT OF ROSE'S STOMACH. He couldn't mean what she thought he meant. He'd spoken quite casually, as if he were referring to some everyday excursion, popping down to Brighton, for instance, or visiting Bath. But it was no simple trip he was contemplating.

"Depends on what? Where are you going, Thomas?"

He turned. "Where do you think, Rose?"

She bit her lip.

"Oh, don't look at me like that," he said. "You know what I have to do."

"You're planning to go yourself? To the Barbary Coast? But you can't!"

"Don't worry, I'm not leaving until after the ball."

"I don't care about the ball—well, I do, but—" She broke off, stunned by his casual carelessness. "You can't go, Thomas. You can't go back to that dreadful place."

"Now, Rose, how else can I rescue my men? I promised them I'd bring them home. You know how important it is to me. I can't do it from here." He made it sound so reasonable, but it wasn't.

For heaven's sake, she'd seen him herself this very night past, shaking and trembling in the grip of a nightmare that she *knew*—whether he admitted it or not—was a direct result of his dreadful experiences there. And he was going back?

"Why can't you rescue them from here? Why not get someone else to go, a trustworthy agent?"

"Because it's not a straightforward transaction. I'll need to find out exactly where each man is and then negotiate for his freedom. It will take a certain amount of local knowledge and a good deal of cunning. And who could I trust with the gold?"

She stared at him, dismayed. "But what if you're captured again? What if someone recognizes you? A tall Englishman with eyes the color of a summer sky is going to stand out. And the minute anyone sees your scars they're going to know you were a slave, Thomas. And they'll take you, they'll lock you up and put you in chains and whip you."

"No, they won't," he said in a horridly reasonable voice that made her want to hit him. "All sorts of people live there, all colors, all sizes, shapes and races. I'll fit right in, I promise. And I'll be very careful, so there's no need for you to worry."

No need to worry, the man said, as if she were panicking needlessly over some minor possibility.

"Now, I've already booked my passage, so there's no point arguing." He opened the door and started down the stairs.

She followed, furious, bubbling with frustration. Why did he have to be so wretchedly *noble*? Because he was

Thomas, that's why. "Well, in that case I hope you got us a nice big cabin."

His head jerked around. "*Us?* You're not going."

She shrugged, as if it were a foregone conclusion. "Of course I am. If you're going, I'm going." With the long skirt of her riding habit draped over her arm, she swept past him on the stairs.

"No. Absolutely not. It's far too dangerous for you."

She made a dismissive gesture. "It's even more dangerous for you. *I'm* not the escaped slave in this family."

He gave her a frustrated look. "I know what I'm doing, Rose."

"Good. That's all right, then. And since you're sooo confident it's completely safe, there's no problem, is there?" She gave him a sweet, utterly hypocritical smile. "Now, what clothes should I take? It's going to be hot, isn't it? Perhaps I should have some light dresses made up."

The front doorbell rang, the bell jangling in the nether regions of the house. "That will be Kirk." She reached to open the door.

He pushed in front of her and gripped her by the shoulders. "Once and for all, you are not going to Mogador, Rose. I won't allow it."

"No, Thomas," she said demurely. She could tell from his wary expression that he wasn't sure whether she meant no-Thomas-I-won't-go-to-Mogador, or no-Thomas-I-won't-obey-you.

She could see he didn't want to ask, and she had no intention of enlightening him.

She opened the door. "Good morning, Kirk. Isn't it a lovely day?"

YES THOMAS, NO THOMAS, THREE BAGS FULL, THOMAS. Always said in such a butter-wouldn't-melt fashion, and with that bewitching smile of hers that turned him inside out and full of knots, hard and wanting and frustrated. And still he had no idea.

He'd commanded ships full of hardened sailors, dammit. He'd fought off pirates, kept five men alive in a hellish journey across the desert by his willpower alone. Survived years in the galleys.

And then, Rose.

A merry dance was right.

He threw her up into her saddle and helped her settle in, then mounted his own horse. Quite a decent hack, too, a thoroughbred gelding. He thanked Kirk. They walked their horses through the early morning traffic to Hyde Park. Rose and Thomas led the way, with Kirk bringing up the rear.

Their argument continued, low-voiced and vehement. She was not going to Barbary. Yes, she was. If he could go, she could go. Danger? If it wasn't too dangerous for him, surely it wouldn't be too dangerous for her? Sauce for the gander, sauce for the infuriating goose.

Tempers were rising. As they reached Lily, Galbraith, George and Ashendon waiting at the gates, Rose trotted forward to greet them. Hugs all round.

Every meeting of the members of this family was like a grand reunion after months apart, when in fact they'd all been together last night.

Rose said something and the three women turned to stare at him. Thomas heard her mutter something about ". . . stubborn, thickheaded, bacon-brained, pigheaded mule of a man." Rose, Lily and George cantered away, with Galbraith and Kirk coming up in the rear.

"Trouble in paradise?" Ashendon said silkily.

Thomas turned to look at him. "How are those scabs of yours coming along?" he said pleasantly. "Should make a nice showing by the ball, don't you think?"

Ashendon scowled and they rode along for a bit in silence.

Lily came trotting up to Thomas. "You're not really taking Rose to the Barbary Coast, are you, Mr. Beresford?" she said anxiously. "It sounds awfully dangerous to me."

"What? You are *not* taking my sister to that hellhole!"

Ashendon snarled before Thomas could even open his mouth. "Are you insane?"

"No, I—"

"Oh, but it's *perfectly* safe," Rose trilled happily as she joined them. "Thomas has assured me that he knows *exactly* what he's doing."

"What I said was—"

"You must be mad." Galbraith joined them. "That place is notorious. A noxious nest of pirates, slavers and worse."

"I kn—"

"Oh, but Thomas knows all about it, Edward," Rose said. "He says it's perfectly safe and I believe him. I'm so excited to be going. I've never been anywhere foreign and exotic."

"I refuse to allow—" Ashendon began.

"Once and for all, Rose, I am *not* taking you with me," Thomas snapped in a voice that could silence a ship full of hardened seamen. The members of her family blinked, looked from him to Rose and back, then visibly relaxed.

But it was water off a duck's back for Rose. "You don't have a choice, Thomas. If you go, I go."

"I made a promise to those men. I gave my *word*. I *have* to go."

"Fine. And I'll come with you."

He groaned. "For the last time—"

"Whither thou goest, Thomas. Whither thou goest."

He glared at her, frustrated. "If you're going to fling biblical snippets around, how about the fact that you vowed to love, honor and obey me."

She wrinkled her nose. "I've never been good at the third one—ask Cal, ask anyone. But I do love you and deeply honor you. And I'm coming with you to—what's the name of that horrid place again?"

He groaned. "Rose, Rose, be sensible. If anything happened to you, I couldn't live with myself."

Her voice hardened. "And what about me, Thomas? How am I supposed to bear it if something happens to you. Again? You left me once before and it was unbearable. And you ended up in an unimaginably dreadful position. So if you think I'm going to let you go alone, let you risk yourself again in that horrid place, well, you've got"—she glanced around for inspiration—"rats in your attic." And she galloped away.

Thomas and Ashendon watched as she disappeared behind a copse—she was a magnificent horsewoman.

"Your sister is a glorious creature, there's no denying it," Thomas said after a while. "You won't hold it against me if I lock her in the cellar the day my ship leaves, will you?"

Ashendon shrugged. "Only reasonable thing to do." He glanced at Thomas. "You will make sure she has some bread and water?"

"Naturally."

"Well, then."

The two men rode on, for once in complete, if silent, accord.

"I THINK WE SHOULD SLEEP AT ASHENDON HOUSE ON THE night of the ball," Rose said as they were preparing for bed that night. By mutual consent the argument about who was going to Mogador had been shelved, unresolved.

It was a standoff between two equally resolute and stubborn people. Their previous accord was slightly stiff now; politeness ruled rather than passion, but Rose was determined not to let their differences come between them. Especially since she knew she was right.

"We?"

She removed her slippers and stockings and stepped out of her dress. "Yes, we. I'll be dressing there for the ball with my sister and George—it'll be such fun, all girls together again—and it's silly to have to change to come back here, or to order the carriage at three or four in the morning, and I'm certainly not going to walk back here in my ball dress at that time of the morning. No, it's much simpler for us to just go upstairs to bed. And then we can all have breakfast together in the morning and talk about how it all went and find out all the gossip."

"But don't you share a bedroom with George?"

"She'll be sharing with Aunt Dottie. It's all arranged."

Dressed only in her chemise, she took the candle they'd brought up to bed and lit several more candles around the room. They threw out a soft glow. Candlelight was so flattering to a woman's skin.

She glanced at Thomas, who was in the process of removing his shirt. Candlelight flattered a man's skin too. She feasted her eyes on him. He had no idea how beautiful he was.

"You all have breakfast together anyway, after you've been out riding every morning."

"Well, of course. Poor Emm can't ride at the moment with the baby almost here, and we don't want to leave her out of things." She turned back the bedclothes. "So are we agreed? About sleeping at Ashendon House, I mean."

"Yes, and you might as well stay on there while I'm away."

"Thomas, we agreed. I'm going with you."

"No, you agreed."

"If that's how you're going to be . . ." She sighed. And took off her chemise. No charming little House of Chance piece of frivolity tonight. Just Rose in her bare skin, fighting for her happiness, and her man.

He groaned. "Rose, Rose, you'll be the death of me yet."

"Thomas, my darling, I'm fighting for the life of you. But let's not talk." She opened her arms and Thomas came to her.

THE DAY OF THE BALL FINALLY ARRIVED. DESPITE THE prospect of an evening that would end in the wee small hours, the Rutherford ladies and their gentlemen—and dog—still went out for their early-morning ride.

The family breakfast afterward, however, was dominated by talk of dresses and jewelry, what other ladies might be wearing, and what interesting snippets of gossip might be discovered. They discussed the gathering of greenery, the arrangement of flowers and decorations, the musical selections. And the dishes prepared for supper. It seemed to Thomas that a ton of food was required—much of it already prepared. Delicious smells had been wafting through the house for the last three days.

Best of all, according to the ladies, several last-minute acceptances had come in overnight and no new refusals. It was certain to be a frightful squeeze—a thing, apparently, to be much desired. Thomas hated squeezes.

The ladies were in a frenzy of excitement, the gentlemen much less so. Galbraith muttered things about needing to visit his man of affairs, while Lord Ashendon, who his wife made plain was required to stay on hand all day to deal with any emergencies, eyed his brother-in-law with a jaundiced expression and ate only two sausages for breakfast— a sign that he was very much out of sorts.

Thomas also made plans for a busy day far away from Ashendon House—he'd call on young Peter and see how he was progressing, visit the bank to see what developments there were, if any. And he'd pack for his trip, away from the prying eyes of his wife, and send his baggage ahead of time, down to the docks.

His ship departed for Gibraltar two days after the ball, and he wanted to leave with a minimum of fuss.

He would return to Ashendon House in time to bathe, shave and change into his formal clothes. Higgins, Ashendon's valet, had offered to attend him. Rose's influence, he suspected, but Thomas was glad of it. He would be under the gaze of the cream of society this night—the nobody who had displaced a duke. He needed to look his best.

Chapter Eleven

❧

*I have had, and may have still, a thousand friends, as they
are called, in life, who are like one's partners in the waltz
of this world—not much remembered when the ball is over.*
—GEORGE, LORD BYRON, IN A LETTER TO MRS.

ASHENDON HOUSE BLAZED WITH LIGHT. AS WELL AS THE
gas lighting in the street and at the entrance of the house,
footmen holding blazing brands stood on either side of the
gate—the flames against the night sky a nice touch of
drama, harking back to the days of linkboys. A red carpet
ran from the edge of the pavement up to the front door, so
that no dainty shoe would be soiled. A canopy had been
erected over it, in case of rain, but the night was warm and
clear.

Inside, the furniture had been completely rearranged to
leave space for dancing, the carpets rolled up and removed,
the ballroom floor polished and then patterned with elegant
chalk designs to prevent slippage.

Gleaming carriages, many of them bearing coats of
arms, were already backed up far down the street. People
who lived just minutes away and not wishing to walk
around the corner in their finery had to wait half an hour or
more just to arrive. A number of ladies arrived in sedan
chairs, their escorts walking beside them.

Inside the house, the graceful line of the staircase was

entirely lost under the masses of people in silks, satins and velvets, inching toward the top of the stairs, where they would greet their host and hostess, meet the guests of honor—Lady Rose and her husband, the nobody—and be admitted.

Thomas ran a finger between his neck and the collar of his shirt. His neckcloth, tied in some fancy arrangement by Higgins, the valet, was far too tight. Or his shirt collar was.

His trousers certainly were. Ollie and the tailor had assured him they were all the crack, but Thomas felt . . . exposed.

Though he'd already noticed several gentlemen whose trousers were even tighter.

He'd also been the recipient of embarrassingly direct glances from a number of ladies. And more than a few inviting, not to say blatant, come-hither smiles.

"And this is my sister's husband, Mr. Thomas Beresford," Lord Ashendon said. Thomas bowed and murmured a polite greeting. He'd lost track of all the names already. The line was endless.

"Not long to go," Rose murmured between introductions. "We'll go inside soon and the dancing can start."

"We don't have to wait until everyone arrives?"

"No. Plenty of people will arrive late, having come from the theater or a dinner or another party. Burton will stand at the ballroom entrance and announce the latecomers as they arrive."

"Lucky Burton."

Rose looked ravishing, even more ravishing than usual in a deep pink silk dress with a spangled gauze overdress. All their dresses, except for Lady Salter's, had been made by the same dressmaker who made the scanty pieces of frippery that Rose wore to bed. Thomas was glad to see that her ball dress covered a good deal more of her, though to his eye the neckline was far too low. Other men kept looking at his wife. Thomas stared them grimly down.

The Rutherford ladies in their ball gowns made a virtual rainbow; Rose's sister Lily wore amber silk shot with silver—a choice that made him realize for the first time that her eyes were gray. The countess wore a low-cut apple-green gown that made no effort to hide her increasing condition. She looked ripe and regal, and the sight of her made Thomas swallow and wonder what Rose would look like, swelling with child like that.

Silvery-haired Lady Salter looked severe and magnificent in shades of gray, and Aunt Dottie looked charming in rich claret silk with blond lace. Lady George, as the only unmarried young Rutherford lady, wore white with a scowl. George hated wearing white, Rose told him.

Thomas's jaw ached from smiling when they were finally freed from the endless reception line. The dancing was about to start.

Since the ball was in their honor, Thomas led Rose out for the first dance; not perfectly conventional, as it should have been according to rank. But then, as Lady Ashendon pointed out, this whole affair was hardly conventional.

Thomas and Rose had put their differences aside for the occasion and though Thomas was a little nervous about his dancing skills—it had been a long time, after all—he was soon reassured that he was adequate to the task.

"Thomas," Rose murmured in a warning voice as they came together in the dance.

"What?" Had he made a mistake?

"Careful, your enjoyment is showing." She laughed at his expression. "Isn't this the most delightful ball?"

"Delightful," he said wryly. It was, as predicted, a frightful squeeze, and while he still found the presence of so many people uncomfortable, the thought that there were rooms upstairs to which he could retire if he wanted to helped.

"Have you noticed your friend over there, with Penny Peplowe?" She glanced to where Ollie was dancing with a tall, redheaded girl. "They seem quite taken with each other. Seating them next to each other at dinner has turned out well, don't you think?"

Thomas nodded. The dinner before the ball had been a

grand affair with honored guests and close Rutherford friends and relations. When asked whom he'd like to be invited, Thomas could only think of Ollie, his sole friend in London. An ally at the table.

"Penny knows everyone and is such a good-hearted soul, and your friend Mr. Yelland not being acquainted with many people, I thought it might be a good match, but now I'm wondering whether it might not become another sort of match entirely."

Thomas looked across at Ollie dancing with Miss Peplowe. They did seem to be enjoying the dance. But his wife was a romantic. It was just a dance.

The first dance came to an end, and now Thomas's duty was to dance with ladies he didn't know. Lady Ashendon, bless her, took him in hand, leading up to his next partner, murmuring her name so he didn't make a fool of himself and generally making it easy for him.

From time to time Burton boomed out the names of the late arrivals. "Lord and Lady Carradice! Lord and Lady Davenham!"

Thomas danced on. He was on his fifth partner, a Roman-nosed matron who reeked of patchouli—Thomas loathed the scent of patchouli—and was wondering how long to supper, when Burton announced, "The Duke of Everingham! The Honorable Mr. Sinclair."

The Duke of Everingham? There was a sudden hush as everyone turned to where the displaced Duke of Everingham, dressed almost entirely in black, stood with another gentleman on the threshold of the ballroom. The duke surveyed the room in an unhurried manner, looking elegant, saturnine and bored.

The Countess of Ashendon rose and glided across the floor to greet him, releasing a buzz of conversation. Rose joined her, and everyone at the ball watched as she engaged the duke in what looked like a brief, but unexceptional and apparently pleasant conversation. A few moments later, he bowed to the ladies and he and his friend drifted off in the direction of the card room.

"Well, that was unexpected." Thomas's partner, Lady Roman-Nose, regarded him with an avid expression. "Embarrassing, isn't it?" Her eyes gleamed with malice.

"Not at all," Thomas said. "My wife invited him." And had no expectation of him coming. What was the fellow up to, he wondered. But he wasn't going to speculate for this lady's entertainment. "Do you hunt, Lady, er, um?"

"No," she responded in a snippy tone. Thomas wasn't sure whether it was because she was balked of any juicy gossip or because he'd forgotten her name, but he didn't much care which. "And my name isn't Lady Er-Um," she added acidly. "It's Lady Toffington."

"Of course it is," Thomas said, embarrassed. "My sincere apologies, my lady. It's just that I've met so many new people this evening, your name temporarily slipped my mind."

"Yes, it must be difficult, being a nobody in such distinguished company."

Oh, she was a charmer, this Lady Er-Um. Thomas danced grimly on, waiting for the wretched dance to finish.

Burton continued to boom out late arrivals. "The Earl and Countess of Wainfleet! The Earl of Brierdon! The Honorable Gilbert Radcliffe!"

The Earl of Brierdon? Thomas stumbled. *Uncle Walter?* He whirled around to face the door but couldn't see his uncle.

"Still learning to dance, Mr. Braithwaite?"

"Sorry, Lady er—" His mind was blank. He scanned the room. *Uncle Walter was here?*

"Yes? You're sorry, Lady *who*?" She regarded him beadily and waited.

"I'm sorry, lady, I have to go." Thomas left her standing in the middle of the dance floor and hurried across to where Burton, the butler, stood.

"Burton, the Earl of Brierdon, where did he go?"

"I'm not sure, sir." Burton scanned the room. "Perhaps one of the card rooms?"

Thomas looked into the first card room. No Uncle Walter.

He checked the second. Not there either. He turned to continue his search when Lady Ashendon touched his arm. "Are you looking for your next partner, Thomas?" He blinked. When had she started calling him Thomas?

"No, it's—I'm sorry, I don't have time to dance. Do you know the Earl of Brierdon?"

"Yes, of course. He was invited, naturally." She looked at him, puzzled. "Is there a problem?"

"Yes, no—I just need to speak to him."

Ashendon appeared at his wife's elbow. "Something the matter?"

"Thomas is looking for Lord Brierdon."

"Why?"

Thomas took a deep breath. If Uncle Walter was here, there was no point in denying the relationship. It was bound to come out anyway. But if Uncle Walter intended to publicly repudiate him, here, in front of Rose and everyone she cared about, he had to be stopped.

"Remember the uncle I said disowned me?"

Ashendon's brows snapped together. "The Earl of Brierdon? He's your *uncle*?"

Thomas nodded. "I don't know why he's here, but if it's to make trouble . . . I won't allow him to embarrass Rose. Or you two."

Ashendon looked grim. "I won't allow it either. Right, I'll get Galbraith onto it. You stay out of sight—better yet, go to the library. We'll find Brierdon and bring him to the library. If he's bent on mischief, we'll soon find out."

It went against the grain for Thomas to let Ashendon take charge, but it made sense to ensure that their meeting took place in private instead of witnessed by a ballroom full of gossips.

He went to the library to wait.

"Thomas?" Rose entered. She hurried to him and slipped her arm through his, a wordless gesture of solidarity. "Emm told me what has happened. Your uncle is here? The one who so cruelly disowned you?"

Thomas nodded. His mouth was dry. He didn't know

what he was going to say to Uncle Walter. He'd take it as it came.

It didn't take long. The door opened. Ashendon entered, followed by a slender gentleman dressed all in white— white knee breeches, a white shirt and a white neckcloth tied in such an intricate arrangement he could hardly turn his head, a white waistcoat and a tight white coat bearing a dozen gold fobs and chains. Galbraith followed, and a moment later Lady Ashendon entered.

Thomas frowned. "That's not my uncle. You've brought the wrong man."

"You said the Earl of Brierdon," Ashendon said.

"Yes. I don't know who this fellow is, but he's not the Earl of Brierdon."

The newcomer uttered a huff of outrage. "I certainly *am* the Earl of Brierdon. Who are you, you impertinent—" His quizzing glass dropped. "*Thomas?* Good gad! It *is* you! My friend Venables did ask me whether the Commander Beresford mentioned on the invitation was any relation, but I told him I had no idea. Lord knows there are enough Beresfords scattered around the country, and I mean, you'd been dead for years, after all." He lifted his quizzing glass and peered at Thomas. "But you're alive."

Thomas's jaw dropped. "Cousin Cornelius?"

"Cousin Cornelius?" echoed Ashendon. "He's not your uncle?"

"No, of course not. He's some sort of cousin."

"Second cousin once removed," Cousin Cornelius said sulkily. "You never did get that right." Thomas hadn't seen Cousin Cornelius since they were boys. He hadn't improved.

"But I heard the Earl of Brierdon announced. Where is Uncle Walter?"

Cousin Cornelius rolled his eyes. "Dead, of course. How else would I be the Ear—er . . ." He trailed off, looking uncomfortable.

"Dead?" Thomas was shocked at the news. Uncle Walter couldn't possibly be dead. "But how? When? He wasn't old, or at least not very old."

"Broke his neck on the hunting field four years ago."

Thomas stared at him, trying to come to terms with the news. Uncle Walter? Dead? And then he realized what else Cornelius had said. "Four years ago? *Four?* Are you sure?" The date had to be wrong.

"Of course I'm sure," Cousin Cornelius said pettishly. "As if I'd forget the date I inherited an earldom."

Rose slipped her arm through Thomas's and murmured, "Lord Brierdon—your Cousin Cornelius, I mean—has been a member of London society for some years."

"But I talked to you about Uncle Walter."

"Yes, but you never mentioned him by his title. I never put the two together."

Thomas turned back to Cousin Cornelius. "Why are *you* calling yourself Lord Brierdon? Gerald is the heir. He should be the earl."

"Gerald died before Uncle Walter," Cornelius said. "Caught some horrid disease in Italy—cholera or something like that. Nasty end. Was shipped home in a barrel, poor sod. The old man was devastated, first his beloved Gerald dead, then you, lost at sea."

Thomas's head was spinning. "But Uncle Walter had to know I was alive. At least—when exactly did he die?"

"Uncle Walter? Fourteenth of June, 1814."

"Fourteenth of June, 1814?" Thomas turned to Rose. "My ship went down on the twenty-fifth of April. I don't know how long it would have taken for the news to reach him, but I do know it took us weeks to cross the desert. I don't know the exact date when I wrote to him, but by my reckoning it was early June."

She saw the implications at once. Her eyes widened. "He can't have received the ransom letter."

"That's right. He was already dead." For most of May 1814, Thomas and his men were still battling to cross the desert. They hadn't even reached Mogador. And when they finally did reach Mogador and sent off the ransom request, it would have taken weeks by ship to reach England.

But the letter refusing Thomas's ransom had been signed by Walter Beresford, Earl of Brierdon. Thomas had seen it with his own eyes. A letter signed by a dead man. Two dead men, seeing that Gerald had died before Uncle Walter.

So who had sent the letters?

Thomas turned to Cousin Cornelius. "You bastard!"

Cousin Cornelius gave an indignant huff. "I'm *not* a bastard! My parents were married!"

"You sent those damned letters! I'm going to wring your scrawny neck!" He prowled toward his perfidious cousin, fists clenched.

"Letters? What letters? I don't know anything about any letters! Don't look at me like that! I didn't do anything! Stay back!" As Thomas approached, Cousin Cornelius gave a frightened squeak and hid behind the Earl of Ashendon. The Earl of Ashendon gave him a distasteful glance and stepped away.

"You refused my ransom."

"What ransom? I don't know anything about any ransom. Help me, Lady Ashendon, he's gone mad!" Cousin Cornelius dived behind the very pregnant Emm.

"Nobody is going to hurt anyone," Lady Ashendon said in her calm way. "Thomas, you know perfectly well I'm not going to allow you"—she glanced at her husband—"or anyone else to wring any necks. I am in the middle of giving a ball, and I will not have my guests brawling, no matter what the provocation."

She gave Thomas a flinty look that somehow combined sternness with understanding. "Thomas, sit down, you're frightening the earl. Lord Brierdon, you sit over here, beside me. I promise, nobody will hurt you."

"Yet." Thomas sat down. He gave Cousin Cornelius a look that made him wriggle closer and clutch Emm's skirt.

Thomas shook his head. "It sounds so wrong, hearing you addressed by Uncle Walter's title."

"That, my dear boy, is because it *is* wrong." Lady Salter appeared from nowhere and inserted herself into the conversation with all the ease of a well-oiled adder. "That title correctly belongs to my *dear* nephew-by-marriage, the seventh Earl of Brierdon."

Thomas blinked. "Who's that?"

Rose slipped her hand into his. "I think she means you, Thomas."

Lady Salter gave a tinkling laugh. "Of course I mean dear Thomas, you foolish child, who else would I mean?" She turned back to Thomas. "Walter Beresford was your uncle, and you are his nephew, his only nephew. A nephew takes precedence over a mere second cousin twice removed." She made a gesture that effectively dismissed such lowly relatives.

"*Once* removed," Cousin Cornelius said sulkily from behind Emm.

"Dear Thomas has always been my favorite nephew-in-law," Lady Salter continued.

Thomas glanced at Galbraith, who until now had been the only nephew-in-law Lady Salter deigned to acknowledge. Galbraith winked.

Lady Salter glanced around the room and added, "You don't imagine my niece would marry a complete nobody, did you? Rutherford ladies have always shown superior judgment."

Rose giggled. "Watch Aunt Agatha rewrite history," she whispered to Thomas.

But despite his amusement at the old lady's complete *volte-face*, Thomas's mind was still reeling. Uncle Walter hadn't repudiated him at all. Neither had Gerald. They couldn't have.

He hadn't been mistaken. He'd been loved, as he'd always believed he was . . .

But who had sent those letters in their name? Who else could it be but the man who'd taken their place? By the time his ransom letters reached England, this white-clad popinjay was swanning around the place calling himself the earl.

He glowered at Cousin Cornelius. The bastard, he'd as good as murdered Thomas in order to steal the title.

Thomas had never even thought of the title in relation to himself—why would he when it belonged to Uncle Walter? And then to Gerald when Uncle Walter died.

Poor Gerald . . . Cholera was a terrible way to go. Thomas was no stranger to death by cholera. But for his body to be sent home in a barrel, it must have broken Uncle Walter's heart. "When you say Uncle Walter died on the hunting field, how exactly did it happen?" Uncle Walter had always been a punishing rider to hounds.

"I'm sorry, Thomas," Lady Ashendon interrupted. "You must have a hundred questions for the—for your cousin, but we're in the middle of a ball here, and I'm afraid it will cause a great deal of gossip if all the principals disappear for such a long time. You know what society is like." She glanced at the clock. "Supper will be announced in a few minutes. We should all be out there." She added, "And perhaps nobody should mention this new development until we're more sure of our facts."

Thomas frowned. "I can't let him just walk out of here." He wasn't going to let Cousin Cornelius out of his sight until he'd wrung the truth out of him.

Cornelius gasped. "You can't force me to stay!"

"I could lock you in a closet," Thomas growled.

"Thomas, you will do no such thing," Emm said.

Galbraith, who'd said nothing up to now, stepped forward. "I'll take him home to my place. Lily's staying here for the night, so she won't need an escort home. How would that be, Cornelius? A nice comfortable bedchamber for the night, instead of a cramped closet." He glanced at Thomas. "I'll keep him safe." In other words, he'd lock him in his bedchamber.

Thomas turned to his cousin. "There's your choice, Cornelius—a closet or Galbraith's hospitality."

"Why can't I just go home?"

"Because I don't trust you as far as I can throw you," Thomas said bluntly.

"Such a frightful ruffian you've become, Thomas," Cornelius said, but seeing that Thomas wasn't going to back down, he gave in with a pout. "Oh, very well, I'll go with Galbraith if I must." He stood, hesitated, then said in a rush, "I have no idea what bee you've got in your bonnet, but I assure you I know nothing about whatever letters you're talking about. And it's not my fault that I was declared the earl. Everyone, even the navy, said you were dead, so you can't blame me."

Thomas, aware of Emm's desire to get back to the ball, stood. "We can continue this conversation tomorrow morning." He turned to Galbraith. "Will you bring him back here at ten?"

"Ten?" Cornelius shuddered. "I *never* arise before noon."

"Then it will be a new experience for you. Ten o'clock tomorrow morning, here"—he glanced a silent query at Ashendon, who nodded—"at Ashendon House."

Cousin Cornelius pouted. "I think you're all being horrid. And I was so looking forward to the ball."

"Come along, Cinderella," Galbraith said. "Pumpkin time."

THEY RETURNED TO THE BALLROOM. THE SUPPER DANCE was in progress and at the end of it, supper was announced. They went in to dine, Thomas escorting Lady Ashendon, Rose escorted by her brother while Lily, most unfashionably, sat with her husband, who had returned, having locked Cousin Cornelius in a guest bedroom and setting a sturdy footman to guard the door.

Ollie escorted Miss Peplowe to the table, behaving in a very attentive manner toward her. Rose caught Thomas's eye and made a see-I-told-you face. Thomas shrugged. It was just supper.

Finally, in a move that caused a great deal of murmuring and subtle nudging, the Duke of Everingham escorted Lady Georgiana in to supper. Lady Salter and her tame escort followed, her smug expression making it clear who was responsible for that pairing. George grimaced at Rose as she passed. Rose laughed.

The supper was a veritable feast, with all kinds of dishes to tempt the appetite: white soup, of course, chicken fricassee, as well as squab and pheasant. There were pies—beef pies, veal pies and fish pies. There was venison, ham sliced paper thin, lobster, prawns and crab patties and two whole baked salmons. There was a range of vegetable dishes, including asparagus and green peas, and there were curd cakes, both savory and sweet.

For those with a sweet tooth there were cakes, blancmanges, glistening tartlets, cream pastries, ices, colorful jellies and brandied custards. For fruit lovers there were compotes of fruit, and the centerpiece of every table held an ornate arrangement of fresh fruit, including grapes frosted with sugar and several whole pineapples.

The tables positively groaned. No expense had been spared.

Remembering his duties to his supper partner, Thomas tried to tempt Lady Ashendon with morsels from the various dishes, but she ate sparingly, even though she was eating for two. He ate without tasting much—though he did enjoy the crab patties. His mind was wholly on the news he'd just received.

Uncle Walter and Gerald dead. And Thomas was now the earl. It was unthinkable.

It wasn't long before Thomas became aware that many of the murmurs and whispers and glances, sidelong and direct, were directed at him. Whenever he caught someone's eye he was treated to a congratulatory smile and a raised glass. It was a strong contrast to the curious and often disparaging looks he'd received at the beginning of the ball.

Lady Ashendon leaned across. "I suspect your secret is out."

Thomas frowned. "But I thought we agreed to say nothing." Cousin Cornelius was safely locked away, so he couldn't have spread the news. In any case, he would hate having to explain his demotion back to plain old Mister.

Lady Ashendon sent a meaningful glance toward Lady Salter. "I'm guessing she's the source of the gossip."

"You mean my dear aunt-by-marriage who always knew I was noble and never once called me a nobody? Or a scarecrow. And certainly never *ever* ordered me to be tossed into a gutter. Twice."

She laughed. "You remember that, do you?"

"When a lady orders you tossed into a gutter, it creates a certain bond," he said dryly. "And twice? Well, that just seals the deal."

She laughed again. "I'm so glad you don't hold a grudge, Thomas—may I call you Thomas, since we are family now? And you must call me Emm."

"Of course." It wasn't true that he didn't hold a grudge. All this time he'd nourished hatred for Uncle Walter and Gerald, swearing revenge against them. And they were innocent.

Who had sent those letters?

However the story got out, it was soon clear that the news had spread like wildfire: Lady Rose's impossible nobody of a husband was in fact the Earl of Brierdon.

Thomas was congratulated right, left and center. People who'd barely talked to him before, people who'd simply looked down their noses at the nobody whom Lady Rose Rutherford had married, now wanted his opinion on everything. If he'd thought the squeeze was bad before, now that the attention was centered on him it was even worse.

"Oh, you are such a naughty man, Lord Brierdon." An arch voice behind him accompanied by a sharp tap on the shoulder caused him to turn. It was the Roman-nosed matron. She gave a trill of laughter and said to the people standing closest, "We are old friends, you know, Lord Brierdon and I."

Thomas looked at her in stupefaction.

She trilled with laughter again and smacked him on the arm with her fan. "Do you know he calls me 'Lady Er-Um,' a little joke between us because when we first met he forgot my name. Isn't that naughty of him?" With a playful titter she smacked him again.

Thomas gritted his teeth. If she hit him again with that thing . . . No. If his first act as an earl were to destroy a lady's fan it would be an inauspicious beginning. Probably. Although quite satisfying. He tore himself away from the temptation.

"Excuse me, Lady Toff-er-um-dammit, I'm needed over there." He pushed his way through the crowd, leaving Lady Roman-Nose entertaining people with tales of his delightfully naughty pretense that he couldn't remember her name.

"Toff-er-um-dammit! Too funny!"

He fled.

THE FIRST ROSE KNEW THE SECRET WAS OUT WAS WHEN people started addressing her as Lady Brierdon, instead of Lady Rose. They were full of congratulations, and there was much talk of how sly she'd been, pretending in the note she'd sent with the invitation that she'd married a simple navy officer.

She wanted to say that she *had* married a simple navy officer, that she hadn't married Thomas for any other reason except love, and that neither of them had known he was the Earl of Brierdon until fifteen minutes ago.

But she didn't want people gossiping any more than they already were. If they knew there was an added mystery, how much worse would the interest be?

She could see that Thomas was hating the attention. He had that grim, granite look she was coming to know so well. "Excuse me, please," she said to the latest batch of well-wishers. "I must speak with my husband."

She hurried across to him.

"Would you like to leave now?"

He brightened. "Can we? It seems awfully early. People are still dancing."

"It's three in the morning. A lot of people have left, but others will stay until the band stops playing, and they will play until four. Or maybe five, I can't remember what the arrangement was. And some of the card players will be here all night. In any case, Cal has already sent Emm upstairs. She's worn to the bone, poor thing. My aunt has agreed to play the role of hostess in her absence."

"Which aunt?"

"The aunt who is soooo delighted with you for becoming the Earl of Brierdon—of course, Aunt Agatha."

"Is Aunt Dottie not delighted with me, then?"

She smiled and patted his chin. "Darling Aunt Dottie has been delighted with you from the very start, earl or not. She's having a fine old time rubbing Aunt Agatha's nose in the fact that she's always had one of her 'feelings' about you—that's a good thing, by the way. Aunt Dottie's 'feelings' are legendary in the family."

"So we can leave?"

"Yes. And if anyone wonders, well"—she dimpled—"we're married and only recently reunited. I think people will understand."

He looked horrified. "I won't have them thinking that we're doing that."

She laughed. "Thomas, of course they're going to think that."

"But we're not—not in your brother's house."

"Why not?"

"With your brother just down the hall? No, thank you. He's likely to murder me in my bed—your bed."

She laughed again. "Thomas Beresford, I never would have picked you for a prude."

"I'm not. Just . . . this is your brother's house."

"Very well, then." She made a careless gesture. "Stay and flirt with Lady Toffington, then. She seemed very taken with you."

Thomas scowled and muttered something under his breath. "Very well, let's go. But understand me, there will be no . . . joining of giblets."

"No, Thomas." She batted her eyelashes at him and led him upstairs to her old bedchamber.

*   *   *

THOMAS WAS SURPRISED TO SEE EVERYONE AT TABLE WHEN he and Rose came down to breakfast the next morning. They were the last to arrive, and he knew full well why.

It was the usual relaxed meal, with everyone helping themselves from the covered silver dishes arranged on the sideboard. Despite her stupendous effort of the previous night, the cook and her staff had not stinted on breakfast, with a dozen hot dishes to choose from.

He was deciding between bacon, sausages and stewed mushrooms when Rose stood on tiptoe and murmured something naughty in his ear.

"What was that, Rose?" Emm had come up behind them. "Did I hear you say something about giblets?"

"Yes, it turns out Thomas is very partial to giblets in the morning." She smiled guilelessly up at him, her eyes dancing with mischief.

"Really, Thomas? *Giblets?*" Emm cast a doubtful glance at a waiting footman. "I'm not at all fond of offal myself, but I suppose we could ask Mrs. Jacobs . . ."

"No, no," he assured her, darting a quelling glance at his beloved. "This is more than adequate. Is Mrs. Jacobs your cook? She and her staff did a superb job with supper last night. I wonder she can provide us with anything this morning, and yet look at all this." He gestured.

Emm beamed at him. "What a lovely thing to say, Thomas. Most gentlemen don't even notice the efforts of servants. I'll pass on your compliment to Mrs. Jacobs."

The rest of the meal passed in discussion of Thomas's new position and how his cousin would deal with it, but, as without any further facts it could only be speculation, conversation soon passed to gossipy chitchat about other things that had happened during the ball. Since these concerned people Thomas didn't know, he didn't take much notice. He was mentally preparing for the meeting with Cousin Cornelius.

* * *

AT TEN O'CLOCK PRECISELY, GALBRAITH ARRIVED WITH Cousin Cornelius, who presented a sulky face and a put-upon air. His all-white outfit was still pristine—no doubt Galbraith's valet had taken care of him. Wearing white was an odd affectation, Thomas thought. He might have to adopt more practical colors, now that the income of an earl-dom was no longer his to squander.

Thomas still found it hard to accept that he was the earl.

They went to the library, where they were unlikely to be disturbed by the busy servants still working to restore the rest of the house to its usual tranquil state. Thomas had invited Ashendon to be present, not only because it was his house but because Thomas would welcome his impressions. Rose's too, of course, because she was better at reading people than he was.

The enmity he'd initially felt for Ashendon had faded a good deal, and though they were hardly bosom buddies, the man was very sharp. And as Rose's brother and head of her family, he had a right to be kept informed.

Thomas questioned Cousin Cornelius closely, but the man's answers were much the same as they'd been the previous night. He claimed he knew nothing of any ransom letters, seemed genuinely appalled to learn Thomas had been enslaved, and was openly scornful when Thomas tackled him about the regular emptying of his bank account. "Why on earth would I bother with some paltry allowance when I had the income of the whole earldom at my fingertips?"

He had a point.

He also insisted he knew nothing about the continuance of the allowance. "Nothing to do with me. Sounds as if the old man—"

"Uncle Walter or 'the earl,'" Thomas grated. "Show some respect." He felt ashamed now for misjudging his uncle.

Cousin Cornelius huffed. "He never liked me."

"I can't imagine why," Ashendon said sardonically.

Cousin Cornelius pursed his lips. "It sounds to me as if the previous earl had arranged it through one of his little pet projects—he was a soft touch, the old m—earl. Ambrose has had the devil of a time sorting them out. Like a squirrel with nuts he was, accounts and legacies all over the place and no central record."

"Ambrose?" Ashendon leaned forward. "Who's Ambrose?"

"My cousin," Thomas said. "A good fellow."

"Cousin?" Cousin Cornelius sniffed. "I suppose, if you don't count the fact that he's 'wrong side of the blanket.' Personally, I don't recognize the relationship." He turned to Ashendon. "The old m— the old earl got him on some maidservant. Made a ridiculous fuss of him, treated him almost as one of the family."

Thomas nodded. "We grew up almost as brothers, Ambrose, Gerald and me. We did everything together, our lessons as well as running wild on the estate." Thomas smiled, remembering. "They were good days. We three were inseparable until Gerald and I were sent away to school, and after that we all went our separate ways."

"Ambrose didn't go far," Cousin Cornelius said cattily, adding to Ashendon, "He's the estate manager now. Runs everything like clockwork, but"—he made a dismissive gesture—"no conversation. A complete country bumpkin."

Ashendon raised a brow at Thomas in silent query.

"Ambrose?" He considered it briefly, then shook his head. "I can't see it. Ambrose has always been like a brother to me." But Gerald had been like a brother to him, too, and for the last four years he'd had no trouble believing Gerald had betrayed him.

Ashendon said suddenly, "What do you know about marzipan, Beresford?"

Thomas blinked, then recalled he was no longer Beresford. He was Brierdon now, which sounded strange: Brierdon was Uncle Walter. Cousin Cornelius was Beresford.

"Marzipan? What do you mean, what do I know about

marzipan?" Cousin Cornelius said irritably. "What does anyone know about marzipan? You eat it. And why the devil have you dragged me here at the crack of dawn if all you're going to do is throw stupid questions at me?"

Ashendon sat back and, meeting Thomas's gaze, shook his head. Thomas agreed. Cousin Cornelius seemed to know nothing. Either he was innocent, or he was a very good actor. Thomas didn't know him well enough to be sure which.

Thomas stood up. "You can go now," he told Cousin Cornelius.

"Well, I like that! There's gratitude for you. I'm dragged out of the ball—and I was really looking forward to it—locked up like a criminal, then hauled out of bed at some ungodly hour to answer a bunch of dashed ridiculous questions, and then it's 'you can go now.' Not so much as a 'thank you' or a glass of sherry."

"Thank you," Thomas said grimly. "Now go, or else I'll—"

"Push you in a muddy puddle," Rose said brightly. "Good day, Mr. Beresford, or should I call you Cousin Cornelius? I'll show you to the door. What a lovely velvet coat that is. So unusual . . ." She hurried him away.

"What do you think?" Ashendon asked.

Thomas shook his head slowly. "I can't be sure. He could be a damned clever actor—"

Ashendon gave a scornful snort.

"Yes, that's what I think too," Thomas said. "He doesn't seem all that bright to me."

"You don't have to be clever to be ambitious."

"That's true." Thomas had witnessed the cunning of the downtrodden, and the most successful manipulators weren't always the cleverest.

"This Ambrose he mentioned . . ."

Thomas made a face. "I can't see it. Ambrose . . . we were always so close, the three of us growing up. And Ambrose was always a gentle soul. He hardly even leaves the estate. Besides, what would be the point? Ambrose is illegitimate; how would he benefit from my death or absence?

He can't possibly inherit. There would always be an earl, whether it was me or Cousin Cornelius, or whoever is next in line after him. It can never be Ambrose and he's known that practically since birth. So what reason would there be for him to plot against me?"

Ashendon shook his head. "Well, whoever's behind your betrayal, this inheritance is certainly going to disrupt your plans. You won't be able to leave tomorrow."

"Why not?"

Ashendon's expression was sardonic. "Because there will be a hundred papers to sign, all kinds of arrangements to be made—you don't just up and call yourself Lord Brierdon and buy yourself a new hat, you know. There's the devil of a lot of tedious paperwork involved. Believe me, I know."

Thomas shrugged. "I'll attend to it when I come back."

Ashendon frowned. "Why wait?"

Thomas met Ashendon's gaze deliberately. "Because all that paperwork might not turn out to be necessary."

A small distressed sound from the doorway alerted him to the fact that they were not alone. He swore under his breath. Rose was standing in the doorway, her face pale and set. She'd overheard what he'd said. And had immediately understood the implications.

"You mean because you might not come back, don't you? See, I *knew* it was dangerous, and finally you've admitted as much. Thomas, you *can't* go. Please, I beg of you!"

"I made a promise, Rose."

"And what of your promise to me—to love me, and cherish me, and keep me?"

"I'll keep that promise too."

"As long as we both shall live, yes—but what if you're dead, Thomas? What if you're shipwrecked or taken by pirates again? How can you keep your promise then?"

He offered her a smile. "At least this time if I'm captured I'll know who to write to."

"Don't! Don't you *dare* joke about it, Thomas! I won't have it." She dashed angry tears from her eyes. "You're determined to risk your life—and my happiness—our happiness—unnecessarily, and now you try to make light of it?" She glared at him, her eyes swimming with tears, and then whirled and ran from the room.

There was a short silence, then Ashendon cleared his throat. "Got a lock on that cellar door of yours, I presume."

Thomas nodded. "Looks like I'm going to need it."

"What time does your ship leave tomorrow?"

"I need to be on board an hour or so before high tide, to take advantage of the current. High tide is just before two."

"Right then. I'll drop by Bird Street some time after four to let her out."

Chapter Twelve

Defer not till to-morrow to be wise,
To-morrow's Sun to thee may never rise;
Or should to-morrow chance to cheer thy sight
With her enlivening and unlook'd for light,
How grateful will appear her dawning rays!
As favours unexpected doubly please.

—WILLIAM CONGREVE, LETTER TO COBHAM (L. 61)

THOMAS AND ROSE RETURNED TO BIRD STREET. "WHAT will you do when I leave tomorrow?" he asked her. "Will you return to Ashendon House, or will you get Lady George or someone to stay with you?"

"I'm going with you," she said. And went upstairs to pack.

Stalemate again.

Remembering his plan, he went down to the cellar to inspect it. As a storage place for wine and spirits it was quite suitable; as a prison, albeit a temporary one for Rose, it left a great deal to be desired.

He found Briggs, their manservant, and instructed him to sweep the cellars thoroughly, paying particular attention to removing every last spider and cobweb. Rose was not fond of spiders. While Briggs was doing that, Thomas carried down the most comfortable chair in the house and a small side table and arranged them in a hidden corner of the cellar.

He caught Briggs looking at him oddly and said, "I sometimes like to sit and ponder my wines."

"Very good, sir, m'lord, sir." All the servants were thrilled by his elevation and were "m'lording" him at every opportunity. Apparently it reflected well on them.

He fetched half a dozen candles, a tinderbox, a jug of water, a cup, a small wrapped loaf of bread, a knife to cut it with, and a book. He surveyed his preparations and wrinkled his nose. Bread and water was just too prison-ish.

He went back to the kitchen and asked his new cook if there was anything nice to snack on. She filled a tin with ginger biscuits and macaroons, then added a large slice of cake wrapped in waxed paper, and some jam tarts, saying, "There you are, sir, that'll keep you going until dinnertime."

Thomas took the tin down to the cellar. The little hidden corner was looking positively homey now. It wouldn't be too much of a hardship for Rose to be locked in there for a few hours.

He thought of something else, and fetched a large china chamber pot.

Now Briggs really did look at him oddly.

"Might grow herbs in it," Thomas said vaguely.

Then he headed off to finalize his arrangements. He called in on Phipps, Phipps and Yarwood, Rose's family lawyers, to make out his will, leaving everything to her, and to make arrangements to collect the gold the following morning. He called in at his bank to see if anything further had come to light about his stolen money—nothing had. He visited Ollie to thank him for his friendship and assistance.

He came home in quite a gloomy mood.

Rose, surprisingly, was quite cheerful. She was full of plans. "I've only packed my oldest summer dresses," she told him. "No point in ruining my new ones with seawater, and heaven knows what maid service we'll get. See what an efficient wife you have? I'm all packed." She pointed to a neat little red leather case sitting by the front door. "I'm not taking much. I thought it might be fun to go shopping when we arrive in Mogador. They have markets there, don't they? I want to get one of those dresses you told me about that covers everything except the eyes."

Thomas had nothing to say about that. His own bags had been sent to the ship already. He brought down a small, neat valise and set it beside hers. Only one of those bags was going onto the ship, and it wasn't the red one.

"Dinner in fifteen minutes," she said brightly.

"I'll fetch some wine."

"Oh, we don't need any—" she began, but Thomas pretended not to hear. He wanted to check the cellar one last time.

Briggs had outdone himself. The floor looked freshly mopped. Briggs had also apparently taken it on himself to rearrange the furniture. He'd brought in a different chair and laid a small rug in front of it. Thomas didn't see the point of the changes but he didn't care.

He selected a bottle of wine—an excellent vintage for what was possibly their last dinner together—and went back upstairs. The dining room was a picture, with a low floral centerpiece in the middle of the table, flanked by two handsome candlesticks. Silver and crystal twinkled in the candlelight.

Dinner was served. They didn't talk much. There would be no further argument. Their positions had been stated repeatedly, and Thomas was determined to make his last night with his wife a pleasant one.

He told her a few stories about his childhood at Brierdon Court. She told him that in the morning Kirk would be coming past with their horses, as usual. That suited Thomas. He enjoyed those morning rides with Rose and her family and the relaxed breakfasts all together afterward. And it would give him a chance to say good-bye to them all.

It was the closest they came to discussing the future, but it sat heavy and unacknowledged at the table with them.

The new cook had outdone herself, but Thomas wasn't much interested in food. They drank and ate and at the end they rose from the table and with one accord went upstairs to bed.

Their lovemaking then was intense, with an edge of desperation—at least that was how it felt to Thomas. He

was memorizing her, he realized at one point, making sure
he knew exactly how she tasted here, how soft her skin was
there, how her breath hitched just so when he did this, and
how she shuddered and clutched at him, making that little
humming noise she did when he did that.

And when he realized he was going over her like a damned
accountant, trying to save her up for the long lonely days, or
more, ahead—as if Rose could ever be summed up in some
kind of list—he threw his mental notebook away and buried
himself in her, losing himself in her, in the world of their bed.
Alone. Oblivious. Together.

Afterward they lay, spent, sweaty and exhausted in each
other's arms. The curtains were open, and faint light from
the waning gibbous moon cast the room in shades of slate
and silver.

"Thomas?"

"Mmm?"

"You do know that I love you, don't you?"

A thick knot formed in his throat. He tightened his hold
on her.

"You love me too, don't you?"

The knot thickened. He couldn't bring himself to speak,
not to speak those words she craved. They stuck in his
throat.

But she sounded so small and uncertain in the dusky night,
so unlike the bold, funny, stubborn, mischievous woman he'd
married. And he was planning to leave her tomorrow, locked
in the cellar, while he went off to who-knew-what. From
which he might never come back.

But saying such things, opening yourself to those feelings, admitting them, it made a man vulnerable, too vulnerable.

Why did women want the words anyway?

Words were cheap. Words could pretend one thing and
mean another. Words could deceive. Words betrayed. It was
actions that counted, not words.

Words did not matter, he told himself as he covered her
mouth with his and poured his feelings into a kiss.

* * *

THEY MADE LOVE AGAIN INTO THE WEE SMALL HOURS, and slept then. But they'd left the curtains open and were woken by the dawn. They made love one last time, leisurely, lingering over each brush of skin against skin, each touch and caress and taste, as if they had all the time in the world. Refusing to acknowledge the inevitable.

"Kirk will be here in twenty minutes."

They washed and dressed swiftly and in silence, watching each other, not covertly but openly, boldly. She watched him shave. It was almost erotic. He nicked himself twice, failing to concentrate, watching her watching him.

He watched the way she luxuriated in the caress of the hot water, patted herself dry then smoothed fragrant cream into her skin, sensuous and deeply feminine. He sighed as she shimmied into her chemise, a delicious quivering of female flesh, slipped on a thin silk shirt, then buttoned her glorious curves into the tight-fitting jacket of her habit. He took her hairbrush from her and brushed her hair with slow lingering strokes and she laughed and shook it out carelessly, a gleaming golden mane to be tucked under her riding hat.

Memorizing again. He swallowed. Four hours left with Rose. He didn't want to waste a minute.

Kirk arrived with the horses and they set off for the park. The crisp, clear morning was a taunt, carrying the promise of summer. He'd be gone by then. They picked their way through carts and barrows and shouting men and darting boys and escaped cabbages. Market day.

"Is it like this on market day in Mogador?"

"In some ways," he said curtly. "Not in others." A cacophony of vibrant colors and odors and noise and people and animals—the same, only different. Very different. Some of the people wore chains.

"I can't wait to see."

He wasn't going to talk about it. Didn't want to think about it.

They met the rest of Rose's family at the park entrance. "Come on, sluggards, race you!" Lady George yelled, and took off on her spectacular black stallion. And so began a wild race through the park, a mock hunt chasing a girl on a swift black horse and a shaggy gray long-legged dog.

Shouts of laughter, mock threats, pounding hooves, the heat of the horses, the blast of fresh air through the lungs. Thomas gulped it all down. Memorizing.

Finally the mad race slowed and they came to a halt, breathless and laughing. "One of these days you'll get us all banned from the park, George," Lily said, laughing.

"Pooh, you didn't have to follow. Anyway, there's nobody around—nobody who cares, at any rate. All the stuffy people are still abed. I'd go mad if I couldn't have my morning gallop, and so would Sultan and Finn."

"I'm going to water my horse," Galbraith said, and they trotted toward the lake, two by two. Thomas and Rose trailed behind. "I'm going to miss this," Rose said. "But they have wonderful horses in Arabia, don't they? George named her horse Sultan because he's half Arab. She raised him herself, from a c—"

There was a loud bang. It sounded like a gunshot but surely it couldn't be, not in a public park. Thomas looked around but could see nobody. He turned to Rose. "What do you think that w— Rose!"

Under his horrified gaze she tilted sideways and would have fallen to the ground had he not lunged across and steadied her. "Rose!"

She muttered something, and her weight suddenly increased. She'd fainted. The horses shifted restlessly and with some difficulty Thomas managed to free her from her side-saddle and half lift, half drag her across to his own saddle.

She lay across his lap, cradled in his arms, wan and senseless. A dark stain was spreading across the back of her jacket. One-handed he unbuttoned it and pulled it down. The flimsy white silk shirt she wore underneath was saturated with blood.

Thomas ripped off his neckcloth, wadded it up and

pressed it against the bloody wound on Rose's back. It turned instantly red.

"What the devil's going on?" Ashendon rode up. He took one look at Rose and blanched. "Oh, my God. Not again!"

Again? It made no sense to Thomas. "She's been shot."

"I can see that. Get her to Ashendon House. I'll fetch a doctor."

"No, a surgeon in case the ball is still in her."

"I know who to fetch," Ashendon snapped. "Just get her out of here."

Thomas was already moving. His every instinct was to ride like the wind, but he had to keep the pace slow and gentle because to jolt Rose any more would worsen her injury and increase the bleeding.

Her eyelids fluttered and she moaned.

"Stay with me, love. I'm here. You're all right, I have you safe." Nonsense, he was talking utter nonsense. Safe? She was bleeding all over him.

Lily rode up beside him. "Rose, are you all right, Rose?" she called distressfully. She brought her horse up close and took one of Rose's limp hands. "You're going to be all right, Rose. Isn't she, Thomas?" Her eyes were wet with tears.

Rose made a little sound and stirred in his arms.

He kept his voice calm. "I know it hurts, love, but I think it's just a flesh wound. I'm taking you home. You're going to be fine, just fine." Flesh wound? He had no idea what kind of a wound it was. He couldn't tell because of all the blood.

They left the park and entered the traffic. His horse sidestepped suddenly to avoid a piece of rubbish blowing along the road, and Rose gasped and clutched at him.

Her pain burned him. "Hold on, love. Not long now."

"Love you, Thomas." Her voice was a thread.

He wanted to pull her tight, shower her with kisses, force her back to wellness, to wholeness, to turn back time. But all he had were words, useless words. "And I—" he began. But she'd fainted.

Lady George had ridden ahead to warn Emm of the

situation, and when Thomas reached Ashendon House he found them ready and waiting. Rose was gently lifted from his arms and carried upstairs to her old bedchamber. Emm and her maidservant peeled off the blood-sodden clothing and washed the blood away. They soaked a clean pad in vinegar and kept it pressed against the wound. Lily fluttered around, useless in her distress.

Rose barely stirred. She was breathing, at least.

Thomas watched, clenching and unclenching his fists in helpless anguish.

"It looks nasty," Emm told him, "but I don't think it's fatal."

Thomas said nothing. Emm meant well, of course, but what would a gently reared society lady know of gunshot wounds? People died all the time of quite small injuries. A tiny cut on a finger, a scratch from a thorn or a fishhook could turn septic for no apparent reason and suddenly the person was dead.

He bent and smoothed back the tumbled golden hair from the pale forehead. Where the hell was that blasted doctor? Not that he would necessarily help. Treatment by doctors often made no difference. There were no guarantees.

"I'm told my own wound looked almost as bad," Emm said quietly, and he stared at her in shock. With an understanding smile, she touched her shoulder. "Just here. I was shot in the park, too, in mistake for my husband."

The doctor arrived then, and shooed everyone out except for Lady Ashendon and her maidservant. "I'll tend to the patient better without having all you people hanging over my every movement," he said brusquely. "A couple of sensible women, that's all I need. No brooding husbands, no fretting sisters."

Thomas didn't want to leave, but Ashendon drew him aside. "He's good. When my wife was shot, he brought her through it without incident." He coaxed Thomas out into the hallway, fetched a couple of chairs from a nearby room, sat him down and poured him a brandy. Thomas tossed it down in a single hit.

"Lady Ashendon really was shot?" Thomas said when he could talk.

Ashendon nodded. "In the shoulder. Long story, but someone was after me, and shot her by accident."

"And this same doctor treated her?"

"Yes, and she recovered perfectly, as you can see."

A slender thread of hope to hang on to. "Did you get the man who shot her?"

"I did," Ashendon said grimly.

"I don't suppose you saw who shot Rose?"

Ashendon shook his head. "Kirk and Galbraith are scouring the park as we speak, looking for the swine."

Thomas sank his head into his hands. "But why? Why would anyone want to shoot Rose?"

"Could be an accident. Might not have been Rose they were after."

"You think they wanted me? Then curse their bad marksmanship. I'd happily die in her place!" He stared at the closed bedchamber door in frustration. "What the devil is taking them so long?"

Ashendon poured him another brandy.

THE DOCTOR HAD FINISHED TREATING ROSE. "I'VE DONE all I can for her now," he told Thomas, adding when he saw how Thomas had blanched, "meaning I'll come back tomorrow and see how she's progressing. I've removed the ball and we'll see how she goes from there. It's quite high, almost at the shoulder, and no vital organs are affected, and as far as I can tell, no bone was shattered. I have every reason to hope she'll make a full recovery."

Thomas breathed again. "Can I see her now?"

The doctor shrugged. "If you like, but don't disturb her. I've given her something to help her sleep."

"And she'll make a full recovery?"

The doctor held up a warning finger. "I never said that. These things tend to run their own course. All we can do is try to manage it. I've warned Lady Ashendon to expect some fever—that's the worst of these gunshot wounds. There's no way to be sure."

"Then what do we do?"

The doctor sighed. "Wait, and pray. When the fever comes, treat it as you would any fever and hope it breaks quickly."

"And if it doesn't?"

The doctor tutted gently. "Let's cross that bridge if and when we come to it." He picked up his bag and left, promising to return in the morning.

Thomas went in and sat down beside Rose's bed. She lay on her front wedged with pillows to prevent her from rolling onto her back. What he could see of her face was deathly pale, but she was sleeping peacefully enough, from what he could tell.

Ashendon poked his head in. "How is she?"

"Asleep."

"And you're just going to sit there and watch her, are you?"

Thomas frowned. What else could he do? Ashendon beckoned. Thomas didn't want to leave. Ashendon beckoned more forcefully, and Thomas sighed, glanced at Rose, kissed her on the forehead and left the room.

"It's nearly noon," Ashendon said.

Thomas blinked. "So?"

"Didn't you plan to be on your ship by now? You can still make it. We'll take good care of Rose, you can be sure of that."

Thomas stared at him. "Are you mad? I wouldn't leave Rose now for—" He shook his head, unable to think of a way to finish the sentence. "I'm not leaving."

Ashendon gave him a long look. "You're sure? You've been set on this thing as long as I've known you."

"I know."

"You're going to abandon your plan to bring those men home?"

"No." He glanced at the door to Rose's bedchamber. "But I can't leave Rose, not like this."

"So you'll go as soon as she's out of the woods?"

"No," Thomas said slowly. Rose's injury and the hours leading up to it had settled something in his mind. He wasn't going to leave her ever again, wasn't going to put her through that worry. His honor was important to him, and he had no intention of breaking his promise, but a man could learn to bend, couldn't he?

He turned to Ashendon. "Ollie says you 'know people.' Do you know of anyone who could go to Mogador in my place, someone trustworthy, who could track down my men and negotiate their freedom?"

Ashendon's expression was enigmatic. "I don't know of anyone like that."

"Damn."

"But I know someone who might."

THE FEVER CAME THE FOLLOWING DAY LATER IN THE early hours of the night. Thomas had barely left Rose's room—George had given up her bed to him—when he heard the first signs: restlessness and agitated muttering. He felt her forehead; she was burning up.

They'd discussed what to do if this happened, and he soaked a sponge in vinegared water, squeezed it out and began to wipe her down. She moaned and muttered.

"Hush, Rose, you're all right." His voice seemed to soothe her. She turned her face to him.

"Thomas?" But her gaze was blank, unseeing.

"I'm here." He kept wiping her down.

The door opened. "I heard voices. What's happening?" It was Emm. She took one look at Rose and said, "She's delirious," and reached for a cloth.

Thomas caught her hand. "I can manage."

"But—"

"You need your sleep." His gaze dropped to Emm's swollen belly, and he added gently, "You're sleeping for two, remember?"

"Thank you, Thomas," Ashendon said from the doorway.

"She'd take on the world if she could, my Emm." He held out his hand. "Come to bed, my love. Thomas will manage."

Thomas sponged and soothed Rose through the night, giving her the medicine the doctor had left, and sips of the willow bark tea they had brewed in case it was needed. And finally, just after dawn, she started to sweat. The fever had broken.

When Ashendon and Emm looked in that morning, Rose was peacefully asleep, her head on Thomas's chest, his arms around her. Thomas was fast asleep, dried tear tracks on his cheeks.

SEVERAL DAYS LATER, WHEN IT WAS CLEAR THAT ROSE was well out of danger, Ashendon approached Thomas after breakfast. "That fellow I said who might know someone? Turns out, he does. Want to meet him?"

"The fellow who knows people, or the someone who might go to Mogador?"

"Both. He'll see us at eleven."

The "fellow who knows people" turned out to be the Honorable Gil Radcliffe, a man who'd apparently attended their recent ball, though Thomas couldn't recall meeting him. His office was at Horse Guards, which apart from housing the Household Cavalry also acted as military headquarters. Ashendon led him through a labyrinth of corridors with a casual familiarity that was revealing.

Radcliffe was a tall, saturnine gentleman who dressed with a careless elegance. The other gentleman had already arrived before them. He sat quietly in a corner seat. Radcliffe introduced him as Wilmott. From the exchange between Radcliffe, Ashendon and Wilmott, it was clear they knew each other from school.

Radcliffe rang for tea and a few minutes later an assistant brought in a heavily laden tea tray. Radcliffe poured and invited them to help themselves to milk, sugar and ginger biscuits. It was all very chatty and friendly and polite, Thomas thought sourly. Lady Salter would have enjoyed it.

While everyone was fussing over tea, Thomas inspected the man who was supposed to solve his problems. He wasn't impressed.

Everything about Wilmott looked . . . moderate, Thomas thought. Mild of manner, bland of appearance. Of medium height, he was slender, with dark hair and dark eyes. Conservatively though expensively dressed, ordinary and totally forgettable. Not at all the kind of man Thomas had expected—or hoped for.

Radcliffe added milk and stirred sugar into his tea. "Now Lord Brierdon, tell Wilmott about your little problem."

Little problem? Five enslaved men was hardly a little problem.

Thomas explained the task and described what he knew of each man's situation. "But it's been several years—anything could have happened to them: sold on, traded, died. Tracking them down won't be easy. And then once you find them, you will need to negotiate for their release—in effect, to buy them from their current owners."

He looked doubtfully at Wilmott. "You'll need to be a skilled and cunning bargainer. Or find a trustworthy local agent who can do it for you. But I warn you, they're sharks."

Wilmott nodded placidly. "Understood." He took another ginger biscuit.

Thomas could hear him crunching it. He clenched his jaw. This fellow would not do at all. He had no idea. "What do you know about that part of the world?"

Wilmott smiled. "Enough, I assure you."

Thomas doubted it.

Radcliffe pulled out his fob watch. "Well, then, that's settled. Sorry to hurry you along, gentlemen, but I have another appointment in ten minutes. Brierdon, if you could give Wilmott the details of your men, and make arrangements for the transfer of the money—"

"No. This is not going to work," Thomas said abruptly. "I need someone streetwise and tough, a man who can handle himself in a fight if necessary, someone who's well acquainted with the culture and the region and the language, not a well-intentioned tea-sipping Old Harrovian. So thank you, but no thank you." He got up to leave.

"So you doubt me, you son of an English dog?" said a voice in fluent Arabic from behind him.

Thomas whirled around.

Wilmott lifted his teacup, sipped genteelly, set it down and let fly a flood of the filthiest gutter Arabic Thomas had ever heard: a torrent of creative, fluent abuse. If Thomas didn't know better he'd swear that a genuine street Arab was hiding under the table.

Wilmott finished his tirade, smiled blandly at Thomas and reached for another ginger biscuit.

It surprised a long hard belly laugh out of Thomas. Ashendon joined in. Wilmott crunched on his biscuit and Radcliffe looked smug. "Never underestimate my men," he said.

"But how?" Thomas asked. "How does an Old Harrovian learn to speak like the veriest street beggar?"

"Oh, I speak perfect cultured Arabic, too, and I read and write it perfectly," Wilmott assured him. "Also Persian and French. If I need to converse with the caliph or the sultan, I won't shame you, I promise."

"But how do you know all this?" Mention of both the caliph and the sultan heartened him. It sounded as though Wilmott might know something of the political setup in Mogador, as well.

"My mother is an Arab," Wilmott explained. "Her father, my grandfather, is a cunning old devil who was determined his grandson wouldn't grow up to be an effete Englishman. I spent half my childhood with him in his palace in Alexandria, where he had me properly educated in the finer aspects of Arabic culture—history, poetry, mathematics, music and so on—and let me run wild the rest of the time. And during plague season, he placed me with the Bedouin, who educated me in their ways. I adored my times with him and have not yet decided which will become my chosen culture—I can fit seamlessly into both, you see." He dusted crumbs from his fingers. "So, do we have an agreement?"

Thomas held out his hand. "We do."

"Excellent," Radcliffe said. "Now I hate to move you chaps along, but . . ."

They thanked him and left. His assistant conducted them to a nearby empty office where Thomas briefed Wilmott thoroughly, giving him the details pertaining to each man and anything else Thomas could think of that might be useful. Wilmott asked questions from time to time and noted everything down in a little red leather notebook in a script that Thomas saw was neither Arabic nor English.

They then made arrangements for him to collect the gold that would be used to buy the men's freedom. "And of course, you must take a percentage—" Thomas began.

"Nonsense," Wilmott said. "Grandfather would disown me if I took a penny for releasing men from slavery. He has no time for Barbary pirates and despises slavery of all kinds. Besides, I'm not going to Mogador just for you; Radcliffe has another assignment for me there."

Going home in the carriage afterward, realizing his men really did have a good chance of being rescued by Wilmott, it was as if a weight had lifted off Thomas's shoulders.

He looked at his brother-in-law sprawled comfortably in the corner of the carriage, staring out of the window, looking slightly bored. "I have to thank you, Ashendon, for arranging that. I can barely believe that such a man could exist."

Ashendon huffed a laugh. "Radcliffe is a collector of men with extraordinary skills. If he doesn't know the kind of man you need, he'll know a man who knows a man who'll know another man who can do it."

Thomas laughed. "What exactly is Radcliffe's job?"

"Making life interesting for the rest of us," Ashendon said dryly. "And don't you think it's time you called me Cal?"

"Cal?"

"It's what family and friends call me, Thomas. You're family now."

"Since when?"

"Since you put my sister before your heart's desire."

"Your sister *is* my heart's desire."

"I suspected as much."

And why could he say such a thing to Rose's brother when he hadn't yet said it to her? Had the terror he'd experienced at the prospect of losing her shaken his reluctance to speak the words loose?

A little uncomfortable at the intimate direction the conversation had strayed into, they each stared out of their respective windows. After a while Thomas said, "Any sign of the swine who shot her?"

"No. Nor any progress on the investigation into the marzipan poisoning."

"I've been giving some thought as to who this mysterious enemy might be, and I've come to the conclusion that, aside from some random madman, it must be either the duke or Cousin Cornelius; the duke in revenge for us ruining his wedding plans, in which case it's not clear whether the intended target is Rose or me. I suspect either would satisfy him. Cousin Cornelius's motive is both more obvious and more likely. He wants me dead so that he can return to being the Earl of Brierdon."

"Your reasoning is sound. Of the two suspects, my money's on Cornelius." Cal leaned forward. "So, do you have a plan?"

Thomas grimaced. "Not exactly. But I'm not going to stay in London, waiting for whoever it is to try again. As soon as Rose is able to travel comfortably I'm taking her to the country. In London every second person is a stranger, and there's no telling who they might be or what their intentions are. In the country, everyone knows each other and any stranger will stand out."

Cal considered it, then nodded. "A reasonable strategy. You're welcome to stay at Ashendon Hall."

"I thought we'd go to Brierdon Court."

"Why there?"

"I grew up there and I think I'll be welcomed as the earl. Rose has never been to Brierdon, so nobody there could bear her any ill will. And it's to be our future home. Now that Wilmott is taking on the rescue of my men, I need to think about becoming the Earl of Brierdon."

ONCE SHE'D TURNED THE CORNER, ROSE'S RECOVERY WAS rapid. The doctor insisted on a week at least of bed rest, lest she reopen her wound, and it was driving her mad. But everyone was so attentive, so kind, she could not complain. Every day flowers and fruit and books and notes arrived from well-wishers.

She and Thomas had decided to remain at Ashendon House for the duration of Rose's convalescence because of the constantly available company there. Lily came every morning and spent most of the day with her, talking and sewing. George kept her entertained with scurrilous tales of the various callers who ostensibly came to inquire after Rose but were really there to nose out gossip and to meet the new earl.

Finn came too, of course, padding across to place his big muzzle on the bed and eye her lugubriously, silently pointing out that people might be injured but dogs still needed to be scratched behind their ears.

They played cards with her, did puzzles with her, read to her, sang to her, and in general could not have been sweeter. But Rose wasn't used to enforced inactivity, and she was finding it very frustrating.

"Take me out in the carriage, please, Thomas," she begged him one morning, when the rest of her family went for their usual ride. "If I can't ride, at least I can watch them and get some fresh air."

But he and Cal considered it still too dangerous. "We don't know if that fellow is still out there, lurking. And until we know who he is, and who he's after—you or me—we're not going to risk it."

She pouted. "But if you knew for certain it was *you* this horrid man was after, you'd go out riding, wouldn't you? It would be perfectly all right then, because you'd claim you were setting a trap for him. But you can't possibly use *me* as bait—oh, no—because it's too dangerous."

He refused to comment on that, mainly because she was one hundred percent right. He didn't mind risking his own neck but he was damned if he'd risk hers.

The day he met Radcliffe and Wilmott was a day they both celebrated. "So you won't be going to horrid Barbary after all?"

"No, I'm staying here with you, always."

"I'm so glad we're not going to that place. It really would have been dangerous, wouldn't it?"

"Yes. But I wouldn't have let you come with me, you know."

"Oh, and how do you think you could stop me?"

So in the spirit of full disclosure, he confessed his plan.

She bridled. "You were going to lock me in that horrid little cellar?"

"Not for long—don't look so horrified—just until my ship had sailed. Your brother promised to come along in good time to let you out."

"*Cal* knew about this?" she said wrathfully.

He made a placatory gesture. "I needed someone reliable to let you out. And it's not horrid, I had it cleaned out especially, not a cobweb or spider left. I put in a comfortable chair, and even provided you with some food and drink. And a chamber pot."

"A *chamber pot*?" she repeated unsteadily. "Thomas, that's outrageous! Ludicrous! Absurd!"

"What's absurd about a chamber pot? Very useful things. You'd have been mighty put out if you'd found yourself caught short in there without one."

"No, I meant your plan to imprison me in the cellar. How iniquitous! How diabolical!" She darted him a mischievous glance. "How coincidental."

He frowned. "Coincidental?"

She giggled. "I told Briggs to mop out the cellar and put in a comfortable chair and table and a little rug. I was planning to ask you to fetch me some wine just before we were due to leave, and then keep you there for hours, until your ship had well and truly sailed. But"—peals of laughter spilled from her—"I didn't even think of a chamber pot."

A WEEK AFTER THE ATTACK ON ROSE THE DOCTOR IN-spected her wound, pronounced it to be healing beautifully and said she could get up the following day and walk around a little, but told her to keep her movements gentle and undemanding. "Definitely no riding for at least another week, probably two," he said when Rose asked him when she could ride out again.

But Rose had been sleeping badly, partly because she could only lie on her side or her stomach and partly because she kept waking up with dreams of being shot again. Thomas knew what it was to live with nightmares; he still had them, though not as frequently as before—and now that he came to think of it, none at all since he'd sent Wil-mott off.

But once nightmares became a regular thing, it got so that you didn't want to go to sleep at all, for fear of what the night might bring. He didn't want that for Rose. And he thought he had a solution.

After the visit, Thomas drew the doctor aside for a private consultation. He asked his question in a low voice.

The doctor's eyebrows shot up. "You what?"

Thomas explained.

"Bless my soul! Young people, eh?" He removed his spectacles, polished them and eyed Thomas thoughtfully. "I would leave it a few more days yet, but after that, as long as you're not too, ahem, vigorous, I don't see why not." He gave Thomas a stern look. "But the moment there's even the slightest twinge, you stop, young man, understand?"

Thomas was well satisfied with the answer, and he hoped Rose would be too.

Three nights later, he put his plan into action. They'd been sharing the bed ever since Rose's fever had broken, but it was all very chaste and . . . frustrating.

They were preparing for bed, or rather he was. Rose had attendants to prepare her for bed, after which the maids departed and Thomas entered the bedchamber.

Rose spent most days in a loose morning gown with a kind of light wrapper over it to protect her dressed wound. But for bed, in case she accidentally rolled over and rubbed the dressing off, Emm's maidservant wrapped a bandage firmly around her upper body, which effectively bound her breasts almost flat, and then slipped a warm flannel night-gown over her.

Thomas removed his coat and waistcoat, hung them up, then pulled his shirt off over his head. He folded it neatly.

Rose sat on the bed watching him. Lord, but she loved looking at him, so lean and tough and hard with those pow-erful bronzed shoulders and arms, and that firm, flat chest. A purely masculine kind of beauty, leashed power, tough-ness and grace.

"People who think that only women can be beautiful are stupid. Men are beautiful. You are beautiful."

He looked at her a little askance, as if he didn't believe her. "If it weren't for the scars, you mean."

"Even with the scars. What was done to you was ugly, but *you* are not the slightest bit ugly. Far from it." Though she would never say it to him, in her eyes the scars only added to his masculinity.

Seeing the way she was eyeing him, his gaze darkened to a molten pewter-blue. Her pulse leaped.

And then she remembered: she was garbed in half an acre of heavy cream flannel with her breasts bound flat. She might as well be a nun. And she wasn't allowed to lie on her back.

"I don't suppose you have any of those little bits of frothy nonsense from your dressmaker lady, do you?"

She made herself laugh, though she was ready to weep. She wanted him so badly and here she was, all trussed up like an Egyptian mummy. "No, they're all back in Bird Street." She posed and mock-pouted. "You don't think this nightgown is seductive enough?"

His eyes glinted. "You would probably be seductive in an old hessian sack."

"Pooh! I wouldn't be seen dead in a hessian sack! That would be deeply unfashionable. Not to mention itchy!"

Dear Thomas. He was trying so hard to cheer her up. He pulled off his boots and sat beside her on the bed wearing just his breeches.

She leaned against him, breathing in the clean dark masculine scent of his skin. He'd bathed before he came to her, as he did most nights. Her lovely, well-scrubbed Thomas. But he hadn't shaved.

She ran her fingers across his bristled jaw. Oh, but she did love the sensation of his bristles against her skin. Pity it could go nowhere with her in her current useless state. Still, that didn't mean Thomas had to do without. She reached for the fall of his breeches and winced at the sharp stab of pain. "I am so fed up with this wretched injury. I hate it. I can't do anything!"

He turned his head and kissed her, long and lingering, and she felt herself melting beneath his heat, the insistent, intoxicating demand.

"Oh, that was nice." She leaned her face against his chest. "How long before we can get back to normal, Thomas? I'm so tired of having to be patient and not going anywhere and not doing anything—and having to be grateful all the time because everybody is so dratted nice."

"No!" He pulled back in shock. "They're not being *nice* to you, are they? How appalling!"

She laughed weakly. "But it is. So unfair when I'm feeling so cross and crabby and have nowhere to direct it at. I'm a terrible person, I know."

"Poor little crab." He kissed her on the nose and removed his breeches. "Now, shove over, little crustacean, and let me in."

"Such a romantic you are." She wriggled over and he lay on his back on the bed. Like a feast spread out before her that she couldn't have. She pushed at him crossly. "Thomas, you're taking up all the space."

"Sit on me, then." He patted his stomach.

Faintly suspicious, she said, "What are you up to?" But she rose on her knees, having to pull up her nightgown a bit to manage it, climbed over him, and sat on his stomach with a little bounce that made him gasp. "Like that?"

"Oof! Yes, like that."

Her thighs bracketed him. He stroked them, slowly, sensually.

The heat of his body soaked into her and she felt a warm tide of desire rippling through her like a wave. This was a bad idea. She was getting all fired up and to no purpose.

She started to move off him. "I don't think—"

His big hand clamped around her knee and pushed it back. "Trust me." He lay looking up at her, his eyes half closed like a big lazy cat. A big, gorgeous, annoying lazy cat.

"Thomas, I—"

"I said, trust me." He pushed the flannel higher, inching it up along her legs, and the sensation of his big callused hands against the soft inner skin of her thighs . . . She shivered deliciously. He pushed it up over her bottom, cupping and kneading her buttocks, all the time with a knowing half smile lurking in his eyes.

The nightgown lay in folds around her waist; she was wholly exposed to him. He slipped his hand in between her thighs, teasing the nest of golden curls at her apex, then cupping her firmly. Her whole insides clenched. She arched her back, but a warning twinge pulled her back to reality.

"It's no good, I—"

"Let's just see. It's stretching your back or your arms that's the problem, isn't it? So try not moving at all."

"Try not moving—" she began indignantly, then broke off as his fingers moved and the ripples intensified. Her breath hitched in a series of gasps.

She bent to kiss him and the sharp pain of her injury brought her smartly upright again. "Thomas, stop it. I can't."

"Have a little patience."

She glared down at him. "Patience? This is Rose here, not Saint Rose!"

He chuckled. "I wouldn't be doing this to Saint Rose, now would I?" He caressed her slick folds, teasing and stroking, sending waves of sensation through her.

"Now, rise up on your knees."

"What? Now?" She was almost at climax point and her legs had no strength in them at all. But his strong hands held her by the hips and lifted her and she had no choice but to raise herself off him.

He moved and suddenly she felt him, hard and hot, nudging against her entrance. "Thomas?" She looked down at where they were not quite joined.

"Now it's up to you. Slide down."

She blinked, not quite understanding.

"You don't need to stretch out or bend your back, so it shouldn't hurt. Just lower yourself onto me." His voice was a little hoarse, his eyes were clenched shut as if he were in pain. "Ride me."

Tentatively she lowered herself and felt him sliding into her. "Ohhh."

She lifted herself up, and his eyes flew open. "For God's sake, don't stop."

Ah, so it wasn't pain at all. She lowered herself again, feeling the intoxicating fullness slide into her, then rose again. Down. Up. And suddenly she saw what he meant by *Ride me*.

She moved, experimenting with angles and movements. And different speeds. He held her tight around the hips, helping her, guiding her. Keeping her steady, protecting her injury.

She squeezed her inner muscles around him and was rewarded with moaning appreciation, and anguish, and jagged, raw need. Oh, this was glorious. Pleasure rocked through her. She rode him slow at first, then faster and faster until he groaned and gasped and bucked beneath her, thrusting himself upward, hard and hard and hard, and she was riding and he was bucking and it was a fierce, hard, glorious mating.

They moved together as one, driven, oblivious, urgent,

and she sobbed and cried out his name as she shattered into a million fiery sparks and if there was pain, she wasn't aware of it, and his big hands held her safe and lowered her gently until she was lying against his chest.

When she came to herself, she was still lying on top of Thomas, still joined to him, boneless and sated and sublimely peaceful.

His deep voice rumbled through her. "How do you feel?"

She sighed happily. "Glorious."

"Back all right?"

She rubbed her cheek against him like a cat. "What back?"

He chuckled, low and deep. "Crab all gone?"

"Mmm, but what I wouldn't give for one of Mrs. Jacobs's crab patties. I'm hungry, Thomas."

"All right, careful now." He lifted her off him, making sure not to bump her injury, and slipped out of bed. He tucked the bedclothes in around her, took a banyan from a hook behind the door—it was one of Cal's—and said, "I'll be back in a few minutes."

"Where are you going?" she asked sleepily.

"Hunting for crab patties, what else?"

She smiled. "A midnight feast? My hero."

Fifteen minutes later Thomas returned with a leg and thigh of cold chicken, a wedge of cheese, a couple of slices of bread, some grapes and two jam tarts. "I couldn't find any crab patties," he began, when a gentle ladylike snore alerted him to the fact that his beloved was sound asleep.

"Oh, well." He bent and kissed her gently. She stirred. "Mmmm, giblets," she murmured.

As he sat down to his own midnight feast, he glanced at Rose peacefully sleeping. An appetite was a wonderful thing.

Chapter Thirteen

❧

We understand death for the first time when he puts his
hand upon one whom we love.
—MADAME DE STAËL

THE ENTRANCE TO BRIERDON COURT WAS VIA AN ANCIENT
gatehouse of unusual design; two houses joined by an ornate
arch. "When I was a boy, Old Newling lived in that one and
his son, Young Newling, who was about seventy, lived in the
other," Thomas told Rose as the carriage pulled up.

A venerable ancient emerged and peered shortsightedly at
them. "It's Thomas, Mr. Newling," Thomas said. "Thomas
Beresford."

"It is not," the ancient responded briskly enough, though
his voice was suspiciously husky. "You're the Earl of Brierdon now, and don't you forget it, young Thomas!"

He peered in at Rose. "And this be our new Lady Brierdon, I'm guessing. Welcome to Brierdon, m'lady, welcome.
A long time since Brierdon Court's had a mistress, and
never one so bonny, I'm thinking."

The old man turned back to Thomas and his rheumy old
eyes filled with tears. "Welcome home, lad, I mean m'lord.
We're all that pleased you're back with us again. T'was a
turrible day when we heard you was dead, turrible. Tears
throughout the length and breadth of Brierdon, there was."

He pulled out an ancient, grimy handkerchief and blew loudly into it. "Get along then, m'lord, m'lady. Mr. Ambrose be expecting you." He waved them through the arch into a long driveway lined with ancient oaks.

"Now that's what I call a welcome," Rose said softly as the carriage moved on.

Thomas nodded awkwardly and didn't reply. He couldn't, Rose realized from his expression; he was too deeply touched by the old gatekeeper's heartfelt and unexpected welcome, a welcome that combined familiarity, respect and a fondness for the boy the old man remembered.

Yet this was the place Thomas thought he didn't have the right to call home, didn't have the right to turn to when he returned to England—after years of unbelievable hardship and loneliness—with nothing; no money, no family, no home—nobody who cared about him.

This old man cared, and he was no relation.

The drive curved around a bend and there it stood, Brierdon Court, ancient and beautiful, built of local stone aged through the centuries to a mellow gold. It was low, double storied, with a carved stone parapet running the length of the house. Two wings spread on either side of a graceful columned entrance, each with a double line of big mullioned windows. Currently they were ablaze with fire, reflecting the setting sun. Half a dozen steps led up to the front door.

"Thomas, it's beautiful."

He nodded silently, his lips pressed tight together, still battling with emotion.

Rose knew from the way he'd talked about this place how much he loved it, but he hadn't so much as mentioned it until after he'd learned he was the earl. Perhaps because he never truly felt it was his home, that he didn't truly belong here. That he didn't have the right to call it home.

Well, now this lovely old house belonged to Thomas and no one could deny him.

The carriage pulled up, and two grooms ran out. The front door opened and a plump, bespectacled man of about thirty came running down the stairs.

"That's Ambrose," Thomas told her.

"Thomas, welcome, welcome." He embraced Thomas, talking nonstop. "I couldn't believe my eyes when I received your letter last week. To think that after all these years of believing you were dead and gone, you turn up alive and well! It's a miracle, a dream come true. A nightmare ended."

As Thomas turned to help Rose down from the carriage, Ambrose exclaimed, "And of course, you're married. This must be your lovely wife. Welcome to Brierdon Court, Lady Brierdon. I am your husband's cous—" He broke off guiltily and turned to Thomas. "You don't mind my claiming the connection, do you, Thomas? Or would you prefer I call you Lord Brierdon?"

"You will call me Thomas, as you always have, cousin."

"And you must call me Rose," Rose told him. She linked her arms with both men, and together they entered Brierdon Court.

"Are you tired? Would you like to refresh yourselves? Holden, the butler—you won't know him, Thomas, he's only been here a few years—and Mrs. Holden, his wife who is also the housekeeper, are waiting to meet you. Holden will introduce you to the rest of the staff."

Thomas turned to Rose, a question in his eyes. They'd taken the journey in easy stages so as not to aggravate her injury, but any long coach trip was tiring, and London to Gloucestershire was, by anyone's reckoning, a long trip.

"I'm not in the least tired," she said immediately. "And I'm looking forward to meeting everyone."

"I'm glad," Ambrose said. "I'm afraid your predecessor wasn't willing to be introduced to any staff except the butler. He, um, had certain attitudes about what was suitable for the earl, and meeting underlings wasn't one of them."

Thomas and Rose exchanged glances. The implication was that Cousin Cornelius had also regarded Ambrose as an underling. Rose recalled that he hadn't recognized the blood relationship between them, either. Harsh, when in fact Ambrose was closer in blood to the old earl than

Cornelius was. But then illegitimacy was an uncrossable barrier.

"He did his best," Ambrose added tactfully. "But he wasn't really up to the task. Not interested in the estate at all. Such a relief that you are home to take up the reins, Thomas."

"Oh, that's right, I ought to make an appointment to go over the books with you while I think of it," Thomas said.

Ambrose laughed. "I wasn't hinting, though of course whenever it suits you, you're most welcome. But give yourself some time to relax, show your lady around the estate while this fine weather holds. The books aren't going anywhere and there's nothing urgent that I can recall. If there is, I'll bring it in at breakfast."

"You'll join us for breakfast, then, as you used to?" Thomas said.

"No, no, very kind, I thank you, but these days I prefer to break my fast in my own cottage. I'm an early riser and like to get a lot of my work out of the way before breakfast. But I'll stay for dinner tonight, if you're asking."

Dinner was a relaxed affair, with excellent food and easy talk, Ambrose encouraging Thomas to reminisce and tell Rose tales about their shared boyhood. "We're not boring you, are we, Lady Brierdon?" he asked several times.

"Not at all, I'm enjoying learning about my husband's misspent youth." Rose laughed. "And please, call me Rose."

"I think we're going to be very happy here," Rose said to Thomas as they went up to bed that night. "I've got one of Aunt Dottie's 'feelings.'"

WORD MUST HAVE SPREAD ABOUT THOMAS'S ARRIVAL because it wasn't long before they were inundated with visitors—calls from the local gentry, cards and invitations and people simply dropping by on the off-chance.

Everyone wanted to meet the new Earl and Countess of Brierdon, to congratulate Thomas on his ennoblement and marriage and to exclaim about his apparent death and miraculous return.

Many people also wanted to express in subtle—and sometimes quite blatant—terms their delight that Cousin Cornelius was no longer the earl.

"Not really at home in the countryside," was the vicar's gentle summing up.

"A most elegant gentleman," said one lady, "but not One Of Us."

Her husband snorted. "Called himself a hunter. Wore a pretty pink coat and turned up on a very showy mount." He snorted again. "Rode with all the grace of a sack of potatoes."

"One of they demmed useless fancypants macaronis," the elderly gamekeeper said, spitting on the ground to punctuate his remark. "Savin' your presence, m'lady," he added belatedly, much to Rose's amusement.

Three days after they'd arrived, Cal's groom, Kirk, and another groom arrived, leading Rose's gelding, Midnight, and a magnificent black stallion whose noble lineaments proclaimed his superior breeding. "What a superb creature," Thomas exclaimed, running his hand over the horse's gleaming flanks. "Whose is it?"

"M'lord sent a letter," Kirk said, and handed over a sealed note. Thomas broke it open and stared blankly at the writing inside.

"What does it say?" Rose asked. Thomas passed it to her. In Cal's distinctive scrawl it said:

Saw this fellow at Tattersalls the other day and thought he might suit you.
We never did get you a wedding present.
From Emm, me and the family.

                                        Yours etc. Cal.

She glanced at Thomas and saw he was stunned by the gift. Dear Thomas, he expected so little and deserved so much.

"Isn't he splendid! What are you going to call him?"

But Thomas was too overcome to speak. He kept running his hands over the horse, getting to know him, letting him snuffle down his front, and feeding him chunks of an apple he had in his pocket.

Rose rubbed her own horse's nose affectionately. "Yes, Midnight, he's very pretty, but you're still my favorite. Can we take them out for a ride today, Kirk? Or will they be too tired from the journey?"

Kirk was his usual phlegmatic self. "I'll give them a drink and a rubdown and a good feed of oats, m'lady. Come the morning, they'll be ready for your morning ride."

"Bucephalus," Thomas said at last. "I'll call him Bucephalus, after the brave horse ridden by Alexander the Great."

After that they rode out every morning, taking a different direction each day. While the beautiful weather held, Rose was determined that Thomas would have a holiday. There was no need for him to bury himself in estate matters, and besides, it was obvious the property was in good condition and Ambrose was doing an excellent job.

Time enough when the weather confined them to the house for Thomas to turn to the books and Rose to redecorating the interior of the house.

One aspect of redecoration, however, couldn't wait: The walls of almost all the public areas of the house were adorned with the heads, horns and antlers of dead animals. With glass eyes that either followed Rose around the room or stared balefully at her. She set a couple of manservants to clearing them out, room by room.

"But what shall we do with them, m'lady?" one of the men asked.

"Whatever you like. I don't want them in the house." Emm had done the same at Ashendon Hall, and the effect was wonderful, Rose remembered. Much lighter and happier. She enjoyed venison, but not with a deer's head staring reproachfully at her.

Thomas approved. He hunted, but only for food, not for sport. "George would like that about you," she told him.

The next few weeks sped past. Each morning they rode

out, and wherever they went, tenants and local villagers came out, giving them a warm welcome, greeting Thomas like one of their own returned to them by the grace of God.

At first they hung back shyly, not wanting to bother the earl, but of course, Thomas being Thomas, he saw and spoke to them all.

He'd left this place when he was sixteen, she recalled, and had gone to sea, and yet he was remembered—and with fondness. And not just because he was the earl. Rose was welcomed as their new countess, and also as Thomas's wife. But Thomas was liked for himself, though he showed no awareness of it.

Wherever they went, people came shyly forward, pressing simple but heartfelt hospitality on them, along with small gifts of eggs, honey, cakes, biscuits, a mug of milk or mead or a tankard of home-brewed beer. And to talk to Thomas and tell him how glad they were he'd returned to them.

Thomas was stunned by the welcome. To Rose, he tried to laugh it off, to hide how deeply moved he was. "Oh, they're just glad they don't have to deal with Cousin Cornelius." But she knew better.

"It's not just because he's the earl, is it?" Rose said to Ambrose one afternoon. "They really seem to like him for himself. Even though it's been more than ten years since he lived here."

Ambrose nodded. "Thomas always did have the gift of seeing people, not simply their role. He listens and he always did, even as a boy. The old earl and Gerald always had a touch of 'high and mighty' about them, as if they were doing people a favor by speaking to them. Thomas never did," Ambrose told her. "People remember that, and when they speak to him now they see that inside the man, he's still that kindhearted boy. So yes, it's genuine, the regard these people feel for him. It's not just for the position he holds."

He said it with a touch of sadness, or perhaps a little envy, and it occurred to Rose that though people referred to

Ambrose often enough in conversation, and did it with respect, there wasn't that edge of fondness for him that was revealed in their attitude to Thomas.

This was what Thomas needed that Rose's fortune could never have provided—to be needed, to have a home, and to have a role that meant something. The people here looked up to him. Ambrose was a good estate manager, but Thomas was a natural leader. Their leader.

The days were long, lazy and golden. Day by day she saw the tension in Thomas visibly lift. They rode out, revisited many of Thomas's boyhood haunts, explored the estate and made love long into the night. And again in the morning.

And if he didn't say the words she longed to hear, he showed her in so many ways that she was precious to him. So she tried not to mind when she told him she loved him, and he replied with a kiss, a glorious, soul-stealing wonder of a kiss. But no words.

It made her a little sad, though she told herself it shouldn't.

He was damaged, he'd told her, outside and in. The damage to his body had healed itself, but the scars still showed. The damage to his soul, his heart? That wasn't so clear.

She felt sure that deep down inside himself he did love her. And it was the scarring inside that prevented him from saying so.

And if she told herself that enough times she might even be able to accept it.

In the meantime, it was foolish to repine over the lack of three little words when everything else in her life was so wonderful.

"This place is the garden of Eden," Rose declared as they rode home at the end of another happy day.

Thomas, looking ahead, slowed. "Don't look now, but I think we're about to meet the snake."

Two carriages had pulled up at the entrance of Brierdon Court. Two extremely fashionable young gentlemen were supervising the unloading of a mound of baggage from the second coach. A third gentleman was draped feebly over the stone balustrade. A fourth gentleman complained in a loud, petulant voice; he was dressed entirely in delicate shades of blue.

Cousin Cornelius had arrived.

"THERE YOU ARE, THOMAS," COUSIN CORNELIUS DE-clared peevishly, as if he'd spoken to Thomas an hour ear-lier, not several weeks before. "We've been kept waiting out here in this horrid weather for eons, simply eons."

Given the state of his horses, "eons" looked to be all of ten minutes.

"We were traveling to Perce's country place for a house party—that's Perce over there arguing with the coachman, a complete ruffian, I assure you!—the coachman, not Perce—but my good friend Venables took sick just past Cheltenham—that's Venables, with the greenish pallor." He pointed to the wan-looking fellow. "And I thought, whatever shall we do? And then I thought, Cousin Thomas will take us in, and so here we are. But your man Holden is proving quite obdurate, and insisting we wait until his lord-ship returns—which is ridiculous. I mean, until a few weeks ago I *was* his lordship!"

"But you aren't anymore," Thomas reminded him. He would happily have thrown Cousin Cornelius back into the street. His turning up here out of the blue was not at all convenient, and more than a tad suspicious.

"I am still your heir, however," Cornelius pointed out waspishly.

Thomas's eyes narrowed. Was Cornelius still hoping to fulfill that role? When Thomas had a wife who would pre-sumably one day bear him an heir?

"Mr. Beresford demanded that this gentleman and his belongings be taken to the blue room, m'lord," Holden in-terjected. "I tried to tell him that m'lady would want to make the arrangements, but he refused to listen."

"I recall nothing about any—"

"Indeed I do, quite right, Holden." Rose slipped grace-fully from her horse and passed the reins to a waiting groom. "How do you do, Cousin Cornelius, gentlemen. Mr. Venables, you do look poorly. Mrs. Holden will have a room prepared for you directly." She glanced at Holden, who inclined his head graciously. "In the meantime, please come in out of the . . . the sunshine."

With the long skirt of her riding habit draped over her arm, she swept inside like a queen, the visitors following meekly like little baby ducks. She ensconced them in the only room still displaying a distressing number of animal heads and antlers. She ordered drinks and refreshments, informed them that their luggage was being transferred upstairs, their carriages removed, their horses seen to and dinner ordered. A servant would conduct them to their bedchambers when they had been prepared. Dinner, she informed them, was at seven. She swept out, leaving them to their own devices.

Thomas regarded her with awe and admiration. "I *knew* there was a reason I married you," he said. "You know, if you'd been born a boy—which would have been an appalling tragedy, by the way—you would have been an admiral by now."

She laughed. "Cal says the same thing, only with him I would have made general. But it's what we're trained to do—be hostesses. And I learned from the best—Emm. Mind you, she would be shocked at my cavalier treatment of guests, but we don't want them here, do we, Thomas?"

"Not at all. I can't decide whether Cornelius really is here by accident or simply wants to puff off his former consequence before his friends—the sour grapes are very evident. As for reminding everyone that he's my heir . . ."

"Rather tactless, I thought."

"Tactless, or very clever—assuming an innocent air."

"Perhaps he's simply availing himself of free accommodation. His friend's illness does seem genuine."

"But very convenient. The sooner we get Venables on his feet again, the quicker we'll be rid of them. I don't like Cornelius hanging around like a bad smell. And I'm not yet convinced he's not behind the attacks. Nobody can be that foolish—it's a blind."

"You think so?"

"I don't want you to be alone with him," he told her.

"But surely the attack on me was a mistake? Why would he want to kill me?"

Because even now she could be carrying his heir, Thomas thought. But he didn't say so. "Just beware of him. I don't trust him an inch."

COUSIN CORNELIUS AND HIS CRONIES, PERCE AND MONTY, soon wore their welcome—grudging as it was—very thin. By day they entertained themselves, riding around the estate—Cornelius acting as if he still owned it—and hunting, though what they could hunt in the middle of the day, Thomas had no idea.

"I don't like them wandering the countryside with guns," Thomas said, "but if it keeps them out of our hair . . . Just make sure you're not out when they are."

They continued their morning rides, because Cornelius and his friends rarely arose before noon.

Their guests played cards and drank themselves into a stupor each night. Rose very correctly left the gentlemen to their port at the end of each meal, and after one glass, Thomas excused himself and joined Rose, leaving them to it.

Even so, they made themselves obnoxious, complaining that life was deadly dull in the country. They complained constantly and were endlessly demanding. Even too-sick-to-travel Venables managed to achieve offense from his sickbed.

Mrs. Holden consulted Rose about him. "Ringing that bell of his a couple of dozen times a day, he is, m'lady. The maids have been running up and down stairs all day and night, and all for the most trivial of reasons; his water glass needing refilling—and the jug not six inches away, his sheets needing to be smoothed, his pillows plumped."

"I'll have a word with him," Rose promised.

Mrs. Holden hesitated, then continued in a rush. "And that's not all. I caught Lucy coming out of his room all rumpled and flustered this morning—and she's a good girl, Lucy, and wouldn't encourage that sort of thing. She says he has hands like an octopus, and the other maids agree. I did try to speak to him, m'lady, but he came across all innocent and kept saying the girl made a mistake. But I could tell he was laughing up his sleeve at me."

Rose stiffened. "I will do more than have a word with him," she declared wrathfully. "From now on, Mrs. Holden, Mr. Venables is to be attended only by a manservant—one manservant, the biggest, meanest, ugliest one you can find. Someone who won't put up with any nonsense. And make my apologies to Lucy and the other girls for the trouble they've been put to."

She marched up to Mr. Venables's room. "It has come to my attention, Mr. Venables, that you've been pestering my maids. This will stop. If you discompose any of my staff again, in any way whatsoever, you will be dumped out on the highway before you know it—and I don't care if you're dying!" She frowned. "Actually, if you're pestering the maids, you're obviously well enough to travel. I'll speak to my husband about it."

Ignoring the man's babbled excuses, apologies and justifications, and his assurances that he was indeed almost at death's door, she swept out.

She told Thomas about it later that day, and to her surprise he sent for all the servants to assemble in the hall. The atmosphere was tense and they whispered nervously among themselves as they waited for him to address them.

He also ordered Cousin Cornelius and his two friends to attend. They flounced in late and sat with their backs half turned away, as if it demeaned them to be addressed in the company of servants.

Rose sat at the front, facing the audience. Ambrose, who had also been asked to attend, sat quietly at the side, his expression quietly curious.

Thomas held up his hand for silence, then spoke. "It has

come to my attention that some of our houseguests have been pestering some of you."

Ignoring the outraged huffs from the guests and the low murmur of surprise from the servants, he continued. "I want you to know that I will not stand for this. No servant in my employ is to put up with any untoward, unfair, unwelcome or bullying behavior from anyone else under this roof, whether they are fellow servants, guests or the king himself. Is that understood?"

There were nods and murmured "Yes m'lords" all around.

Cousin Cornelius and his cronies rose. "Well, really, this is the outside of enough," Cornelius declared. They stalked from the room, the picture of offended dignity. The servants exchanged glances, and a low murmur followed.

Thomas continued, "Anyone who feels threatened or distressed in any way is to speak to Mr. or Mrs. Holden, or if you feel uncomfortable about telling them, come directly to me or Lady Brierdon. I promise you, we will investigate the matter and act on it. Agreed?"

At the chorus of agreements and nods, he dismissed them.

They filed out, leaving Thomas, Rose and Ambrose alone. Ambrose looked stunned. "I never thought I'd hear an Earl of Brierdon speak like that on behalf of servants."

Thomas lifted a careless shoulder. "I doubt any previous Earls of Brierdon were slaves and understood what it is like to live at other people's mercy. Or lack of it."

Ambrose stared at him for a long moment, his complexion ashen. "A slave, Thomas?" he repeated weakly. "Is that what you became?"

Thomas nodded. "It changes you."

Later Rose said to Thomas, "I thought Ambrose's reaction was a little strange, a little extreme, didn't you?"

He shook his head. "No. Ambrose's mother was a maidservant."

THE IDYLLIC WEATHER WAS COMING TO AN END. THE LAST few days had been dry but overcast, but as Thomas and

Rose came in from their morning ride, a damp wind brought spatters of intermittent rain.

"Looks like this afternoon might be a good time to begin going over the books with you," Thomas told Ambrose. Despite the weather, Cornelius and his cronies, showing a surprising resilience, had headed out after luncheon, dressed to the nines in their hunting outfits.

"Or were you going out?" he added, noticing that Ambrose was wearing a thick outdoor coat, hat and leather gloves.

Ambrose grimaced. "I was, as a matter of fact. The gamekeeper told me our friends have bribed a couple of the local lads to dig up a badger's sett."

"A badger's sett?" Thomas frowned. "For baiting, you mean?"

"I'm afraid so." He screwed up his face in a distasteful expression. "Cornelius organized a badger baiting here last year. I despise such sports, as you know, but—"

"It's not sport, it's carnage. Setting a pack of dogs onto an innocent animal. It's obscene."

Ambrose's expression softened. "You always did like badgers, didn't you?"

"Where is this sett?"

"I can deal with it, Thomas."

"No, I will. It's my responsibility." And he doubted Cornelius would listen to Ambrose. "So where will I find this sett?"

Ambrose thought for a minute. "Remember the old hide you and Gerald used to use?"

"At the edge of the clearing near the big old oak?" Thomas said, recalling a giant tree that was several hundred years old.

Ambrose nodded. "That's the one. The sett is just near there. In fact, you could probably see it from the hide, though heaven knows what state that's in after all these years." He added thoughtfully, "I should probably have it pulled down. Don't go into it, Thomas, I'm sure it's dangerous."

Thomas nodded. Animal baiting sickened him and the thought that Cornelius had dared to arrange anything of the sort without a word to Thomas—and on *his* land, with *his* badger—had set his temper blazing. He grabbed his coat and hat and headed out.

He found the hide without any trouble; it had been a favorite haunt when he was a boy. It didn't look in too bad a shape. He scouted around and found the sett. There was no evidence of digging. Good, they hadn't caught the badger yet.

His cousin's unlikely braving of the elements earlier was a dead giveaway; he'd be coming here this afternoon with the local boys to dig out the hapless sleeping badger.

Thomas would catch them in the act. Let Cornelius try to wriggle out of that.

He glanced at the hide. It didn't look nearly as dangerous as Ambrose had said, but then Ambrose always had been the overly cautious type. Thomas opened the rickety door at the back and stepped inside. Dead leaves and cobwebs, mainly, and some ancient animal scat. Nothing to worry about.

The hide faced out to the clearing and gave an angled view of the location of the sett. There was even an old wooden box that would make a convenient, if grimy, seat.

He was about to settle down to wait when he decided it would be better to relieve himself first, rather than get caught short at an inconvenient moment. Cautiously, in case Cousin Cornelius was close by, he slipped from the hide, took himself to a nearby tree and began to unbutton his breeches.

CRASH!

Thomas whirled. The hide was no more; a huge branch had crashed down onto it, reducing it to a pile of splintered matchsticks.

He stared at it in shock. A moment earlier and he would have been inside it. Dead. Squashed like a beetle.

He heard a faint crunching sound in the distance. Footsteps? He looked around but saw nobody. He moved cautiously forward, skirting the fallen branch, looking upward at the tree from which it had fallen. And saw a smooth cut with a jagged finish.

He examined the fallen branch and found a rope tied to it.

The accident was no accident. Tie a rope around a branch, then use a saw to cut the branch almost all the way through. Wait until Thomas was in the hide, then pull down on the rope, causing the last bit to break.

He swiveled around, scanning the surroundings, all senses alert. The culprit had to be lurking close by; they would have to remove the rope so it would look like an accident.

Cornelius knew how he felt about badger baiting. He'd set this whole thing up.

"Cornelius!" he roared. "Come out, you filthy coward."

But only the wind answered.

Thomas stormed back to the house. "Where's Cornelius?" he demanded as he entered the house. "Cornelius!"

Rose came running. "Thomas, what is it?"

"That swine Cornelius just tried to kill me!"

"Are you all right?"

"Yes, he missed me, but where the hell is the villain? Cornelius!" he roared again.

Holden emerged from the servants' area. "I think he and his friends were going to the village, m'lord. To the public house. There's a skittles match on. They'll be betting, I'm guessing."

"Skittles match? I'll give him skittles match." Thomas stormed out.

He arrived at the public house, strode into the taproom and peered through the fug. "Where is he? Where is that weaselly little rat?"

"Would you be meaning your cousin, my lord? Mr. Beresford?" the landlord asked politely.

"That's the one."

The landlord gestured. "In the private sitting room, my lord. He and his friends don't like to mix with the likes of us."

"And we don't like to mix with the likes o' they," someone called from the corner. There was a general laugh.

Thomas threw open the door to the private sitting room and found Cornelius seated with his two friends, playing cribbage at a table by the fire.

"There you are," he snarled.

Cousin Cornelius jumped. He eyed Thomas nervously. "Is something the matter, cousin?"

"Cousin? Second cousin twice removed, is it not—"

"Once," Cornelius muttered.

"As far as I'm concerned, that's not damned well removed far enough," Thomas snapped.

There was a muffled sound from the landlord, who had followed him in. Thomas turned around with a savage look, and the landlord's face became instantly blank.

Thomas turned back to Cornelius. "How dare you!"

"Dare what?" Cornelius said nervously.

"Firstly, you tried to arrange a badger baiting on my land. With one of my badgers."

"No, I didn't."

Thomas said in a voice loud enough to be heard by the ears no doubt pressed against the door, "All animal baiting is from now on forbidden on this estate; no badger baiting, no bear baiting or anything else of that kind. Is that clear?" Not a peep was heard from outside, but the landlord nodded.

"But you're wrong about me," Cornelius insisted. "I did organize one last year, it's true, but I didn't realize what it was going to be like. It was horrid, hideous, disgusting." He shuddered. "Never again."

Thomas was inclined to believe him. "Secondly," he said in a lowered voice, "you tried to kill me this afternoon."

"*Kill* you?" Cornelius's eyes almost popped from his head. "I didn't, I swear I didn't. This afternoon, you say? I couldn't have. I've been here all afternoon and haven't moved." He gestured to his friends. "Tell him, Perce, tell him, Monty." His friends frantically concurred.

Thomas glanced at the landlord, who nodded to confirm

it. "Hasn't left the place since he arrived a good four hours ago, my lord."

"See, Thomas?" Cornelius began in an aggrieved tone. "I think you owe me an apol—" He broke off, seeing Thomas's expression. He held up his hands pacifically. "No, no, it's nothing. Don't owe me anything, Thomas. Never said a word to you. Was talking to Perce here who owes me a monkey, don't you, Perce?"

Perce nodded.

"See, Thomas? No offense taken and none given, I hope." He gave Thomas a sickly, placatory grin.

Thomas leaned over their table and in a steely soft voice said, "I've had it with you. You and your friends are leaving first thing in the morning, Cornelius."

"But Venables—"

"Can die in a ditch for all I care. Ten o'clock and you're out of here."

"Ten? But that's an outrag—"

"Nine then."

"But that's even more inhum—!"

"Eight o'clock. And if you're still here by five past eight, I'll have you and all your belongings thrown into the street. Understand?"

"Yes, Thomas."

SO IF CORNELIUS HADN'T TRIED TO KILL HIM, WHO HAD? Thomas worked it out on the way back from the village. Ambrose. The thought made him sick to his stomach.

It couldn't be. His oldest living friend—or so he thought. He had to be mistaken.

But he knew he wasn't. Why else would he tell Thomas that Cornelius had bribed some village boys to dig up the badger's sett if it wasn't true?

There was no answer to that.

The case against: He'd specifically warned Thomas against going into the sett.

Knowing full well that such a warning would prompt Thomas's curiosity.

It had to be him. There was no one else.

But why? The question pounded uselessly at Thomas's brain. *Why?* What good would Thomas's death do him? There was no advantage that Thomas could see.

Did he hate Thomas? Had he hated him all these years? And if so, why?

He'd always considered Ambrose his friend. His cousin. His only living relation, apart from Cousin Cornelius.

It dawned on Thomas with sickening certainty that it must have been Ambrose who sent those letters, purporting to be from Uncle Walter and Gerald. Condemning Thomas to life as a slave.

The memory of Ambrose's chalky complexion when Thomas had mentioned his slavery came back to him. *A slave, Thomas? Is that what you became?*

Had he not realized the power of those damned letters? He must have. Surely.

It was Ambrose. Ambrose had condemned him to slavery. Ambrose had sent the poisoned marzipan. He must have shot Rose in mistake for Thomas. And today he had tried to crush Thomas with a doctored tree branch.

The realization was devastating.

But the question remained: *Why?*

Chapter Fourteen

❧

Nobody can tell what I suffer! But it is always so. Those
who do not complain are never pitied.

—JANE AUSTEN, *PRIDE AND PREJUDICE*

ROSE WAS WAITING FOR HIM WHEN HE REACHED THE
house. "Well?"

"He didn't do it."

"Then who did?"

"Ambrose."

"Ambrose?" She stared at him in shock. "Are you sure?"
He nodded.

"But why?"

"That, I can't even guess at, but I'm going to confront
him about it now."

"Shall I come with you?"

"No." He kissed her. "This is one thing I must do on
my own."

He went to Ambrose's house and knocked on the door,
but there was no answer. He peered in the windows, but it
seemed deserted. He tried the door, just out of frustration,
but to his surprise it opened.

"Ambrose?" he called out. It seemed wrong to intrude
upon the man's home, even when it belonged to him. Even
when the man had—it seemed: his heart still struggled

against it—tried to murder him several times. And didn't apparently mind if he got Rose by mistake.

The door to the estate office was closed. Thomas opened it and looked in. All neat as usual. But a folded note sat on the desk, on top of a pile of ledgers. It bore his name. He opened it.

I'm sorry, Thomas, more than I could ever say. But these books, dull as they are, will tell the tale.

> *Ambrose*

Thomas glanced at the pile of books. Account books. Was that what it was all about? Money?

Where was Ambrose? He was starting to worry. Thoughts of suicide were loitering at the edge of his mind. He refused to entertain them.

He returned to the main house and questioned the servants. The Holdens hadn't seen him for a few hours. "He went out just before you did this afternoon, m'lord. I haven't seen him since." Went out, no doubt to pull down a great branch on Thomas's head.

Thomas went to the stables, half expecting to see his cousin dangling from the rafters. "Mr. Ambrose, m'lord?" one of the grooms said in answer to his question. "He took the good carriage and four out, mebbe about an hour ago. Took a portmanteau and a little trunk as well. Saw him pack it."

"Any idea where he was going?"

"Don't know, m'lord, but old Mr. Newling at the gatehouse would know whether he turned right or left."

"Good man," Thomas said. Ambrose had taken the traveling chaise and four horses, which meant that he'd be traveling at speed. "Saddle my horse and bring it up to the house, as quick as you can."

He raced back to the house. "He's gone, taken the good carriage," he told Rose. "I'm going to follow him."

"But it'll be dark soon. It's dangerous to travel at night."

"If I don't go now, I'll never find him. I'm only an hour

behind him." He glanced at the sky. "It's a few hours yet to sunset and there's twilight for thirty or forty minutes after that."

"But you don't even know where he's gone."

"Old Mr. Newling will know which way he turned. If it's left, he's making for Cheltenham and possibly London after that. If he turned right, he's heading for Bristol."

"Bristol? You mean the port?"

He nodded. "My guess is he's planning to leave the country, and the quickest way to do that from here is to catch a ship from Bristol. Leaving at high tide tonight, unless I miss my guess."

"I'll come with you."

"No, you can't ride to Bristol in that flimsy—though admittedly very fetching—dress, and I don't have time to wait for you to change. Ambrose could leave the country in a matter of hours, and if nothing else, I have to know why he's done these terrible things." As he spoke, the groom ran up with his saddled horse. "Here's my horse now. I'm off. Don't worry." He kissed her, a hard, swift possessive kiss.

"But what if he has a gun?"

"I know how to take care of myself." He leapt lithely onto his horse and galloped down the driveway.

ROSE WATCHED HIM TURN THE CORNER AND DISAPPEAR from sight. "Saul," she called to the groom who was walking back to the stables. "I gather Mr. Ambrose took the traveling chaise."

"Yes, m'lady."

"What other carriages are left? I'm going to follow his lordship."

He wrinkled his brow, thinking. "There's the old master's carriage. Creaky old thing it is, but. Probably fall apart if you hit a bad bump, m'lady. And there's the dogcart, of course, though that's missing a wheel at the moment."

Rose stamped her foot in frustration. "Isn't there anything else?"

"Only Lord Gerald's curricle."

"Lord Gerald's curricle?" she exclaimed. "Does it have all its wheels?"

"There are only two wheels on a curricle, m'lady."

"I know that, but are they both working? Is the curricle fit to drive?"

"Yes, m'lady, but you can't go off in Lord Gerald's curricle."

"Why ever not?"

"Because you're a lady, m'lady. A sporting curricle is not a fit vehicle for a lady."

Rose clenched her fists and breathed in a deep calming breath. "Hitch your fastest pair to the curricle and bring it around."

"But m'lady—"

"Just bring it around, Saul." She hurried upstairs to put on something warm. The mood Thomas was in, he was likely to kill Ambrose. And if he did . . . Oh, Lord. She prayed she'd be in time to stop him.

THE PALE PEARLY TWILIGHT WAS JUST STARTING TO FADE when Thomas rode into Bristol. He'd made good time. Like his namesake, Bucephalus showed stamina as well as speed.

Thomas knew the Bristol docks well; he'd sailed from Bristol on his last ill-fated naval voyage. He made his way to the wharves where he thought Ambrose would most likely be headed. His nostrils flared as he scented the sea, mixed with the other smells of the docks; oil, fish, sweat, spices, rotting wood and more.

The last shreds of twilight rewarded him when he spotted a familiar-looking traveling chaise and four tired horses, drawn up close to the wharf entrance.

He dismounted and looked into the carriage. Empty. No sign of Ambrose or any groom. Blast the man, was he just going to leave his exhausted animals to their own devices? Their sweat was still wet; they hadn't been here long.

Farther along the docks he could see the usual flurry of

activity that accompanied a ship getting ready to sail. He tied Bucephalus's reins to the carriage and grabbed the attention of a passing boy, the kind of lad ubiquitous to the seafront, alert to any opportunity. "Here, lad, if you mind my horses—those ones over there—and fetch them some fresh clean water, I'll pay you well."

The boy looked him over. "How much?"

"A gold sovereign. Half a crown now, and the rest when I come back."

The boy's eyes bulged. "A yellow boy? You're on."

Thomas tossed the boy a half crown. "I don't suppose you saw the man who came in that carriage, did you?"

The boy nodded. "Geezer carryin' a portmanteau and a little trunk. Went along there." He jerked his chin.

"How long ago?"

"Coupla minutes."

Thomas went in search of Ambrose, praying he hadn't already boarded his ship. He searched. It wasn't easy—the wharves were a blaze of light where the work was going on, studded with pockets of intense darkness where no lights were needed.

At last he saw him, standing waiting in the shadows. The ship's master must be making the last-minute passengers wait until the cargo was loaded. Thomas would have missed him except that his silhouette stood out against the light farther along the wharf. Thomas approached him stealthily.

"Ambrose," he said when he was a few feet away.

His cousin started violently, grabbed his luggage and tried to run, but he tripped and went sprawling. He scrambled to his feet and reached again for his luggage, but Thomas put his foot on the smaller piece, the little leatherbound trunk.

Ambrose stared wildly around, then pulled a pistol from his pocket. "Give me that trunk."

Thomas shook his head. "Not until you've explained."

"Isn't it obvious? I'm leaving. What more explanation do you want?"

"I want to know why, Ambrose. Why you've tried to kill me, several times. Why you left me to rot in that Barbary hellhole."

"Because I needed to get out, go someplace else, get away from that god-damned place. Travel."

"Get away? From Brierdon? But I thought you loved the place."

"I hate it. I always have."

Thomas was stunned. It was the last answer he'd expected. "But you could have left any time you wanted. I never knew you wanted to travel."

Ambrose snorted. "You never asked."

"Surely you knew I would have helped you. The three of us were always so close, more like brothers than cousins."

"When we were children, perhaps, sharing the same tutor. But it was an illusion. You and Gerald were sent away to school, and even though I was clever and worked hard and did well at my books, I was kept at Brierdon and given to the old estate manager to learn his job. Nobody ever asked me if I wanted to go away to school. I did, desperately."

"I didn't realize."

His voice was bitter. "Why would you? It was always understood that I would take over and manage the estate on Gerald's behalf—well, you and I both know that Gerald cared only for his poetry and his painting."

Thomas nodded.

"And then when you were sixteen, and it was clear that Gerald would be going to Cambridge, the earl asked you what you wanted to do."

Thomas remembered. For him, as the son of a younger son, the choices were to enter the church, take up politics or become a military man. And since Thomas's father was a navy man, Thomas chose the navy.

"So again, you two went away, on your chosen paths, traveling the world, meeting new people. And me? I was clever, but did I get the chance to go to a fine school? Or attend university?"

Ambrose gestured angrily. The pistol barrel glinted, catching the light of a lantern. "Nobody ever considered that *I* might want to go to university. Gerald frittered away his time there, painting and scribbling—dabbling, he had no real talent, we both know that—and drinking away the nights with his friends. I would have killed for the chance he had to study at university."

Interesting choice of words, Thomas thought.

"Nobody ever asked me what I wanted to do. Nobody considered the bastard son might have dreams of his own, oh, no. My ordained place was at Brierdon, serving the needs of Brierdon, doing what I'd been trained for from birth."

His words and the bitterness with which he spoke them hit an unexpected chord in Thomas. *Doing what I'd been trained for from birth.*

"I asked my father once for leave to go and travel—to see something of the world—and you know what he said? He laughed, and told me the day I walked off the estate was the day I left it forever, that I'd have to find work for myself. He told me he wouldn't give me a reference. Or a penny extra. Or take me back. That if I ever left, I'd be on my own—forever."

And he was Ambrose's *father.* Thomas was shocked. He'd never much thought about the relationship between Uncle Walter and his illegitimate son. He'd always treated Thomas with careless kindness—of course he'd favored Gerald in all things, but that was natural because Gerald was the heir. But Thomas had assumed Uncle Walter had treated Ambrose much the same as he'd treated Thomas. Apparently not.

"All those letters you used to send from strange and exciting foreign places. I'd never even been to London until last month."

"Last month?" Thomas narrowed his eyes.

Ambrose sighed. "Yes, I fired that shot at you in the park. I'm sorry. Hitting Rose was an accident. It frightened me."

It frightened *him*? The sympathetic feelings Ambrose's explanations had aroused in him drained away.

"I suppose it was you who sent us poisoned marzipan."

"Yes, though I gather it didn't work." He sounded irritated, rather than regretful.

"It worked all right," Thomas said grimly, remembering the sight of young Peter sprawled on the cobblestones in his own vomit. "It almost killed a young worker in our house." And it could so easily have been him or Rose.

"But you didn't eat any!" It sounded like an accusation.

"No, I don't like marzipan."

"You used to love it. I remember you scoffing it down as a boy." He sounded aggrieved.

Thomas's voice was hard. "You're missing the point, Ambrose. What if my wife had eaten it?"

"Oh, I would have been very sorry about that," Ambrose assured him. "She's a lovely girl, Rose. No, no, it was you I intended it for."

Thomas stared at him incredulously. Did the man not care that he'd endangered others? Apparently not. "But why try to kill me in the first place? I never did you any harm in my life."

"Thomas, don't you understand? It wasn't about you, it was about me—it's always been about me."

He gestured with the pistol. "I was the eldest son, and I got nothing. Nothing. The old man forced my mother—did you know that? *Forced.* It wasn't her choice to have a babe out of wedlock—she was a decent girl, a virgin before your uncle had his way with her—but she had to live with the shame of it every day of her life.

"And was *he* ashamed of what he'd done? Not a bit—he thought himself a devil of a fine fellow, siring two strong sons six months apart. And oh, didn't he pride himself on his generosity in taking me in, his base-born brat, and raising me to be useful in the service of the family? Yes, *useful.* I did everything. And my reward? Oh, I got a house to live in, and was fed and clothed and shod—but none of it was mine. Payment?" He snorted. "I was paid a pittance, because what did I need money for? Everything I needed was provided—as long as I stayed in my place, doing my job, like a good little well-trained bastard."

His story struck a chord deep in Thomas. He'd known some parts of it as a child, and had accepted it then with a child's understanding. Now, as an adult, a man who'd suffered his own injustices, he gained a new perspective on Ambrose's situation. Some of his anger began to drain away.

"I had no idea . . ."

Ambrose's voice was bitter. "No, once you grew up, you never thought of me as a man, did you, with my own dreams and desires. I was just a boy you used to know, your uncle's steward. And then Cornelius's. And then I was yours—handed down like a piece of property."

Thomas swallowed. It was true. A thought occurred to him. "Did you kill my uncle? And Gerald?"

"No, Gerald really did die of cholera in Italy. And the earl broke his neck of his own accord—though admittedly he'd been drinking and was more reckless than usual. It was losing Gerald, and then you, that finally got to him. He kept saying, over and over, that he'd lost everyone, his whole family. As if I weren't standing right there in front of him, his own flesh and blood."

He considered that for a moment, his pistol drooping, forgotten. "If I'd known back then that you were still alive, none of this would have happened. You were always more reasonable—you would have listened, I'm sure. But when Cornelius inherited I realized I would be trapped forever. You know, I asked him to increase my pay and he refused."

"Cornelius is a fool."

"Yes, he is a fool and lazy with it, and that's when I realized that he was never going to check the books, never going to take an active part in managing the estate."

"And so you started helping yourself."

"Yes, at first it was just helping myself to your allowance—I never stopped it. Cornelius didn't know about it. It was so easy."

"You forged my signature."

Ambrose shrugged. "You know I was always good at drawing—better than Gerald if you want to know the truth. And I had some of your old letters and a couple of old documents. It was easy to copy your signature."

"You wrote those letters refusing my ransom, too."

Ambrose nodded. "That was easy. The earl often got me to sign unimportant documents on his behalf. And I had some of Gerald's old letters—not that anyone on the Barbary Coast would know whether a signature was genuine or not. But by then I had the house seal. For some reason foreigners set great store in an impressive seal."

He seemed quite proud of his cleverness, Thomas thought savagely. Had he forgotten who he was talking to? What he was boasting about? The "cleverness" by which he'd sentenced Thomas to a life of slavery.

Thomas's fists knotted. He shoved them into his pockets. Much as he itched to thrash the smugness off his cousin's face, this was not the time to lose his temper.

"When I realized what a lazy sod Cornelius was, I came up with my plan—to amass enough money to enable me to buy land and make a start elsewhere. And by the time that letter arrived, saying you were alive and demanding ransom, I was too deep in to stop. I'd had a taste of freedom, and started to amass enough money to start a new life."

Ambrose must have seen something in his expression. "I'm sorry, Thomas, but I was up to my neck in embezzlement by then, and I knew if I brought you home, you'd discover it pretty quickly. As I expect you did earlier today, if you looked at the books. I wasn't happy about leaving you there, I assure you." He shrugged. "But it was you or me."

Thomas gritted his teeth. "So you left me to be a slave in a foreign country for the rest of my life."

Ambrose gestured indifferently. "I never really thought about it. I wasn't thinking about you, I was thinking about me. If you came back I'd be ruined."

His lack of concern for what he'd done, the ease with

which he'd sacrificed his cousin, his boyhood companion, stunned Thomas. Had he ever really known this man?

"I might have understood, might have given you a decent portion."

"I wasn't prepared to risk it. Now I suppose you're going to fight me, have me hauled off to prison, or transported. Well, I warn you, I won't go easy." He lifted the pistol and trained it on Thomas.

There was a long silence, broken only by the distant sounds of men shouting and talking as they loaded cargo.

It would not end like this, Thomas decided. He'd lost all desire to kill Ambrose, but he wasn't going to forgive him either. And he wasn't going to let him get away with his ill-gotten gains, for whom so many innocent people had suffered.

He eyed Ambrose and his gleaming pistol. When had Ambrose ever stood up for himself except in some sneaky, backhanded manner?

Thomas began to walk toward him.

Ambrose backed away, his pistol wavering. "No closer, or I'll shoot. I will, Thomas. I will!"

"No, you won't." Thomas kept walking. "You're not going to shoot me, Ambrose, not face-to-face and in cold blood. That's not the way you operate. And we might be relatively unobserved at the moment, but the instant that gun goes off this place will be swarming with people. You know you'd never get away with it. You'd hang for certain then."

In three swift steps he reached Ambrose, grabbed the pistol, wrenched it from his grip and tossed it into the sea with a splash.

"Don't hurt me," Ambrose whimpered, and cringed away from him.

Thomas's mouth twisted in disgust. "I'm not going to fight you, Ambrose. Don't get me wrong, I'd like to strangle you, and if you'd managed to hurt Rose, I would kill you now. But she's unhurt, and I'm free, and so, against my better judgment, I'm going to let you go."

Ambrose frowned and glanced around uneasily. "What's the catch?"

"No catch. I owe you, the family owes you an apology at least for the way you—and your mother—were treated."

"I don't understand."

"I can't speak for what happened before you were born, but I did think of you as a brother—or at least a cousin, growing up. You never gave my situation in Mogador a thought, but I realize now that I never gave your situation much consideration either. You should have been asked what you wanted to do. You should have been given choices, as Gerald and I were. You should have been given a handsome wage for all the work you've done on behalf of the estate. And because you were my uncle's son."

Ambrose narrowed his eyes. "You do understand that I've embezzled a substantial amount."

Thomas shrugged. "I don't know the precise amount, but the estate can bear it."

"I tried to kill you."

"You didn't succeed. But you almost killed my wife, and that I won't forgive. So get on that ship, do what you will, live the life you've always dreamed of living, but don't ever come back. If you do, I'll have you charged with attempted murder."

"You won't make it stick. There's no evidence it was me." He was right, but his certainty was infuriating.

"Then I'll kill you myself. I warn you now, I'm this close to killing you anyway for what you've put me and my wife through." He held up his thumb and finger.

Thomas still itched to give Ambrose the hiding of his life, to beat him to a pulp, but he knew once he started he might not be able to stop. And killing Ambrose wouldn't change the past, wouldn't take away the suffering he'd caused.

But killing him would most definitely ruin Thomas's future. He wasn't about to lose everything he'd gained in the last few months for the sake of some petty revenge.

Besides, he'd learned something tonight. They said *to*

understand was to forgive. Thomas wasn't ready to forgive, not by a long shot, but . . .

"You're letting me leave? I don't believe it." Ambrose stepped back, scanning the surroundings suspiciously, as if expecting the shadows to disgorge a dozen armed men.

Thomas said, "You think I don't understand what you've just told me, about being trained from birth to be useful to the family? About being prevented from living the life you chose? About having no choice? I do. I understand it more than you can imagine. Now don't test my patience any longer. Leave this country and never come back. If you do, there will be a warrant waiting for you."

Ambrose hesitated and glanced down at the small trunk at Thomas's feet. "I'll just take my trunk, then."

Thomas bent and picked it up. "No, that stays here." The weight of it confirmed his suspicion that it contained the ill-gotten gains, the money that Ambrose had tried to kill him for, and had almost killed Rose and a young boy for. He would let Ambrose escape with his life, but he was damned if he'd let him take the money as well.

Ambrose hesitated, as if considering whether to fight Thomas for it.

Thomas hefted the trunk onto one shoulder. "You exchanged my life for this money," he told his cousin. "Now I give you yours." He turned his back on his cousin and walked away.

Something moved in the shadows. Thomas tensed.

ROSE STEPPED INTO THE LIGHT. "YOU'RE LETTING HIM GO? Just like that?"

Thomas blinked in surprise. "Rose? How did you get here?" He glanced around as if in search of an answer.

"I drove," she said impatiently. "Don't change the subject, Thomas. You're letting Ambrose go, after all he's done?" She'd overheard the last part of the conversation between Thomas and his cousin and was hopping mad. After all Ambrose had done—he'd tried to kill Thomas three times! And that after sentencing him to a lifetime as a slave! She wanted him punished, boiled in oil, strung from the rooftops. At the very least beaten to a pulp.

But she understood perfectly well why Thomas wouldn't do it. She knew all about his fight with Cal and how it had ended. Ned had told Lily, who'd told Rose. Still, he could have him arrested.

"Why did you come after me?"

"I thought you were going to kill him. Which I would have understood perfectly—except that then we'd have to flee the country." She shook her head. "Don't look so surprised, my love—I couldn't let you hang for murder. But I don't understand, Thomas, why are you letting Ambrose go? He ought to rot in prison at the very least."

There was a short silence. "It's complicated," he said at last.

"It's not complicated to me."

He shook his head. "Let it go, Rose. I have my reasons."

As far as Rose was concerned, it was a wholly inadequate answer. She gazed up at him. His face was in partial shadow, dimly illuminated by distant lanterns farther along the wharf, but there was a world of pain in his eyes. The knowledge that the last person in his family left alive, the one person he'd always trusted and loved, had plotted and schemed so cold-bloodedly against him—for money!

A lump formed in her throat. *Oh, Thomas.* So much suffering caused by that evil little worm, and Thomas was prepared to forgive him.

I warn you now, I'm this close to killing you anyway for what you've put me and my wife through.

She understood why he hadn't killed Ambrose, and was grateful for it. But to let him walk away, untouched? Impoverished but unharmed, in what was almost forgiveness?

Because that was Thomas, her noble, wonderful Thomas. She ached for all the pain he'd suffered and taken inside himself. She loved him and trusted him, and if he'd decided to let Ambrose go, she would respect his decision.

But Rose was not nearly so noble. Nor so forgiving.

Ambrose still stood at the edge of the wharf, watching them. He was going to get on a ship and sail away. "I'll just have a quick word with him," she said, and before Thomas knew what she was about, she ran up to Ambrose. "Cousin Ambrose, I understand you're leaving the country? So suddenly?"

His mouth gaped open in surprise. He darted a suspicious look behind her, but Rose hurried on in case Thomas was behind her and would try to stop her. "I just wanted to bid you good-bye, and give you a little something to remember me by." And with that she smacked him as hard as she could across the face. She followed it with a good hard kick to his shins. How providential that she'd worn her sturdiest boots.

He hopped around, swearing. "What the devil—?" Rose smacked him again. Harder. And then kicked the leg he was hopping on.

"Good-bye and good riddance," she said, and shoved him as hard as she could off the edge of the wharf. There was a loud yell and a large splash.

Rose turned and found Thomas behind her. "Your cousin fell in the water," she said innocently.

"So I see."

They peered over the edge of the wharf. In the dark they couldn't see much but they heard a lot of swearing and splashing.

"Can he swim?" Rose asked.

"Unfortunately, yes—we all learned together as boys. But that water is really filthy. It contains all the effluent of the port and surrounds."

"Oh, so he'll be filthy, too? What a shame. He's quite the dandy, your cousin Ambrose." She looked at the portmanteau still standing on the wharf. "I suppose he'll need his other clothes then." And she tossed it in after Ambrose. It must have hit him, because as well as a splash she heard a yowl of pain or outrage, Rose wasn't sure which. Nor did she care. She turned away from the water and linked her arm with Thomas's. "Now, shall we go home?"

"So, you'd flee the country with me, would you?" he asked as they walked back. He sounded surprised. "If I'd killed him, I mean?"

"Of course I would, Thomas. How could you think otherwise?"

After a moment he said, "But you'd miss your family, terribly."

"I know. I would hate not seeing them." She hugged his arm tightly. "But you're my family too, Thomas. My husband, who I love very much. And whither thou goest . . . Always." •

They walked on in silence. A small part of Rose ached, because again he hadn't said it. She shouldn't need him to speak the words, she told herself. Actions spoke louder than words, and his actions ought to be enough for her.

They *were* enough for her. Thomas was protective, supportive, and affectionate. And he made love to her like a dream. He was a wonderful husband. It was foolish to cry for the moon as well.

They reached the place where they'd left the horses and found Thomas's urchin horse-guardian arguing fiercely with Kirk, the Ashendon groom.

"This big Scotch bugger was tryin' to pinch your horses," the boy said as soon as Thomas got near enough. "But I stopped him."

"I wasna trying to steal them," Kirk began with asperity. "I was checking to see—"

"I watered 'em, din't I? Just like the man tole me to. *And* I rubbed 'em down with a bit of straw."

Thomas repressed a grin. "Thank you. You did a fine job. You may hand responsibility over to Kirk now."

"You know 'im?" said the urchin suspiciously.

"I do. Here's your money. You did a splendid job." He handed the boy a gold sovereign.

Kirk blinked. "A yellow boy, just for minding your horses?"

"He prevented you from stealing them, didn't he?"

Thomas said mildly, and walked over to the curricle. He placed the small trunk on the floor and turned to Rose. "You drove the curricle?"

"If you tell me it's not a vehicle for a lady, Thomas, I'll scream. First Saul and then Kirk—he insisted on coming with me—"

"For which I'll thank him later." He lifted her into the curricle and climbed in after her. He called to Kirk, "We'll spend the night at the White Hart in Broad Street. There's a livery stables close by. If you don't know the way, I'm sure our friend here will guide you for a small fee."

"Half a crown," the urchin said immediately.

Leaving Kirk and the boy haggling over the price, Thomas picked up the reins and moved off at a walk—the horses were very tired.

Rose slipped her arm through his. "You don't mind, do you, that I hit your cousin? I just couldn't let him leave without giving him a piece of my mind."

"I know." They left the docks area and headed into town. Thomas wasn't sure that he could explain his decision to let Ambrose leave, unpunished. It had been an impulse of the moment, but the more he thought about it the more he felt it was the right thing to do. Even though it went against everything he believed. Or thought he believed.

The man had tried to kill him three times at least, by poison, shooting and tree branch. He'd forged Uncle Walter's signature and sentenced Thomas to a life in slavery. He'd embezzled money from the estate he was employed to administer. On all these counts he deserved to be imprisoned, if not hanged.

"I hadn't planned to let him go. I was all ready to drag him back and make him face justice. But there's no evidence that it was him who tried to kill me, and shot you and poisoned Peter."

"Didn't he admit it?"

"Freely—to me, in the dark, with no witnesses. But that won't hold up in court. We could get him for the embezzlement—that was the reason for it all—to cover up the fact that he's been stealing from the estate—and me—for the past four years."

"And the bank account mystery?"

"Yes, that was him, too."

They turned into Broad Street and made their way toward the White Hart Hotel. "He'd be jailed, or most likely transported for the forgery and embezzlement, but that's all."

"Better than nothing." She looked at him thoughtfully. "But you're saying that it's not worth pursuing him for the sake of justice?"

Thomas didn't respond. They consigned the horses to the care of the hotel ostlers, booked rooms for themselves and for Kirk, ordered dinner for three to be served in their respective rooms, and went upstairs.

Rose didn't pursue the matter. Thomas was disturbed enough by what had happened with Ambrose. And they were both tired. A good night's sleep was what was called for.

The next morning they made their way back to Brierdon, a much more leisurely drive, sparing the horses who had performed so valiantly the day before. It being a fine, clear morning, Rose and Thomas decided to take the curricle with Bucephalus tied on behind—a position the horse made clear he did not like. Kirk followed with the chaise and four.

"Now," Rose said when they were out on the road and clear of traffic, "tell me the real reason you let Ambrose escape."

He glanced at her. "I don't know if it will make any sense to you. It barely makes sense to me." He drove on for a few minutes, then started to speak. "It occurred to me, as we were talking last night on that dark wharf, that Ambrose had been a slave, or as good as one. Bred by my uncle on one of his servants—he raped a maidservant, who then bore him a son. My uncle took that son in and trained him, almost from birth, to serve the family.

"I never realized it until now, but Ambrose was never given a choice, never given the freedom to decide his future. And right up until my uncle's death, he was kept dependent on my uncle in order to do his job." He looked at her. "That's how slaves in other countries are treated. I saw it. I lived it."

"And you think it's the same thing?" Rose couldn't see it. Ambrose didn't have any whip scars. He'd lived a fine life as far as she could see.

"He wasn't treated with the kind of brutality I experienced, no. And I don't think my uncle would have recognized it as a kind of slavery, and neither did Ambrose, though from his bitterness about his life, I'm sure he felt it. But when you've lived slavery, even for a short time as I did, you recognize it."

"And so you let him get off scot-free?" She wasn't as good a person as Thomas. She wanted Ambrose to pay.

"I let him leave with his life. He doesn't get to keep the money he stole. He can start a new life. Jailing him would have been—well, it might have been justice by some people's lights, but I couldn't have lived comfortably with it."

That was all that mattered, Rose decided. If Thomas was satisfied she would try to be.

"I'LL TELL YOU SOMETHING FUNNY ABOUT THIS PLACE UP ahead," Thomas said as they approached a small village. "It's where Jemmy Pendell comes from. His wife was the hardest one to track down. We knew he was from Newport, but as it turns out there are quite a few places in England called Newport." He broke off, frowning. "Is that horse trotting oddly?"

She looked. "I think it is."

"Blast, I think it's lost a shoe." He slowed the horses to a walk. "I hope this place has a blacksmith."

"You were saying, about Newport," she prompted. "Jemmy Pendell's wife lives here?"

"Yes, we searched the country far and wide, through

several towns called Newport, and it turned out she was right on my doorstep. I never even realized this little place was called Newport, and yet I've driven through it a dozen times heading to Bristol from Brierdon."

There was a coaching inn ahead and he pulled in. An ostler ran up and Thomas stepped down to consult with him.

"I'll just stretch my legs," Rose said. Mrs. Pendell lived here.

When Thomas had told her about his men, she'd felt for all the wives who had, like Rose, for the last four years believed themselves to be widows. She felt especially for Mrs. Pendell, who, if her husband was only nineteen, must be even younger. And she'd had a baby on the way when he left.

She wandered into the taproom and found a woman mopping the floor. "Do you know a Jemmy Pendell?"

"Aye, used to," she said. "Went to sea and drownded, he did."

"I'm looking for his wife."

"His widow, you mean. Lives up there with Jemmy's old granfer. House at the end of the lane." The woman ushered her through the yard and pointed to a small stone cottage.

Rose strolled up the lane and found a neat, plain cottage in a garden bursting with vegetables, fruit and flowers, mainly roses. Not an inch of space was free of something either productive or pretty. It was both practical and charming.

Rose knocked. A pretty young woman answered the door. "Yes? Can I help you?" A small piquant face peeped out from behind her skirts. A little girl, about three years old, with wide blue eyes.

Something caught in Rose's throat. If her baby had lived it would be about this little girl's age.

"I . . . I was just admiring your roses," she said, because of course she couldn't admit her real reason for coming.

Mrs. Pendell looked heartbreakingly young to be a widow, and wore a drab, faded purplish gray dress that washed all the color from her face. Poor people couldn't afford to buy new clothes in black when they were bereaved;

they simply dyed all their clothes black. And after a few washings, the black turned into this drab purplish-gray. The little girl was dressed in the same dreary gray.

"I'm sorry, I should introduce myself, Lady Rose Brierdon. And I wondered, could I buy some of your beautiful roses?"

Mrs. Pendell's eyes widened. She bobbed an awkward curtsey. "Oh, m'lady, I couldn't sell them. You're welcome to have them for nothing."

"I wouldn't dream of it," Rose said firmly. "But I would love some." She waited. Dreadful manners, but she'd had an idea.

"Well, if you insist . . ." the young woman said uncertainly. She produced a pair of shears from inside and walked around the garden, cutting roses. The little girl followed, picking daisies from the grass verge and handing them to Rose.

"My grandfather-in-law grows the roses and he'll be right sorry he missed you. His pride and joy, them roses." She gave a little laugh. "He'll be cross with me for selling them. He says roses come from God and should be given away for love, not money."

"A lovely thought but not very practical," Rose said. "I couldn't help but notice, are you a widow?"

She nodded. "Four years now we lost my Jemmy at sea." She indicated the little girl. "Suzy never knew her da."

"She's a lovely child."

"That she is." Mrs. Pendell rumpled her daughter's curls fondly. The lump in Rose's throat grew.

"That's perfect," Rose said when a dozen roses had been picked. She gave the young woman a ten-pound note.

"Oh, no, m'lady, I couldn't accept that—it's far too much."

"Nonsense. They'd charge more than that in London. Besides I don't have anything smaller."

"Then take them for nothing, please, I couldn't—"

"I have an idea," Rose said briskly. "I was once a widow too, and I cannot bear to see a pretty young woman such as yourself—nor a dear little girl like yours—dressed in widow's weeds, especially as your mourning period is well and truly over. It would please me greatly if you used some of this money to make yourself and Suzy a pretty dress in your favorite color. You do sew, don't you?"

"Of course, m'lady, but I really couldn't accept—"

"Please," Rose said. "It would make me so happy." She put her hand on Mrs. Pendell's arm and added in a coaxing voice, "Wouldn't you like to see this little darling in something pretty for a change?"

The young woman's eyes filled with tears. "I would. Thank you, m'lady," she whispered.

"Good. Next time I come through here I'll expect to see you both wearing something pretty. Promise?"

Mrs. Pendell gave her a misty smile. "I promise."

"I HAD A NICE LITTLE WALK," ROSE SAID TO THOMAS AS they drove out of Newport, her arms full of roses. "Horseshoe all fixed?"

"Yes. Where did you get those?" His eyes grew dark with suspicion. "Rose, you didn't go looking for Mrs. Pendell, did you? It would be cruel to get her hopes up."

"As if I would do any such thing, Thomas." She lifted the roses and inhaled the scent. They really were superb.

She glanced at him. He was back to worrying about his men, she could tell. She hoped there would be some good news soon.

THE LETTER FROM WILMOTT CAME TWO WEEKS LATER. Thomas seized it with trepidation, scanned it rapidly and gave a shout of joy and relief. "He's done it! He's tracked them down. My men are coming home."

He seized Rose around the waist and whirled her off her feet. "They're coming home!" He set her down, dizzy and laughing, and picked up the letter again. "Wilmott says, '*By the time you read this they'll be on their way, making for*

Southampton on a ship called the Aurelia. *I'm sending this letter by an earlier ship in the hopes that you'll get it in time to meet them when they arrive.*'"

Rose had never seen him quite so elated. The unfettered relief in his eyes was an indicator of just what a weight he'd carried all this time, as if he didn't deserve true happiness while the men he'd promised to bring home remained in captivity. "I'm going, Rose. I'll leave today."

He rang the bell for Holden and ordered the traveling chaise to be prepared.

He made no mention of taking Rose with him, and though she would have loved to go, to witness the men's reaction when they reached their native shores at long last, after years of hopelessness she recognized that this would be a private moment, a bonding experience that only they should share. To have a stranger there, however well intentioned, would only inhibit them.

So she helped Thomas pack his bag and sent him on his way with a kiss and a smile and a heart full of love.

Chapter Fifteen

❦

It isn't what we say or think that defines us,
but what we do.
—JANE AUSTEN, *SENSE AND SENSIBILITY*

THE *AURELIA* DOCKED AT SOUTHAMPTON ON A COOL, GRAY, drizzly morning. Thomas stood in the rain, waiting, staring out over the water as if he could speed them ashore by concentration alone.

He was as tense as a bowstring. What condition would they be in?

They came ashore in a jolly boat. The oars dipped and pulled. The little boat skimmed so slowly across the water, it was agonizing. Half a dozen men in the boat, apart from the rowers, all head down against the rain—no, there was one tanned young face turned up to it, receiving the rain full on his face as if it were a miracle, a blessing.

And so it is, Jemmy Pendell, so it is, Thomas thought, his own sight blurring. He recalled his own reaction to rain after years under a scorching, pitiless sun.

The boat came on in an eerie silence, the only sound the dip and creak of the oars, the slap of the waves against the pilings, and overhead the mournful screech of gulls. Usually when sailors returned home there was much laughter and talk, men eager to get home.

But nobody was laughing, nobody was smiling. And nobody was talking at all.

The silence and the stillness were disturbing.

Thomas's chest was hollow. Why so silent? He peered through the drizzle, trying to make out their expressions.

And then he realized: Jones was not among them. Only four of the five men were coming home.

But Wilmott's letter had said that he'd found them all. So where was Jones? Had he died on the voyage home?

Thomas felt sick at the thought.

The boat drew closer, their faces became clearer and he realized why everyone was so silent and why there was no laughter or talking.

They were trying not to cry. The men's faces were working silently, their lips pressed tightly together. Their eyes were wet, and not just from the rain.

The jolly boat reached the wharf. Dyson climbed up first. He looked thinner and browner, but otherwise much the same. He looked around him in wonder, as if unable to believe his eyes.

O'Brien was next, agile, brown and wiry. He took two steps ashore, sank to his knees and kissed the ground dramatically, half joking, half sincere.

Jemmy Pendell climbed the ladder, still skinny, but not as scrawny as the last time Thomas had seen him, on the auction block. He stood staring around him, like Dyson, in wonder and faint disbelief.

Thomas remembered how that felt.

Dodds came last, his bald head shining in the rain. He stepped ashore, looked up at the sky, held out his hands, rolled his eyes and said, "So here I am, back in England after all these years and it's *still* bloody raining, wouldn't you know it?"

It broke the ice. The men all burst out laughing. They hugged each other and danced around in the rain. "We're home, we're really home!"

"England!"

"Never thought I'd see the old country again."

And then they saw Thomas. "Commander, Mr. Beresford, sir—you came!" They crowded around him, a little awkward, then Jemmy stepped forward and hugged him. Thomas hugged him back, tears streaming down his face and he didn't care who saw it. They each hugged him in turn, even O'Brien, who finished it with a light playful punch to the shoulder. His eyes were wet with tears as well.

Dyson hugged him, thumped his back and then shook his hand. "I dunno how you managed this sir, but I'll owe you for the rest of—"

"Nobody owes anyone anything," Thomas said gruffly.

"But the ransom—we know it weren't the navy. It was you, wasn't it, sir?"

"It was a gentleman who wishes to remain anonymous," Thomas said. "He was leaving the country and decided to do something worthwhile with his money." Ambrose's little leather-bound trunk proved to contain very close to the sum that he'd sent Wilmott off with. He'd paid it back into Rose's account.

"Well, whoever paid the money," Dyson said, clearly not believing Thomas's tale, "we know it was you who brought us back, sir. I didn't believe you could. I heard where you got sent and well, it's a life sentence ain't it, the galleys? I figured that was the end of that and I'd spend the rest of my life in that place."

"You promised you'd bring us home and you did," Jemmy said, fighting his tears. "Dunno how, but you did."

"I didn't bring you all home, though, did I?" he said. "What happened to Jones?" He braced himself for the bad news.

Instead they laughed. "After all the girls Jones played fast and loose with, he got himself caught by a pretty little Arab girl," Dodds said.

Pendell nodded. "He converted, sir—genuine, it was, not just to get hisself released. You know how Jones always was on about religions?"

Thomas nodded. Jones was always getting into arguments with the other men. He'd always assumed it was just to stir up a bit of excitement on a boring voyage.

"He took to Mohammedism all the way. Got himself freed, started working in a bakery, and next thing you know—typical Jones—his eye's on the boss's daughter. Next thing he's married."

"He's got a couple of little doe-eyed daughters of his own now. Besotted with them, he is." Dodds grinned. "Serve him right. He'll be worrying himself sick over them twelve years from now, the randy beggar. Nothing like a former rake for knowing how wicked men can be."

"Mr. Wilmott made him write a letter to you, telling you all about it. Mr. Wilmott said you'd be worried otherwise." Dyson produced two crumpled bits of paper from an inside pocket and handed them to Thomas. "There's a note from Mr. Wilmott, too."

Thomas swallowed. Mr. Wilmott was right. He pocketed the letters to read later. So all his men were all safe and where they wanted to be. It was a weight off his shoulders.

"Come on now, let's get you out of the rain, or you'll catch your death of cold," he said. "I've booked rooms for us all at the Star."

Dodds whistled. "Bit fancy for the likes of us, ain't it, sir?"

"Not in the least. After what you've all been through—"

"What we *all* went through, sir," Dyson interrupted. "You included, if you don't mind me sayin' so."

They piled into the chaise and headed to the Star Hotel.

First it was hot baths all round—as much to prevent a chill as for cleanliness—followed by a night of celebration and storytelling. They fell on roast beef, mashed potatoes and Yorkshire pudding with delight and washed it down with good English ale—none of them had the digestive problems he'd picked up from the bad food on the galleys. The drink and the stories flowed late into the night.

Next morning they told him their plans. O'Brien and Dodds were planning to set up as woodworkers together. Dodds was a ship's carpenter and O'Brien had been sold to a master woodworker and had learned from him. "We thought we might set up shop here," Dodds said. "Looks to be a prosperous town. I'll fetch the wife and kids—better for them than London, I'll be bound."

Dyson was going back to Yorkshire. He might emigrate, he thought. Would see what his wife thought about it.

The men were eager to be reunited with their families, so Thomas put O'Brien, Dodds and Dyson on the stage to London that morning. To his surprise, they all had their own money; Wilmott had divided up what was left over from the ransom between them. Compensation for all they'd lost, and something to help them get started.

He set off home, taking Jemmy Pendell in the chaise with him.

"AND WHEN WE REACHED NEWPORT, HE DIDN'T EVEN give the chaise time to stop, he was out of it and running madly toward his cottage, yelling out 'Jenny, Jenny'—his wife's name is Jenny—Jenny and Jemmy Pendell, can you imagine it?"

Rose poked him in the ribs. "Get on with it. Jemmy is running madly toward his cottage, yelling out 'Jenny, Jenny,' and . . . ?"

"So, he's yelling out her name like a banshee, and then she comes out of the cottage and she sees him, and for a moment she doesn't move. Just stands there stock-still. And then, and then . . ." He paused, deliberately.

Rose elbowed him again.

"Then she starts running toward him, and she's crying and calling his name and—"

"What was she wearing?"

Thomas stared down at her. "What does that matter?"

"It matters to me. What color was her dress?"

He rolled his eyes. "Blue, I think. With white thingummies." He made little curling motions with his fingers.

"Dark blue or light blue?"

"Light blue—like a summer sky, like your eyes." He moved in for a kiss.

She held him back. "And her little girl, what color was she wearing?"

He frowned. "How do you know there was a little girl?"

"Of course there was a little girl. What color was her dress?"

"Pink," he said, baffled.

"Oh, that's perfect. And then what happened?"

"You don't want me to describe what Jemmy was wearing?"

"Don't be ridiculous. So when they met . . ."

"They kissed, and he whirled her around and then they kissed again, and, well, you get the idea."

"No, you'll have to show me later."

His eyes glinted. "If I must."

"And when the little girl met her daddy?"

He grinned. "You should have seen her, Rose. First she hid behind her mother's skirts, peeping out at him from time to time, but every time Jemmy tried to talk to her, she hid again. And then he sat down on the ground—in his brand-new clothes—are you sure you don't want to know about his new clothes? Because they were very smart."

"No. He sat down and . . . ?"

"Pretended not to look at her, and she crept out and just looked at him, right up close as if he were some insect she'd just found. Then she reached out and shoved at him—quite a hefty push for a little fairylike creature—and he rolled right over and fell back on the grass as if he were dead."

She sniffled. "Oh, he sounds lovely. Jenny Pendell was weeping by this time, I take it."

"Yes, just like you are now." He passed her his handkerchief. "Then the little girl came and tried to wake him up. She pushed at his face and pulled his hair and poked him on the nose and he didn't move a muscle. She stood there frowning down at him for ages and he didn't stir, not so much as a flicker of an eyelid. And then, you'll never guess what she did next."

"She kissed him, and like Sleeping Beauty he woke up?"

He stared at her in amazement. "How do you know these things?"

Her mouth curved in a mysterious smile. "I'm a woman."

He looked down at her. "You certainly are . . ." And he bent to make sure of it.

"You're going to give Jemmy a job here on the estate, aren't you?" she said after a while. "Because there's nothing for that family in that little village."

"How did you—? Never mind. Yes, we arranged it on the trip up from Southampton. There's a spare cottage with plenty of room for him and his wife and daughter and—"

"And his grandfather."

"His grandfather?"

"Yes, I want to employ him to build me a rose garden."

"Do you now?"

"Any objection?"

He laughed. "Would it do me any good if I did?"

"It might. It depends."

"On what?"

"On how good you are." She pulled his head down for a long, luscious kiss and one thing led to another and they made love again, slowly, thoroughly, until he was sated and exhausted and he couldn't wipe the smile off his face.

"I love it when you smile like that," she said sleepily. "I love you so much, Thomas."

The sound of Thomas not responding hung in the air.

He swallowed. It was all very well for him to tell himself that the words didn't matter, but they mattered to her. If they didn't, she wouldn't be telling him all the time that she loved him.

And if he were honest with himself, every time she told him she loved him he felt warmth coil in his chest and spread all the way through him. A small healing. A benediction.

So he was lying about the importance of the words. Lying to himself and by omission, to her. Because he did love her, more than words could express.

He opened his mouth to tell her so. But to his chagrin, she flinched, and pressed her fingers over his mouth.

"No, don't, I'm sorry. I wasn't pressuring you. I don't

need you to say anything, Thomas. I'm all right, truly. I don't need to know."

He took her hand and kissed her on the palm. "Yes, you do. And I need to tell you. It's just . . . I'm not very good with words."

"You don't need to—"

"Hush. I do. Rose, you're . . ." How to describe something so immense, so powerful? He groped for words; impossible, flimsy, parsimonious, feeble words.

"Of course I love you." So inadequate. Useless.

"And I—"

"I'm not finished." He'd barely started. He took both her hands in his, held them cupped against his heart as he lay on the bed facing her, all defenses down. Vulnerable. Open. "Rose, when I was shipwrecked, the thought of you kept me afloat. When I was dying of thirst in the desert, you were my water. When the other men were lost, barren of hope, wishing to die, I refused to allow it because I was strong, because I had you in my heart. You were my beacon, my hope, the very flame of my being.

"You were with me in the filth and degradation and brutality of the galleys, keeping me sane, keeping me strong. Reminding me that there was another world, clean and good and wholesome because you were in it. Through my darkest days, the knowledge that you were here, waiting, gave me heart. I knew, with unquenchable certainty that somehow, someday I would get back to you. And though I didn't realize it, since my return you've freed me from the invisible chains that bound me still. My dearest girl, I love you, more than I can say, more than any words can ever express."

"Oh, Thomas." She was awash with tears. "But if you felt like that, why did you keep telling me to take the annulment?"

"I didn't think you wanted me. I was damaged. I didn't want to drag you down to my level."

"Oh, Thomas, never think it. I always loved you and I always will. I loved you when I married you, and—"

"And I loved you."

Her face crumpled. "Really? It wasn't just because you were protecting me? Because of the possibility of a baby?"

"No, I loved you then and I love you now. From the moment I first saw you in the pump room in Bath, I knew you were the only woman for me."

"When you told me you'd been damaged, I believed you, but I still loved and wanted you." She wiped tears from her eyes. "But, Thomas, you've been through the most horrendous experiences, and I don't know how, because God knows it should have destroyed you, but somehow you've emerged from it a fine, strong, decent, beautiful—yes, beautiful, don't argue with me—kind and loving man. I don't deserve you, but I'm selfish that way and no matter what you say or do, I'm keeping you."

There were no words after that. Thomas's heart was so full it felt ready to burst. All he could do was show her how he felt in the best way he knew. By loving her.

Epilogue

❧

To see the world in a grain of sand, and to see heaven in a
wild flower, hold infinity in the palm of your hands, and
eternity in an hour.
—WILLIAM BLAKE

THE LATE-AFTERNOON SUN WAS SOFT, MELLOW WITH THE
hush of autumn. A faint scent of wood smoke hung in the
crisp air. The trees surrounding Brierdon Court were thin
of leaves, a mere smattering of gold and claret and brown
against the stark tracery of branches. Yellow birches,
golden larches, tawny oak leaves drifting down to lie in
damp carpets and become one with the earth.

Seated on a rustic wooden bench, Rose gazed out over
the place that would become her rose garden. She and old
Mr. Pendell had spent many a happy hour designing it and
poring over rose catalogs. They'd decided on a walled
garden—roses were tough, but in a sheltered, sunny spot
they'd flower more and longer, Mr. Pendell said. And a
walled garden would make more of the scent—stop it from
being blown away. The perfect place for a lady to sit. Or a
lady and her gentleman, he'd added coyly. He was a romantic, old Mr. Pendell.

Now the walls were finished and stone flags had been
laid, forming the pathways that wound romantically through

the garden. The beds had been dug, manured and dug again, and trellises constructed for the climbers. Several pretty arbors had been built with seating beneath—in time the bare wood would be covered by roses.

Everything was ready. Only one rosebush had been planted so far, a transplant from Mr. Pendell's garden. Rose had chosen it especially. It was her special rose, and though it was just a bundle of sticks at the moment, in spring it would blossom with white roses, tiny, sweet-smelling buds. The rest of the rosebushes would be planted tomorrow.

But Rose wasn't thinking about roses. She wasn't thinking about tomorrow at all, but about a time in the past when she'd been young, and ignorant and alone.

"I promise I won't forget you," she said softly. "You were with me for such a short time, but you meant all the world to me. I loved you then, and I love you now. And though I have more to love now, it doesn't mean I'll ever forget you, or love you any less. You'll always have a place in my heart, your own special place."

"Who are you talking to?" Thomas came up from behind and sat down on the bench. She turned her face up to him and the smile dropped from his face. "Rose, darling, what is it? What's the matter?" He pulled out a handkerchief and began to wipe her cheeks.

She took it from him, scrubbed at her eyes and then blew her nose. "It's nothing. I was just thinking." She hadn't even noticed the tears running down her cheeks.

"You were talking." *To nobody.* She could see the concern in his eyes.

She looked at the little lone rosebush. "I was talking to the baby. The one I lost when I thought I'd lost you."

He slipped his arms around her and gathered her against him. "Ah, don't be sad, love. You'll have a baby one day, I'm sure of it. But if not, don't worry . . . I can't bear it when you worry."

His words caused her eyes to fill again. "I'm not sad, or worried, truly I'm not. Quite the contrary. I'm just . . ." Unable to find the words to explain the turmoil of emotions inside her, she simply took his hand and placed it on her belly. And waited.

Thomas continued, "I know you've been fretting for weeks now—and it's been worse since Emm had her baby. I know you don't want to talk about it, but it really doesn't matt—" He broke off. A strange look came into his eyes. He glanced at her belly, then looked at her. "Rose? Did I just feel—?" He broke off again. His big hand was warm against her belly.

She nodded, laid her hand over his and said mistily, "There's a baby in here, and it's alive, Thomas. My baby is alive. And kicking."

"A *baby*? But how—I mean when?" The baby kicked again and he stared, wonder dawning in his eyes. "How long? I mean, do you know when he—she—when our baby will be born?"

Our baby. She loved hearing him say it.

"In three or four months."

"*Three or four months!* You mean you've known—" And then he realized. "And all this time you've been fretting and worrying? Without saying a word." The arm around her tightened.

She bit her lip. "I didn't want to say, unless . . . until I was sure everything was all right." She'd felt the first faint flutters weeks ago, but still she hadn't dared to believe . . .

"Ah, love, you should have told me. But it's going to be fine, I'm sure of it." He glanced down at her belly again. "A baby! We're having a baby!" His silvery eyes blazed with emotion.

She smiled mistily, and he pulled her closer, one hand cupping her jaw as he kissed her tenderly, the other protectively cupping her belly, and their baby.

Author's Note

❧

DEAR READERS, THANK YOU FOR READING ROSE AND Thomas's story. I hope you enjoyed it.

Most of my stories take me in a different direction from the one I expect at the beginning, and while this is part of the pleasure in being a writer, it also throws up some challenges.

One of those challenges is to present history that is true to its time through characters that modern readers can identify with. We can't rewrite history, we can only try to understand and learn from it. And try to do better.

So many changes have occurred in the past two-hundred-plus years: for women, whose choices for an independent life or expanded identity were so limited by customs and expectations and access to their own funds; for people of different origins and ethnicities who were certainly seen as less than equal; and how our notions of what it is to be human have altered (perhaps not quickly enough!).

Thomas's time as a slave changed him and gave him a greater understanding of and sympathy for the lives of people in less fortunate positions; servants, poor people, people dependent on others or bonded by things less obvious than chains. Because of this, he's not a typical earl of his time.

But his experience of being shipwrecked, captured by tribesmen and taken across the desert to be ransomed or sold was the kind of thing that really did happen.

There are many accounts of people captured and enslaved by Barbary pirates (or corsairs) from the sixteenth to the nineteenth century. For Thomas's story I borrowed from the true-life account of Captain James Riley—*An Authentic Narrative of the Loss of the American Brig* Commerce: *Wrecked on the Western Coast of Africa, in the Month of August, 1815, with an Account of the Sufferings of the Surviving Officers and Crew, Who Were Enslaved by the Wandering Arabs of the Great African Desert, or Zahahrah*.

I had Thomas and his men experience much the same as Capt. Riley and his men, right up until the point where Capt. Riley was ransomed and sent home. His ransom was organized by William Willshire, the British vice consul to Mogador from 1814 to 1844.

Since I did not want Thomas to be ransomed, I removed William Willshire from my tale, and thus sentenced poor Thomas to four years of slavery. But the real William Willshire deserves a mention (see next page) because he was a hero.

The rest of Thomas's experience (and that of his men) was also typical of what happened to many people taken by Barbary Corsairs.

Here's how historian Prof. Robert C. Davis explained it: "These freebooters took their captives from merchant ships, fishing boats and any village they could sack, selling them in the slave markets of Salé on Morocco's Atlantic coast, or in Algiers, Tunis and Tripoli, on the Barbary Coast. Some captives—the very wealthy and many women—were bought by dealers who specialized in ransoming and were often well treated, more as hostages than as slaves.

"The great majority were properly enslaved, though, worked hard by their masters, regularly beaten and sold when they were no longer fit or profitable.

"At least an eighth of the captives were allocated to the state, its share in recompense for supporting the corsairs. They were set to work on state projects—building the harbor, or fortifications, digging in quarries, serving as longshoremen; or rowing in the galleys.

"Those sold to private masters were either used as house servants or farm laborers or rented out to potters, tanners, construction bosses or water sellers. A lucky few managed to run shops or taverns, paying their masters a monthly fee for the privilege. Women not suitable for ransoming generally ended up in the harem of wealthy corsairs or the ruling pasha, either as serving maids or concubines."

(Robert C. Davis, *https://publicdomainreview.org/2011/10/03/slavery-in-north-africa-the-famous-story-of-captain-james-riley/*)

WILLIAM WILLSHIRE

At age twenty-four, Englishman William Willshire was sent to Mogador as an agent of an English trading company. Shortly afterward he was appointed the British vice consul in Mogador. He made a success of his business, but his name is remembered today because he redeemed, cared for and helped repatriate hundreds of Christian sailors—not only Englishmen—who were enslaved in the sultanate of Morocco during the early part of the nineteenth century. The town of Willshire in the U.S. state of Ohio was named after him, in thanks, by Capt. James Riley.

The fictional character of Wilmott in my story, though he organized the care and repatriation of Thomas's men and his name sounds similar to Willshire, is not based on any real historical character. I often like to include characters of mixed background, especially since there was a lot of travel and interaction between people of different nationalities, races and cultures in historical times, as well as now. Also, Wilmott was one of those characters who simply sprang to life and refused to be relegated to a quiet corner of a novel.

If you want to know more about this background history, simply search for *Barbary pirates*, *Capt. James Riley*, *William Willshire*, *Barbary slavery* or *galley slaves* on the web, and you'll find masses of fascinating information. But be warned—it's an endless warren of rabbit holes.

WHAT'S NEXT?

Next in my "convenient marriage" series is George's story. As you will no doubt have guessed, she's about to lead a certain cold-eyed duke on a merry (or possibly quite grumpy) chase . . .

Thanks again for reading *Marry in Secret*.

Anne Gracie

ABOUT THE AUTHOR

Anne Gracie is the award-winning author of the Chance Sisters Romances, which include *The Summer Bride*, *The Spring Bride*, *The Winter Bride* and *The Autumn Bride*, and the Marriage of Convenience Romance series, including *Marry in Scandal* and *Marry in Haste*. She spent her childhood and youth on the move. The roving life taught her that humor and love are universal languages and that favorite books can take you home, wherever you are. Anne started her first novel while backpacking solo around the world, writing by hand in notebooks. Since then, her books have been translated into more than eighteen languages and include Japanese manga editions (which she thinks is very cool), and audio editions. In addition to writing, Anne promotes adult literacy, flings balls for her dog, enjoys her tangled garden and keeps bees. Visit her online at annegracie.com. You can also subscribe to her newsletter.

Ready to find
your next great read?

Let us help.

Visit prh.com/nextread